The
Master of
Counterpoint

Book Disclaimer:

This book is a work of fiction. That means the characters, events, and places in the story are made up by the author. While some parts may feel real or remind readers of real people or situations, everything in this book is created for storytelling. If anything seems similar to real life, it is a coincidence.

The book talks about serious topics like murder, abuse, stealing, adultery, false accusations, and other moral or criminal acts. It also includes ideas about justice that come from mysterious or supernatural forces. These events are not real and are not meant to tell people how the world should work. They are only part of the story and imagination.

The book also shows different opinions, beliefs, and reactions from characters. These views do not represent the thoughts or beliefs of the author or any real group. They are only there to make the story more interesting and meaningful.

This story is not based on any real religion, political idea, or country. It does not try to teach or support any real-life system. The goal of this book is to make readers think, imagine, and reflect — not to offend or target anyone.

Because the story includes sensitive and mature themes, it may not be suitable for all readers. Reader discretion is advised. Some parts might be upsetting or emotional.

Twin Hammocks

Books by JK Worth

The Hungry Horse

Columbia Falls

The Kootenai Lodge

The Master of Counterpoint

Coming in 2025

Lying Awake in Whitefish, Montana

Kootenai: The Restoration

Sequel to The Master of Counterpoint

JK Can be reached at: **jkworthauthor@gmail.com**

On X: jk_worth

I write my books while aboard Big Sky. I couldn't do it without my two friends and captains of the vessel. They make it possible for me to write without worry in the affectionately titled "Floating Writer's Lounge" located on the aft deck, next to the bar and Ice maker. Trisha and Ben are from Lake Charles, Louisiana and taught me about the culture and the people. I lived in their beautiful home and city for two months on my boat and learned all I know about the Cajun world from them. It's a huge part of this book. Thanks, guys. Keep us afloat!

The
Master of
Counterpoint

By

JK WORTH

TWIN HAMMOCKS PUBLISHING, LLC
Miami, USA   2025.

1

Outside Beaumont, Texas

1/1/2026

It was just after midnight; the lights in the prison were ablaze. Alarms were blaring as the crisis exploded. Prisoners were screaming over the dead bodies locked in their own cells. A few guards were lying on the floor, and some were sitting upright in chairs. They were dead. The living guards tried to help their fallen partners first. They panicked as they saw their faces. Their dead eyes were wide open, and their eyeballs were bulging as if they were about to burst from the sockets. Those eyes gave each face the most hideously frightening expression. This happened in Cellblock A.

There were five other blocks, and the distant screams told the living that this was not an isolated mass casualty. The entire prison was affected.

The penitentiary was on its usual night lockdown at midnight when this horror erupted. The warden would not lift it until they had answers. After witnessing the mental state of the prisoners who were still alive, they would remain locked in their cells. The guards were in shock and not able to perform their duties. He had no options but to leave everything as he found it. He certainly was not inclined to open the cell doors to deal with the hysterical, living prisoners.

Warden Darkenwald ran to his office to call the governor and the mayor. It was 12:20 a.m.

"I'll tell the governor; he'll call you back." The phone operator sounded annoyed. The same story with the mayor. His next call was for ambulances. No need for doctors, except to pronounce the dead, well, dead.

He ran back to Cellblock B and saw it was a reprise of A. The same with the rest. They all had dead prisoners and a few dead guards. The best he could quickly calculate in the panic was that 40% of the prisoners and 4% of the guards were dead—all at the exact same time and in the exact same state. No visible signs of trauma. Just the haunting eyes and hideous expression. Some of the guards tried to close the dead guards' eyes to reduce the shock of looking at them. They couldn't close them! It was as if they were glued open.

The governor returned the call from the party he was attending. "Scott, what's going on over there?" He sounded a little agitated to be disturbed by a prison warden at 12:30 a.m. on New Year's Eve.

"I don't know, sir." He paused a second to try and formulate a sane response to the insanity he had witnessed. "Half of the prison population is dead, and some guards are too!"

"How did the prisoners get out of their cells? How could …"

"They didn't," he interrupted. "They're all in their cells, and the guards were at their stations. No signs of trauma, no indications of violence."

"Are you drunk?" That was all he could think of. He would apologize for that comment later. This scenario was impossible.

"And here's the strangest part: they all have incredibly bulging eyes. They have a look of sheer terror on their faces." He stopped and caught his breath. "I'm gonna need the National Guard, sir. I have prisoners locked up with dead bodies in their cells. My guards are not equipped to deal with this. Almost half of the population is convicted murderers!"

The governor didn't think he sounded drunk. He couldn't come up with any explanation for this.

"Call the mayor."

"I already did. I'm waiting for his callback."

"Okay, good. I'll get the National Guard over there. How many cells are affected?"

"Maybe two or three hundred; I have over six hundred."

"I'll get three hundred soldiers over there as soon as possible. I'll see you in about an hour."

The governor called the Sheriff's Department and woke the commander. He wanted another set of eyes on the ground while he was preparing the National Guard. The warden sounded sane, but the situation was insane. He needed some sort of verification before he committed three hundred men and women.

Fifteen minutes later, the sheriff called him back.

"Send the troops. This is real. I saw a few dead bodies on the streets around the prison on my way in. I stopped and looked at one. He had cash and small packages of drugs in his pockets. He was dead, and his eyes were about ready to come out of his head. Same inside the prison. This is unreal, sir!"

"They're on the way. Stay there and give me updates. Anything happens, I want to know about it."

"Yes, sir. Ambulances are already here, and so far, no survivors from the 'wounded' guards. They couldn't resuscitate a single victim. I called up all my officers to get to the prison. I don't know what else to do."

"There's nothing to do until the Guard gets there and sets up shop. Try to calm the surviving prisoners. Some are in cells with a dead man in the other bunk?"

"Yes, sir!"

The sheriff went in to talk with Darkenwald. He wanted to be ready the next time he talked with the governor.

"Scott."

"Mike, good to see you—this is crazy." Nobody had even a hint of a reason for any of this.

"The governor called me and wants us to try and calm the prisoners. The Guard is on the way."

"That's what we're doing now. We told them to cover the dead and stand by the door. We're delivering water. I'm going to make an announcement over the PA system. I'm trying to figure out what to say. Seriously, what is there to say?"

He had no idea what he could tell them that they didn't already know. Hundreds of dead prisoners with bulging, terror-stricken eyes and expressions. Prison guards too.

"I asked Henderson to make a list of all the dead—prisoners and guards alike. There must be a connection. I have no other leads. It seems so random. I don't know where else to start." Darkenwald was struggling.

"There's a few on the streets too. Same eyes. Same expression." He stopped for a minute to think. "I'm gonna have my men check the hospitals and the streets for others. We'll get their identities and look for any correlation. There must be one."

2

An incoming helicopter was heard in the distance. It was the governor. The pilot landed in the yard. Darkenwald made sure it was cleared before allowing it to land. He walked over to the governor and gave him an update while shouting over the chopper's rotors. It wasn't much, but it was everything they had or knew about. They walked into the secured prison and up to Cellblock A. The yelling and screaming had settled down after the guards did their best to calm the prisoners. When they learned about the dead guards, they knew whatever happened wasn't directed solely at them. That helped a little.

"The National Guard is still about an hour away. Keep them locked up until we figure things out."

"I will. I was about to address the prisoners from the PA system."

"Let's go." The governor tried to remain calm in this chaos.

Warden Darkenwald picked up the mic and started to speak without really knowing where he was headed with this "pep talk." He knew he had to keep them calm and let them know that the National Guard was on the way. He shaded it as a sort of rescue operation and said it was to make sure the prisoners were kept safe. The governor nodded in agreement.

He pushed the talk button on the mic again. "We don't know what happened. We have no idea. No one escaped their cells; the dead guards were all at their stations. The witnesses said they just stopped breathing, and, well, you know the rest. I asked Officer Henderson to make a list of the dead prisoners and guards so we can see if we can find any connections, any consistencies—anything that will help explain this. The sheriff told me a few bodies were on the streets. All were very close to the prison, not even a thousand feet away."

He didn't want to tell the prisoners the rest of what the sheriff knew. The sheriff told him it looked like a pattern, with the prison in the center of a circle where the outside dead were found. He couldn't imagine what would cause that. His men were plotting the location of the dead on a street map and would have a better understanding in an hour. The governor would soon be even more perplexed.

The mayor finally showed up and was relegated to a question-and-answer session with Henderson. Both the warden and the governor were miffed at him.

"At least he's not on one of his junkets."

"Might as well have been. I called him almost three hours ago. He still hasn't called me back."

He burst in on them as he sidestepped Henderson.

"Governor Willoughby. And you must be Darkenwald."

"Warden Darkenwald," the governor shot back.

"What's going on here? The stories I'm getting are crazy."

"Glad you could finally make it." The governor was not in a mood for the mayor's pomposity.

"Can we be civil?"

The two of them were on opposite sides of the political spectrum. Mayor Richt would have let all the prisoners out without bail if he had his way.

"Did your guards do this?" he asked in a demeaning and demanding tone.

"Don't answer him," the governor jumped in. "He doesn't deserve an answer if that's how he asks it. As far as I'm concerned, you can read about it in the newspapers, you little piece of …"

Henderson burst out laughing and quickly stuffed it back in from where it came. Darkenwald had enough wisdom to at least turn his head away before smiling.

"Go ahead and laugh, but be assured there will be a full investigation, and you will all be held accountable."

"Thank you, Mayor," the governor said. "Now go about your investigation; just don't mess up ours that started three hours ago while you were partying. A sheriff will walk you through. Don't interfere with anyone, and don't touch anything. We're having a meeting as soon as Henderson gets us the list of the dead. That is being compiled now. I will let your aide know the time to meet. You are more than welcome to join us and bring along any bit of evidence that you might stumble over."

"I'll be there!" he asserted.

They parted ways and watched the mayor start his "fact-finding" tour of the dead. In less than two minutes he would be ashamed of his arrogant language and threats. He wouldn't be humiliated enough to apologize, though; he was too conceited to let that happen.

❖

Henderson had the information on the dead. All the prisoners were convicted of premeditated murder. The guards were still a mystery that needed more investigation. The bodies outside the prison were identified by fingerprints found in the FBI database. They were either awaiting trial for murder, out on bail for murder, or awaiting sentencing for murder. The six were on a path to prison for homicide. When the governor saw that the outside bodies were within a circle, he stopped the meeting and kicked everyone out of the room except for the warden.

"We need to get the Feds in on this. Something is so far out of the realm of reality that we need help, Scott." He was totally confused by the data. "Get to work on the dead guards' backgrounds."

"Yes, sir. You can use my office for your calls to Washington."

Governor Willoughby followed Darkenwald up to his office overlooking the floodlit yard. He thanked him and started a series of calls that would eventually reach the President before breakfast. He thought it had national security implications. It couldn't be anything other than a top-secret incident that would be classified within hours.

The Beaumont Penitentiary was in Texas. It housed the highest level of violent prisoners. Its population dropped by 437 prisoners in less than one minute, including 4% of its guard roster.

Information on the dead guards revealed a connection to murder. Two were investigated for the murder of their wives. The evidence was not enough to pursue charges. Another was suspected of intentional "friendly fire" on a soldier in his battalion. No witnesses, so that ended before it started. Two were ex-gang members involved with street sales of drugs. Those DEI hires had no record of murder charges in their past. The last was involved with an investigation into the beating death of a motorist that resulted in his firing from the Houston Police

Department. They couldn't convict, but most believed he beat him to death.

"So, the legal system labeled them as not guilty of murder, but they were all investigated for murder except for the two ex-gang members."

"That's accurate, Governor." Henderson wasn't surprised. He had run-ins with some of these dead guards before. "And just because the gang members were never charged with murder doesn't mean they didn't kill anyone. It was to be expected in that line of work."

Willoughby thanked Henderson as he left the office.

The governor turned around and faced the outside prison yard and shook his head while speaking with Darkenwald.

"Every one of the dead is connected to a murder. Convicted or not, they had a direct line to a murder. The few prisoners that weren't connected probably got away with it." Scott agreed. "I want you to call every prison in the state to see if anything strange happened in the last day. I'm sure I would have heard already, but I want to be sure. I'll need answers for the Feds—answers I don't have. Oh, one more thing: the five prisoners that were in for murder but survived unscathed? They were all in the process of filing for a rehearing. The Innocence Project lawyers were defending them."

No other reports came back from other prisons in Texas. The only place this happened was in the area south of Beaumont. It made no sense.

The National Guard started arriving. Darkenwald would organize a systematic release of the living prisoners, and the Guards would escort them, one by one, to the yard. He thought about the danger of leaving them alone after this traumatizing event. He ordered that the dead guards not be moved so that as the prisoners walked past them, they could see that the dead were not only prisoners but also guards.

Each cell block was opened, and the terrified living were separated from the terrified dead. The guards walked them out, and the soldiers, in hazmat suits, did a quick search before relocking the cell door. Darkenwald didn't know if the dead could infect or cause others to be stricken with whatever it was that killed them. He didn't want to move them until the proper authorities examined the bodies. This was a crime scene, and he treated it like one. Who the "proper authorities" were was beyond his knowledge and experience. He never investigated the crimes of his prisoners; he was only in charge of their incarcerated lives after their conviction for crimes.

The liberated prisoners were not a behavioral problem. They were happy to be out of their cells and headed to the yard. Most of the remaining prisoners were in for financial crimes or fraud convictions. The most violent criminals were dead and lying in their bunks covered in sheets. That's when it dawned on Scott that almost half of his prisoners were "early released" for "dead" behavior. "Probably all are in hell," he thought. His job, although difficult now, would get much easier in a week, and hopefully somebody would have answers by then—answers to the hundreds of questions.

The transfer of the prisoners was an easy transition. No incidents occurred in the yard. The prisoners were still shaken, but the real reason was that only the "good" prisoners were left. Word traveled fast among the survivors. It didn't take long to figure out that all the murderers were dead. The most violent were dead. There were still violent prisoners left, but the elimination of the most violent made them worry they themselves might be on a "watch list" of some unexplained power. Besides, with the hardcore element gone, the oppressive fear that thrives in prison was dissolving.

The Beaumont Municipal Airport was listed on half a dozen newly filed flight plans from Washington, D.C. Senior officials from the FBI, CIA, DEA, DHS, NSA, and the Center for Disease Control and Prevention were all headed to the same regional airport in their government-issued Gulfstream jets. The single air traffic controller, who was called back to work, was perplexed at his small airport's rise to prominence among the top levels of government. He reopened the runway and manned the control tower. The three-letter agencies were jockeying for command of this enigmatic investigation. The President had to make it clear that the CDC was to go in first and not be challenged or interfered with by the others.

The prisoners were all transferred to the recreational yard as dawn lit the grounds. Darkenwald thought about getting them food and coffee. No prisoner had an appetite. He put it out anyway. It was there if they wanted it. The food got cold, but the hot coffee was soon gone.

One at a time, the Feds arrived. They had to wait for the CDC— President's orders. Darkenwald brought them to meet with the governor in the parking area and to explain everything that he knew. When he finished his oral report, the Deputy CIA Director asked him to leave him alone with the governor. Darkenwald looked at Governor Willoughby as if to let him stay and got no help. He left things to those with a higher intelligence and security classification. Soon, even the governor would be excused. This was big.

The Assistant Deputy Director of the CDC arrived and suited up with the scientists she brought along. The first thing was to close off the prison and detain everyone on the property. The National Guard had about 25 men on site. They would have to stay. The governor was included in the quarantine.

Air samples were taken in each cell and labeled. This was identified as a Cluster Outbreak. The governor agreed it was a cluster, but the four-letter word he used following "cluster" was not "outbreak."

All the dead were located on a site plan, including the ones on the street, thanks to Henderson's work. No new cases were discovered. The Case Definitions part of the investigation was easy. Those considered part of the outbreak were all dead. Not much detective work was needed to figure that out. There were no "slightly dead." No wounded. You were one or the other: dead or alive.

Data collection included DNA sampling all the bodies. They sealed four in plastic body bags to be shipped off to Atlanta. Autopsies and biological testing would commence in the afternoon out of Georgia.

The other agencies were directed away from the cells and the other prisoners. The reason for that directive was not because of what they knew, but because of what they didn't know. Hazmat suits would now be required. Tents and cots would be set up in the yard for the surviving prisoners. They couldn't return until the "all clear" was signaled after the sanitizing operations were completed. The remaining bodies would be placed in portable cold storage trailers by sunset. The inmates would be able to return the next day if all went well.

A local news outlet picked up on the radio chatter and sent a camera crew to the prison. No one would give an interview. Rumors were circulating about a mass casualty. The police were fielding calls from family members. The only story for the local news was video of the National Guard amassed around the prison and dozens of black SUVs with white government license plates. The governor was planning on addressing the media at 7:00 p.m. The FBI would censor it and spin a story about the air-conditioning system dumping freon gas into the cells. This emboldened conspiracy theorists to spin their own misinformation. Prisoner advocates were throwing out charges of brutality, and they would not stand for a cover-up. It would have been so much easier to just tell the American people the truth.

Protesters were arriving from all over the state and throughout the South to chime in on the mistreatment of prisoners. Some of these protesters died and wore the "Face" upon entering the circle that surrounded the prison. They must have committed murder at one time. This "thing" must still be punishing murderers that entered the circle. Governor Willoughby had enough! He called into the TV station and told the truth. He then ordered the Feds out of his state. The CDC was allowed full access. Texas would not be complicit in the government lies.

3

The Second Day – Houston in the Circle

1/2/2026

The Houston Evening Late News carried the prison story and was demanding answers from the Warden and the Governor. They closed the broadcast insisting on a press conference. It was just before midnight, 24 hours later.

In under one minute, the same scenario would play out in Houston and the ever-expanding "Circle of Death." Now it was an exact 200-mile perfect circle. Ground zero was the same as last night, in Beaumont. They would learn later that it did not cross the border into Mexico, Arkansas, or Louisiana.

Reports of more deaths in the expanding circle were coming from the greater Beaumont area and everywhere within the larger radius. The police precincts were flooded with calls from panicked citizens. Gangs were decimated. Upstanding family members were found dead. The same horrific expression on their faces gave away their secret life as a murderer. Hundreds of undocumented migrants, especially from Venezuela and Central America, were dead.

Some gang members thought immediate revenge on rivals and snitches was necessary to save face. These were the remaining gang bangers who were still alive. It was very hard for them to locate any rivals still living. When the rare target was found and aim was leveled in their direction, the would-be assassin died immediately. The second night, the circle was devoid of any murders. It was impossible to try to kill someone without killing yourself with an instant-karma-style retribution.

Just as the night before, a lot of surprises occurred. Some sketchy cops were dead. A pastor and a nurse had the mark of a murderer on their faces. By tomorrow afternoon, everyone would understand that the people who died were actually killed because of a murder in their past. An invisible vigilante was dishing out quick justice on an unheard-of scale.

No one was spared. Big cities, small towns, and the prisoners were all paying the ultimate penalty for murder. Many were hiding in plain sight, and that was the biggest shocker. Airlines reported passengers with the "Face" dead in their seats, even on planes that didn't land in Texas. Evidently the airspace above Texas was in the circular dome, and that was enough to prosecute this new justice. Reports came in from ships traveling in the Indian Ocean: dead sailors and passengers had the identical terror-stricken look on their eye-bulging faces. Airlines reported mysterious deaths on their aircraft over the waters between Australia and India. Nowhere else in the region, just the middle of the Indian Ocean. Two unrelated places on the planet: the Indian Ocean and parts of Texas.

Reports from Houston were insane. Ninety-five percent of the gang population was wearing the "murderer's face." Street corners were littered with fallen drug dealers. They qualified because of their customers' overdose deaths and the murders they committed defending their turf. Thousands were dead, and each passing hour, more were found. Morning would reveal the devastation delivered to the evildoers within the Circle.

A man and woman who lost a child to street violence were included with the other murderers. They were suspected of being involved in a crime when their toddler took a stray bullet. An ex-fireman accused of arson was found wearing the "Face." No one was spared who was guilty of murder. Motorcycle gangs had their fair share of this special revenge, which trimmed their ranks.

Governor Willoughby was on his plane from Beaumont to Houston to see for himself. The CDC had no answers for any of it. Not a thing. No virus, no poison, and no reason that explained any of it. The four bodies were negative for anything unusual except for the protruding eyes that couldn't be closed and, of course, the terrified expressions. Picking up the bodies was the most difficult task. They couldn't perform autopsies on that many bodies, so they didn't bother. Cause of death was labeled "Fear."

The press stopped blaming the governor and the prison wardens. No apologies were offered. Since they couldn't figure out who to blame, they had to actually investigate their stories. Lack of practice made the hard work of real journalism difficult. It wasn't like riding a bike. Most new reporters hadn't yet taken off the training wheels of activism they learned from J-school.

4

Dallas, Austin, El Paso, San Antonio, Brownsville to Amarillo

Day Three 1/3/2026

The rest of the state waited to see what would happen when it was their turn. The airports and bus stations were busy selling tickets to some real characters and some very scary people trying to outsmart their destiny. Some drove to Louisiana, some to Mexico to escape the punishment they knew they deserved. They would soon find out if their schemes were successful. Two guys booked a flight to Spain; they thought the longer distance would be a workaround.

Beaumont hadn't experienced a murder in two nights. All crimes were down to a fraction of normal. It was too soon to tell in Houston. Tomorrow would be interesting. The police were on alert—all hands on deck this evening. A lot of people were holding their breath. Others couldn't wait for the anticipated justice that the courts, very good attorneys, and rogue prosecutors had denied victims and their families.

Most households intended to stay up until midnight. The television news stations decided to expand their news coverage. The ratings would explode as the rest of the citizens of Texas—and now the nation—sat on the edges of their couches to watch the unfolding and unscripted reality show. For most Texans, tomorrow's water-cooler discussions would be epic. Instead of worry and fear, the good citizens of Texas couldn't wait to see justice delivered. After the excitement of watching people get what they deserved, more forward-thinking citizens were very concerned about the origin of this bizarre realignment of good and evil. Who could be behind this? What else could they do? It was 11:45 p.m. "Grab some popcorn," was shouted throughout the state.

Sports bars were packed, but the screens were not focused on sports. They were all tuned to the news broadcasts. This was the new entertainment for a state that had had enough of crime and illegals causing a massive amount of that crime. Having virtually no border was a tough pill to swallow for most of the citizens. An open border without the criminal element was a reasonable substitute and would be a welcome relief to the chaos.

Midnight arrived. Nothing happened. Was it over? Would there be no more justice for the guilty? And then the cameras that the media set up in parts of the various cities—ones seedier than most—showed street "vendors" dropping to the sidewalk. The bars broke out in cheers. More cheers than at a lot of Texas college football games—even Dallas Cowboys games.

Now it was happening across the state. Every city and town felt the wrath of "something bigger than they were." The entire state was being cleansed of murderers. Texas was now the safest place on Earth, Antarctica included.

The people who thought they could outsmart their destiny were mistaken. No matter where they were hiding, they died from the "Fear." The two on their way to Spain died over the Azores. Side by side in first class, they wore the "Face" that they couldn't outrun.

The Mexican government had a cleanup on the border to deal with. Hundreds of bodies were strewn on the sidewalks, streets, and bars south of Brownsville and west to San Antonio. Mexican cartel members were starting to get a little concerned that this reaper might demand justice in their own pueblos and ciudades.

Politicians were not exempt. Neither were Christian housewives, school principals, and charity workers. There were no loose definitions of murder in this Shakespearean play. Not much comedy, but a lot of tragedy.

The National Guard was pulled from Beaumont and moved to Dallas. The governor didn't think it was really necessary. The prisoners who were left behind were incredibly well behaved. The undetected murderers in the rest of the state might be a lot more trouble for society than imagined. Their bodies would be found everywhere one could imagine.

The citizens of Texas would have no need for police who were once required to preserve civility just two days ago. Prison guards and private security guards in high crime areas were unnecessary now. If this kept up, Texas would be the safest and most popular state in the union. But would this play out in petty crimes and street violence? Would crimes other than murder increase with this new reality?

The weird and unexplained part of this "uncrime" wave was the mystery behind it—what or who was running this operation?

Now the entire world was watching the events unfolding in Texas. Many attached a Judeo-Christian religious component to it. The Old Testament's "eye for an eye" rectitude seemed plausible. Almost as many attached an Eastern religion karma aspect to it. Most religions tried to claim it as their own. Nobody knew. The unknown left a cloud hanging over this, so far, well-received "street justice." Most of the rest of the nation wished it would expand into their neighborhoods.

The watch parties started to wind down. As the sports patrons headed home, they were greeted with police and ambulances' flashing lights. The downtown Dallas area was strewn with bodies. It was shocking how many murderers lived among them. These were the ones wanted by the police and the unknowns. This was what was running around their city just two hours ago. People living in secure and safe apartments and condos were horrified as they watched a few of their friendly neighbors being wheeled out to awaiting ambulances the next day.

Mental institutions were hard hit since many housed convicted criminals who were spared prison because of their insanity evaluations. Half were probably fakers. It didn't matter to the powers, entities, or gods controlling this purge.

Meth cookers, fentanyl, and "tranq" dealers were especially hideous looking. Since their coroner's photos would be public record, TikTok accounts parading them were the new rage. A lot of illicit drug customers were "jonesing" hard now that most suppliers were exhibiting the "Fear." Many tried to go it alone with what meager drugs they had left. Soon, the withdrawal survivors would be drug-free and living a new life with positive possibilities.

The massive numbers of bodies being recovered would take months to gather DNA and get the results analyzed. The CDC was insisting on sample collection from each body recovered exhibiting the "Fear." An accompanying photograph would be included. The latest unverified total numbers tallied from the past three days had surpassed 10,000 bodies. The governor's biggest problem was what to do with so many. The few recovered bodies without the "Fear" expression were set aside and separated from the murderers, then handled with dignity before being turned over to family members.

5

The Great State of Texas

1/16/2026

As soon as it started, it was over. With every murderer or accomplice dead and hauled away from the communities they terrorized, Texas was a totally new experience. No murders had occurred since the third day of the purge—almost two weeks ago. One could walk down any street, day or night, and not worry about being killed. Street crime was still prevalent but was greatly diminished by fear of retribution from the mysterious judge, jury, and executioner responsible for the cleansing.

People were moving to Texas in greater numbers, causing the real estate market to explode. Texas finally had a border wall. Not a wall to keep out illegals, but a state-line safety boundary delineated by a simple line on a map. Some cartel members tried to challenge the safe areas and were immediately dropped at customs and carted away, suffering from the "Fear." They were politely returned to Mexico in zippered black bags.

Police didn't need guns anymore. A billy club was a sufficient threat for skirmishes and petty offenders. Domestic violence calls were easily handled by simply breaking down the door and apprehending the perp.

Bulletproof vests were hanging in storage closets in the precincts. Cop spouses slept better at night.

6

Calm

1/19/2026

The DNA profiles for the Beaumont prisoners were completed and analyzed. Nothing was noted as unusual or connecting this to anything ever seen before. When cross-referenced with the FBI database, it confirmed the innocence of twenty-three prisoners from around the country. They would be released after the paperwork from the various prosecutors was completed and confirmed by judges so it could be recorded with the courts.

The Feds still had no explanation for what happened nearly three weeks ago. Some crazy theories were batted around and quickly thrown out. Most laypeople settled on the supernatural, whatever that meant to them.

Life was settling down, and folks were getting used to the new world of Texas justice. Petty thefts, shoplifting, and car thefts began to increase slightly as the separation between the event and the current day grew longer. These types of crimes were still much lower than before that reckoning day in Beaumont, though.

Quite a few family members wouldn't be sitting down to Thanksgiving dinner or celebrating Christmas in Texas this year. They knew they couldn't survive stepping across the border. That shocked a few families who figured things out.

Insurance costs were starting to drop, and some retailers could offer lower prices because their "shrinkage" was much lower. Shrinkage is the euphemism for shoplifting in the woke world. The actuaries were fluctuating weekly as crime statistics were digested.

They still had problems in Texas, but the rest of the country was seriously jealous of the "New State of Texas."

David and Nicole were recently married and hadn't thought much about starting a family yet. They lived in a part of Houston that was in a higher crime zone. That played a big part in their decision to put things off for a while. They would have to move to a better part of town. Now they were rethinking things. Besides, their two little dogs needed some kids to play with. Their neighborhood was safe now. No drugs were being sold. Dealers knew that if someone overdosed from their product, they would catch the "Fear," as everybody referred to it now. Marijuana was about the only product for sale in the city, and that testified to the lower risk. Many of the drug users who were in the neighborhood just weeks ago had relocated to another state to resume their old habits or stayed willingly and gone cold turkey.

David used to carry a handgun while in his car. Too many carjackings required the deterrence that a revolver in the glove box provided. Not needed anymore.

Nicole still carried; she didn't want to get in a tussle if she was targeted. It makes a big difference to know that you won't be killed if you fight back. It gives a potential victim a psychological advantage over the once-advantaged attacker. Self-defense didn't count against the shooter in this new order. Even a walk to the store late at night was very safe, especially if you had a gun on your belt. If a thief wanted to rob you, they had to assume you had a weapon on you. The potential victims and their attackers also knew if a crook drew and tried to shoot, it would be immediate suicide. No one wants to die with the face of "Fear" adorning their body. Police investigations ended before they started when they saw that look on the dead attacker.

Funerals with closed caskets were now code for "murderer inside." An open casket would not be comforting to the families and friends of these dead.

It was such a weird new reality. There was an underlying sense of doom, though; nobody knew what the reason was or who was behind this. This power had no side rails. It caused a lot of worry along with the relief and safety it brought. Those emotions are not supposed to run together. They did in Texas.

The list of "Fear" deaths was long and unusual. Professional athletes and college football players were missing from their teams. Many murders spawned by business competition ended careers and lives. Many abortion doctors who crossed the line discovered the new normal. A new emoji showed up on Apple iPhone updates. The little yellow happy faces offered a dark new option: the face of "Fear." It was super popular and available in a dozen skin tones.

Some of the attention and attraction was wearing off. No new events in two months. Whatever it was appeared to be finished. There were so many questions that it was best to just let it go and get on with life. Sort of a "Move it along, nothing to see here." Even the media was bored now. Paranormal television shows were scouring and scouting the state for a show angle. They were the only ones that still cared to "gin up" their viewers.

Church attendance increased considerably along with the offerings that came with the returning wayward and new seekers. Belief in God gave relief to many. There was no other explanation that could challenge this explanation.

7

Stealing

6/30/2026

Six months after the first death brought nothing new from Texas. Every now and then a misinformed or stupid murderer would try to enter the state. They would be immediately torched like a fly in an electric bug zapper. "The force was still with them," like the old Star Wars movies, was a common observation. The governor considered warning signs at the border, but after thinking about it, he decided that was not a very good idea.

The three-letter Fed agencies were still stumped. In that first week, quite a few of their agents ended up with a case of the "Fear." They quickly declared anyone involved in assassinations or murder, persona non grata in Texas. A retired CIA agent up in Dallas came down with the "Fear" on the night that hit his sector. Everyone knew he was somehow involved in the Kennedy assassination. Now they knew it was more direct than they were originally led to believe. A lot of cover-ups and lies were being exposed. "Why was this only happening in Texas?" the FBI Director wondered. He had no plans to visit the state. He didn't want to take any chances.

Same with all the other agencies. The higher-ups stayed away after the first agency cases of the "Fear" occurred. No reason to take unnecessary chances. Too many past actions might qualify them for a special surprise.

7/1/2026

Midnight arrived. And then it happened again. This time it was not lethal. It was as confusing as the first "Fear" cases. Certain people found wrapped bundles of cash in their homes. Others had their bank accounts drained. Insurance companies transferred money to policyholders they had cheated in the past. Insurance cheaters suffered a sudden loss of funds that matched the insurance scams they ran. Some of the bolder scammers lost everything they had. Even real estate was transferred in the legal way. Properly notarized deed transfers were recorded with the state. The new owners received their compensation in the form of their scammer's property.

As the asset and property "losers" realized what happened, some tried to confront the winners. Many attempted violence that was thwarted by an immediate and devastating self-inflicted wound in the exact proportion to the intended damage they hoped to deliver.

The next day, it became clear what was going on. Stealing was now targeted for special attention. Shoplifters were stopped in their tracks, and their penalty was the amount they attempted to steal. It was removed from their banks or cash they had on hand. The sudden transfer of ill-gotten gains left many penniless. It was justice time again in Texas.

Old thefts were included in the tabulations as well. The last criminal elements were seriously considering leaving for states with less oversight. That would help to open up housing for the many who wanted to move to Texas. Some decided it was time to get a job and use whatever skills they had to earn an honest wage. Alarm clocks would be, for many, used for the first time in their lives.

People started to notice refunds from years-old apps that they couldn't figure out how to cancel. Cancellations were made almost impossible to navigate. Many of these tech outfits declared bankruptcy, but not before all the money was transferred out to their once-handcuffed customers. Many banks took a major hit on their bottom line when unfair or hidden charges were immediately returned. Some institutions tried to take it back from their customers' bank accounts but found out quickly that that tactic would fail and impart even more pain and loss of money to their bottom lines.

Telemarketing scammers lost everything, and many were jailed by their own whistleblowers' testimony against them. People can turn on you quickly when you don't pay them what you owe them. These scammers didn't have a dime left for payroll.

Car dealerships ran into difficulties too—not all, but quite a few. The aftermarket sales in "closing" rooms were always a place for hidden fees and excess charges to be attempted. Special paint treatments or rustproofing or extended warranties. Not anymore. Out-of-state buyers skyrocketed because of their new, albeit forced, honest approach.

Stolen elections ended after the illegal votes were mysteriously moved to the opposite side of the aisle. It went both ways.

Everything from lunch money thefts in elementary schools to mob shakedowns of businesses came to a halt. Loan sharks were devastated when they saw the money evaporate.

In a matter of weeks, insurance costs would plummet, and the savings would be passed down to businesses and individuals.

Security companies weren't needed anymore, nor were safes, locks, and police. The taxpayers were able to self-police now. Municipalities' expenses dropped dramatically. Soon property taxes and other fees wouldn't be as necessary. Quite a few city government workers and council members were involuntarily paying back the money they took from the citizens. Productivity increases exploded. Mayors stopped going on taxpayer-funded work trips. When you have to pay it back, the luster of a "work" vacation wears off rapidly.

Especially hard-hit were the politicians who took bribes or traded with insider information. The ones who made it through the first round six months ago were not forgotten. That wrecked a lot of lopsided marriages. The age difference couldn't be overcome without all the money needed to feed it. When that dried up, so did the "love."

Texas was now a true sanctuary state—a sanctuary for honest and hardworking Americans. Living in Texas as an illegal alien carried no negatives now. You couldn't survive if you weren't honest and hardworking. The chaff was winnowed down to the good people from all nations. Running into another race or culture on a dark street was nothing more than a nonchalant and friendly encounter. People helped each other without reservation. The new normal was a potent balm for people who were abused by crime and fraud. Drivers were even picking up hitchhikers, something not seen in years, and some women even dared to hang a thumb out.

Rampant voter fraud was revealed as new elections overwhelmingly confirmed mostly conservative victories. Maybe it was just because the more liberal voters left the state in their cars or coffins. The Latinos left behind voted the most conservative, as seen in all the statistical evidence. With election fraud washed away, candidates had to rethink the verity of their platform strategies and allegiances.

Louisiana, and especially New Orleans, wanted the new justice where they lived and worked. Some politicians modeled their new legislation to mimic the results in Texas. It had emboldened some of the weaker elected. Representative Clay Higgins led the way. He was not one of the weak. He knew he could dole out sentences to better fit the crimes. If it overcrowded Louisiana's prison system, it didn't matter. Texas had quite a few "vacancies" that could be brought into negotiations.

A funny thing happened after a crime crackdown announcement was made from the congressman's office. When Higgins reminded criminals that they were likely to be rotated into the Texas prison system, the smarter ones realized that they would instantly become part of this new normal. All their past crimes and all their undetected crimes would be adjudicated at the exact moment they crossed into Texas. How many would suffer the "Fear" in that moment was conjecture. Higgins knew it would be astronomical. His career before politics was within the leadership ranks of the police. Nothing would shock him.

Crime came to a stop like a train hitting a truck blowing through a railroad crossing. The more stupid criminals were warned by their friends and families that crime in the State of Louisiana was a "dead-end" occupation. Many decided to move to Mississippi to avoid the correction that would certainly come if they maintained the status quo. Louisiana started transporting prisoners as a matter of course through a circuitous route to county or municipal lockups—a route that would take them into Texas, even if for a mile or two. It was the perfect cost-cutting and cleansing algorithm for the times.

When that story hit the media, what little crime was still occurring was whittled down to a sliver. Now an undetected Louisiana murderer or any other class of criminal understood that if they didn't walk a straight line, an arrest for littering could end up causing the "Fear."

Higgins laughed as California and Illinois passed laws outlawing the transfer of prisoners to Texas. Those two states added another type of sanctuary for the downtrodden. They were now a sanctuary for murderers and other criminals. Not surprising, crime exploded to new heights never imagined by these well-meaning and "savvy" politicians. For the first time in years, U-Hauls were headed back into these new sanctuaries. These out-of-state "outlaws" were treated with suspicion and worried their new neighbors.

8

Pedophiles/Traffickers

9/1/2026

It happened again at midnight. The Texas "solution," as it was now called. Bodies were everywhere. Not on the streets, but in homes and apartments. Like everything else surrounding this enigma, this was another unknown. The murderers were all dead from the first day that this Force cleaned house. Who was in this new dead group? Why were they not already in their final resting place? Why were they added to the rolls of the punished? The answers would be known in the morning.

"Pedophiles Are Next" was the two-inch-tall headline in the Dallas morning newspaper. It didn't take long to compare the names to sexual predators who were charged or convicted of crimes against children. This new dragnet scooped up any deviant who touched or harmed a child. Way too many activists who proclaimed pedophilia should be normalized were gone for good now. These "minor-attracted" activists were obviously more "hands-on" than they claimed. Most weren't part of any new wacky gender group. They were living as mothers and fathers, public school teachers and priests, Boy Scout leaders, babysitters, Sunday school teachers, and camp counselors. Day care workers and drag show "girls" were also hard hit, along with a lot of Disney media workers. Quite a few filmmakers living in Texas and lured by tax incentives were wearing the "Face." The filming industry collapsed on this day in Texas.

Pediatricians, dentists, doctors, and therapists had their businesses closed by the sudden deaths of their owners or staff members. Lawsuits killed the straggling surviving practices as the huge compensatory verdicts were read in courtrooms across the state. The level of pedophilia shocked the nation and the world. Any person involved in trafficking these children was "gone" now too. Pornographers who abused children paid the price for their wickedness. Internet porn was directed away from Texas internet. Too risky for the declining rolls of online perverts they serviced.

Parents were at ease letting their children out of the house unsupervised. They had lamented that their past childhoods were so carefree compared to modern America. Now their kids could enjoy the safe and carefree lifestyle that any child should experience.

9

Adultery 11/1/2026

Once again, things quieted down. All they could do was wait and see. These punishments always occurred on the first day of the month. As was customary, sports bars changed the stations to news just before midnight. It was a Texas tradition now. Most of the world that was in reasonable time zones at midnight on the first day of the month was watching the clock and the television sets too. Super popular in Australia. It was the number one show in Shanghai, Singapore, and Tokyo.

People on the fringes were really getting nervous now. How deep would this cleansing go? So far, the crimes have been the big ones. The really big ones. Would they stay aimed at those targets? Every midnight caused a lot of interest along with a lot of worry. The smarter media companies had text announcements available for those who signed up to their apps. If something happened, phones would be dinging by the millions around the world.

Nancy Zemanski and Jerry Ward met in a small group for marriages and families destroyed by adultery. They were both technically married and awaiting the courts to complete the dissolution of their once "perfect" bond. Jerry's wife reconnected with her high school boyfriend on Facebook, and Nancy's love of her life was tarnished by a one-night stand that went on for two years. Their homewreckers both intended to marry their new lovers at the "right" time. Their text messages revealed their motives and explicit language and sexting.

Nancy's husband was on the first night of a five-day, out-of-state business trip when the clock struck midnight. Jerry's wife was planning a second trip home in just a month to visit her mom. Her childhood house was two blocks away from her lover's home. He was married and had his own family. They went to the same church as children. He lived in the same house he grew up in. She was packed and ready for her plane flight in six hours. She would be back in her old neighborhood by 10:00 a.m. She woke at 3:30 a.m. to get ready and felt strange. Really weird, she thought, almost numb. She couldn't put her finger on it, but something was different. She just wasn't as excited as she was the day before, fantasizing about her upcoming sex while pleasuring herself next to her sleeping husband in bed. He wasn't asleep; he knew what she was doing.

Jerry drove her to the airport. She didn't kiss him goodbye; she hugged him, looking away to avert unnecessary and convicting eye contact. She would miss two weeks of her Bible study groups while away. Ironically, she was the leader of both church groups.

Brook Hepinstal's husband was an airline pilot for a European airline. He was tall, handsome, and away from home for ten days a month. He took advantage of his wife and of the opportunities for affairs during those ten-day stints. He was a well-known philanderer in pilot circles. They lived in Kemah, Texas.

Brian Foley's wife was basically a very oversexed woman. Not the kind a husband dreamt about. She was the other kind—a nymphomaniac driven by porn and the excitement that danger provided. Her husband worked over forty miles from home and never came back early. She had an impressive run of male visitors to her home. She loved when an appliance broke down or a plumber was needed. She knew whom to call, and they knew what was expected. She was, like many nights, out with girlfriends at the local sports bar to watch the news at midnight. Her husband was home in bed. He had a tough workday the next morning.

The bar patrons were counting down the seconds to midnight. You'd think they were watching a space launch. The same countdown was playing out in thousands of bars around the world. Was this going to be the night for another midnight visit? They all wanted it. This was real, not a phony reality television series touted on the legacy networks.

Everyone was chanting. Three, two, one. The bar got very quiet. It usually took a few minutes to know for sure. This time nothing happened for hours. The fans went home empty-handed. They would try again next month when they returned to the "Fear Factor," as it was now known. A fitting name from another TV show of the past.

Something did happen at midnight, though. It wasn't as obvious as a body dropping down dead with a contorted face. It was much more subtle to the ones not affected. It was devastating to the receivers of this special discipline. It wasn't the end of their life; it was the end of their lineage. These were the adulterers of the world—the destroyers of vows and families. These were the homewreckers, betrayers, and cheaters. This caught a lot of people off guard. It also affected the non-married through their illicit link to the married offenders. It struck millions in Texas.

The punishment for this was a divorce without retaining any assets or valuables. You were left penniless and homeless. The affected partner got it all: the house, the cars, the money, and the children. There was another component to the punishment, though: it was the impotence that befell these cheaters. They could never be satisfied sexually. They couldn't feel a thing. Not one part of their body could experience a sexual or even a sensual feeling. To many, it was a death sentence—just like the death of their marriage. Neither cheating spouse wanted to live anymore. The women lost their children, as did the men who thought they would never be caught. It was heartbreaking for the kids.

Most people thought of adultery as a minor infraction. Nothing like murder and pedophilia. It wasn't, though; it was a crushing blow to families that would survive, and the betrayal would live on through multiple generations.

This one frightened people still in the game. They worried about what would be next or who would be next. They wondered if they would be in the sights of this unknown force when the next midnight bell tolled.

Murder, stealing, pedophilia, and now adultery. This was getting close to the list of Moses' commandments from thousands of years ago. Throw in lying, bearing false witness, graven images, and coveting, and the rest of Texas would be thinned and culled like the varmint coyotes or prairie dogs that plagued ranchers. After all, everybody did those "things." Would lusting be categorized as subject to adjustment? Lying was a way of life for Americans. Especially politicians. How many husbands lied to their wives about their weight or beauty to keep the home from becoming a war zone? Bearing false witness was a serious problem, especially if it falsely convicted an innocent. But wasn't gossiping like bearing false witness? This was suddenly getting real to those committing the "minor" infractions. This was going too far. It was fun and satisfying to watch the serious offenders get what they had coming. Everyone was reanalyzing their lifestyles and lives now. A large contingency decided the risks were too great for the lower-level crimes they were committing. They headed out of state—as if they could outrun their bad choices.

The wedding business in the state took a major hit to its bottom line as cancellations started rolling in. Texas had over 175,000 weddings the year before. This year that number would be cut in half. The "Save the Date" announcements, which usually went out in advance of the invitation mailings, caused a lot of arguments, accusations, confessions, and sadness to the married and their families. Many parents of the bride or groom wouldn't be able to attend their own child's Texas wedding because they were cheaters. They would soon know the punishment that would emerge upon entering the Lone Star State. The offenders didn't want to be anywhere near Texas or flying through its airspace now. Even the Indian Ocean was too dangerous.

Nancy's husband was in Las Vegas when he learned about the latest midnight surprise. His paramour was as numb as a gum after a shot of Novocain. And he was totally impotent. No Viagra could help his predicament. Their arrangement ended immediately. He would soon have no more money to keep her. There was no love in their arrangement. They confused love with sex.

Jerry's wife suffered the same fate as everyone else who played on the field of betrayal. Her lover was as soft as a jellyfish. The lovers never got together again. No desire was more potent than impotency.

Brook's husband came home, and he moved in with his mother. She was devastated by the cheating and wasn't swayed by his pleas. It took her years to recover. It still haunted her dreams and lived in her nightmares. She met a wonderful man and lived for him now, and he cherished her after his wife was caught. Those who were exposed were distinguished by a small mark on their ring finger—almost like a tattoo. The mark "/\" was on their left ring finger, on the underside and in red. A sort of subdued and modern shout-out to Nathaniel Hawthorne and his *Scarlet Letter* of old.

Brian's wife left the bar feeling awful. She couldn't define it. She canceled her soirée set up with the bartender after closing. She had no interest in him now. He had no interest in her either. She arrived home earlier than usual. That made Brian happy. His happiness wouldn't survive her soon-to-be-exposed infidelity. She would be on the street soon; she wore the mark.

A tech guy from Austin was stunned by his new wife's infidelity. He didn't sit around moping; he developed a matchmaking app for the faithful and made a fortune putting destroyed lives back together by connecting them with a new mate. The whole process consumed him and made it possible to forget what his two-year marriage once meant to him. He was a successful entrepreneur, but so distraught he considered suicide. He crawled out of his brokenness and turned it around. He would not be defeated by the sociopath he wed. Narcissists and their antics were exposed by the tens of thousands. Many spouses took them back. Years of control is a mighty yoke that isn't easy to cast off. Even a lot of the physically abused wanted their cheating spouse back. At least the abuse would be stopped and turned back on them if they tried it again.

The spouses and families affected by adultery are always shocked and hurt—a hurt that can't be quickly salved. Trust cannot be easily regained. It usually never can be regained when such a horrific betrayal is exposed. The offenders don't care about what pain they cause; they just care about themselves. Most therapists in this type of family counseling specialty know that reconciliation is normally unobtainable, even if a voluntary stop to the cheating is promised. If the offender doesn't take full control of the process and the healing and act like they mean it, it's sunk. Even if they do all the right things, it may take decades to fully trust again. That's a pretty tough road to travel down. Most simply run out of gas before the journey to reconciliation is complete. The old saying "once a cheater, always a cheater" certainly didn't help.

How many fathers have told their sons that your good name and your word and your trust are all you have in life? How many disregarded that advice and ruined their lives and their families' lives and their grandchildren's lives? In Texas, quite a lot.

Who is behind this reckoning? Why is this only happening in Texas and in a faraway ocean? What's next? When will it stop? Will it touch me? Almost every citizen was "sucker-punched" by this realignment. When adultery was added, it affected everyone's families and their friends' and their neighbors' families too.

10

Tourism was in free fall. Nobody wanted to expose themselves or even take a chance on being in the state when the next edict would be revealed. A new edict that could indict them for past actions. What began as a huge win for law and order was turning out to be an economic catastrophe for much of the state and especially the tourist industry. The most popular T-shirt in the tourist shops had the words: "I Survived a Visit to Texas" displayed over an outline of the state. They sold them by the thousands. Unfortunately, hotel and restaurant bookings were at an all-time low. People were starting to hurt from this almost as much as the judgments and punishments.

Large corporations stopped considering Texas for relocation or expansion. Higher-ups in out-of-state and global subsidiaries would refuse to visit the home office. It also killed mergers and acquisitions— too risky for the bottom line and not worth the headache. Back-room operations that required honesty and integrity made sense, and those outfits were left in Texas. New accounting and purchasing departments opened in Texas in the hopes of stopping embezzlements or under-the-table payments for priorities given to unscrupulous sellers.

People were starting to demand answers that no one had. Church leaders struggled to find scripture or anything else that could be pulled together to explain this phenomenon of biblical proportions. Some churches described it as a modern-day, old-fashioned plague. It made sense, except that now innocent people were touched by it. Up until recently, this plague "passed over" the righteous. There was nothing you could put on your doorframe to save you from this Passover.

There was an outbreak of praying that comforted many. Murder, pedophilia, stealing and theft, and now adultery. Add a few more, and you'll have the complete moral code given to the wandering Jews in the desert. God wasn't talking to His worshippers about this. No church leader claimed inside knowledge. No layman experienced a connection.

There were a few religious charlatans who thought a quick buck could be made. Unfortunately for them, they were done with their scams when the first dollar was put into their pockets. They were stealing and defrauding—not allowed in Texas nowadays.

November 27, 2026

New cults were observed in the state, staking a claim. Mostly religious, but some satanic ones. It depended on whom you worshipped. Texas was getting to be weirder than Portland, Oregon. "Texlandia," they called it.

Sydney was married the year before, and so far, so good in the midnight judgment department. She was a fine person and loved God. She and her husband Carter lived in Austin. They were visiting family in Ft. Lauderdale for the holiday and staying in her parents' home. The soccer trophies and ribbons were where she left them in her bedroom.

This Thanksgiving took on a whole new and intensely deep significance. The prayers before the feast went on a long time. Nobody cared this time. They liked it. Lately, Sydney was having strange and uncharacteristically ominous dreams. Not nightmares—intense dreams that she really couldn't recall in the morning. She just knew she was experiencing something from a higher place. They didn't frighten her, although she was worried that they might as the nights passed and the episodes continued. Carter calmed her enough to not worry. They were both aware of the judgments in their home state. Sydney guessed they might be connected to her nights now.

The dreams subsided the next week. She was relieved in a way but wondered where they were leading her before they stopped. She was able to make a little sense out of some of them. She did feel they were somehow connected to the judgments in Texas. Now they vanished.

Nancy and Jerry's divorces were finalized. Their spouses were out on the street. Both moved in with each other's parents. Luckily, they didn't have an attraction to cheating.

A great sense of ease washed over them. They started to officially date, and that was a great way to help them get over the shock of not being wanted by their spouses. She was the sweetest thing he had ever met. No anger was detected even though she earned that right. Jerry was a shy man, and being burned by his ex-wife wasn't good for his self-esteem. He didn't gain any happiness knowing that she was living back at home. He actually was relieved that he didn't have to worry about her welfare—her physical welfare, not her emotional. She pleaded to be let back in. He was not having any of that. He now had a new friend who experienced the same insult, and the future was a lot brighter than when the adultery was first revealed.

They enjoyed each other's company and went out at least twice a week. After a month, Jerry kissed her. It happened at the back entrance of her home, next to the washing machine. It was like the first kiss he ever had—pure and clumsy. It was perfect. He saw a pathway out of his depression and anxiety. Nancy smiled later when she realized she'd had her first teenage kiss in her parent's laundry room as she leaned back against the washing machine and closed her eyes. She too had a flood of emotions and a great release from the hell she had experienced at the hands of her ex-husband. They began to regain their health and restore their hearts. It was the inverse for their exes.

Jerry hadn't talked about his wife's cheating with anyone except a therapist or three. That didn't help him get over it or understand it. He needed Nancy to listen to his story. He needed someone he could sit next to and touch while he tried to make sense of it. He knew how lucky he was to find another companion so swiftly. It wasn't built upon a foundation of quickly getting married or sex or showing off to his ex-wife that he was happier than she was—although he was much happier than she was. He didn't have to move out with nothing. She did. His pain was still more piercing than her physical pain. She inflicted some serious damage on the man she married. His younger brother was killed in Iraq, and he was devastated by that hole left in his heart. This heartbreak was worse. It was physical and psychological.

His heart knew before his brain knew that his wife was cheating. His heart hurt. It was literally broken and was physically damaged. Three visits to the emergency room for heart attack symptoms confused him when the doctors ran the usual tests and declared that he was healthy. They asked if he was under any stress. He didn't think he was and said no. He thought the undetected heart problems would soon kill him. He made sure his "things" were in order. The large insurance policy, the legal papers and titles, and the bank account passwords were all cataloged so that his wife would have an easier transition when he died.

He would learn that "heartbreak" was a real physical assault on his body. Thousands of years of poems, romance tales, and stories about this condition were all true. These old and ancient stories weren't copied and forged over and over again like an easy and lazy plagiarism. Each battered love story was different and came in hundreds of layers filled with painful memories, broken hopes, and destroyed dreams. All aimed at the heart and leaving an open wound that seemed fatal to the maimed lying in ruin.

It was coming to an end—like a multicolored sunrise slowly appearing over the ocean. The straight and perfect horizon was the flawless line of demarcation that separated the night from the light. The breezes and winds that move unobstructed over oceans always lie down at dawn out of respect for the daily new creation. It bows to give it the recognition it deserves. A pause before life returns to the chaos that is exposed by the new day's sun hidden by the night. Jerry was rising from under that horizon.

Nancy was better equipped than Jerry to leave the road behind her. Her married "road" was always under construction. Warning signs on the side, flagmen waving red flags that she often ignored. Sometimes traffic flowed smoothly without interruption. The last few years, her highway department must have run out of money. Detours, flashing lights, flags, bumps, and warnings to be prepared to stop took the joy from her journey. Her roads were washed away by her husband's infidelity and betrayal. She knew but decided to ignore the obvious. She didn't really ignore it so much as pack it away to deal with later. Nancy would often stare at their wedding portrait to see if there was a telltale sign—something she could have seen to predict her future. He was just too damn handsome. When they dated, women would try to snatch him from her. He was always a citadel that needed to be defended. She wasn't enough of a warrior to withstand the constant assaults on the walls of her marriage. He was even less equipped and eventually raised the white flag in defeat. He paid his tribute when he conceded everything he had for short bursts of illicit pleasure.

Nancy was decimated by his disloyalty. She went through the same emotions that most women internalize in cases of the devious mishandling of trust by their life mates. His was complicated by narcissism. He was unable to empathize with what his wife's emotions might be if she found out. He thought it would never matter. She would never find out. Typical narcissist. Everything was all about him and his desires. She had a breakdown at first, but after the tears were drained dry, she felt a relief that it was over. It wouldn't be easy, she thought, but she was prepared to lick her wounds and move on. It would be difficult, she thought. But not as impossible as trying to rebuild the sacrificed trust that always haunts a reconciliation—even a sincere, remorseful, and repentant reconciliation. Most people who separate and divorce from destroyed trust won't live long enough to put the affair back into a sealed bottle. It's too easy for old wounds to be reopened by something as simple as an unanswered call or the ever-present infidelity in most movies, television series, and literature. Those were the hardest—watching infidelity portrayed as an innocuous diversion for the sophisticated relationships of our times.

She had no intention of ever seeking another relationship that could reopen her wounds. It just didn't interest her in the least. Until Jerry. She didn't know where this would go, but she understood where his heart was after his wife's backstab.

Now Brook was very different. She loved being married. The ten days a month in Europe seemed to make their relationship better. Sort of an "absence makes the heart...." You know the rest. It did, even after the babies came along. She hired a nanny to help. That was a blessing. When her husband returned home from his last flight, the reuniting was made more intense. She would spend hours getting dressed to set the stage. A late-afternoon arrival gave her time to visit her hairdresser and get her gel-coated nails touched up. Makeup and lipstick were carefully applied and checked in the mirror. Lovemaking was always on the agenda and usually instigated by him immediately after passing through the front entrance. She didn't want to interfere with the schedule. Having a nanny was appreciated even more when they closed the door to their bedroom.

As the news reports about the mental neutering of the cheaters traveled around the world, he understood what happened to him. He called his wife to confess and ask for forgiveness. She was all he had now. His mistress had the same affliction and was angry because she knew that he had groomed her for months before she gave in to his relentless attention. She knew he was married and had children. Brook hung up on him.

Brook would realize later that his super-charged affection for her had two names: Love Bombing and Affair Fog. She learned about it in the infidelity communities on Reddit. It was commonly used by cheaters to hide their guilt and used to cloak their infidelity. That realization really pissed her off.

Within three hours, everything he owned was thrown into a pile on the oil-stained garage floor. The next day the locksmith had changed every lock and key. The security cameras were installed inside and out, and then a 24-hour recording schedule was set up. She sent him a text message ordering him to make arrangements within three days of his return to Texas to "get his crap." If not, it would be picked up by the Salvation Army. She told him that the garage door code was the same, but that everything else was new and secured. She advised him about the security cameras that would watch his every action.

The next steps she took were textbook in their decisiveness. She blocked his cell number and texts. Email was no longer a workaround; blocked. She called her mother-in-law and laid out the betrayal. She told her that only questions about their children would be allowed and that any questions should be handled through his mother. A 180 strategy was next. She also learned about that during her research on Reddit.

This strategy can be used to either lead to reconciliation or to detach from emotional dependence and take back control. Limiting communication is the first step, and Brook already had that in place. She would have communication limited to the subject of the children. She would be calm with her mother-in-law as she cut off any chance to negotiate or reconcile. She was finished with this relationship and threw it on top of the pile with their wedding portrait and his crap in the garage. She would imagine him carrying it out and loading it into his car with all the other stuff. This woman did not intend to take a prisoner. He would be his mother's problem now.

Thanksgiving was the first holiday that was taken away by this "force." Others would soon follow as daily life walked slowly through the stumbling blocks on the calendar. So many citizens of Texas were affected by this midnight madness. Some felt they were unequally selected. They weren't.

Food stores noticed a significant drop in turkey sales and Thanksgiving favorites. Most out-of-state family members were not interested in visiting Texas to spin the roulette wheel. The ones complaining the most about going to Texas were obviously guilty of something. It destroyed many relationships. Over half of the out-of-state invitation recipients declined this year.

The talks around the dinner table were focused on a single question.

"What do you think they did?"

11

The handsome, gray-haired old man sat alone in the church. He was intrigued by the preacher's style and manners. The music that launched the service was loud, and so was the preacher. It was a new style to him, but he liked it. The music got your attention, and so did the boisterous sermon that blasted through the hanging speakers. This was not a new-age church. It was an old-age one—not referring to the age of the worshipers, but to the age of the words spoken. The sermons may have been written the night before, yet those words were supported by over 2,000 years of scripture. Some Sundays, it was bolstered by 7,000-year-old words—words that survived time and many "cross" examinations.

Pastor Ed was as solid as they come. His church was, too. Fifteen years ago, it barely survived an attack from its mortgage and a previous pastor's marriage that fell into default. They were in trouble. The old man remembered that dark time in the history of "The Island," as the church was known. He recalled praying for them and was happy to be sent there to check on them. He was glad he had pressed for their survival. Gabe was pleased with what he saw.

The sermon this Sunday was similar to many others that were concerned about the power behind the Texas turmoil. Ed talked about the "Fear" and what he thought it meant to Christians. He didn't know. Nobody did. He believed it was spiritual—it sure had the markings. People were nervous about this unexplained phenomenon, and they prayed long and hard this Sunday.

Gabe enjoyed the Orange Beach area of Alabama, the people who lived there, and the visiting tourists and young families that vacationed on the Gulf of Mexico. It was a few miles west of the Florida state line. "The Island" was in a growing and very popular place. That had nothing to do with its recovery. That was thanks to the new pastor's leadership and sermons.

Sun, boat, and water worshippers were drawn to the National Seashore and its protected, Caribbean-colored waters. It had everything, including hurricanes. Sally was the last one that blew in, causing serious damage. But like most communities that suffer through larger hurricanes, it pulled through with the help of its citizens. "The Island" rose up through the flooding and wind damage and was a blessing to those who were suffering. Gabe liked that; he remembered Sally. He was there.

December 2026

This Christmas was filled with trepidation and fraught with concern. Past holidays tended to carry worry, but that was usually nothing more than fretting about all the money spent on gifts. Many families were affected by the "Fear," and that put a somber blanket over the normally festive time. How do you deal with this ominous guillotine hanging over your head?

"Am I next?" was privately mulled over.

"Are you next?" That made you think.

The Defense Intelligence Agency (DIA) had been looking into this since the first "outbreak" last January. The little-heralded agency was as close as the government came to supernatural investigations. They still relied on science and seemed to be outside this realm. The Defense Department was investigating too, more to figure out a way to harness this power than to explain it.

The European Union, NATO, The United Nations, Mexico, and Canada commissioned teams to investigate this "matter." The Catholic Church took a more simplistic tack: this was either divine or satanic— one or the other—and they leaned toward divine.

Russia and North Korea suspected it was some kind of communist-style purge from the last century. They would try it themselves if they thought they could get away with it. Putin was the most impressed. In his mind, it had to be from the state, since no god existed to them.

India was investigating the ocean south of its country. This huge area in the ocean was the only other place on Earth where this phenomenon occurred. Ships and air traffic tried to avoid the Indian Ocean, but no recognizable boundary existed yet to go around. As more reports came in, a boundary was being plotted, but it made no sense. The International Space Station came down with a case of the "Fear" as it crisscrossed around Earth—an American from Florida. That happened early on, though, and since then no other reports of the unexplained in space were noted. Things were settling down again, as they had before. And like before, it kept citizens on low alert, along with a low-level anxiety.

12

The Middle East was starting to pay attention. They didn't want this turned against them. They were certainly vulnerable to every one of the midnight surprises. The religious leaders didn't like to think that their directives to deal with infidels would be classified as murder. Their edicts were in the name of their god, after all.

Israel's religious leaders determined that this definitely had the markings of the Old Testament—right out of Exodus, Chapters 20 and 34, to be exact. Many Christians agreed with that assessment. The Old Testament is the word of God to both religions, except for the more liberal ones that don't like to discuss that pesky place known as Hell.

The Uyghurs of Asia looked on with anticipation. They were subjugated and killed, and their conquerors had to be whistling as they walked past that graveyard. The Uyghurs felt they had earned this kind of dramatic justice.

The European Union's citizens were struggling with the hordes of immigrants that were invited in by their leaders. Crime and violent assaults of every kind were exploding, just like in the US. The citizens felt no one was listening to them; no one cared about their suffering—only the "newcomers" and their virtue-signaling enablers in government benefitted. Many overrun towns, villages, and cities were desperate to return to sanity. The insanity of their elected officials' own making needed a course correction. The citizens liked what they saw coming from Texas and hoped they would not be forgotten.

Gaza, Palestine, Congo, Sudan, Houthis, Hezbollah, Hamas, Ethiopia, Iran, Israel, the United States, and others were labeled as supporting genocide by the UN and by each other. Some thought the UN should have included itself. Politics aside, if that's possible, a "solution" might be coming their way. The leaders of each of these countries knew their nations were guilty of assassinations and murder. How far up the ladder a "correction" might go was a worrisome thought. Better that it be left in Texas.

Johnny Rentschler's older sister Linda won the National Geographic Bee years before Covid. He wanted to win it too. He studied and studied, and he loved everything about geography. When the National Geographic Society decided to cancel it due to lack of interest after Covid, he was heartbroken. He wanted the recognition again for his middle school.

His bedroom wall was covered in wallpaper featuring a huge Mercator Projection of the world—9 feet by 18 feet. He went to sleep looking at it and woke up looking at it. He knew every country, continent, ocean, lake, river, province, state, and region. His parents gave him permission to correct the misnomers caused by name and boundary changes. He hated wars; they could overthrow boundaries while toppling governments. His fine-point marker was ready to record the changes.

Johnny had seen a news program about the Texas midnight surprises on his birthday. He was confused like everyone else. The Indian Ocean was always intriguing to him. He looked over the data about the location of ships when they "crossed the line" and coughed up a body or two with the "Fear." It was a weird combination of straight lines and jagged ones running through the vast ocean south of India.

He looked in his atlas to revisit Texas. He had a hunch. He determined the longitude and latitude of straight lines and various points along the Rio Grande. Next, he reversed the numbers to the negative and placed these antipodes on his wall map. It was the exact boundary and size of Texas—just on the other side of the world and inverted. The antipode was a straight line through the center of Earth. It was as if you could look through the planet and see the underside of Texas in the Indian Ocean. The shape was upside down. Little Johnny cracked the code that others had tried and failed to solve before.

He surmised that the exact shape and size of Texas determined the area of the plane. The boundary lines pierced the Indian Ocean on the other side of Earth. He bet that a physical survey would show it to be an exact match in the ocean—just the underside.

He remembered that the International Space Station had an outbreak of this "justice." He researched the station's location in orbit at the time. It had just entered the "airspace" of Texas outside of San Antonio. In the three-dimensional map of Texas he imagined, this force escaped through Texas and the Indian Ocean and kept going into space. He was not a student of space; Johnny was still learning about the Earth that was on his wall map. He called his brother and asked him what he thought. Wells studied at the Lawrence Berkeley National Laboratory. His PhD program was in astrophysics, and he was in his last year. Another lab was working on the Texas phenomenon. Two scientists there were searching for answers but had yet to explain anything. Well's baby brother just did.

"Johnny, you're a genius!"

"Don't make fun of me, Wells." He was miffed.

"I'm not, buddy. I'm serious. You cracked the Indian Ocean conundrum and the space station death."

"I thought for sure you guys knew this already. Don't forget to credit me when you win the Nobel!" Johnny felt pretty smart now. So did his soon-to-be-PhD brother in California.

Wells ran down the hall and over to the "Project" building up the hill, surrounded by eucalyptus trees. He needed security clearance to enter. After he left a message with the director, he started to walk back down the hill with his "Top Secret" information.

"Wells! Wells!" He turned after hearing his name. "Get over here!"

He was granted access and brought up to the private office of the director.

"I got your message. Where is your report?" The director seemed surprised Wells didn't have a notebook full of equations.

"No report, just a simple explanation." That got the director's attention.

"I'm listening."

"The Force is a three-dimensional map of Texas. It pierces the Earth and carries out into space."

"The space station death," the director said, thinking aloud. "Okay. What else do you have?"

"The shape of the Indian Ocean zone is the exact size and shape of Texas. It's just a reverse image."

"Like looking at Texas from underneath?"

"Exactly. It's that simple," Wells said proudly, thinking of his little brother. "He was right."

"What method did you use to figure this out? Our guys have been working on it for a while now." The director was intrigued by the data and calculations.

"My thirteen-year-old brother called me a half hour ago and told me he cracked it. I don't even know how he did it."

"May I call him?"

"We can talk to him right now. I'll get him."

Johnny answered his brother's call. "What, you need more help with your elementary education?" He was on speakerphone. Wells and the director laughed out loud. Wells explained who was on the line, and Johnny apologized. He was famous now—at least inside the esteemed Lawrence Livermore labs. It wasn't as famous as the Fusion Ignition breakthrough in 2022, but the next best thing. He explained that his calculation was simply reversing the longitude and latitude and giving them a negative value. The answer was discovered that easily.

"After I plotted them, it revealed its location in the Indian Ocean. Next, I overlaid the known shipboard locations where someone died from the 'Fear.' It wasn't exactly the boundary of a reversed Texas, but it was close enough to see the pattern. I figured the fuzziness was from slight errors in the ships' reports." Johnny spoke too fast and had to slow down.

"In order to verify this from another source, I plotted the space station death based on the time and location. I calculated a straight line from the station through the center of the Earth. It traveled through San Antonio's border with Mexico, straight through to the Indian Ocean. Bingo."

The director was impressed. So was Wells.

If any laboratory could whittle down this mystery a bit more, it was the one on the hill above Berkeley, California. They had the tools and the minds. Director Wharton couldn't wait to tell his disciples about little Johnny—and to rub it in a little.

13

New Year's Eve provided the parties and wide-screen TVs to watch and wait. Drink specials in bars served as old-fashioned spielers to lure customers inside. The "Fear" show kept them in their seats and on barstools until closing.

Midnight struck, and everyone remained focused on the screens to hear the reporters offering a play-by-play that would have made Vin Scully proud during his days calling Dodgers games. Vin could always fill the airwaves with great stats and stories during more boring matchups. Midnight tonight was boring; they already knew the stats. They wanted to "play ball."

Nothing! It wasn't written off quite yet, as some of the corrections took a while. The loyal fans would stay until they were sent home empty-handed.

The first business day of the new year revealed what happens when you give false testimony or, as some very old literature refers to it, "bearing false witness." That's right—the Ninth Commandment. This was either a very clever way to disguise these punishments as the wrath of God, or it was the wrath of God.

Either way, the results were biblical. Lumped together under that broad category was lying. Papers began to land on judges' desks implicating thousands of Texans involved in criminal and civil cases. Lying under oath was given more weight. Fibbing or white lies counted, but they were at the bottom of the discipline scale.

Judges read the statements and began to release thousands of prisoners who had been falsely convicted of crimes. Their prison replacements would soon experience the pain and suffering they had caused, as the liars took over the bunk space from the wronged. Most of these were men involved in police investigations, as well as businessmen involved in fraud. Politicians who had survived by not taking bribes were busted for their lies, however. They were fact-checked and given a lifetime score for lying: 0 to 100. That sure changed political ads in Texas.

Many gun owners who lied on their applications were jailed and banned from purchasing guns after their release. Even notary publics were punished for knowingly falsifying documents with their seals and signatures.

Hundreds of rape convictions were overturned, and the lying accusers placed in prison. Thousands of divorce cases were revisited after lies and deceit from the complainants were revealed. Children were returned to the other spouse, and assets were transferred to those unfairly treated by the court system. Many apologies would be forthcoming from family members and friends to the recipients of false-witness damage.

Texas was not only the safest place on the planet, but it was also now the fairest.

Still, there remained the "little liars." They got off easy, but their lies were exposed to their friends and family. An A-through-F grade was found on the underside of the ring finger, in some cases right next to the adulterer's mark. It would take a lot of work for that grade to be upgraded. It would show on the finger as a change as people "cleaned up" their image.

This last midnight madness affected everybody. Very few had an A. It was like restaurant ratings. Smart owners would get right on fixing a bad rating; the same went for liars. Lots of people were holding their tongues to reduce the negative ratings. Salespeople were proud of their B ratings and would show them off to prospective customers. Bluffing in negotiations wasn't strictly enforced unless they were up against an unequal combatant—let's say, a grandma vs. XYZ Corporation. Poker games were not included. Everyone knew it was all about lying by expression and mannerisms.

Regular, non-adultery cheating was not on the "do not disturb" list.

This correction was different from the others. So many surprises in families, businesses, churches, social media, political campaigns, governments, and medicine—so many lies wouldn't allow for the truth. Fortunes were turned upside down. Deceit failed now. It was exposed.

Gabe left Orange Beach and traveled to Texas. He wasn't worried about the invisible border line. He looked at it like a checkup—a maintenance stop along the way. He had a sense of humor. He left from the Pensacola airport and chuckled as he went through the metal detectors and pat-downs. Texas had an exemption for flights originating in-state. No need anymore.

He landed in Houston to visit old friends. Den-O's sports bar was an old hangout. Gabe's old friends were also very old, and this bar was even older. He met them at 5:00 PM, and they sat down at a corner table in the main room. They talked about the "good old days" because that gave them the most comfort. Jack was worried about what was going on in Texas; that's why Gabe had come to town—to help his buddy get through the last years of his life without much worry. Jack lived alone now; his wife died last year, and he was floundering. He was thankful for his old dog, Ricky. He knew Ricky kept him going. He loved that mutt more than anything now, and the thought of losing him was another worry. Jack wanted to die on the same day Ricky died. He didn't think he could survive without him.

Gabe reached across the table and grabbed his right hand. "Let's say a prayer, Jack. You need it, old buddy." They closed their eyes and slightly bowed. Gabe prayed for Jack for over five minutes. Jack must have said "amen" twenty times or more. When they opened their eyes, Gabe stood up and hugged Jack.

"I really needed that," Jack said. "Thanks, Gabe."

"Finish your beers. Let's get outta here and get some grub. Jack, come with me in my car."

They all left, got in their cars, and headed to Ninfa's for Tex-Mex. Their fajitas were the best, and they even claimed to be the first American restaurant to serve them.

Donny was confused. While they were praying, he didn't hear anything. Not a word. Gabe was praying, but he couldn't hear it. Chuck had the same experience.

"That's the religion I like best," Chuck sniggered.

"What do you mean?" Donny asked.

"The quiet kind of religion."

After dinner, Jack and the boys left in Chuck's car, and Gabe drove his rental to the airport. He was headed to New Mexico. He hadn't visited in quite a while and remembered it fondly.

Chuck teased Jack about the silent prayer and said he could deliver one of those.

"What are you talking about, you old fart?"

"The silent prayer." Jack was confused. "Are you having a stroke?"

"The prayer at Den-O's. Gabe didn't say anything."

"Donny, what is he talking about? Did you hear anything?" Jack was startled and shook his head side to side.

"No, it was silent." Now Donny thought Jack had a stroke.

"He said a prayer, and I heard every word," Jack insisted. He wanted to get home to his dog, Ricky, who would comfort him.

They dropped Jack off at his small house. He was confused. Donny and Chuck were worried about him.

On the Mexican side of the border below Brownsville, an American man was shot and killed. He lived on the US side, and he had not been singled out by the Texas mystery. He wasn't protected on the other side of the border. Living in Texas didn't inoculate you against violence outside its boundaries and borders. That made news, and Texans took notice.

New Mexico police were mimicking Louisiana, and the level of all crimes was dropping. It didn't take long for criminals and violent offenders to get the message that a drive across the border to Texas would be on the itinerary either before trial or after. That caused thousands to move out of state. California was the top recipient, thanks to its new sanctuary laws.

The Ninth Circuit Court in San Francisco was hearing an emergency case promoted by district attorneys from multiple large cities in California. The end game was the Supreme Court of the United States. They wanted the practice of law enforcement bringing prisoners across state lines into Texas stopped. They wanted that border closed to criminals—a border inside the US.

Appellate attorneys around the nation had some great countering ideas. Kent Wirth, a D.C. appellate pro with Arnold & Porter, was questioned by the media: "I'd have the alleged perpetrators sign a notarized document declaring their innocence. If they really were innocent, they would have no worry. If they signed and then got the 'Face,' that meant they had lied on a sworn statement. The other option would be to plead guilty, with a guarantee from the prosecution to remain in the state." Representative Clay Higgins liked his logic. Louisiana would be calling Arnold & Porter. He thought New Mexico should simply bus the convicted to California and let them enjoy their freedom in the sanctuary state. They would have to take the long way to get there.

Pastor Ed in Orange Beach needed to add another service. Three weren't enough. Now all four were standing-room only. His television broadcasts on the CW station were breaking records. His internet servers for online broadcasts needed to be upgraded to handle the traffic.

The same resurgence was happening in every state. Some estimates placed regular churchgoers up 20%, now nearly 50%. Not since WWII had such high numbers been seen.

❖

Tammy and Dalton O'Rourke lived in El Dorado, Arkansas, and both knew that a visit to Texas would end poorly. They had turned their lives around three years earlier. They got off meth and stopped cooking and selling it. Dalton worked at a convenience store and went to night school at the community college. He wanted to be an EMT.

Tammy cleaned houses in the nicer part of town. She was really good at her job and was as responsible as any good mother. That would come in handy since she was already one day pregnant. They decided to have children now that their lives were on the right track. She wouldn't learn about the baby for another month.

They both knew their past was shameful and reckless. Just before they quit the "business," as they called it, one of their fentanyl customers overdosed and died on the local high school bleachers. They knew it was a dangerous drug. They knew people were dying from it, yet they kept selling it until they were investigated following the death of one of their buyers. They didn't even remember him. The police didn't have enough to charge them.

Jesse Williston was 18, had just graduated from high school, and had a bright future. A tiny purple pill put an end to it. His football scholarship to Missouri was a dream come true. He was so excited that he and four friends decided to take some pills to celebrate. Jesse was a big guy; he took two. It was his first time taking drugs, and now he was dead.

Those same two pills killed his parents, his big sister Stephanie, and his younger brother Will. His girlfriend and his grandparents on both sides were emotionally destroyed too. The entire Williston family was shattered. It would take decades for them to heal. They wanted justice almost as much as Tammy and Dalton wanted forgiveness. Neither had achieved their opposing goals yet.

They started attending church two years ago, and after a rocky start, they were regulars each Sunday. Tammy was a volunteer, cleaning houses for those who couldn't—people recovering from surgery, broken bones, or strokes. Dalton was always available to help seniors with broken toilets, clogged drains, and yard work. These "little things," as they called them, didn't accomplish what they had hoped. They couldn't "buy" their way out of their past. They both learned that "good works" weren't enough to escape their guilt.

The Texas correction haunted them. They did their best to live with what they had done, but it hovered, disrupting sleep and peace. Their home was not far from the Texas border.

14

2/1/27 Sexual Assault

Another midnight on the first of the month. It wasn't the same entertainment attraction it used to be. It was easier and cheaper to stay home and watch. YouTube would have it up as soon as something happened. When something did, it wasn't like the original first-timers. No immediate gratification for the audience after the third round.

This month there was another event. It became evident in the morning. For those punished, it wasn't unexpected. They knew it was coming for them; they just wondered when.

Once again, it showed up in a lot of cells around the state. The screams were as loud as that first night in Beaumont. The difference was the screams were coming from the "corrected." The screamers were still alive and yelling. Some were crying. Some were missing their sex organs. The men were castrated. Everything was gone. Impossible to rape again. Not that they ever would have the chance. These scumbags had followed the news and knew violence of any kind would bring retribution. They knew their raping days were over. Women rapists were treated differently. Nothing was removed, but all desire was taken away. It was difficult to determine how many women got "fixed" until time passed. A lot of schoolteachers were affected. It was evidently more common than previously thought. The falsely accused had already been freed during the liar's correction. It didn't bring true joy to the victims, but it did bring relief and a meager kind of satisfaction.

Bobby Johanson was in prison for rape. He had been falsely accused while in college. The accuser waited a month before filing charges and, since this was in the early "Me Too" craze, he was convicted well before his trial. He should have been released. Bobby's case slipped through the cracks when his prosecutor misplaced his papers under the mess on his desk.

When the other prisoners were screaming about losing their genitals, Bobby was silent. He was sound asleep with his earplugs jammed in his ears. When the lights came on and the warden walked through, he stopped at Bobby's cell.

"Why aren't you screaming like the rest?" he demanded. "You're a rapist."

"No, I ain't."

"Well, you're in prison for rape."

"I know, but I ain't no rapist, sir."

"Drop 'em and let's have a look at your junk." The warden was serious. "Do it!"

Bobby followed orders and dropped his pants. There it was, his "little buddy."

"I always suspected you were a good kid, Bobby. Do you have someone who can pick you up tomorrow or the next day?"

"For what?" Bobby asked, confused.

"You're getting out of here. You're innocent, son!" The warden grinned. "That little dick of yours got you off the hook."

Bobby always hated that he was not of equal "stature" with the other guys. Right now, though, he wondered how his "small but mighty" friend freed him from prison.

Bobby wouldn't know what to do when he got out. He had just started college six years ago and was still a freshman. He was targeted in prison and within a week was seriously injured by another inmate. Bobby suffered a head trauma that left him mentally disabled. His family and friends abandoned him after his conviction, and he had nowhere to go. He wished he could stay in prison. It felt like home.

The Berkeley Lab at Livermore was stymied by this unknown power. It appeared to emanate in the center of the Earth, pierce the crust, continue through Earth's different atmospheres, and then off into infinity. None of their instruments could detect a thing. None of their minds could deliver a reason. This would be more difficult than unlocking cold fusion. The answer to this enigma would have to be reverse-engineered. To solve this equation, they needed a theorem as a basis, drilling down until they hit a solution or a dead end. No theorems existed at the moment, other than spiritual ones.

Nancy and Jerry were married in a small ceremony in the Bahamas. They liked it so much they bought a little house on the beach—two bedrooms and two baths, the perfect size for their new lives together. It was paid for by their ex-spouses' confiscated spoils. They spent every winter in their little hideaway. They both lived into their 90s. She died within four hours after Jerry's death. She was found on a chaise lounge on the beach in front of the little house. Jerry lay in bed with a smile on his face. Nancy had one too.

A year passed, and no new corrections were seen—no midnight entertainment. It seemed as if it was over. That was a great relief to many who wondered where they stood at the table. Those were the ones who were generally good people with a few aberrations along the way, a few blips on the radar.

Most people had friends and family who were affected by this powerful power. No one was left untouched. The joy of the first few surprises gave way to the others that were serious but not on the same top tier.

The most disruptive was adultery. It affected almost everyone, and that was a rude awakening to the reality of human nature—the animal side of life on Earth. Children were the most hurt and affected by this ancient attraction. It caused much damage, especially for the littlest ones.

It was reasonably easy to handle the death of a friend who was a murderer—they deserved it. The children did not. The damage to families seemed punitive to the innocents. It must have been very important to whoever or whatever was running this operation.

Brook's husband continued to fly and retired at the mandatory age of 65. He took his job more seriously now. It was all he had. His old life was gone, along with his marriage to Brook. He became a check pilot for his airline, and he had a reputation as one of the best. The rookie trainees considered him a very wise man. He wished he'd had that wisdom before he ruined everything.

Brook never remarried. She went back to school and became a therapist. At first, it was to understand her predicament. It helped her realize it wasn't her fault; it was his. She needed that clinical evaluation to keep going. She accepted an offer to join a group of psychologists and soon became a beacon in her "industry," a beacon of hope for marriages in decline. She lived in Texas, so none of her clients were adulterers. The odd thing about that setting was the marriages she tried to help weren't riddled with mistrust, making her work more satisfying, as confirmed by her success rate. It was so much easier to repair broken things if betrayal wasn't involved. That was a high hurdle, and she had personal experience and expertise. She became a well-known author and spoke to large audiences who sought help. She signed her books and gave good advice to the broken. She was as happy as when she first married.

Brian's life continued without his wife. He threw her out, changed the locks on his house, and closed off his heart. She didn't fare well once her preoccupation with cheating ended. Brian noticed that the home repairs, which had been so frequent when he was married, were no longer needed. He hadn't had a repairman at his house since his divorce. He canceled his home repair warranty. It was as bad a deal as his marriage had been.

He ran into a friend from elementary school, and they hung out on weekends. She had never married or had a relationship. She wasn't as attractive as his former wife, but he liked this "model" better. Her name was Matilda, and he called her Tilly. She was much more dependable than the old model. Although they never had children, they loved to sit in the park and watch families play together. There was no worry about creeps anymore; problem perverts were not around these parts— at least not above ground.

Tilly had been afraid to go outside alone before she met Brian. She had been attacked by Antifa while attending school in Oregon. She hadn't been protesting any cause, just walking through campus when a very large woman with a skinhead randomly punched her. Her face was covered by a burka and tattoos. That violent group of "protesters" wasn't a worry anymore. They didn't last long after they found they couldn't control the streets without violence. Now, they were ridiculed and relegated to a waste bin in Texas. It really changed their "protesting" techniques when they couldn't hurt anybody. They weren't missed.

Most every relationship changed in the state. The troublemakers were either gone or retrained by the punishment they'd received for their errant behavior. It made it much easier and less stressful to pursue more meaningful friendships at any level.

Yet there was still this overarching cloud of the unknown covering the state, one that time had trouble mitigating. Church attendance was still growing, and so was the belief in a bigger power. It was a strange concoction of light and dark.

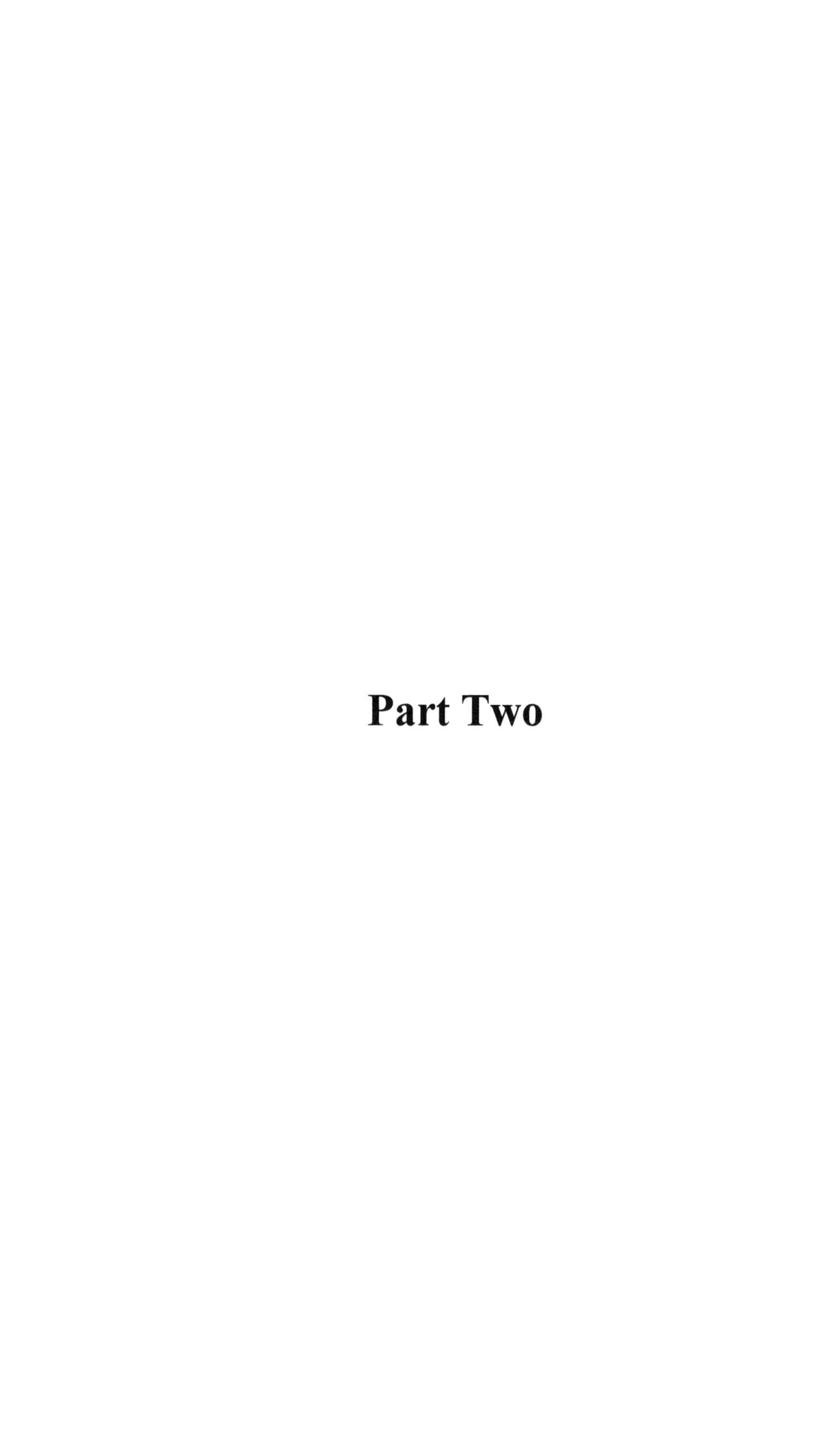

Part Two

15

1/1/28

Two years had passed since the first "Fear" casualties. Nothing new happened on the first of this month anywhere. It arrived with a bang and left without even a squeak. Texas was still the only place on Earth, along with that strange footprint in the Indian Ocean, that was affected. The power was still enforcing its past edicts. New Year's Eve parties were returning to normal.

The Supreme Court still hadn't ruled on the challenge by Louisiana. Jurisdiction complications sent the challenge back and forth. The parties hoped to sort it out before the summer. In the meantime, prisoners were brought across the border. That helped push the crime rate way down in states surrounding Texas—way down.

Berkeley had nothing. The director shut it down and used the scientists on more pressing investigations. The Air Force base in Roswell, New Mexico, took over. They seemed like the right place to hand off this unidentified object.

3/01/2028

That morning, reports from prisons came pouring in from New Mexico. The "Fear" was back with a vengeance. Prisons and cities over the entire state were feeling the effects at the same time. Midnight surprises were back in business.

New Mexico's population was just over two million, compared to Texas's thirty million. The difference made their cleanup more manageable. It was exactly like Texas two years ago—except everything happened all at once.

In the following days, wild stories and rumors were confirmed. Identical events. On the opposite side, it penetrated through the Indian Ocean. One French-controlled island was the only land mass in the expanded boundary—the Kerguelen Islands. They are French-controlled, with only a handful of scientists there. No casualties were reported.

Gabe was watching at midnight in an old bar in Santa Fe called El Farol, serving customers since 1835. Gabe had stopped in dozens of times over the years. He had a few bad memories, but mostly good ones. El Farol means "the Lantern" in Spanish. He liked that name and the metaphor of darkness lit by lanterns. All the owners knew him well, and he was always welcome. They went back a long, long time.

Santa Fe was his base for the last two years. He visited all the western states from his new home. He'd been in Arizona for over a month before returning to New Mexico. He was getting old, but he still had a lot left in him, and traveling was something he'd been doing forever.

Johnny Rentschler heard it on the internet. He quickly determined the coordinates for each corner of the state and reversed them to figure out each antipode. He plotted it in the Indian Ocean next to the reverse footprint of Texas.

Google set a record with searches for New Mexico, causing some servers to overheat and crash from the demand.

Arizona greeted the new year's morning with its own announcement: it was next. The population of the United States was being reduced to levels that made the budget office recalculate funding and adjust for the reduced Social Security base. It was not good news. Dead folks didn't pay taxes.

The population of Arizona was seven million. The "Fear" would have another national consequence. The border antipodes remained in the Indian Ocean. So far, the impact had only been felt on US land in three states—and on ships and planes crossing the Indian Ocean zone. And, of course, the extended reach into the universe.

California would be rethinking its sanctuary-state platitudes previously spouted by the very people elected to keep them safe, prosperous, and free. Starting now, criminals crossing into America from Mexico would be self-funneled through the southern border of the "Golden State." Most military-age, single men would stop crossing in the usual places. Voluntarily or by a sudden case of dropping dead.

The governor of California had had enough. He declared a state of emergency and authorized the National Guard to barricade the border. He just shut it down, turning everyone away. The unspoken message: "Try Arizona if you have the guts—or if you're not on the laundry list of grievances handed down by this unknown 'Power.'"

Until now, our government had told us the border couldn't be shut down without congressional action loaded with hundreds of unrelated giveaways or political agendas. A lot of egg yolk ended up on a lot of faces in Congress and the Senate. Citizens now knew that talking point had been pure BS, and this quick remedy proved it.

This midnight surprise caused many families to be divided by geography. Quite a few of the people visiting their relatives in Mexico had a problem. They knew who they were—they were the ones who would instantly pay the price for their murders and crimes if they entered through the wrong state. Many simply picked up and went back to their families in their home countries. It was getting too complicated for the bad elements of society to keep track of safe zones. Most assumed California would be next, prompting a hurried departure.

Thousands of apartments had vacancies, left fully furnished because those fleeing had to abandon anything that wouldn't fit in a car or pickup. Banks temporarily closed as the massive wave of withdrawals strained the system. It didn't take much to shake the foundations of financial institutions—just like an earthquake, this new force gave little warning before unleashing calamity.

Various Mexican, South American, and American gangs now faced a dilemma. If they abandoned their territories and income streams to leave California, only to find later they didn't need to, what kind of turf battle would explode in their neighborhoods and barrios upon return? Tough business decisions for these street vendors. These "business leaders" had no backup plan—no forecasting think tanks. They shot their pistols sideways for show, sacrificing accuracy and, often, longevity. Their business plans boasted the same ridiculous vanity.

Scores of politicians returned to D.C. to avoid embarrassment and potential poverty. They thought they could distance themselves from the house cleaning that was coming to the House. They would be mistaken. Those from the three "lucky" states were already purged—some in the first murderer cleanup and others in the lying, cheating, and adultery departments. The follow-up elections were truly fair, free of the ads that flooded airwaves with lies and misinformation. Candidates now had to discuss their plans and projects if elected. Each ad carried a mysterious truth rating. It was mysterious how it appeared on every political billboard, lawn sign, and video. A well-known Seattle law firm lost a lot of business because that couldn't spin and lie for high-paying political clients anymore.

The sheer number of lawsuits was massively reduced in the "affected" states. Once deposition and witness testimony was fully truthful, there was no wiggle room for barristers inclined to bend the truth for their clients. Attempts would be exposed and would affect their honesty ratings. It was far better to be honest in this new world (or at least in these three states).

Politicians and attorneys with good ratings finally gained the respect each deserved. So did the ones with bad ratings—just not the kind they wanted. Some had to make huge changes in their methods, while others needed none.

Millions of citizens were having difficulty dealing with this mystery and punishment. They knew they wouldn't be passed over. The "wait and see" was, to some, more painful than the actual discipline that might cross their doorsteps. Unless you committed murder or adultery, the wait was acceptable compared to the alternative.

Mental health problems surfaced but were mostly ignored. Some innocents were affected too. They worried about their family and friends who might not be as incorruptible. Suicides exploded in the 47 states still waiting for their turn. Many did it to save their families from the disgrace of their past. "Anchoring" was one method some used— renting a boat and "falling" off into the water, first wrapping the anchor chain around their necks. That popular phrase— "conveniently closer to Hell"—showed up in bars and on T-shirts. Nobody was fooled, though, when divers recovered most of the bodies. Those who jumped into deep saltwater were often never found, but a boat left floating without its chain and anchor gave away their intentions.

16

4/1/28

Gabe watched the midnight news at El Farol. Nothing surprised him. He decided to fly to California for a few weeks to visit two old friends and cruise around the state. Most of his friends there were long dead. He rented a car in San Diego and began his journey. He was shocked by the homelessness and rampant crime. He knew about it, but seeing it up close really drove it home. He felt sorry for California. His memories made it even worse. He walked through some of the homeless camps and spoke with the people who weren't too high to string a sentence together. He was in a rough neighborhood, but he wasn't scared. He prayed with those who allowed him to. He warned them of what was coming. They knew. They had heard about it from everyone.

He prayed with Slim and Mabel. They lost their jobs during Covid, and when the money and welfare ran out, they moved to the streets. Gabe wrote out a phone number for them to call—a job would be waiting for them. His old friend didn't yet know he'd be hiring, but if Gabe wanted it, by golly, Gabe got it. He would also make sure they had a safe place to sleep, though he needed a bit more time to work out the details.

As he drove up the Pacific Coast Highway, he smiled at the beauty of God's creation—a creation he felt was in decline. He wasn't focused on the scenery; he was thinking about the people who lived there and how their lives were filled with unnecessary pain caused by misguided leaders and their voting enablers. "How could things get so out of whack?" he thought.

He went to the ever-expanding seedy part of Hollywood and talked with gang members who were obviously selling drugs in plain sight of the police. Again, he wasn't afraid to be in dangerous places. Most of the street thugs he spoke with were surprised at his stupidity—or courage. They weren't sure which. Some thought it was a trick set up by the cops sitting in their car down the street. He spoke fluent Spanish and asked them point-blank why they were harming people. "Don't you have brothers and sisters and parents? ¿No tienes hermanos y padres?"

They pushed him away and laughed. Gabe walked off disheartened and heartbroken. As he headed down the sidewalk, a younger gang member suddenly sprinted toward him. Gabe noticed his shoelace was untied and bent down to retie it. The kid launched himself into the air, just as Gabe knelt to grab his laces. That's when Gabe saw the teenager fly overhead and land face-first on the concrete about ten feet away. Gabe ran forward to help him. The boy was embarrassed and frightened by Gabe's perceived superhero move. The street gang behind him laughed so hard that the kid got up and ran in the opposite direction toward his home. He was only fourteen.

Back in Arkansas, Dalton was now working as an Emergency Medical Technician. It made him feel a little better about himself and his past. He was genuinely remorseful and repentant about his earlier life. He always carried Narcan—at least a dozen doses in a zippered bag. "Maybe I can save a life," he thought. Narcan could have saved Jesse's life.

He suffered through nightmares, as did Tammy. They both volunteered and helped dozens of lost souls around town and older members of their church in El Dorado, Arkansas.

Tammy had hired more than sixteen people she found loitering outside the Home Depot looking for work. They were all full-time now. She showed them how to save money and even had taken them to her bank to open accounts. Once a month, she started the morning with a refresher course on saving and planning for the future. Since none of them had ever had a real future before, they needed this kind of direction to break the cycle of living paycheck to paycheck. She gave them a month-end bonus with the stipulation that it be deposited into a separate savings account, untouched unless they consulted her first. She also required them to bring in their bank statements to prove it. It wasn't so much about controlling them as it was an excuse to protect them from spouses or family members who felt they should share in that "wealth." They wouldn't be asking for a gift, of course—just a "loan" that would never be repaid.

Gabe drove up the coast past Ventura and stopped in Santa Barbara. He found a motel and went to his room. He was visiting an old friend, Earl Winnis, who loved live music and charities and often melded the two by hosting charity concerts featuring well-known acts. Earl was retired, and this was the perfect way to stay sane. He loved Montana and enjoyed visiting the Kootenai Lodge outside Bigfork.

Gabe wasn't visiting Earl to cheer him up; he wanted to see where his spiritual head was. Gabe knew big changes were coming to

California, and he worried for his old friend. He wanted Earl to be prepared. He didn't want him to suffer. He couldn't tell him everything he knew, but he could offer clues.

They reminisced for a while, then went to dinner overlooking the ocean. The sun slowly set over the unusually calm water. It was a nice respite before the coming storm.

After dinner, Gabe headed back to his motel. He thought Earl got his coded message and hoped he'd think about getting ready.

Jesse's younger brother, Will Williston, was thirteen. He hoped to be a doctor one day. Will made a pledge on his brother's memory never to take drugs. He kept that pledge his entire life without hesitation. He wished Jesse were still there for advice and leadership. Fentanyl had taken him away. Will planned to wear his brother's jersey number one day if he became a football star too. That was his dream now.

Will's sister and parents were still heartbroken about Jesse's death. His sister's wedding, six months after Jesse died, offered some distraction. Their pain was diminishing slightly, though Jesse remained on their minds, just not every minute of the day. Seeing Will play football and watching Jennifer (his sister) welcome a new baby offered the family a diversion they sorely needed.

Gabe followed the Pacific Coast Highway and then headed east on I-80, toward Tahoe and into Nevada. He didn't stop in San Francisco this time; he used to love visiting there, but not anymore. It had become too weird for this old man. The 1960s music scene had been the best—The Grateful Dead, Jefferson Airplane, and Big Brother and the Holding Company with Janis Joplin. Those Haight-Ashbury days of peace and love were authentic and pure until Madison Avenue got its hands on them. It reminded him of what developers did to Tahoe. He didn't mind that both made money. The "root of all evil" wasn't money itself, in his eyes—it was the worship of it.

He enjoyed the freedom to do whatever he wanted. He liked choosing how to handle his missions and destinations. He'd traveled the West too many times to count and missed the beauty and grandeur of the landscapes. Tahoe was a favorite. The Nevada side was the place he stopped to look around. It had huge hotels and condos now. He remembered when there was nothing. He didn't care for the changes, but he understood why people wanted to visit and live there—for the same reason he stopped by. He loved the vistas and the lake.

He found a church on Sunday morning in Tonopah. The Tonopah Community Church delivered a message that resonated with him. Revelations was a book that frightened some people who had minimal exposure to God. It seemed wacky to some, filled with colorful descriptions and warnings, and it didn't sit well in a more liberal setting. But here, it did.

The pastor was talking about the End Times, the same talk that had been going on for almost 2,000 years. All it really said was "Be ready for the return of God." It was sobering. Some congregations tried to soften the blow by "putting lipstick" on it, but Gabe thought to himself, "Good luck with that."

He sat next to a young family—Molly and Luther—who were clearly struggling. Their baby started to fuss and cry.

"Can I hold him?" Gabe asked. Children liked him for some reason.

"Are you sure? He's pretty grumpy." Molly handed the baby over. He immediately calmed down.

"What's hurting you guys?" Gabe asked gently. "I don't mean to be nosy; I just want to help. I can see things aren't going well. It's more than money. You can tell me. You can talk to me."

Luther looked at Molly for a moment, then finally spoke. "We are on the run from a very bad man," he said, glancing at his wife, who nodded. "He's from Chicago. We were selling marijuana for him two years ago and decided to get out. We wanted a family; we wanted a normal life." He paused, noticing Gabe's calm expression. "We left for Texas, and last month, we learned he was looking for us." Luther couldn't believe he was telling this to a stranger. Gabe somehow made it easy for people to open up.

"Why?" Gabe asked.

"We found out he was trafficking children. Selling them. We don't know the details, but we can guess. I went to the police and told them everything I knew about his operations. They must have had a mole. My buddy Cholly—he worked with me selling—tipped me off. He told us to run as far as we could and hide." Luther stopped and looked at Molly.

She continued, "Cholly was killed. The guy found out he warned us, so they shot him right on the street. We got out of Chicago in ten minutes and drove straight to Texas. We stayed with a guy who used to work for that trafficker. He was on the run too. He got the 'Fear' when it was the pedophile's turn. We left Dallas that day and headed west to Nevada, where I was born. We used up his stash of money. Now we're broke, and that man is still after us."

"Why were you in church?" Gabe asked, though he had a feeling he already knew.

"We're lost. Desperate. We're looking for help," Molly said, tearing up. Gabe looked at her gently, and she stopped sobbing.

"Where are you staying?" he asked.

"In our car," Luther admitted. He felt ashamed.

"I have a motel room nearby," Gabe said, "and I'm putting your family there. I'll give you some money. I have to leave this evening for Idaho, but you can stay as long as you need. I'll take you now to get food and diapers for your baby—and groceries for you two. There's a refrigerator in the room."

Molly and Luther were speechless. "Who was this guy? Why was he helping us? He doesn't even know us. What's his angle?" Luther wondered if it was too good to be true.

Meanwhile, Johnny's dad found him on the soccer field by the old school and honked. He ran over and got in the car, waving goodbye to his buddies.

"The President wants to speak with you," his dad said, heading out quickly.

"Tell him I'm playing soccer," Johnny joked.

"I'm not kidding. Wells called. He's in a meeting with the President, and the President wants you to call him." His dad drove home a little faster than usual, expecting no trouble from the police if they got pulled over for speeding on such an errand.

"Hi, Mom. Dad says you have a phone number for me to call. The President, right?" Johnny laughed.

"Call him," she replied.

He dialed the number and connected with the meeting in progress. Wells heard his voice, confirmed that Johnny had left the message, then introduced him to the President.

"John, nice to speak with you," the President said. "Great work on the Indian Ocean solution. Your brother tells me you believe Idaho is the next state to get a visit from whatever is causing this. Why Idaho?"

"Mr. President, I'm just an amateur geographer," Johnny began. "That's how I figured out the Indian Ocean boundaries. I have a wall-sized Mercator Projection of the world in my bedroom. I colored Texas red when it got the 'Force.' Then New Mexico, then Arizona. Then something really strange happened." He paused, choosing his next words carefully. "When I woke up after midnight, I saw that Idaho was colored red. I didn't do it. Nobody did it. My door was locked, and nobody could have sneaked in. Later, I called Wells to tell him, but I had to leave a message. Then I went out to play baseball and soccer with my friends. That's it." He paused. "Oh, I also had dreams about California being next—until last night. Now I'm dreaming about Idaho."

"I was hoping for something more concrete than a dream and a colored state on a bedroom wall," the President muttered.

"I know, sir," Johnny said. "But the only way to see if I'm right is to wait for whatever happens. Or if anything happens."

"Thank you, son." The President ended the call with Johnny. Wells was still on, and he said goodbye to Johnny, promising to call later.

The President turned to his agency directors and the California team. "So this is all we have—an eighth-grader coloring states and having dreams?"

❖

Molly grabbed diapers; Gabe added two more packs. Baby food, some clothes for everyone, toiletries, shampoos, body wash, toothbrushes, razors. On the way out, he grabbed snacks and stuffed animals for the baby. Twelve hundred dollars later, they headed out and over to their new motel home.

They unloaded and stocked the fridge. They put their new clothes in the drawers and closet.

"Okay, guys, I'm leaving now. I'll call you tomorrow. Do you have a phone?" Gabe asked.

"Yes," Molly answered. "But we're out of minutes." Gabe handed her a thousand dollars in cash.

"I'll take care of the phone minutes," he said. "One more thing— on the 31st, Nevada will be in turmoil after the midnight visit by our 'friends.' Once it's done, you can go back out safely. Stay in Nevada, though."

Gabe knew they would be okay. They'd been living in Texas when that state got its surprise. They should have stayed there, he thought; they already passed the test. Before he left, he prayed with them, and they thanked him. Gabe said goodbye.

He stopped by the office, told the clerk they would be staying in his room, and gave his credit card plus a hundred dollars in cash.

"Thank you, Mr. Arch. I'll take care of it," the clerk said.

"Please, call me Gabe."

"Yes, sir."

Gabe got in his car and headed north to Idaho. It was April 29.

Wells took a call from Johnny in his office. "Hi, buddy, what's new?"

"Nevada turned red," Johnny said. "It happened at 1:00 a.m. while I was sleeping. I woke up Dad, and he aimed a video camera at the wall. At 2:00 a.m., Nevada snapped red. Idaho's in play, and now Nevada is too. I also had another dream about Idaho and Nevada. I'm getting scared, Wells. What's going on?"

"I don't know, John," Wells admitted. Johnny had asked to be called "John" after the President addressed him that way—it made him feel older. "Nobody knows. Let me call you back, buddy. I need to pass this along."

Wells called Director Wharton to report Nevada's addition. It was the 30th now. Wharton passed the info to his team and the Pentagon task force. All they could do was wait. Wells didn't know much about "the Project," as they called it. Wharton's team had set up every detection instrument they had all over Idaho after the first joint meeting. If anything was measurable, they'd catch it.

The governor of Idaho was informed about the "hunch," as the team called it.

Wells called his brother back. "Hi, John, I let the people in charge know what you found. They don't tell me anything because I don't have a security clearance."

Tammy and Dalton kept working hard and helping people who needed it. They saw what happened in Arizona and New Mexico, and it frightened them. They wanted to start a family but didn't want their child to become an orphan. They knew what fate might await them; they just didn't know when Arkansas would be "on deck." It hung over them constantly, not giving them a moment's peace—not even for an hour. Still, they kept working and helping others. Tammy won community awards for changing broken lives. She wished she could change her own. She wished she could go back and rearrange the decisions she and Dalton had made when they were younger. She wished they could have a mulligan on the hundreds of bad choices they'd made. One day at church, they saw the new message on the lawn sign:

"Are You Next?"

It summed up their worries and fears.

17

It was the 31st. The bars were back in business after New Mexico and Arizona "came on board" last month. California was the top betting pick—odds were so high, it slowed down wagers because of the low payouts. Traffic jams stretched for miles at the southern border. The U.S. Border Patrol and Customs asked Mexico to expedite admissions into their country to ease the lines, but Mexico declined and told their border agents to slow it down. "Let the fleeing murderers, pedophiles, traffickers, and drug dealers die on the American side," the president of Mexico thought privately.

California had 39,000,000 residents, plus another million who had shown up to escape the "Fear," thanks to the new sanctuary status.

Thousands of Oakland residents headed north to Oregon, hoping to dodge the convictions they knew were coming. Portland seemed like the perfect refuge for them—Antifa could recruit from this sudden influx of murderers. Their new recruits soon staged a hostile takeover of Portland's Antifa, killing off any old members who opposed them. Ironically, the old Antifa now found the violence it had once unleashed returning like a boomerang. This "new and improved" Antifa was on steroids, and its violence and intimidation skyrocketed. Female members fled back to their parents' basements, unwilling to remain for the rapes their new leaders introduced to these "mostly peaceful" protests.

Bars and restaurants filled up by 10:00 p.m. It felt like those first nights, when massive crowds gathered in a kind of wild, fearful celebration. Around the world, people prepared and waited.

Cameras were set up all over California, mostly in the seedier parts, to capture any midnight mayhem. The camera crews hoped it happened soon; they hated risking their lives in dangerous neighborhoods just for the sake of "entertainment."

Molly and Luther stayed in Gabe's motel room, trying to relax. They kept the TV on, waiting for news. Nobody mentioned Nevada as the next target; all focus was on California. They wondered how Gabe had come by his predictions.

It was 10:40 p.m. in California. The countdown was starting. Drinks were being ordered in bars. Alarms would soon go off across the country as midnight approached.

The president was awake in the White House, watching. The California team was on standby. The agency directors weren't sleeping either. "What if Johnny was right? What if Nevada and Idaho were next?"

At 11:04 p.m. California time, news broke from Boise, Idaho: it was happening there.

"Johnny was right. How did he know? Get Miller on the phone," the president snapped before remembering he was in bed with his wife. He called his chief of staff and told him to get Miller from the NSA.

"I saw it, too, Mr. President. Johnny was right about Idaho, but not Nevada," Miller said, not realizing Nevada was in the Pacific Time Zone while almost all of Idaho was in Mountain Time.

"Different time zones, Miller. It's not over yet. Call Wells. Let him know agencies will be descending on his parents' house in the morning. He might want to warn them."

Down in L.A., Fox News was ready with less than a minute to go until midnight. "Five, four, three, two, one…"

California was quiet so far.

"Just wait," a reporter cautioned. "It can take a minute or two before we see anything on the streets." Three minutes passed—still nothing. Then the news broke from Nevada. Las Vegas was in chaos. Bodies were dropping in casinos and on the downtown streets.

The governors would face a long day. Idaho wasn't as hectic as Nevada, but it still had its fair share of wrongdoing, from random crazies to small clusters of white supremacists in the woods. Meanwhile, in Nevada, a few lingering mobsters and numerous rackets and prostitution rings added to the confusion.

Miller called Wharton, who'd been waiting.

"We're sending a team to the Rentschler home," Miller said. "So far, that's all we have." The president had countless questions for Johnny. "Call his brother, too. We'll send a jet for you. Keep this quiet. The agencies arrive before lunch. I want Wells there to handle his family, help relocate them if necessary."

"You're going to relocate the family?"

"We need to set up shop in the house and get to the bottom of the 'magic map' in Johnny's bedroom. I also want Johnny at the lab so we can monitor his dreams."

"Understood. We'll gather any data we've collected from those states by 11:00 a.m."

Luther and Molly woke up the next morning and turned on the TV. Sure enough, it hit Nevada, just as Gabe had predicted.

"How did he know?" Luther asked, baffled.

"Idaho, too," Molly added. "He said he was driving there. He called us from Idaho last night."

Luther gave her a strange look. "I was thinking about our phone—he recharged the minutes for us. But I never told him our number or which company we use. How could he do that?"

"I don't care who he is," Molly said. "He was the kindest person we've ever met. He's an angel to me. He's the only one who bothered to help us."

"I'm not denying his kindness. I just can't figure out how he knew Nevada was next. Or how he got our phone info."

Gabe made a few stops in Idaho to visit old friends. He saw firsthand the effects of the "Fear." Thousands of deaths, plus punishments for adultery. Fortunes changed hands as liars and cheaters were forced to make restitution. Just like in Texas, there was no more violence, murder, cheating, or lying. The United States was becoming "un-United." A self-regulating boundary on the map did what no fence or wall had managed: criminals knew what awaited them if they crossed the "wrong" state line. Washington, Oregon, and California were now cut off from the rest of America by this invisible perimeter, trapping criminals in those states.

The only ways into the West Coast "trinity" were through Canada, Mexico, or the Pacific Ocean. Mexico had become extremely picky about who crossed into its territory. After a few million "bad guys" arrived and caused chaos, they closed their border and built a wall. Every vehicle was checked. Trade between Mexico and the U.S. took a massive hit. Tourism collapsed—no one wanted to risk a vacation there.

Canada was also dealing with a spike in crime from its new arrivals, so it clamped down on its borders. Everyone faced thorough screening before admission.

Gabe phoned Molly and Luther to let them know he'd be back in a week and asked them to stay put until then. They agreed. He said he was going to drop off his rental car and fly out of Boise to Little Rock for some unfinished business.

18

Wells called his mom and dad to tell them what was about to happen in their lives during the next 24 hours as the federal government swarmed into their world. His dad answered the phone.

"Dad, I'm coming home this morning to visit." He hated disrupting their lives without much warning or planning. His dad was a planner and didn't do well when someone or some event tried to push him. He pushed back.

"Great son, are you in town for a meeting?"

"No, dad. You heard the news about Nevada and Idaho?"

"Yeah, of course."

"And Johnny's wall map that turned those states red?"

"Yes. I know. That sure is a weird thing. I don't think he's doing it, but what else could it be?"

"We don't know. I mean, I don't know." Wells was stalling. "I called Dr. Wharton at the National Laboratory to tell him about Johnny's prediction about Nevada and Idaho and his dreams. They're coming to the house with scientists and all sorts of testing equipment to try and see what's going on."

"They're coming here. When?"

"This morning, dad, I'm sorry, they told me just now."

"Wells, we must let them do their thing. Anyway, what's the big deal? I don't mind a few scientists setting up equipment here. We can live with that. It's for our country, I get it."

"It's more than that dad, they want to move you out and quarantine the house while they investigate the map."

"Oh. I better tell your mom right away. She won't be happy, but she'll survive; I'll handle things on my end. You do what you must."

"Do they know anything about what's happening? Does anyone have any idea what's going on?" His dad hoped for an update.

"I don't think so, dad, but I don't know. I don't have a security clearance and that keeps me out of the loop."

"I better get your mother moving. What time will you all arrive?"

"I'm heading to the airport now. I'll see you around 10 this morning. The guys from DC will get to the house before noon. Keep Johhny out of school. He's gonna be investigated, too."

"Why on earth is that?"

"His dreams about this."

"Oh yeah. I get it. I think he's gonna like all the attention."

"Thanks, Dad. I gotta go. See you in a few."

Wells was glad his dad didn't freak out. He was All-American from head to toe. Served in Nam, too. He was willing to die for his country then. This would be more of an inconvenience for his country.

Wells met Dr. Wharton at the Oakland Airport and boarded the 12-passenger jet to his hometown in Lake Charles, Louisiana.

"My dad took it pretty well."

"I know." He replied, before he thought about what he said.

"How do you know." Wells was surprised. He didn't say anything about it.

"I meant I know it's gonna be a pain for your mom and dad." Wharton recovered quickly. "It's a major hassle for them."

Dr. Wharton had been told just before boarding the plane that the family wouldn't be a problem. The NSA had been tapping their land lines and cell phones since the day that Wells told them about Johnny.

Wharton was trying to get Wells a security clearance. The FBI was on it this morning. The vetting wouldn't take too long. They would have to go over all the phone recordings from the house and cell phones. They also would revisit all of Wells' private and work-related calls to finalize the rigorous background check. His calls were also being "listened in on" since the day his connection to this map event was first disclosed.

Gabe was at the Boise Airport and sat in the waiting area. He decided to trade in his first-class ticket for a coach when he saw a young woman in a military unform in the waiting area before boarding. He went up to her and thanked her for her sacrifices and offered to exchange tickets with her. She had only flown once in her life, and it wasn't in first class.

"Serious," she said while smiling back at the stranger.

"Serious," Gabe replied. "Let's go to the ticket counter and get it done. My name is Gabe.

"I'm Sally. I'm please to meet you, sir."

"You forgot my name already; it's Gabe." They both laughed.

Gabe handed his paper boarding pass to the ticket agent. He always had a paper pass. He knew it was old-fashioned, but his battery died one time, and it held things up for everyone. He asked the ticket agent to swap seats with the young soldier.

"Mr. Arch, I can't do that just before boarding."

Gabe gave her his hundred-dollar angelic smile.

"OK, let's see what I can do." Gabe looked back at Sally and winked.

"Mr. Arch, do you really have 12 million Sky Miles with Delta? I think I can take care of this right now." She leaned over to the agent in charge and told her about the swap. She looked over at her screen and said. "The seat is open next to his; just upgrade the soldier to that seat first. Let's keep this customer happy."

The agent typed for a few seconds and printed out a boarding pass for Sally and gave Gabe his back without changes. "The seat next to you is open, we upgraded your friend to first. Have a great flight." She looked at Sally. "And thank you for your service, soldier."

They started boarding passengers that needed assistance and then those in active military service. That was Sally. The gate agent looked at her and she waived him off. She wanted to board with Gabe.

"Do you really have 12 million Sky Miles? Sally thought Gabe must live on planes and in airports.

"Yeah. I don't use them; I donate them to the "Make a Wish foundation," I gotta remember to do that. It's almost been two years since the last time."

❖

6/16/28

A black Chevy SUV picked up Wells and Wharton from the small airport in Louisiana. Lake Charles was originally named Charleston. It was changed around the Civil War years to, some say, avoid confusion with Charleston, South Carolina and distance itself from the two different cultures. It was originally Charlie's Lake and named after Charles Sallier. It's in the heart of Cajun country and the people are mighty proud of that.

They drove past the Loggerhead Bar and Restaurant and continued to the Rentschler home on Pickerel Lane. They drove in the long driveway that led down to the house and bayou. A boat slip and dock held their yacht called "Contraband." Four families lived on the street and were known as "The Hood." They had a few honorary Hood members that didn't live there anymore. The frequent parties and dinners were the time to bring them all together. It was a fun place to live. The bayou was stunningly beautiful.

Calcasieu Parrish was one of the 22 official parishes that made up French Acadiana. Crab boils, gumbo and boudin are as common as the native Zydeco style of rousing music.

Wells arrived home and introduced Wharton to his father. Johnny peeked around and Wells introduced him next. "Dr. Wharton, this is Johnny."

"It's John, sir."

"It is very nice to meet you, *John*." Dr. Wharton liked this kid.

"Wanna see my map, sir?" Johnny took him first around the back to see if he could find Fred. He was hiding in the bayou. Fred was an alligator and also a member of the hood. Wharton noticed the yacht's name. "The agencies are not gonna like that!" He chuckled to himself.

❖

Nevada and Idaho were struggling through their "correction" period. California thought they "dodged a bullet." If you used that phrase in California, you had to give a "trigger warning." How funny is that? They release violent criminals back on the street without any warnings and somehow that doesn't qualify for a "heads up."

The federal agencies that handled these things were getting pretty used to it and for the most part, kept things running smoothly. You couldn't smooth over the sadness and shock that was brought to the families and people of these two very different states. This new "Department of Corrections," as the agencies involved affectionally called themselves, would now be split between the two states.

Las Vegas was hit the hardest and took 50% of the agency's attention. Refrigerated truck trailers were standing by before this latest surprise happened. They didn't have to scramble and scour to get the equipment they needed. The agency was "good to go" now.

Just when things were quieting down at the CDC, they got the call to arms. Call to bodies was the reality. More DNA testing and photographs of the dearly departed would commence in a few hours.

Californians knew they were on borrowed time. The closed borders funneled everyone through the overburdened customs and immigration stations. Not coming into the US, but on the Mexican and Canadian sides. There were so many trying to enter Mexico that the US Government removed sections of their newly constructed walls and took down Mexican ones so the "undocumented migrants" could flood into our neighbor's country. It was like the water pulled out to sea in a tsunami, only to get hit even harder by the returning waves. The waves were returning now, and the damage to Mexico was just beginning to be exposed.

It was a humanitarian decision, the government claimed, while trying to hide a smile on their government faces. Oh, how things change so quickly and so ironically. The Mexican president threatened to make America pay for the chaos they dumped on their friendly neighbor to the south. You can't make this up.

Gabe and Sally had a wonderful trip from Boise to Little Rock. He learned that she came from a very poor rural background. She was going home to see her family after surviving boot camp. It was pretty easy for Sally. The Army lifestyle certainly was easier compared to her meager life up in the hills. Gabe loved her spirit. She was no spoiled teenager. She was a full adult and acted like a mature one.

The pilot came out of the cockpit and walked down the aisle to Gabe and Sally. "Welcome aboard." He thanked Gabe for his Delta Diamond status and Sally for her service. Sally didn't feel like she deserved being thanked for her service. She just got out of boot camp and hadn't served anyone yet, let alone the nation. After he flirted with the flight attendants, he remembered to be careful in this new world. He returned to his seat on the left side of the cockpit.

Sally leaned over and asked Gabe what he did for a living. She had been doing all the talking and trying to answer all his questions about her life.

"I'm in the messenger business and security, too. It's a big outfit; we're everywhere."

"Do you like it?"

"Yes, I do, very much. Do you like the military so far?

"Yes, I do, very much. I never had any order in my life. It makes me feel safe."

Gabe was an expert in changing subjects. He never lied, and this strategy helped keep his score perfect.

John took Dr. Wharton up to his room. His mom was cleaning it.

"Mom, this is Dr. Wharton."

"Nice to meet you. I guess you wanna look at Johnny's map." John didn't correct his mom. "I'm finished in here, just straightening things up a little. You know, boys."

"I have two, Ma'am."

John showed him the red states. He explained how he marked Texas red first, then added New Mexico and Arizona. He then showed him Nevada and Idaho. "Can you see the difference? The ones I colored are not at all like these. The others look like they were printed and mine looks like it was out of a coloring book."

"I can see the difference. You're right."

"My dad setup a video camera right after I told him about Idaho. It was a little after 1:00 am here two days ago. You can see on video what happened next. Nevada just sort of flashed to red. I was asleep. It was 2:00 am here. Nevada happened at midnight, Pacific Time Zone."

"It's strange that Idaho happened at 11:00 pm in the Pacific Time Zone. The others all happened at midnight."

"I know," Johnny said. "I figured the same thing, so I thought to check and see if the time zones were different. Guess what? They are. Only a small western part of Idaho is in the Pacific time zone. The rest is Mountain Time Zone. It all comports."

"Smart Kid." Wharton thought to himself.

The other agents were beginning to arrive. They would land at the old Chennault Air Force Base nearby and drive over to the "Hood." The Loggerhead had a dozen or so cabins to rent. The feds rented all of them. That made the servers and the bartenders happy. Jim, the owner, couldn't complain either.

Gabe and Sally landed in Little Rock. He offered to drive her home to see her parents. "It's over two hours south of here, thanks anyways. I can take the bus." I'm heading to southern Arkansas. I can drop you nearby if it helps."

"Are you sure?"

"Come on, I'll get you home. I'm harmless."

Sally turned her woman brain on before answering. She wasn't worried about him being harmful. She was trained in hand-to-hand combat, and he couldn't have gotten on the flight with a weapon. Alright, she thought, he passed.

"Okay. Thank you so much, Gabe," she liked Gabe. "Where are you headed?"

"El Dorado."

"I know where that is; it's pretty close to my home? You won't need a map. I know how to get there. It's a big city; they have a Home Depot."

<h1 style="text-align:center">19</h1>

Wells helped his mom and dad get their things to the car. The agency had a hotel room for them in the casino. His dad thought about staying with his sister in Lafayette. His barber was there, and he did need a haircut. Wells talked him out of that. They wanted Johhny nearby for the hundreds of questions they had. He would be hooked up to a lie detector. They all teased him about being in the room with their own questions. They all laughed at that. His older sister, Linda, was supposed to come home from school over the weekend. The agency said they would make sure she had her own room. Wells had called her earlier and told her to stay put until this blew over.

"What school does she attend?" The agent graduated from Mississippi State.

"What do you mean what school, it's the only school. LSU, of course!"

The agent kept his college a secret.

They drove away from the Hood and straight to the Casino Hotel. The manager was waiting for them out front to personally handle their arrangements and baggage.

"Don't you need us to stop at the desk?"

"No, sir. Everything is taken care of. Your bags will be up in a minute."

They all got into the elevator and Johhny asked to press the elevator button like all kids his age. The manager said yes, he had two kids with the same affliction. It always caused a fight.

"What floor?"

"P"

"What's that?" asked Johnny

"The Penthouse." Mom and dad looked at each other and giggled.

The doors opened to an opulent floor that was different from the rest of the hotel, and the hotel was a very elegant property. They walked down the ten-foot-wide hall toward these enormous double doors at the end.

"Where are we going?" Johnny asked.

"Do you see those two big doors? That's your room."

"Cool."

The Manager opened the door and walked them into a huge room with windows overlooking the lake. It had a powder room, a large bar area fully stocked, a dining table for twelve, a living room with three upholstered couches and two big chairs surrounding the massive coffee table. On the opposite side was an open video room with a 96" TV. It was next to the full kitchen.

"That will save us some money. Do the couches pull out for beds?"

"No, no, no. There are four bedrooms. I was told your daughter might be visiting. And anything you want to order from room service or while dining in one of our five restaurants is carte blanche."

"What's carte blanche?" Johnny never heard that phrase before.

"It means everything is comped; everything is free," Wells explained.

"Including a 20% tip." The manager proudly announced as if he were the one comping their stay. "You will pay nothing except for gambling." He smiled at the boys before seeing the frown on Mrs. face.

"Let me show you your bedrooms." He showed them the rooms and Johnny squawked, "I call dibs on the master." The Rentschlers all shook their heads.

Gabe and Sally were approaching Warren, Arkansas. Salley directed Gabe to Bradley 25 Road outside of town. They drove up the hill to her house and stopped in front. Her mom and dad came running out. She introduced Gabe and invited him in. He thanked them, apologized, but insisted he had to get to El Dorado. He didn't want to interrupt their homecoming.

He thought about all the different people he'd met all over the world and was always amazed at how many good people were out there. The ones you never hear about. The ones drowned out by the bad that take up all the time, the oxygen and the news cycles. Sally was one of the good ones and so was her family. She didn't think twice as Texas exploded onto the news a few years back. Those were big city problems that seemed so foreign to God-fearing folks surviving in small towns and "hollers".

Gabe drove down to El Dorado and found a motel room. He would get back to business in the morning.

Wells and Johnny drove back to the house to meet the newly arrived agents. They wanted to interview Johnny right away. The president was pushing for answers; really anything would do. Something to start their investigation.

The latest "reason" was aliens. Yes, aliens were controlling crime before they would colonize and enslave humans. Another good one was the government found a way to bypass the pesky court system. That had a big hole in it, since politicians controlled government and they were the most corrupt as witnessed in the corrected states. Russia was always a good country to blame. Ask any democrat. And the all-time favorite, Elon Musk. That only left God and that was gaining a lot of grip. You could see it in church attendance and in people beginning to self-police themselves.

Wells pulled up to the house and had to park on the lawn. Too many black SUVs with white license plates were blocking the driveway. They went in and johnny went toward the stairs before he was stopped.

"I want to see what you're doing in my bedroom."

"I can't let you go upstairs. They're working."

Johnny sat down next to Wells and waited like a good boy. Wharton walked over to get them for the polygraph test. It was setup in the dining room. The agent giving the test asked Wells to stay in the living room.

Wells was a little surprised and asked. "Will you be recording the questions and answers?" He asked.

"No, why?"

"Then you're not gonna test him today. Come on, John, let's go." He grabbed his hand and started for the front door. He was well aware that his government had changed over the years and could not be trusted.

"Wait, you can't leave." He tried to strong-arm Wells.

"Watch me!"

Wharton intervened and tried the same tactic. It didn't work. "Don't jeopardize your career, Wells. You've worked too hard to get where you are."

"Here's my resignation." He lifted his right hand as he walked away but stopped before displaying the "bad" finger. He let the view of his back going out the door serve as a more polite substitute.

Let's go, Johnny. They hurried to their car. He was glad he parked on the lawn, and it wasn't blocked. It would have spoiled his dramatic resignation and "stage" exit.

Gabe woke up feeling refreshed. He slept the whole night without the usual jostling and turning. He always liked Arkansas. As he aged, he liked towns and people that moved at his slower speed. He felt synchronized in Arkansas.

He was looking for some friends that owed him money. Not to collect on the debt, but to check in on them to see how they were doing. Gabe didn't need money; he was set.

The population there was less than 20,000, so it wasn't a big town. He drove to the last known address that he had. No one was home. He was glad to think that they both had jobs and were at them instead of sleeping in or hanging out on the couch. The were sketchy that way. Gabe drove off and looked for a place to have breakfast.

He headed to the main street in town. It was called Main Street. The perfect name to describe the kind of place El Dorado was. Small.

Just as he began to turn left onto Main, a dump truck without brakes was honking to warn others. He had no control of his 15,000-pound load.

He slammed into a Kia and Gabe watched it sail through the air in front of his rental car. It landed fifty feet down Main Street. The engine went farther down the pavement. The Kia was leaking from its recently filled gas tank. It was ready to blow.

Dalton was in an ambulance on his way back to the fire station after delivering a five-year-old girl named Della to the hospital with a compound fracture to her arm. He was travelling behind the dump truck and stopped at the light. He watched in disbelief at the horrific wreck down the street in front of him.

He turned on his lights and siren and drove up to the scene. Not too close as he learned from his training. "Potential Fire" was the term on his exam. He jumped out and ran to the car to pull out the driver. She was unconscious. He got her away from her car and ran back to make sure no one else was trapped.

Running back, he noticed the "Baby on Board" sign dangling from inside the rear window and pulled out his seat belt cutter from his belt as he forced the driver's seat forward. It wouldn't budge. He noticed he was standing in gasoline and watched as his partner backed off and ran away. Dalton was able to get his back against the rear of the seat and using his legs, was able to break it and push it forward. He stuck his head in and cut the seat belt holding the four-month-old baby boy. No one was helping him. Six iPhones were recording the drama, but no one stopped recording to help, not even his partner.

Dalton finally got the baby out, still in the car seat. After a quick scan inside the car looking for others, he ran as fast as he could to get away from the "Potential Fire." He selected that multiple-choice answer correctly on his exam.

It wasn't fast enough, though. He got about twenty feet away from the car before the blast pushed him face forward to the ground. He pitched the car seat forward as hard as he could before the flames could harm the baby. Dalton's shirt back was on fire. Steph's baby was out of danger, sliding and spinning away from the inferno.

Dalton's partner grabbed the fire extinguisher that he had pulled from the ambulance and had it in hand when the car burst into flames. After his initial panic attack, he rebounded, and he ran to him and extinguished the flames. He emptied the red cylinder and grab his arms and pulled him away to a safer place. His hair was burned off on the back of his skull and his shirt was melted with the skin on his back.

Gabe's eyes were closed as he prayed for Dalton, Steph and baby Jess. He stayed behind to give a witness report to the police that were screaming down the street toward the wreck.

The three were loaded into the ambulance. No need to triage these victims. One was unconscious, one badly burnt and one crying but unhurt. Dalton and Steph Townsend were on gurneys and the baby was strapped in the front seat. Steph came to and yelled for Jess.

"He's okay; he's in the front buckled in."

Steph looked at Dalton and at the EMT that ran from danger. "Who is that?"

"He saved your life and your baby's. He's burned pretty badly. Your car exploded into flames."

"What happened? She didn't remember a thing.

"A dump truck ran a light and hit you. He pulled you out of your car and then went back for your baby."

She wished she could look at his face and thank him. His face was held in place, facing down to protect him from moving.

Gabe talked with the police and told them what he had seen. The dump truck driver was unhurt, but badly shaken. He watched Dalton's heroics and saw him get burned. It was my fault, he thought; his brakes failed, but it wasn't his fault. Gabe went over to him to comfort him. He didn't speak English. He was a Czech Republic immigrant working for his uncle. Gabe spoke to him in his native language and calmed him down enough to be able to talk with the police.

With Gabe's testimony, the distraught driver was only ticketed for operating a vehicle with faulty equipment. The policeman thanked Gabe for translating and for giving a detailed description of the accident. He asked the cop what hospital they were taken to and after waiting for the driver's uncle to show up, he headed to the emergency room while praying for the injured.

Wells and Johnny drove back to the Casino and went up to the penthouse suite to tell his dad what happened. He had already heard from Wharton. He wanted to hear Wells' side.

Both he and Johnny gave a complete description. Word for word except for the cancelled middle finger gesture. Now, his dad was angry.

"I'm glad you did what you did, son. I'm happy you didn't take any crap from them." Wells' father was as patriotic as you could get, and the events of the last few years that pointed to a corrupted cabal of three letter agencies never caused him much concern until now. "I'm calling my attorney right now."

"Hello, Jackson, Kilroy and Simpson. How may I direct your call?" Jim Jackson was a college buddy who was drafted for the "Conflict Overseas." He was in the same unit in Nam. It was a coincidence that they both enjoyed.

"Jim, please, this is Kevin Rentschler." A few seconds later, they were talking.

"Kevin, how's it going, old friend? How's the family?"

"That's why I'm calling you Jim. Do you have a moment?" He was throwing out ideas in his brain as to how he would explain this. How far back should he go?

"Sure do. What's going on?"

He decided to start at the beginning. "You remember when all this "correction" stuff started?"

"Of course."

"My Johnny has a map on his wall of the world. He figured out the Indian Ocean aspect of this and then started having dreams about the next states that would be affected. His brother Wells took that information to the National lab in California, and they ran it up to the DC agencies and the next thing you know, the President is asking to speak with Johnny. Evidently our government hasn't a clue about the origins of this phenomenon or even what it is. Johnny predicted Idaho and Nevada when everyone assumed California was next."

"How did he do that?"

"Okay, are you ready?

"Let me have it, Kevin."

"First, he had dreams that he clearly interpreted as an omen concerning those two states." As he explained it, he thought it sounded kind of crazy, but he kept going. "He colored Texas, New Mexico and Arizona in red on his wall map after they became relevant. He woke up at 1:00 am two days ago and saw Idaho was colored red. He didn't do it; it just showed up on his map. He woke me up and I put our little Wyze camera in and turned it toward the wall. We wanted to know when the next state changed to red on his map. We went to bed, and in the morning, Johnny saw Nevada was red. When we reviewed the camera video, it showed a distinct flash on Nevada and then it snapped to red. That happened at 2:00 am."

"Wow. That's weird and kind of scary."

"I know." He was glad he didn't say it was crazy, although it sure sounded crazy. "Johnny called Wells, and he ran it by the NSA director. They are in our house with a dozen agents and scientists from different agencies." He stopped to breath and to try and slow things down. "They kicked us out of the house to investigate the wall map and to set up equipment in an attempt to gather some sort of information to explain all of this."

"You know they can't do this without your permission."

"We gave them permission and now I wished we hadn't."

"What happened?"

"They wanted to give Johnny a polygraph examination. Wells took him back to the house to have it done. When Wells asked to be present, they said no. When he asked if the procedure would be video recorded, he said no again. That's when Wells decided to end it cold. They tried to strongarm them, but Wells stood his ground. His boss at Berkeley Laboratory threatened his career. That was when Wells quit his research job and walked out and ran to the car to get away. Now we're leery of this whole thing and we have our house taken from us and I've got to tell you, I'll bet there will be some retribution. That's the way our modern government deals with its citizens."

"Jim, Wells did the right thing. Did he really quit his position at Cal?"

"He sure did. Just like in a country music video, too." They both laughed a little. Mostly from nervousness with what the next step might be from "our" government."

"Where are you now?

"In the casino hotel room. The presidential suite."

"I want you to get out of there and come over to my place. I don't like you being in their luxury prison."

"Okay. We're on our way."

Steph Townsend and her little baby were recuperating quickly. Jess was barely touched and was laughing and gurgling and doing the usual baby stuff. Steph's parents picked her up and took her home after two days of observation. She was badly bruised and sore. It didn't bother her. Jess was safe and sound. Grandma and Grandpa kept him fed and changed.

Steph's husband was in the Air Force, serving in Germany. He would get home the next week. First Lieutenant Ronnie Townsend wanted to meet the man who saved his family. That would have to wait.

20

Las Vegas was returning to some sort of normal. It could never be normal, but now with the bad elements on the ropes or dead, it would at least be safe.

Idaho took it fairly well. It didn't have the same number of "clientele" as Vegas.

California, that was a different story. The southern border was a disaster with so many people trying to get out and slide into Mexico. Quite a few didn't understand that their fate was not dependent on where they are now. The long arm of correction would find, judge and convict, if necessary, based on where you were. Most got it and just wanted to go back to their families to wait it out. Nobody wanted to risk a trip to a "hot" state. So far there were five and the "Force" appeared to be on the move.

Crime was over the top. Every cop that could, retired. They knew that when their state's time to "Face the Fear," they wouldn't have a job anyway. The already defunded police were about to see what no cops would deliver to their doorstep.

Parents were keeping their kids out of school. Too dangerous to chance it. Traveling at night was a big risk. Walking wasn't exempt either. So many attacks made that not worth it. The only people with guns were the bad guys and that made the good guys easy to pick off. No one worried about being arrested anymore in California. It was more of an inconvenience to the perp and not worth it for the victim to bother. The state was now a failed experiment.

Same in Oregon. Lawlessness rose to new levels never anticipated by the politicians that had previously allowed it. How hard is it to figure out that if you have no consequences for your actions, you do whatever you want? The people of Portland were not the type to return their shopping carts to the cart corral. The term self-policing was a word in a foreign language to them.

Washington State had a backlog of gate crashers at the border waiting to get out. Canada didn't want them. Maybe they were too liberal or too crazy even for our northern neighbor's taste. They would choke up the inbound process to slow down crossings. Crime escalated to "High" on the misery gauge everyone internally carried along. It was sad to watch the once-great city of Seattle slip into chaos. This chaos was different from the five hot states. An end was in sight for those. Washington, Oregon and California hadn't passed into that phase yet. It was forecast, but the predictions were as weak as the climate change ones. At least those were predictions from "models."

Molly and Luther spoke with Gabe the morning after Nevada's membership in the new order commenced. He told them it was safe for them to go out. He told them to take the baby and enjoy a nice meal in a restaurant. They earned it, he said.

"When are you coming back?"

"In a few more days." Great, we want to thank you for everything in person. "Luther is looking for a job in the service industry. He's hoping for an offer tomorrow."

"I'm happy to hear that Molly; I'm very happy to hear that. Is everything OK at the motel?"

"Yes, thank you so much." She still couldn't believe what luck they had to meet Gabe. It was out of nowhere, she thought.

Gabe parked at the hospital and asked about Dalton and Steph and her baby.

"Are you family?"

"Aren't we all?" he said while giving her his best angelic smile. He had a way with people, and they would do what he wanted.

"I guess we are."

"Dalton's in the ER. He's going out on a chopper to the Houston Burn Center. He's stable but burnt pretty badly on his back and skull. Do you know his contact person?"

"I do, will you call. Her name is Tammy." He gave the nurse her number and sat in the small lobby by the ER."

Fifteen minutes later, Tammy came running into the lobby and asked about her husband, Dalton. The nurse explained that he was soon going to a Houston burn center. That's when she lost her hold on holding it together. She broke down crying. Gabe approached her and said that Dalton would be alright; he was in stable condition and soon would be in a hospital that would finish healing him.

"Do… Do I know you?" she stopped wailing and settled a little after looking into Gabe's eyes.

"I knew him as a child, before he…." Gabe stopped before he said it.

"Were you in the business?" She thought he was either an old customer or an old supplier. "We don't do that anymore."

"I know, I know." He looked into her eyes and conveyed a message that he was there to help and not to judge. That Dalton would be okay, and he would make sure of it.

The emergency staff came in and gathered all of the IV bags and lines that were dripping into his veins and moved him to their cart. He was face down and his wounds were exposed and awful. Gabe wouldn't let Tammy see them. He pushed her away and stood in front of her to block her view.

"I want to go with him!" Tammy yelled as they were wheeling him to the elevator and up to the roof. "Please, I want to go with him."

"I'm sorry, we have no extra room. There is no space for you."

She broke down again and Gabe wrapped his arms around her to keep her from falling or passing out. He brought her over to a chair and gently lowered her down.

"I have to go to Houston. I have to be with my husband. I can't stay here!" Gabe told her that he would take her there and get her in to be with Dalton. "Stay here while I get the information where they're taking him. I'll be right back."

Gabe waited for her to settle in and walked over to the nurses' station to get the location and address of the burn center. He used the Delta App to look for a way to get to the Houston Hobby Airport. He knew it would be safe for them to travel to a hot state. He knew that they asked for forgiveness and had received it. They didn't know that.

"Oh my God." She gasped. She looked at Gabe and told him she couldn't travel to a hot state. "Dalton will die when he crosses into Texas. My Dalton will die."

"Listen to me; he will not die. Dalton will not die. He is forgiven and so are you."

"How can you know, who are you?" Tammy was confused. She couldn't understand what was going on. "How can you know that mister?"

"Call me Gabe; my name is Gabe." He paused and looked straight in the eyes again. She calmed down. "I just know. If you want to wait to see if Dalton made it alive to Houston, I'll oblige and wait. We can take a late flight."

"No, let's go. I don't want to live without my Dalton. I couldn't live without him. Let's go then. I don't know why, but I trust you; I believe you."

They jumped in his rental and drove to regional FBO airport to get to the burn center. He would have to fly private. The airport was not serviced by commercial airlines.

Tammy called her second in command at her housecleaning business to let her know what happened and to deputize her as the boss. Gabe was impressed with her sense of responsibility. They went through the large hangar, met the pilot and got on the plane. It didn't take long for the three-hundred-mile flight. Tammy did not get the "Face." Gabe only told her their location after they were fifty miles inside Texas.

They landed in Houston and taxied to the terminal.

"Why are you doing this? Who are you?

"I told you I'm a friend of Daltons. I met him in El Dorado."

"Let's go, they're opening the door."

They grabbed a rental car and drove to the hospital. He found a parking spot right next to the entrance. Gabe always found a good parking spot.

"Where is Dalton O'Rourke?" Tammy asked at the information desk. "I'm his wife."

"Upstairs, third floor. They just took him to his room."

"He was alive!" She hugged Gabe so tight it hurt him.

The Rentschler family was packing the car and driving away as they noticed two black SUVs coming in the entrance side of the parking area. They didn't see them. They drove toward Jim's house and as they were turning off the expressway, Jim called them.

"Stay away from the house. Two black SUVs are sitting down the street. They're waiting for you. My phone must be tapped. Nobody knew you were coming except me and Betty. She saw the cars from the second-story bathroom. Get out of town and call our friend. You know who I'm talking about. He'll get your message back to me." Jim hung up and waited for the inevitable agents that would soon show up at his office.

"Looks like we're going to my sister's house in Lafayette. They know we're on the run."

"This is pretty cool dad, this is really cool." Johnny declared.

"To you, Johnny, to you it is." He thought. "Everybody shut down your cell phones." Dad would have been a good contract asset for the NSA.

The Rentschler family made it out of Lake Charles before the feds nabbed them. They took the back roads to Lafayette and drove up the long drive to his sister's home. They knew they couldn't stay long. They felt threatened and tricked.

"Dad." Wells had an idea. "Let's drive to Texas. It's a hot state; they can't kidnap Johnny there. They can't hurt us, and they certainly can't kill us. Heck, they can't even lie in Texas."

"Brilliant! We need to have cash; we can't use credit cards. I saw that in a movie. We need a different car; they'll be looking for us." Kevin was enabling brain cells that hadn't been used in years. "You're right, Johnny; this is kinda cool." He thought about a rental car, and then he remembered the Suburban SUV behind the barn and under the shed roof. It runs like new and is titled to his old LLC. "Let's take the old Suburban and hide our car in the barn."

"We better hurry. These guys seemed to be pretty good at what they do." Wells was all in. In five minutes, they had the old truck loaded and borrowed $500 from Kevin's sister. The Rentschler family was on the run, headed for Texas with the government lawmen hot on their tail.

Tammy was allowed into Dalton's room. The nurse prepped her about what she was going to see. She told Tammy that he was better than he looked, and in a few months, he'd be walking around with some scars on his back and the back of his skull. She told her that his hair would grow back, but his back would be scarred.

"I accept your terms," Tammy smiled. She was happy her husband was going to pull through. She was happy crossing into Texas didn't kill Dalton or herself. All things considered, she thought it was a pretty good ending for a very bad start to the day.

"He's not able to talk now. I just want you to see him and see that he's alive." Did you know he saved a young woman and her baby? They're both doing fine. The chopper pilot told me about it. Your husband tossed the baby out of the fire that engulfed him. He went back in to save that baby, and he knew that the gasoline all around the car could ignite at any second. His partner panicked; Dalton did not."

With the Mexican border closed into America, they soon had a backlog of over half a million migrants waiting to get into the US. That was not going to happen. Now, Mexico had to feed, house and provide medical services. They immediately started mass deportations of the illegal aliens, swamping Mexico's social services and crashing communities unable to handle the sheer numbers. The southern border was sealed tight to halt the out-of-control inbound migration. When Mexico was just a pass-through to America, everything was fine. It wasn't fine anymore. They got a dose of reality of what was happening in the US, and they were not pleased.

Congress was eager to hold hearings about this in Texas. Democrats and a few Republicans tried to block the venue. They knew that witnesses couldn't lie in Texas anymore. They knew that their imported, undocumented Democrat "voters" scheme would be exposed. Everybody knew what the scheme was anyway. It was so obvious. What other reason made sense other than hating the country so much that they wanted to destroy unique American culture?

Military-aged men were sent back to the countries they left behind. To countries from all around the world.

21

Tammy's business and hard work were starting to collapse. She couldn't concentrate on anything except Dalton. Her loyal staff were trying to keep things positive, but nobody could run things like Tammy and now she was incapable.

Dalton was doing much better. He was in excruciating pain still. Mostly because he didn't want to take the morphine the doctors wanted to push into his veins. It reminded him of his old life, and it scared him.

He couldn't help with supporting Tammy now that he was incapacitated. He signed on as an independent contractor with the city. He didn't have insurance or an income anymore. The O'Rourke duo would soon be out on the streets.

Tammy had to get it together and fast. Dalton was coming home in ten days. He sent her home to save her business and their home. "I'll be alright, honey. I need you to save what we have left. I'm fine as I can be, considering. The doctors think so too if they are gonna send me home."

Tammy left for El Dorado. The utopian name for a mythical city of wealth and abundance. She felt neither now. She had work to do and she decided to stop feeling sorry for herself. She worked on a strategy while on the Greyhound Bus back home.

Gabe set up a "GoFundMe" page and seeded it with $5,000. Steph and Ronnie matched it. They would have given more, but that was all they had. Steph's mom and dad added $20,000 to help them out. They too wanted to meet this man that saved their daughter and grandson. They all prayed for him every night without fail. They didn't even know his last name until they read about the new fund-raising campaign.

The Rentschler clan made it through Louisiana on Interstate 10 and arrived unscathed in Texas. They noticed four black SUVs a couple of miles before the border to Texas. Kevin was sure glad he swapped cars. He knew they were waiting for them. It was a great relief. The feds might find them but now the playing field was a little more level. The feds didn't operate as well in bright lights and sunshine as they did in darkness.

They called their "mutual friend" to let Jim know they made it out of Louisiana safely. Jim was glad they didn't go to his place or Kevin's sister's house. They were both visited by men in suits and since no one knew where they were headed, the men in suits couldn't glean anything helpful. Kevin's daughter was told to stay at school and things would be explained later.

They drove to their condo in League City to wait for the eventual visit by whatever three-letter agency got there first. Wells put his money on the NSA. He was a little surprised they weren't already waiting inside. "Not as together as in the movies," he laughed.

He wished his dad hadn't taken the "Contraband" back home to Lake Charles. He fantasized how great it would have been to load it up and head out for a two-week cruise. They had a slip behind the condo that could have been a perfect getaway for the Rentschler pirate family to load up the ship. He remembered that John Lafite had long ago plied the freshwater bayous in the Lake Charles area and hid out amongst the cypress trees until things cooled off. The Rentschlers were resuscitating history, just on dry land for now.

Luther got a job in a huge hotel/casino in its Environmental Services Department. He was a janitor. Molly found work babysitting. Her only stipulation was that she was allowed to have her own baby with her. That wasn't an issue. What's better, a 14-year-old watching after your baby or a mother with her own baby watching yours? After a few days, she was passed around the upper-class neighborhoods and she came with an A+ rating. Molly had more business than she could handle. She remembered getting 2 bucks an hour when she was a teenager. Now, she was getting a hundred bucks an evening. She and Luther went looking for apartments to rent. They felt rejuvenated. Gabe came back and helped them move in and helped with the first, last and security deposit. It was actually more than help; he paid it in full.

Luther had two things that confused him. "How did you know my phone number and how did you know Nevada was the next state."

"Lucky guess," Gabe chortled.

Luther was good with his answer. He didn't want to press a gift horse. His mom had a different way of saying it. "Don't spank the baby that ain't crying." When his mom was younger and still had a few teeth, she used to say, "Don't bother with a dentist if you don't have any teeth." She didn't bother with a dentist and now she had no teeth.

Johnny liked the condo in League City. It was on the water and near enough to the beaches of Galveston. He grabbed the old Road Atlas from his bedroom and brought it to the living room to plan their escape route if needed. He liked being a fugitive on the run. The only thing missing was a shotgun on the floor and a couple of side arms in the glove box of the old Suburban.

He flipped to the Texas page and had fun looking at all the places they could hide out. He flipped back the US Map and saw Texas, New Mexico, Arizona, Nevada and Idaho were in red. That's weird, he thought. And then he saw Illinois was red, too. Illinois must be next, he thought. He hadn't dreamed about it, though. He showed Wells. His eyes almost bulged out like the dead.

"Johnny, where did you get this?"

"It's my old atlas that I kept in my room."

"Don't play with me. Did you do this?"

"No, Wells, I didn't and I'm more scared than before. This is freakin' me out."

"Okay, okay, Sorry." Wells was dumbfounded. He didn't know what to do. Should he call the feds? It would give away their location if he called. How could he tip them off? He felt he had to. "Dad, I need to talk to you!"

The feds got nowhere at the Rentschler's house. The map never changed, and no electromagnetic waves or anomalies were detected. Nothing from nearby radio stations was unusual coming into the bedroom. Nothing from deep space. Normal cell tower transmissions were about it. They setup sensors in the ground and in the bayou. Nothing.

"Wells called a friend at Berkeley and asked them to leave a handwritten message for Dr. Wharton."

Wharton opened it and read it. "Illinois is next," he looked at it again. "**Illinois is next**." Johnny has a road atlas, and the five hot states were red on it. Just like the bedroom map, only Illinois was added.

Wharton called the Lake Charles team and told them. "Our map doesn't have Illinois in red. Are you sure?"

"No, we can't be sure until the end of the month. Next weekend should be interesting."

Dalton came home by ambulance from Houston. Gabe made the arrangements and went along for the ride. Tammy heard about the GoFundMe page and told Dalton about it. There was over $370,000 raised and waiting to help with the crushing bills that were now relegated to just "pesky bills."

They couldn't believe that people could be that kind. Gabe reminded them of their kindness to others in their community. It was being paid forward now. Their hospital bills were picked up by one of the Wal-Mart Waltons that lived in Arkansas. They also pledged to pay for any other expenses that went toward his healing. That was a relief, because he was headed to the hospital in El Dorado for at least another month.

Tammy was so happy and relieved to have her "baby" back home. Even if he was in the hospital. He'd be home soon enough and back on his feet. The local newspaper was about to run a story about Dalton with a picture of him and Tammy. It had quotes from Steph and her family including a picture of her and Jess and Ronnie. It would make the community even happier and prouder to live there.

7/1/28

It was near midnight in Texas and Illinois. The bars were busy but not as much. The novelty was wearing off a bit. The drink specials weren't enough to fill the seats. It still had a festive feel to it, though.

The Rentschlers were all around the TV to see if the Road Atlas and Johnny's dreams about Illinois over the last few nights were predictors.

Wharton and the feds were doing the same thing. Watching and waiting to see if Illinois was next.

The usual countdown began and then the two-minute pause to see if it was happening. It did.

"Illinois!" The Newsmax announcer yelled. This should be a big one!" Not as big as Texas, but with almost 13,000,000 people it was big enough. Images and videos should be rolling in any moment. It was party time in America again. Not everywhere in Illinois, though. Tomorrow morning would provide all the gory details that most loved to hear about. It was like a bloodsport that was almost of Roman gladiator quality. Now, it was creeping toward the eastern part of the nation. Clay Higgins of Louisiana felt cheated again.

DC was nervous now. Very nervous.

"What are we going to do with Johnny Rentschler?" Director Miller wanted his agency to interview him. He told Wharton that he would handle it himself. The NSA was "above the fray." He thought. His agency was the premier one in the nation. That's what the CIA and the FBI thought of themselves, too.

He knew where they were. He already had eyes on them in League City. He decided to just call Wells and try to repair things with the Rentschlers.

Wells' phone rang and he let it go to voice mail. The area code was from DC. He waited a few minutes to let it finish and touched voice messages to listen. He put it on the speakerphone so his dad could listen.

"Wells, this is Director Miller. I heard about what happened in Lake Charles and I want to apologize. I want to set up a meeting with you and your dad's attorney, Jim Jackson. We need to interview Johnny and of course you and your parents can be in the room, and we will video the answers and the equipment results. Hell, I wouldn't leave my 12-year-old alone in the pediatrician's office. Maybe in Texas," he quipped.

"Whatever terms your family and your dad's attorney want, we'll abide by. No games and no spy movie BS. We need your help. We need Johnny's help real bad." He threw in that little folksy part at the end. "Please call me back. We can come out to meet with you in League City or wherever you like. I hope to hear from you soon."

"What do you think, Dad?" Kevin looked at his oldest son and his wife before speaking.

"I think we need to help. I'll call Jim Jackson and run it by him, and I'll let him set it up. Don't call him back; I'll have Jim make that call."

Dalton was healing and Tammy infused her much-needed management skills to save her company. It wasn't really as desperate as her employees made it out to be. Her customers knew what was going on with their lives. It was in the newspaper and on television. They were famous in El Dorado.

The article about Dalton and his heroics was in the *El Dorado News-Times*. It had pictures of Dalton and Tammy and another with Steph, Ronnie and baby Jess. Tammy loved it. The Townsends and their parents, the Willistons, planned on stopping by later in the afternoon to thank them in person. Tammy wanted to thank them for their generous GoFundMe gift. She didn't know what to say, except "Thank You."

As Tammy read the article, it talked about the loss they suffered when their son died from fentanyl. Tammy froze and then started shaking violently.

"Tammy, what's wrong." He pushed the call button for his nurse.

"Dalton, It's them. It's Jesse's family. He's the boy we killed!"

Jim made the arrangements to meet with the NSA. He would be present along with Johnny's family and Wells. He arranged things to protect Johnny and gave the entire family blanket immunity for anything they said and for any "untruthful" answers as determined by the polygraph machine and the examiner. He rejected the arrogant man they had the run-in with and chose a new examiner after reviewing his resume and experience. Miller, the examiner and Jackson would fly the short trip in a government jet and meet at the condo.

The Willistons had the article and read about Tammy and Dalton. Steph realized immediately who they were. She read their last name and put the photo together with it and couldn't believe it. It was them. The number one suspect in the death of Jesse. Her brother was the person she named her baby after. They were going to meet with Jesse's killers and Steph and Jess' savior.

22

Gabe showed up at the hospital to visit Dalton and Tammy. She broke down crying when she saw Gabe walk through the door.

"What's wrong, honey?" Gabe knew that she knew.

"It's the boy we killed. It's his family in the article. I can't face them; I can't look at them in the eyes without dying. I can't handle it. Oh, Gabe, we need your help again."

"How weird is this? This is not an accident, Gabe. Is God doing this? Is this part of our repentance? Is this a punishment?" Dalton lamented.

"If it is, just remember that God will never give you more pain than you can handle. It may be really close, but it is never more than you can handle. You just have to deal with it and ask for forgiveness."

Gabe looked at both of them and spoke. "They know who you are. They certainly have read the article. If they walk through that door this afternoon, you can bet they forgive you and are thankful that you were and are a part of their lives." He looked over a Dalton.

"You saved Stephanie's life and her baby Jesse's life. You almost died for them. Don't you think they are as grateful as you are ashamed and sorrowful and penitent? Don't you think they have forgiven you this very day?"

Gabe knew the answer. He visited the Williston house that morning. He had the same conversation with them about Tammy and Dalton. He told them how Jesse's death saved them too. His death saved four people. It turned their lives around. He told them that these events were no accident. They believed him. They had genuine forgiveness in their hearts. All the Willistons did, including Ronnie too.

The white Gulfstream jet was approaching Galveston. It had no markings. It didn't have a tail number. The air traffic controller would identify it with the transponder squawk code. The pilot confirmed it and was permitted to land. It taxied to the Island Jet Center.

A Black SUV with government plates was waiting on the tarmac to drive them into League City to meet at the condo. Inside was a wrapped gift that Miller asked for. It was delivered from the Johnson Space Center a few minutes before. Jim wondered how many black SUVs the government owned. They seemed to be everywhere.

The Rentschlers greeted Jim and Miller and the polygraphist. The technician liked that name better than "lie detector guy."

Jim brought copies of the agreement he constructed with the NSA attorneys and the executed immunity documents from the State Department and a gift for Johnny and flowers for the Mrs.

He gave Johnny a big box covered with NASA spaceship wrapping paper. Johnny opened it and pulled out a heavy, autographed space helmet from the 1980s. "John Young signed it before his death in 2018. He was one of the most accomplished astronauts in history. He flew on Apollo missions, moon landing missions and commanded the first space shuttle mission. Oh, and he walked on the moon as the commander of Apollo 16. That small, clear Lexan case has a moon rock in it from his mission."

For once, Johnny was speechless.

Mrs. Rentschler loved the huge live orchid she received.

"Wells, your desk is waiting for you back at Berkeley. I heard about you quitting. Very impressive, son, well done."

That worked much better than Wharton's approach. Miller wasn't as smart, but he had way more common sense than that geek.

The Willistons arrived at the hospital to see the O'Rourke's. Gabe snuck out just before. They didn't need him.

Steph was holding Jess as she quietly knocked and peeked in.

"Come in, come in," Tammy said while holding her breath.

Steph ran over to Dalton and touched his cheek. She wanted to pick him up and hug him. That would be a few months off. "Thank you, Dalton. You can't imagine how grateful I am that you came to our rescue. I am so sorry for all your pain."

He wasn't sure that she knew who he was. He didn't know. He wanted to tell her that his physical pain was nothing compared to the emotional pain he inflicted on her family. He just blurted it out and closed his eyes for whatever was coming his way.

"We know who you are. You didn't know who I was when you saved my life. When you ran back to check if someone else was in the car. When you were standing in gasoline trying to get Jess out to safety. You didn't know and I didn't know. You just ran into danger and almost made it out. You threw Jess, buckled in his car seat, across the pavement to safety as you were on fire from the explosion."

Tammy ran over and hugged Steph. She was crying so hard, and she couldn't stop. She finally took a breath and said. "Thank you, Steph, for forgiving us. I dreamed about this forgiveness that I thought would never come. Thank you."

"This is the first step. I want to be your friend!"

"Can I hold Jess?" Steph smiled a huge grin and handed Jess to her. "I'm pregnant!"

"What?" Dalton screamed. "Sorry, Babe, I was gonna tell you tonight. When I saw little Jess, I couldn't hold it in. Are you happy?"

"This is the best day of my life, honey. I love you so much!"

The rest of Steph's family was in the hall. They decided to talk with them later. They didn't want to pierce the reconciliation that they all needed. They knew they would have a lifelong friendship and that there was plenty of time to talk. Mrs. Williston broke down and cried. She was as happy as the day before Jesse died. It felt good.

Gabe was around the corner listening. Nobody knew he was there. "All in a day's work."

Johnny asked if he could wear his new helmet during the interview. Wells laughed, but not enough to embarrass his little brother. "Alright, I'll put it down."

They hooked him up to stick-on electrodes of some sort. The man calibrated his machine and asked a few easy questions to fine-tune things.

"Okay, Johnny, what's your full name and address?" Johnny answered.

"A little slower. Don't be nervous; I'm not gonna bite you." Alright, do you like your gift from Director Miller?

"I hate it! He laughed, watching the arms swing wildly across the moving paper.

"Perfect, Johnny, you just calibrated a lie for me. Are you ready?"

"Yes, sir." He thought this was pretty cool.

'When did you first hear about this phenomenon?"

"New Year's Day, 2026." The pen arms didn't move much.

"What did you think it was?"

"I thought it was a poison gas until I learned that the deaths were selective. That was really strange, I thought."

"When did you figure out the Indian Ocean conundrum."

"Almost a year later, after data from ships and planes reporting the location of the deaths. They weren't very accurate because of the delay in determining the exact time of death. That made the plotting very fuzzy and concealed the true boundary."

"How did you work around that?

"Kind of by accident. I was concentrating on the Texas boundaries and then It occurred to me that the Indian Ocean plots had a vague resemblance to the size of Texas. It didn't look like Texas, but the size, the area was so close. I then picked certain obvious parts of the Texas boundary to look at closer. The straight lines and the corners, the panhandle and the Rio Grande irregularities. I gave those latitudes and longitudes a negative value and then plotted them on the map. Bingo.

It was Texas from the underside. It was backwards. The Indian Ocean incidents all lined up nicely. The antipodes of Texas were in the Indian Ocean."

This went on for two hours. Johnny was giving precise answers to the questions. Not once did he cause the arms to flail on the machine. The only time was when he asked to go to the bathroom and the examiner asked if he could hold on for a little longer. He said Yes, it was an obvious lie. They disconnected him and he ran to the toilet. He barely made it in time.

After it ended, Mr. Rentschler asked if he could question his son about a girl he liked in his class. Johnny ripped the electrodes off and smiled. "Not today, Dad, not today."

The arms were banging around the machine like the old black and white *Lost in Space* TV show robot in full panic mode.

Illinois' population declined overnight by more than 12,000 people. That didn't include pedophiles. The State law enforcement was working on those numbers. It was bad if you were a criminal. It was very good if you were an upstanding citizen.

Everything played out just like the other five states and like the last four, the punishment came all at once. Whomever was behind this decided it was best to just rip off the band-aid and get it over with. They could handle it. It wasn't a new thing anymore; it wasn't unexpected.

Illinois was and outlier. The other five states all touched each other and made the boundary into a very long one. Illinois was in the middle of the Midwest. Its boundaries were like an island, like a moat surrounding a castle. In the new state of Illinois, you either sink or swim, crossing that moat.

23

The five "after" states suffered losses in business and hiring from the "before" states. Adultery seemed to be the biggest culprit. A wayward wife or cheating husband killed the prospect of them relocating. Colleges "suffered" a similar fate and found that they had to reach out to a more conservative brand of professor to "guide" their young adults. It seemed that those with the more liberal mindset weren't really bothered by rules and regulations until this new and mysterious "ruling class" majority stepped in to reestablish order. Applications and interviews dropped 75%. So many far-left professors left the "after" states that the universities were going through demographic upheavals at the highest levels. Most university presidents, deans and leadership were hammered by the "Force."

As more conservative "second stringers" were called up from the bench, the usual protesters planned their countering rallies. It was humorous to watch free speech assemblies now. The once "peaceful protests" that burned, blockaded and rubbished buildings on campuses were now actually peaceful. It was humorous to watch the polite and orderly groups now that they couldn't harm or push or harass anyone. The man-bunned "men" and blue-haired "women" looked completely out of context with civility and courtesy restraints placed on their First Amendment-protected freedoms. Just as the liberal professors were packing up their stuff and heading to the "before" states, so did their mindless followers. As these wagon trains of whackos headed out, the adults in the room headed to their new homes and positions in this new six-state alliance.

This education upheaval reached down to elementary, middle and high schools too. The school boards flipped overnight to resemble something that the overwhelming majority of parents wanted instead of the activist driven agenda that was reshaping minds to accept the perversions it declared "normal." The candidates couldn't hide their hidden agenda anymore. Truth exposed and removed them from leadership. People could now tell you the definition of "Woman" once again. No more agonizing word contortions and jumbling of meanings stood in the way of clarity. Even the little things, like returning your shopping cart from the parking lot to the store, felt comforting to the earlier non-serious offenders.

It was much cheaper to live in the new USSA. The "United Six States of America." Auto insurance costs dropped 80%. No thefts or break-ins and it seriously reduced accidents. People were now obeying laws. Even the cost of health insurance was dramatically slashed. The greatest health improvements were in the mental health field. After the initial "correction" shock passed, common ailments like anxiety, depression, fear and helplessness evaporated and freed many from their once heavy loads and mental prisons. "Jail-breaking" as it was called by mental health professionals.

It was the small things that seemed to matter. Remembering you didn't lock your car or back door in the middle of the night was not important. Protection orders from abused spouses weren't bothered with anymore. When people are considerate of others, no matter the motive, life is a joy. Nobody was moving out of state anymore. Why would you want to go from protected, safe harbor waters into a tempest? You wouldn't.

On the other hand, California was suffering. Worse was Oregon. That was the number one attraction of the crazy left. It was spreading into farm communities that used to be a buffer to them from the families and God-fearing. Crime was so out of control that Oregon was dubbed "Clockwork Oregon." The value of farmland was escalated by the real estate sales records that were broken every month. Many of the farm families sold and moved to more suitable locations. Almost all to the USSA.

Washington State didn't fare much better. Home break-ins were so frequent that you couldn't leave your house. City dwellers didn't own guns for protection; the city leaders made sure that only the criminals owned guns. In the outlying areas, where guns were in the right hands, crime was up, but nothing a bullet couldn't stop. The state at first tried to prosecute people defending their lives and property but gave up after the USSA offered "sanctuary." It was humorous to see the state newspaper editorials denouncing these sanctuaries that were "undermining" a civilized society.

All these positive changes were embraced by the average American. But the lack of drug sales had the most reformative effect. It was obvious that "Reformative Justice" was a failed ideology that sought to explore and research the many diverse reasons for drug abuse. Turns out the reason is very simple: availability of drugs. When the drugs aren't available, drug use stops. Who would have thought that? It wasn't worth the risk selling or transporting to the USSA. The liberal laws were overridden and cancelled by the new way of conduct. Drug companies weren't exempt either. They suffered great losses of scientists that pressed for profits above people. Profits used to be a call to action for the left years ago. Now, they forced people to take vaccines if they wanted to have a job. Even gave the corporations immunity for the false claims of virus vaccine immunity. The left of the sixties was the real far-right of the 21st century. They just couldn't see it staring back at them. Pressing for censorship was the most hilarious part of these "non-nazis," and "non-fascists," and "non-constitution" types claimed as their high ground. Nobody was listening to this nonsense anymore and it seemed they weren't listening to their own words. Words that convicted their demands as ironically flawed and absurd on their face. The first amendment was the first for a good reason and not to be trifled with for bad reasons. The second was there to ensure the first survived the mobs and to survive that good old and reliable enemy of the left: unchecked government. The exact type of government they now adored and even worshipped.

Politicians, DAs and the new breed of prosecutors had a difficult time reconciling that the USSA didn't have crime because there were no criminals on the streets anymore. The threat of punishment was a real deterrent there. Wouldn't it be the same in the rest of the nation if the criminals were simply taken off the streets? Did anyone ask, "How can we do that?" The concept of separating criminals from society via a jail sentence was cruel and unusual punishment to these "intellectuals." But wouldn't that have the same effect? Wouldn't that be better for the other 95% of the citizens victimized by crime and violence? Why couldn't they be protected from cruel and unusual crimes? Why were they left unprotected? Pretty simple math here. Pretty straightforward logic.

Who's next and who's doing this were still unanswered questions. The big unanswered questions.

24

The Rentschlers were allowed to go home to Lake Charles. The four-hour drive lacked the excitement of being on the run. Johnny fell asleep with his 4-pound NASA helmet on.

They drove past the Loggerhead and turned left onto Pickerel and drove up the long driveway that ended at the house and docks on the bayou. Fred greeted them and then darted under the water.

Johnny ran up to his bedroom and was surprised to see his map had Texas and the other five "after" states neatly cut out and missing. A note explained that a drywaller would repair his wall the next day.

Wells had to get ready to return to Berkeley. They didn't send him a private plane this time. He didn't know it, but he would find a package on his university desk that explained his security clearance. The name of his dad's boat caused a temporary freeze until research revealed it was the name of a local festival celebrating the famous pirate John Lafite and his boat called "Contraband."

Like the other levels of security, he would have to demonstrate a "need to know" before gaining access. Signature, affidavits and disclosure documents awaited his execution along with a designated witness. Because of the unusual Top-secret classification that Wells had achieved, the witness to his signature required a minimum-security clearance level of "Secret." That was just below Wells' classification. The name listed as a witness on the documents was Wharton. Wells would have a higher level of clearance than Wharton the second he signed on the "dotted line" of the witness signature page. Wells would not take a revenge type of pleasure watching Miller sign his papers, but he would always cherish this "Kodak" moment.

They were expecting a sleep monitor technician later in the day to hook up Johnny. He would install video cameras focused on Johnny's bed and another on Johnny's map. The monitor would indicate body movement, sleep and awake times and brain wave changes. Normal and not normal. It couldn't identify the paranormal, clairvoyant or telepathic; no current technology could.

Johnny had his Rand McNally Road Atlas with him. They let him keep it with the caveat that if another state changed to red, he would let the DC boys have it to examinate. "Yes, sir." Johnny felt a part of the team now and liked that they trusted him.

Kevin's attorney, Jim, suggested they hire a "bug sweeper" to go through the house. Kevin wasn't concerned. He just assumed they would be monitored every way they could. Even in ways a "bug sweeper" didn't know about yet. So much was classified by the NSA that it wouldn't be discovered by the public until it was obsolete.

Kevin agreed with Jim. He remembered a friend who asked the CEO of a large military munitions provider to the army, about the "silent helicopters" that dropped in on Osama bin Laden when he was killed.

The CEO told him that they were silent but offered no other details. "I can't talk about what I know," he said with a small smile. "Do you remember Desert Storm when we saw the stealth fighters and bombers for the first time?" He nodded yes. "That technology was obsolete years before. The only thing I can add is that when you put your head on the pillow at night, sleep tight. Everything will be ok in the morning; the US Military has your back."

Kevin appreciated that story, even if it was only somewhat true. He liked the days when he respected the military and our government. After a rocky start from the last few days and recent events, some of his trepidation was melting.

Johnny was "hooked up" before bedtime, and the video cameras recording different light waves and radio spectrums were calibrated.

He said he would stop by in the morning to check in on things. He showed Johnny how to disconnect from the equipment for whatever reasons he needed.

On the third night, he disconnected so he could use the bathroom and when he came back, he saw the map on his wall was different. Louisiana, Mississippi, Alabama and Florida were as red as a ripe tomato. 36,000,000 citizens of these four states would join the USSA if Johnny's predictions held. It would temporarily be named the United Ten States of America. The population of the UTSA would be 80,000,000. A little less than a quarter of the total US. Things were starting to move rapidly and now would be heading east if the map on his wall was as accurate as before. His road atlas was not colored red. The four new states were only on the bedroom wall map.

Wells was woken by Johnny with the news. He walked him to his room to show him. His dad was already looking at the wall map with six cut-out holes and four new red states. "What are we gonna do, boys? Wells knew. He had Millers' cell phone. He grabbed it off the charger and touched the recent from his last call.

"Wells. What happened?" No point in pleasantries.

"We have four new states on the wall map. Louisiana, Mississippi, Alabama and Florida."

"Holy sh..?" He blurted.

"We're on a speakerphone with my dad and Johnny," Wells informed him.

"Oh, sorry. Can I have Phillips come over to look at the recordings?"

"Please, yes. Johnny wasn't hooked up to the monitor when it happened."

"Why, you know we nee…" Wells cut him short.

"He went to the bathroom. He was offline for a minute, maybe. That's when it happened."

"Interesting coincidence, I'd say." Miller had the same thought the Rentschers had. "Okay, I'll call Phillips now and tell him to run over to your place. I'll call you back in a minute."

"He's on his way and so am I. See you in five hours or so. I may bring a few associates with me. We need to strategize how to handle this." Miller hung up and jumped in the shower after alerting the pilot to get ready to fly to the "Pelican State."

Phillips checked the videos, and he saw the flash and then the four new red states emerged. He also saw Johnny get up and leave to visit the bathroom and return after the states flashed to red. "Just like before, Johnny said," Phillips confirmed that Johnny didn't somehow color the states himself.

"Any dreams yet?"

"No, sir. It's usually a day or two before the correction. They're not frightening dreams; they're just regular dreams about the states."

Johnny wanted to be as helpful as possible; after all, he was part of the team. Not an adversary that Wharton created a few days ago.

Phillips decrypted all the electronic equipment and came up empty-handed. Nothing. He wished he had the data when the flash occurred. That was probably the time for a spike. He decided to build a cable long enough to reach the bathroom. He needed to know if anything changed during the flash.

Miller arrived at 7:00 am and was driven to the Rentschler's home. He set up shop in Kevin's office. He wanted to come up with a cover story and be ready when the four states turned at the end of the month. He had no doubt about Johnny's predictions and the veracity of the map.

Wells came into the office and asked if he could talk alone with Miller. Phillips got up and walked around the large deck overlooking the bayou.

"I know I'm not versed in how government handles these types of situations, heck you're probably not either. This is like a UFO. It's only with real evidence."

"I can't talk about UFOs. By the way we reference them as Unidentified Aerial Phenomena now; UAPs."

"I don't want to talk about UAPs either. I want to talk about notifying the four states ahead of this event and addressing the nation honestly with a press conference. Don't you think it would be best to just be honest. If for no other reason, when it hits DC, any false statements will count against you on these crazy honesty ratings. When that happens, and we all know it will, you'll have no credibility and that goes for the president too."

"Interesting approach. We don't normally tell the truth when big things happen. We try to protect our citizens from panic."

"Or yourselves from scrutiny."

"Well played." Miller was considering something that was unusual in modern politics, and he knew all the three letter agencies were on the political treadmill. It's the nature of the game now.

"You have a call from the President," Phillips yelled.

Miller picked up the phone. "Mr. President."

"What's the latest? I hear we have some more movement."

"Yes, sir, four new states."

"I heard about them. Did you find anything from the monitors or videos?"

"Just the video. We saw the flash just before the states turned red on the wall map."

"It only turns red when Johnny is nearby. He is certainly a key to what's happening." Miller looked at Wells and put his finger up to his mouth and zipped his lips. Wells understood that secret code.

"Sir, I think it's time to be honest with our citizens. I think we need to bring them into our problem. They should know that we don't have much to go on except for a map in a bedroom in Lake Charles and a thirteen-year-old boy that is the receptacle for our advance notice. I think we should notify the new states immediately and offer our help. We're pretty good at this now."

"I hear you and I can see your point. Let me bounce it off the other boys. I'll call you back before lunch."

"I think he'll do it. I think he agrees with you, Wells. I think he sees that he's better off telling the truth now than later, coming off as a lying idiot who only wants to cover his "you know what." He nodded his head up and down and asked, "What do you do at Berkeley? I'm sorry I forgot."

"Astrophysics, sir."

"If you're half as smart as Johnny, I think we could use you at the NSA." Miller laughed, but 80% of that statement was true.

The rest of the day was filled with people from black SUVs talking with Johnny and Miller and a bunch of folks in DC.

Gabe returned to the hospital to say goodbye to Dalton and Tammy. It was people like them that made the world a better place. He especially loved the ones that screwed up the most and when confronted by their own legacy, owned it and made a conscious decision to change. Dalton and Tammy sure fit that description. They were headed toward a great life together and unlike some of Gabe's friends that struggled through life, they would be a lighted walkway for all that crossed their path.

Gabe was on his way to Louisiana. Lake Charles, to be exact. He had an important message to deliver. He drove to the El Dorado FBO and boarded the small plane to the Lake Charles Regional Airport. The last time Gabe was in the city was August 23rd, 2020, just before two hurricanes slammed into town. First came Laura, on August 27th. She was a 150+ windspeed behemoth that was a direct hit on the Cajun city. Delta followed in October and caused more damage to the structures that had been severely damaged and were left covered with blue tarps. Its 100 MPH winds finished off the properties that barely made it through Laura. It would take years to get back up to fight another day.

Gabe was there to help evacuate people before the storm hit. He had a way with strangers that put them at ease and made them able to trust him. Some said it was his blue eyes; others claimed his comforting voice. He was credited with saving a lot of lives. The newspaper ran a story about his passion to help others. They only knew his first name, and nobody could find a photo of him. The reporter had taken dozens of photos of volunteers and remembered Gabe convincing "old timers" that had "hurricane experience" to shed their bravado for this girl that was headed to town. She would not be impressed. Those pictures were somehow missing. Gabe left Lake Charles at 6:00 pm on the 26th of August. Seven hours before Laura came to town.

He got off the plane and walked out to grab a taxi. He ran into Lee. He was a pilot and had just finished a flight for the Calcasieu Parish Sheriff's Department. Lee was part of the "Hood" and was a volunteer with Gabe during Laura. Lee asked him if he could give Gabe a ride into town.

"If it's not trouble."

"Not at all. Where are you staying?" Lee had his GPS ready to input Gabe's destination.

"A place called the Loggerhead Inn on the English Bayou, North of town."

"Lee laughed. It's next to my street. Let's go."

Lee and Gabe walked to his car. He threw his one bag in the back and got in.

"I remember you from Hurricane Laura. Everybody wondered what happened to you. You just disappeared. We thought you must have left to board up your own place. We didn't even know your last name."

"Arch," he said. "Gabe Arch."

"Good to see you again, Gabe. Good to see you."

They drove through the city and Lee pointed out the empty spot where the thirty-story office building used to stand. It was demolished. "Four years after Laura, it sat there dying. It was an eyesore with half the windows blown out. It was damaged beyond repair and after a few strange deals were floated, the city sued and made the owners demolish it. That felt like the turning point in our rebuilding." Lee held the same sentiment as most of the residents.

Gabe didn't miss the irony of demolishing something to feel like you were rebuilding. He thought about the thousands of people he came across that were as damaged as that building in Lake Charles. How they tried to scheme their way out of their broken lives and couldn't. They couldn't until they realized that their brokenness needed to be demolished. Imploded. Blown to bits before they could rebuild their own lives. It was a turning point for them, too.

"Do you have plans for the evening?" Lee liked Gabe.

"No, just grabbin' a burger in the bar."

"You're coming to my house for dinner. All the neighbors will be there. Ten or twelve of us live on the street and we get together whenever everyone's in town. Greg's frying shrimp and Mike's making one of his Cajun specialties. Not sure which, but they're always excellent. We'll even have personalized pizza from the pizza oven. Ben and Trish will bring the cocktails. They're both boat captains and well, what can I say, they enjoy adult beverages. Don't tell 'em I said that."

"Thanks, Lee, that's very kind of you. Thank. you."

"I'll get you at six."

Lee notified the Hood about the new guest.

The President called and told Miller he liked his idea. "I'm the only one that liked it, but I'm also the only one with his head on the block. I'm gonna do it. I'm calling for a 1:00 pm press conference tomorrow. I'm going to level with our people. I'm gonna tell them the truth. It's time for honesty."

Miller thought that an odd statement. "It's *time* for honesty." He chuckled and thought to himself, "Soon, it won't be a choice; it will only be a time for honesty."

The Rentschlers brought Miller with them to meet the Hood. He hadn't had any decent Cajun food yet. The pizza that Tammy made at the RV Park and gas station was great, and the boudin was a new experience, but he needed something authentic. The Hood will provide it.

Lee ran over to the Loggerhead to fetch Gabe for the meet and greet at his house. The Hood was in full attendance and accounted for. Dr. Dave and his wife laurie from Moss Bluff. John and Rhonda, (More names XXXXXXXX) were already there. The Hood in residence were: Mike and Buffy, Lee and Laurie, Greg and Annette the Captains Ben and Trish and the Rentschlers, who rounded off the perfect attendance. Everyone was in town and together for the first time in a while. They were at Lee and Leeann's beautiful new home on the bayou. The way the party flowed through it would make one think they designed it for the Hood parties.

Wells missed the fête. He was back in California, longing for the good food and the crawdads that he was weaned on. He was eating a West Coast "fusionally confused" meal of quinoa and microgreens. A salad with a macadamia nut dressing topped off with a hint of matcha and a dusting of bee pollen. He had to laugh about the food he was missing on the English Bayou. It may not have been as ridiculously healthy, but it most certainly was ridiculously tastier and cheaper than the $70 fare he was staring at while daydreaming about boiled crawdads.

Johnny was the guest of honor. At least, it seemed that way with all the questions he was pelted with. They knew about the mystery map and Johnny's mystery predictions. Miller knew the President would make an announcement in the morning, Louisiana time, and when Johnny looked at him for guidance on the questions that were walking too close to the line, Miller nodded either okay or negative. He loosened up the secrecy a little bit for the Hood. That made Johnny really feel a part of the team and it showed in his newly acquired adult mannerisms of pride and standing a little more erect to gain a half inch in height as he disclosed the government "secrets" that the Hood was now privy to. He had never felt so important in his lifetime. "Bigshot" is what his mom called him that evening.

Buffy asked a question she knew even the highest levels of government couldn't answer. She looked at Miller and asked straightaway, "Who is doing this? What kind of power is this? Miller didn't have an answer. The Hood all chimed in together. "God!"

The "unwashed and unclassified" always had an answer, Miller thought to himself before noticing his eliteness stinking up the party. That was out of character for him. He was used to DC parties with political celebrities and power mongers all vying for a better seat at the "table." The Hood was more to his liking. All the seats were equal except maybe for Mike's Barcalounger back at home facing the largest TV screen for miles.

Gabe sat and talked to Johnny. He enjoyed his youthful exuberance and innocence. He was somehow tied up in all these unexplained phenomena. Johnny couldn't explain it because he didn't know why he was selected. Gabe could see the underlying fear he had and told him to not worry. When Gabe looked into Johnny's eyes, he felt immediately more relaxed and at ease.

"Don't worry about anything, young man."

"Matthew Chapter 6?" Johnny remembered those verses that he memorized last year. He liked a girl and worried about not being accepted and not knowing how to act in front of her. He talked to his dad about it, and he told him about the verse and advised him to memorize it. Johnny did and now Martha was his secret girlfriend.

Gabe loved his answer and his maturity. A minute ago, he was worried about the young man sitting next to him and how he would handle these things he was involved with. He had no worries anymore. Gabe had his questions answered. Gabe thought it was ironic that he was worrying about Johnny and that he might want to revisit Matthew for his own wellbeing.

They all headed home around midnight. Lee dropped Gabe back at the Loggerhead. The Hood walked back to their homes as the honorary members drove to their own places around Lake Charles.

Gabe checked out of his room and headed to Nevada. His work in the Bayou State was complete.

25

Illinois was taking it hard. Thousands of mommas and daddys were mourning their sweet and young little "murderers" deaths. They didn't know that their lack of direct parenting caused it. Single mothers were twice as affected as their midnights rang in. A "polite society," as our founding fathers called it, was back in Chicago. Southern Illinois was already polite. Not much going on there except in the Universities. Mostly drugs, pedophilia, adultery and indoctrination.

Interstates 90 and 94 had less cars and fewer long-haul trucks than thirty years ago. Some speculated it was less because of murder and more adultery to blame. The well-known truck stops that provided extracurricular activities for exhausted and not-so-exhausted drivers were totally quiet. All agreed that a night in "heaven" in the privacy of their truck sleeper wasn't worth the hell that would be inflicted on their "tackle" and libidos for the rest of their lifetime. Those married drivers who had partaken during their travels, avoided crossing through Illinois. They knew who they were, and they bid on short hauls that didn't take them through the "Danger Zones." Prices nationwide increased substantially and affected inflation. Freight trains became very popular for west coast shippers heading east. After heavy recruiting and training replacement engineers, they were back to 100% and expanding.

Financial sectors were trying to negotiate a safe route through the unknown. Some short-sellers cherry-picked the obvious. Condom makers, bullets and ammunition, weapons, pornography, security companies, lock and safe manufacturers, insurance companies and law firms specializing in slip and falls, personal injury and divorce. The "before" states were even affected. Most knew what was coming their way. It may take a few years, but they know it's coming their way eventually. Gold prices were trending up for years.

The military lost a lot of soldiers and not from combat. Married enlisted and officers alike that were tempted by and succumbed to adultery, and those ordered to report to bases in the "after" states refused and were court-martialed and kicked out. New recruits hit levels so low that national security was severely weakened. When the rest of the states join the new union, America would have to withdraw virtually everywhere around the world and be pulled back. When the Pentagon realized that was causing even more chaos because too many returning decided to refuse. Pay cuts were offered to US-stationed soldiers to relocate to foreign bases with a promise to stay away from the Indian Ocean and the US during operations. It was a forced isolation that isolationists approved.

These "after" states didn't only lose business and employees, they also lost cultural events, sporting events, entertainment and tradeshows. Billions of dollars stayed away because of the known risks and immediate repercussions that would ruin their day and beyond. Sports teams in Texas, Arizona, Nevada, Florida and now Illinois were decimated. Rapists lost their testosterone along with their genitals. That didn't make for an aggressive sportsman. They couldn't find many replacements from the "before" states. Teams refused to enter these new states, causing forfeits and profit losses that shut down multiple NFL teams overnight. Some of the mediocre college teams in the south were suddenly contenders. A forfeit was the same as a win for them. When Penn State, Ohio State, Georgia and Oregon refused to enter the "no go" zones, they technically lost. That upset everything.

The three Pacific western states were desperate. The law-abiding citizens started to understand that order had completely broken down in their part of the American dream. Californians especially watched as everything they sacrificed in order to build a good life was decomposing into waste. Thousands crossed into Nevada to purchase defensive weapons. Legislators tried new laws and ways to stop them. They probably would have worked in the past. Now, the police were on the side of their weary friends and neighbors who just wanted a fighting chance to save their families and property. Guns were cheap in Nevada. Gun stores were full of used guns that weren't needed for their citizen's safety and protection. Supply and demand set the prices low. Nevada passed laws to relax residency requirements for these new Second Amendment supporters. They knew that bad guys wouldn't cross the state line to buy guns.

Colleges and universities were struggling. Evergreen University in Oregon was the first to go down. It wouldn't be missed except for the entertainment value it always provided. Antifa, Stop Oil, BLM, Anti TERFS, Gaza, Palestine, Anti Zion and whatever new popular derivatives evolved, made college too dangerous. Walking through campuses wasn't worth the risk. If you weren't a part of their group, then you were considered the enemy and the recipient of bullying and injury. Parents were conserving their money. They might need it for the collapse that surely was coming. The luxury of a useless college education lost its shine and ranking in things considered worthwhile.

Wells Rentschler had enough. He didn't join in with the gun-buying frenzy. He had top-level security clearance and didn't want to break any laws. He didn't know it, but his Top-Secret classification would allow him to buy and carry a gun in any state. He was technically a federal employee, and the feds did whatever they wanted. Legal or not. Wells decided to leave the chaos of California, head home and work for Miller at "ground zero." It was conveniently located down the hall and next to his old bedroom in Lake Charles. Miller couldn't be happier; he had no other good news to report in ages.

The governor of Florida planned for his state's turn. He was as ready as you could be. This wasn't a good old regular and reliable hurricane. His state had them figured out and set the standard for preparedness and "repairedness."

The thousands of bodies were picked up and moved to refrigerated warehouses that sat empty for over a year, waiting for the dead to arrive. Prison security teams had been trained and ready when called up. The prisoners were ready and waiting since the classes and lectures told them what to expect, what would happen and tell them the order of restoring order. When midnight came their way, they almost took it in stride. Except for the unbelievably grotesque facial expressions of the dead that couldn't be mitigated by lectures or literature that tried explaining it and showing it, to lessen the impact and shock. All in all, the job was accomplished, except maybe for that last part.

Florida was under control in a few days of the initial stage of this upheaval. They moved into to help them the other states with the cleanup. Louisiana, Mississippi and Alabama benefitted from Florida's success and followed their lead. The four southern governors spoke daily on video conferences and online apps. They reported twice a day to the press and people in order to calm things down. It was a success. The rest of the debris that came along later would now be easier to deal with. Wells was particularly happy with the newly styled "honest" approach to press announcements from state governments. He wondered when the feds would get on board. They were trying, but decades of lying and deception were cooked into the culture. It was for the good of the stupid masses, they said to ease their guilty consciences that they couldn't trick.

Most Christians knew in their hearts that this was spiritual. These "end times" weren't explained in the same way as the *Book of Revelation*. But the date and time were open-ended and not predicted. Unless "in the future" was considered a prophesy.

Churches held meetings across the country and the world to better understand what was happening. They set up boards to investigate prophetic testimony and unexplainable miraculous occurrences. There wasn't much to work with. No apparitions, miracles or divine evidence of any credibility was yet to be found. They had reached the same dead end that Miller and the NSA had. The consensus was unanimous. God was behind this and soon Jesus would be coming, riding on a chariot to gather his believers, or maybe something not quite so dramatic. Their unsuccessful scientific approach was slowly giving way to prayer. That was a needed dose of comfort and peace.

Atheists were all in for the alien explanation. Definitely from outer space. As usual, making claims with no evidence whatsoever.

Gabe landed in Las Vegas and checked in with Molly and Luther and the baby. They moved into their apartment and were getting settled. Molly's younger sister was in a foster home and having nightmares about all the upheaval in the nation. She was only thirteen, and the uncertainty of the nation was like the uncertainty of her family life that changed every six months or even sooner. One of her foster parents died of the "Face" the second day she arrived. He was a pedophile who had damaged every child placed in their home. His wife was in Reno, and she died the same day. She was a compliant and complicit partner. Maggy was placed in a temporary home for the seventh time in two years. Her foster pervert hadn't touched her yet.

Molly wanted her to move in with them. She needed to find out where she was. She hadn't spoken with her since Chicago. She would ask the only person she knew that could help her and her sister. Gabe, of course. There was nothing Gabe couldn't do, she thought.

They all sat down at the new dinner table they bought in the used furniture store. Las Vegas had a lot of good options for cheap furniture and possessions of all kinds that were pawned or sold for next to nothing and made available to buy for the next set of new owners.

"Where's the little one?"

"He's napping. Don't worry, you'll hear and then see him pretty soon."

They talked about the turnaround in their lives and thanked Gabe a little too much.

"Okay, you guys, I get it, you're thankful. Enough, please!" Molly smiled and touched his hand, pursed her lips and nodded in obedience.

Gabe asked about Luther's job and his and promotion after only ten days on the job. He was a crew chief now and was making $28 per hour with hospital benefits. That was a relief to him and Molly. They never had insurance for anything except and old pickup truck that rusted away two years ago. That insurance expired a year before its demise.

Molly served the spaghetti that one of her babysitting clients taught her to make. Debbie Halberman was the sweetest woman and quickly saw that Molly needed some "wife" lessons. Molly had plenty of "Life" lessons under her belt. When Molly babysat, she wouldn't relax when the baby or toddlers took a nap. She brought the baby monitor into the kitchen and started there. After that was cleaned, she went through the house, straightening things and even cleaning the bathrooms. She had an excellent work ethic and Debbie was struck by that. She never had a sitter like her before. Molly had a female mentor now. She thought of Gabe as a mentor too, but he was a man. Debbie was perfect for somethings and Gabe was perfect for other things. Molly thought Gabe was the man for her next request.

"Gabe," Molly smiled at him sincerely. "I'm gonna need your help again." Gabe made a joke by reaching for his wallet. "Don't worry, it won't cost you anything this time." Gabe laughed at that and so did Luther. "I want to get custody of my little sister who is in state care somewhere in Nevada. I want her to live with us so I can take care of her. I don't even know where she lives."

She explained it all to Gabe. "I'm in. Give me all the details and I'll get to work on it in the morning. You better get her room ready; Maggy is movin' in with you very soon."

He meant it. Gabe had connections with the state's social services department. He knew just the person to call. Maggy would have a quick hearing after the state investigated their living conditions. After passing a background check and reviewing references, they would deny or approve the request. Gabe knew the answer before dessert was served.

Clay Higgins was busy helping with the cleanup on "aisle Louisiana." He had sifted through quite a few dead already when they took a "wrong turn" toward Texas over the last two years. The Supreme Court case was moot now. He called Arnold & Porter to let Wirth know immediately. He wanted to avoid more crazy legal bills. They were a good value in his mind, but they gained prominent stature when they became a line item in the state's annual budget. Wirth would be up for partner after his fine work for the state of Louisiana.

New Orleans already had a new ad campaign "in the can" awaiting their turn to experience the correction. Police would still be needed for the overindulgent partiers on Bourbon Street. Mostly to get them home safely. They would not be needed for violence even if the partiers threw a punch in their direction. That would be a self-fulfilling prophecy. The new ad campaign touted the great family vacation destination and showed tourists enjoying their late-night strolls through the historic neighborhoods that surrounded the center of town. The NFL team had its troubles, just like any sports franchise. All that was left in the New Orleans Saints lineup now were saints. Good for humanity, not good for sports.

The rest of the world was getting very unsettled. As each new state joined the "after" states, it made a lot of correctable people nervous all over the world. Long-term plans were not really a thing anymore with that crowd. The US administration was offering free jet transportation out of the US to their homelands. The new flight plans were interesting and lengthy. Routing the planes over Canada to escape or through the eastern seaboard of the US and out to the Atlantic. Tens of thousands of "newcomers" were returning home and killing the tourist industry along with anyone who got in their way. *El Tren de Araguas* was now booking flights on *El Avion de Araguas*. It was a fun trip for the Border Patrol. Nothing better than a plane full of ruthless killers as your passengers. No flight attendants on these planes, just US Marshals and a lot of handcuffs and leg chains. Their passengers were all advised to use the bathroom before boarding. No potty breaks would be allowed during the flight. Needless to say, the planes would have to be thoroughly cleaned upon return to the US.

Venezuelan dictator Maduro still held control of the government even after losing the election. He refused to accept the "good citizens" he sent to the US over the last few years. That standoff lasted about twenty-four hours. The US confiscated everything with ties to the socialist country that was desperate for hard currency. He changed his mind the next day and had them imprisoned and then executed after filling the prisons. Plenty escaped with the help of tools. The paper tools were green and had large numbers on them, usually the number 100. Ironically, the state of California did not put out a welcome mat for them to visit their sanctuary state.

The UTSA was the safest place on earth now and the surrounding states saw a drop in crime of 50%. California experienced a 250% rise in violent crimes and a 500% increase in thefts and shoplifting. Stores were wiped out and never reopened. Soon, shoplifting would be at the lowest rate ever. Everything was already stolen.

Trade with China was at a standstill. The economies of both nations suffered. Since China was more dependent on the US, they absorbed the brunt.

The European Union was now the number one destination for border crossings in the world. Since the US was too risky and not worth chancing deportation, they needed a new drop-off point. New routes and methods were used by the coyotes to get them there. It was business as usual, just on another continent. Easy transition for multinational criminal organizations.

26

Drugs virtually stopped crossing into the US from Mexico. They traded borders with Canada. Our neighbors above were swamped with drugs and criminals trying to help their declining bottom line. The northern border was open from Montana to Maine and that's where they targeted their entry points. These were the states with borders that until now, were out of the action. The White House had made it too easy to get in through Mexico. Now, the cartels had to work to smuggle their China-supplied drugs into America. Prices increased to new highs, but profits were reduced by the low flow rates that choked the "pipeline." Europe would soon be flooded with the deadly powders and pills.

Gabe found Molly's sister, Maggy, three days later. She was in state custody in the Carson City, the capital of Nevada. He called a man that owed him a favor and he was able to facilitate awarding temporary custody to Molly and Luther. They would have to agree to the state monitoring their home and completing a background check. They heartily complied. Maggy would be coming to live with her older sister after years of being shuffled around the state in foster homes.

Gabe drove them to Carson City the next day and by the afternoon, Maggy was released to her new family. She was thirteen years old, and this would be the most stable home she would have in seven years. Gabe's old friend met them at the state offices to help. His name was Isaiah.

"Gabe, you look the same as you did forty years ago. You never age." Isaiah was eighty years old and showed it. "You look like your forty." He was amazed.

"I feel like I'm forty. Clean living, I guess." Gabe gave him a hug and thanked him for his help. He hadn't seen Isaiah since 1987.

"How did you ever find me?"

"I didn't know exactly the address, but I knew you'd be in a casino." Gabe laughed. "I described you over the phone and everybody knew you. I didn't take long to track you down. I'm glad you quit smoking."

"That was over thirty-five years ago. Thanks for pushing me; it seemed that you were the only one that cared about me." He looked at Molly and Luther and little Maggy. "He picked me up off the streets and found me a place to live and got me a job. I haven't seen him since, but I always felt his presence. I always knew he was looking in on me. It was a comforting feeling I had."

Luther looked at Molly like they finally understood Gabe. They had the identical feeling. He was just a good man who cared about others. Especially others in trouble. He still didn't know how he knew his cell number when he loaded minutes back in Las Vegas, kinda like Isiah's address. He didn't need to know or care anymore. Isaiah put his thumb on it. Gabe was watching over Isaiah and him and Molly and now Maggy.

Gabe handed the large manilla folder to Molly and Luther to hold. It was all Maggy had. Luther looked at the files and all the various places she lived. He reached out and held her hand. "You don't know me, Maggy, but I'm gonna watch over you and never let anything bad happen again. You don't know me yet, but you'll see, just like Gabe, we'll be keeping watch over you."

He handed the package to Molly and gave her Maggy's birth certificate after glancing at it. "You were born on New Year's Day, pretty cool!"

"I remember mom went into labor that night. We drove her to the hospital just before midnight. I was worried about drunk drivers. I remember holding Maggy and seeing her sweet smile. I swear, she smiled at me." In the meantime, she would get to know her niece. Molly's baby girl was almost two and was paying attention to Maggy. She kept reaching for her and that really pleased her new thirteen-year-old aunt. She was smiling at her.

They all thanked Isaiah again and headed home to Las Vegas. It was now an actual "pretty good" place to raise a family. They didn't care. They had Maggy to watch and they knew Gabe would be watching over them. Molly and Luther understood they had a big job ahead. Maggy was having bad dreams. She kept her eyes focused on Molly. She didn't want to be left behind again. She didn't ever want to move again. She had a lot of traumas bottled up.

The Willistons and the Townsends were happy to have met Jesse's "killer." They hated that word for Tammy and Dalton now. It was unspoken, but Jesse's death was somehow traded for Steph and her baby's lives. If you were keeping track, it was 2 for the life of 1. Jesse made a decision to take drugs, and it killed him. The O'Rourkes were somehow and some way now heroes. They couldn't be angry with the fearless man who almost burned to death saving Steph and her baby. They were grateful and felt genuine sadness for his pain and disfigurement. The permanent scars could be covered by a shirt. The permanent loss of Jesse could be covered by forgiveness and the future that was saved for Steph and her baby.

Dalton would be released next week and be home with Tammy. He was happy to become a father in the next six or so months. When his baby was born, he would understand how Steph felt about almost losing Jess. He would understand how she could forgive him. He would understand a lot of emotions he could never understand before the day he would become a father.

Mr. Willistons invited Dalton to join him at Will's Pop Warner football games. He was in the Pee Wee Division. Dalton hesitantly accepted the invitation at first but was happy he did. He hoped he could take his boy in a few years. He got to know Will after a few games and surprised him with a New Orleans Saints jersey. The number on it was 9. Will knew right away whose number that was. His favorite NFL player, Drew Brees. Dalton was going to wait until his birthday, but Will's dad told him not to wait. January was too far away. It was such a big deal for the Pee Wee athlete.

Will was glad to have Dalton at his games. He was starting to get over his older brother's death. His nightmares about drugs killing him frightened his parents as much as they terrorized Will. His nightmares were giving way to dreams now. He had vivid dreams about places around the world instead of a drug dealer forcing him to take drugs. His bedwetting stopped when he defeated the bad guys that came to him at night while he slept.

Tammy was doing great with her cleaning business. The GoFundMe money wasn't spent. They didn't need it. They both decided to keep it and if everything worked out, they would give it to folks who really did need a hand. They would make themselves happy and certainly Gabe happy. They would consult with the Willistons and Steph and Ron to make sure they would be okay with that. They would change the name on the account to "The Williston, Townsend and O'Rourke Helping Hands." Their moto was "Changing Ways and Saving Lives." It was a perfect name and motto. Tammy and Dalton now understood what being saved was all about.

The Rentschler's had Wells living back at home again. Neither he nor his parents expected that. In normal circumstances, this would be strange. These were strange circumstances and having Wells back home seemed normal. Nothing materialized on Johnny's map or with the monitoring devices that were set up throughout the house and grounds. Even the "Contraband" had equipment installed just in case a signal to the map missed its mark and landed on the yacht. Wells patrolled the equipment with care and dependability.

Johnny was still having dreams, just nothing worth calling Director Miller about. All was quiet on the home front. Maybe it was really over this time; maybe it would end without fanfare. Most of the planet could only hope for that unlikely finale.

The Hood was asking about Gabe. Lee said he didn't know anything since he came to the neighborhood dinner. They wanted him back for another visit. They wanted to show him around town and the bayous and waterways. Greg wanted to show him the casinos and Annette their hothouse vegetable garden. Lee wanted to show him his church, airplane and the town. Mike wanted to show him his barbeque collection and a few risqué photos of Buffy. He always blamed it on Buffy. So much he named his boat, "Blame it on Buffy." Ben wanted to show off the industrial part of town. He knew everybody that had a business it seemed. Terri and Joel at A&L Bolts. George at Homsi Boudin stop. Mark at Mac's Tire in his Moss Bluff… At his Moss Bluff car repair shop and of course Los Panchos Mexican Restaurant for the Margarita 2 for 1 special. Cherokee was always cheerful, with a carefully curated tip-enhancing cute smile. She was always ready to take care of her customers. The Rentschlers didn't know where he was, but they had his cell phone number. Johnny offered to call him. He liked talking with Gabe. There was something about that, Gabe. He would be a good non-voting member of the Hood.

The United Nations wanted answers. They demanded access to findings, research and origins evidence. They obviously thought it was a US psyops program. The new President didn't have anything to tell them, and he didn't want them to know he didn't have anything to tell them. He sent a polite letter thanking them for their interest in matters of state and he promised to include the UN at the appropriate time if the US elects to renew their membership. That made them angry and anxious. Imaginations ran wild with crazy assumptions and scenarios. He also reminded them that they should collect the dues from the delinquent members before demanding action from the non-delinquent members. It would be better for world stability if it was thought the US had the kind of power they imagined.

President Hennessy was the president-elect. He easily won the November election and helped the outgoing president draft the UN letter. One of his top priorities was the great mystery that handled crime and punishment in the new order of things. He was setting up his senior leadership candidates to fill the 4,000 appointed positions in the US Government. His top priority was to get answers to America's questions about the ten states. He chose Director Miller of the NSA. They were old friends from a previous administration. They would strategize immediately. This was the highest priority for the new administration. All leads, no matter how insane, would be fully investigated. So far, Johnny Rentschler was the only connection, and his maps and premonitions were the only advance notice. Wells Rentschler was picked as Miller's right-hand man. The antipodes of the ten states were all still in the Indian Ocean. Illinois' was just off the coast of Australia. It was having a deadly effect on ships in the area. Airline schedules were adjusted to accommodate the expanded area of influence. It was still a small portion of the planet, but it seemed to be closing in tighter with every new reveal.

The incoming president set up hotlines and a web site to share any information that could help. The UN thought it was a smokescreen to hide their real intentions to use this new power to somehow dominate. Pretty ironic coming from an organization that uses member dues as a "charity" to fund terrorism and other dark operations.

11/25/28

Thanksgiving landed on the 25th this year and the first manned Starship landed on Mars.

This Thanksgiving was mostly close-knit family members that lived in the state and had survived the crime cleansing. It carried more meaning and genuine thanksgiving this year as the "thanksgiving" part of the day was elevated each subsequent November. Almost as important as the football games that day.

Molly, Luther, Maggy and the baby were planning their first real Thanksgiving. Plenty of help was offered and accepted by Molly. Her cleaning customers were all mothers and experienced holiday hosts. They would help her elevate her family game. Molly would soon "test out" way beyond her first year's progress and the nervousness of her first big dinner would be replaced with the joy of creating a feast for her expanded family. Luther and Molly were more thankful than most this holiday. This was only a dream a few years ago. They wished Gabe could be with them this year. Maggy barely knew him, but she liked his kindness and his comforting smile. Her dreams were becoming vivid but not enough to disclose the places and landscapes to her. She was young and had little worldly experiences to draw upon. The nightmares were mostly gone now. She was in the comfort and safety of her family.

The Rentschlers loved Thanksgiving too. It was their favorite family time. This year, Wells would be with them and that would help with that "thing in the basement." Johnny took it in stride. He always had a heads-up. He always knew before everyone else what was coming. No one on Earth would know before he would. That gave the boy a sense of control, even if it were a false sense.

The Willistons didn't need any other reason to be thankful. Because of Dalton, a daughter and grandson were spared. It seemed so unlikely to William and his wife that their family was saved from another loss by, of all people, Dalton. Spared a double loss. They knew God saved their family even more pain and released the horrific torment suffered by the O'Rourkes. From this day forward, nothing in their lives would be taken for granted. They truly believed that nothing happened by accident. It was all part of some bigger plan. Will asked about Gabe. The mysterious man that nobody knew, but somehow, he was their friend. He wondered where he would spend Thanksgiving this year.

❖

Space Exploration Technologies Corporation was now onboard. He and the new president would tackle this new, unknown and uncanny force. Hennessy admired his work and the speed with which he accomplished the impossible. They became friends during the last election. SpaceX had the technology and the workforce that no other company in the world could claim. After a slow start in 2026, they safely landed a rocket on Mars. For the first time, the pros were on the case. Miller called Wells with the great news. "We have SpaceX on the team, or should I say they have us on the team!" Miller was thrilled to have a real genius working on the solution. The project would now be called Orion. A fitting name for the hunt. The Orion Constellation, also known as The Hunter, had two very bright stars in its celestial figure. Most thought the reference was to the two CEOs. The President-Elect of The United States and the 3 in 1 job description of Head Engineer, Chief Designer and Chief Executive Officer of SpaceX named E. Reeves Musk. Musk had a little extra time since the successful Mars mission. Miller would be the new Operation Officer and report directly to the president. He would defer to other's decisions, especially personnel that would be selected to staff this new project. It was classified Top-Secret. Everyone had that top-level status already. The president wouldn't wait until January 20th. The outgoing president bequeathed the top classification as an early parting gift. Unlike all others, he would not be required to provide a "Need to Know" disclosure before looking at sensitive documents.

Starlink satellites were already configured to gather radio waves and signals from deep space. It was a side gig for a satellite company and sort of a hobby for the forward-thinking CEO. No one knew what to expect, but everyone had great expectations. Wells couldn't help thinking of Wharton back at Berkeley. He was not invited to join the team. He was never considered a "big leaguer." A woman working for Wharton was invited onboard. That really hurt his fragile ego.

Miller and Musk got along nicely. When Miller made a rookie miscalculation one very early Monday morning, Musk renamed him Miller Light. He was the second smartest man he knew; after himself, of course, he would joke. Miller called him George, after the first 1950s TV Superman George Reeves. Reeves liked the idea that he was an immigrant from a faraway planet called Krypton. He would name a spaceship after the make-believe planet.

Thanksgiving began with Johnny waking from a dream about the Whitehouse. It was different than the other premonition type dreams he recalled. He wasn't ready to make a call on DC yet. Wells made a call to Miller before 8:00 am. His map didn't change to red in the District.

Molly and Luther were woken by Maggy at 7:00 am with a dream about the Lincoln Memorial. She had never been there, but she described it as if she had. It frightened her a little bit because it was so vivid and intense. She crawled into bed with them and slept with her arms around Molly and her foot in Luther's armpit. It was a picture of a true family. They got another thirty minutes in before the baby woke them up for breakfast.

Will woke up at 7:00 am with a wet bed. He was so embarrassed and didn't want anyone to know. He tore his sheets off the bed and panicked when he saw the large wet circle on the mattress pad. He grabbed that and put everything into the washing machine. He came back in clean pajamas and threw his wet ones in with the load. He had a dream about George Washington in battle and crossing a river. He saw hundreds of Revolutionary War soldiers shot and bayonetted alongside the British. It wasn't clear who won. It jerked him awake and when he felt the wetness, he hated himself. His mom heard the commotion and found him in the laundry room, sitting alone in the corner. She knew what happened when he said he was doing his laundry. She didn't know he dreamed about Washington. She put her arms around him and sat with him so she could help with his laundry and his ego.

Gabe was on his way to the Williston's house. He would make a surprise visit. He had nowhere to go on Thanksgiving. He ate alone a lot on holidays. Something told him they needed him there.

27

There was a weird quietness around the world. It was like everyone was waiting for something good or bad to happen, which one depended on your circumstances. Most things that seemed important a few years ago, now didn't. The activist-protesters seemed tired and like a watch dog that has nothing to protect, except for himself, it just wanted to sleep under a tree or in their crappy little house without a door and wake up only to yell at a passerby or two. That's what happens when you don't care about the old things that used to matter. Especially if nobody besides you cares anymore. You're nothing more than a drooping sail on a windless day. Global warming-mongering was a flop. PETA drilled all the way down to put insects on their signs after the city rats they elevated for special care were mocked by literally every person on the planet. Throwing soup on heritage art to stop heritage fuel usage came crashing down when some silly girls thought that it was a really good way to get people to stop filling up their vehicles. They will be sleeping in a cell for two years. Hopefully, that will give them time to come up with a more compelling strategy.

This whole "ten-state" thing in the US seemed like a massive meteor heading toward earth. The trajectory confirmed. The timing still uncertain. The more that was learned about this phenomenon, the less long-term planning was well planned. Its uncertainty was suffocating and like a corporate takeover that demanded instant profits for its shareholders, this was demanding instant attention from its stakeholders and was unpleasantly interrupting daily routines.

Worldwide, "warring" was not as important anymore. Even the Middle East was quiet. North Korea was unusually quiet, too. Managing this "crisis" was handled by staying out of the Ten States and the Indian Ocean. Trade routes were disrupted to Europe from Asia. The Panama Canal couldn't handle the increase in volume. Rail lines were built to work around the danger zones as cooperation with multiple nations worked out the logistics. Freight forwarders utilizing cargo ships and planes figured out that they only needed to have captains, pilots and crews that were "clean." A worker clearinghouse was set up in Texas to weed out the unwashed. All it took was a plane flight to Texas or over the Indian Ocean to determine the *bona fide* of the new workforce.

Gabe knocked on the Williston's door and waited to explain his unannounced visit.

"Mr. Arch, what are you doing in town?" Will was glad to see him. "Come on in."

"Please, call me Gabe, Will."

"How about Uncle Gabe? I'm more comfortable with that." Will had never called an adult by their first name before. It felt foreign and weird to him.

He walked Gabe into the busy kitchen and looked at all the Thanksgiving preparations.

"Mom, can Gabe eat with us?"

"Of course, he can. What a surprise, Gabe; what brings you around here? I want to thank you again for orchestrating things with the O'Rourks. They're coming today. We eat early, the dang football games, so I hope you're hungry." That was as close as she ever got to a course word, let alone a curse word.

William jumped from his football chair and walked in to say hello. "I thought I heard your name. Great to see you, Gabe. Are you staying for the feast?"

"It looks like it. Are you sure?" Gabe winked, knowing full well that he was busted for intruding.

"Great. Do you like the Cowboys?"

Gabe thought for a minute about some of the cowboys he knew over the years and although he liked a lot of them, some were very bad people and even outlaws.

"The Dallas Cowboys!" William laughed.

Gabe laughed when he realized how stupid he looked. "Only when they don't beat my Detroit Lions." It was a quick and flawless recovery.

The meal had it all. Turkey, of course. Will loved the huge drumsticks since he was six. Dressing: four casseroles, scalloped potatoes, mashed potatoes to hold the gravy, yams, green beans, breads and three salads and Pumpkin Pie with whipped cream. All presented on dishes that only get used twice a year.

The only talk about Jesse was in the prayer that was meant to commemorate him and to forgive the O'Rourkes sitting next to Gabe and to thank God for everything. It was more healing.

The football games started, but the beloved Cowboys didn't kick off until 4:00 pm. They finished the feast and Gabe stayed at the table to speak with Will. He knew he was still hurting from the bedwetting incident. Will talked about his dream of George Washington on the Potomac River.

Gabe told him that he might be able to prophecy.

"What do you mean, Uncle Gabe?"

"You might have advance information on the next 'place.'"

Will knew what he meant and had already wondered if that was possible. He looked at Gabe as his dad walked into the kitchen to help with the cleanup. Gabe thought it best that he tell him.

"I'm talking with Will about his nightmares that turned into vivid dreams. You know that I know Johnny Rentschler?"

"The kid in Louisiana that predicts things."

"He only predicts the affected states a few days before they light up his map in red." Gabe didn't want to alarm him. He wanted his permission to tell Miller and Wells about Will and his dream.

"Ya, that's alright. Do you think Will has the same ability?"

"Probably not, but you never know. He could." Gabe knew it was real. The answer to the next question would change their family in more ways than even the death of a son could. "Do you think Johnny's brother could talk with Will?"

"I think so, I guess." He looked at Will. "What do you think, buddy?"

Will thought it was a great idea.

Wells picked up the land line in Lake Charles and heard a hearty hello. It was Gabe; he loved land lines over cell phones. Much clearer for an old guy to understand things. "Happy Thanksgiving, Gabe. Are you in town?"

"No, I'm with some friends I want you to speak to. Is Johnny nearby?

"I'll get him." Wells knew where this was going.

Johnny got on the speakerphone with Wells.

Gabe started. "I want my friend Will to meet Johnny. His dad, William, is next to me."

"Hi, guys." They both said together. Nice to meet you and Happy Thanksgiving." After a few back and forths, Gabe changed the subject to the one everybody was there for.

"I think Wills might be of interest to your team. He's having more focused dreams about Washington, D.C. and he reminds me of Johnny. He was eleven, too."

Wells choked and tried to gather himself. It took him a minute to speak. Johnny took over. "Me, too. When did yours happen?"

Will looked at Gabe and his dad. Almost as if he understood that everything in his life would be different from this moment forward. "I was woken up this morning by it. It frightened me at first."

"This is incredible!" Wells struggled to sound normal again. "Will, I would love to have Johnny meet with you and bring you on the President's new team. You can also meet E. Reeves Musk."

Orion had a new member. Will Williston, from El Dorado, Arkansas.

Gabe left the house and his first Thanksgiving dinner in years. He enjoyed every minute.

❖

The knock on the door surprised Molly. If that had been a year ago, she would have panicked at the thought of "Chicago" coming for retribution. Not anymore. Nevada was safe.

She opened the door and hugged Gabe. "What are you doing here? I am so happy you are standing at my door. Come in, Gabe, come in." She was so excited she yelled a little too loudly for Luther; it scared him at first and then he realized Nevada was safe. It still took a while for people to forget the old state and its bad stuff.

"What?" he yelled back from Maggy's room. "What?"

"Gabe's here."

Luther ran straightaway to see him. The thing he was thankful for the most just showed up in person on Thanksgiving Day. "I can't believe it. I can't believe you're standing in front of me. How did you get here?"

"I just flew in from Arkansas, and boy are my arms killing me." The oldest flying joke in the world. Luther repeated that tired old Las Vegas nightclub joke from the 50s too many times over the years. This time, Gabe revived it so Luther could have a chance to laugh at his bad joke.

"You're staying for dinner, right?" Molly asked it as if it were a question, as if it were up to him to decide. It wasn't a question; it was a sugar-coated demand.

"I would love to." He smiled back as he looked over at Maggy coming down the hall.

"Hi, Gabe!" Maggy had no problem calling him by his first name. She ran up and jumped into his arms. He sure had a way of shortening the "getting to know you better" part of a new relationship. "I missed you!" She said while hugging him.

"Do you have a suitcase? Are you staying a while?" He was pelted with three or for other questions before Molly took a breath.

"No, I'm flying out this evening to New Mexico. I'll have to leave around 6:00 pm."

"Man, your arms are really gonna be killing you tonight." Nobody laughed with Luther except Maggy, it was the first time she heard the joke. Molly and Gabe did laugh at him though.

They all settled in around the new TV. Every month or so, after paying bills and padding the savings account a little, they added a convenience or a fun new thing to their lives. This month, it was the TV, just in time for the football games.

"I hope you like the Vikings, Gabe!" He wouldn't be caught off guard again. He quickly stopped recollecting about some of his old Norwegian troublemakers from the past and remembered the football Vikings.

"As long as they don't beat my Detroit Lions."

His second Thanksgiving dinner of the day was not quite as good as the Williston's, but pretty darn close, considering it was a reprise.

Gabe sat next to Maggy, and they talked about her "new family." She was so much happier now. She was safe and felt like this would be her last home until she grew up and got married.

He asked about her nightmares.

"Almost gone. I haven't had one in a while, at least I don't think so."

Gabe knew what she meant, but he wanted her to tell him. She began to speak.

"I had a dream about this huge building with an even huger man sitting in the middle of it. I drew a picture of it for my sister. She said it was the Jefferson Memorial in Washington D.P."

Luther chimed in. "D.C. and it was the Lincoln Memorial."

Gabe knew she would be the newest member of the team. She had the "gift." Molly and Luther obviously were fully aware of Johnny Rentschler and when Gabe asked if he could tell Wells, they agreed. Gabe asked Maggy and she agreed.

Wells picked up the landline in Lake Charles. "Hello." Two calls on the landline in one day; it had to be Gabe, he thought.

It was. "Gabe, I'm glad you called; I have some questions for Wells. Can you put him…"

"I'm in Las Vegas." He interrupted and said before thinking. He never lied. "I'll explain later."

"Wells, I want you to meet Maggy and her family, Molly and Luther."

They talked about Maggy's dreams and then Wells stopped to get Johnny on the speakerphone.

"Johnny, this is Maggy and her family."

"Hi guys, what's up?" Johnny didn't know what to expect.

"Gabe, here, we may have another team member."

Everyone got quiet. "Are you still there?"

Wells spoke up. "Yes, you surprised me. I had to process it first. We're still here. Tell us about it."

Molly started to tell Wells and then Maggy took over. She explained what she saw and how she felt and exactly when it happened. Johnny tried to make her a little less nervous by telling her his story. It helped her. Johnny's experiences were so similar to Maggy's, except for the map business.

Johnny asked her if she was going to help them. "Do you want to help us? There's only two of us now and we sure could use another friendly face. Oh, and you get to meet the spaceship guy. Musk."

"Sure, I'd love that; what can I do?

Nobody knew the answer to that yet. They would be monitored 24 hours a day, hooked up to a small satellite signal relay. When Musk heard about the old contraption they had on Johnny, he felt sorry for the NSA. They were so behind. He quickly had his team create an easier way to keep an eye on the kids and had it installed in less than 24 hours, "including shipping," he bragged.

Wells was tagged to figure out a way to get everyone together in 48 hours and keep the kids and the families happy. It would be the first "all hands" meeting of Orion. Texas seemed like a natural, since most of the team were there. The President-Elect wanted to be in this meet and greet and get a feel for the progress. He called the outgoing president to give him a head's up and he was quickly invited to bring everyone to the Whitehouse in five days. Nobody had time for that delay except for the outgoing president. Musk rejected it out of hand and invited him to Texas instead. He passed on the trip. Miller wondered why; he was a lame duck and had a clean slate until the inauguration. It took Musk twelve seconds to crack that code.

"He can't come to Texas. It would expose whatever he was hiding." Campaign lies were not tolerated in Texas anymore and politician's mysterious grades that followed them brought down a lot of careers.

"Maybe he had a Vince Foster moment in his past." Musk stopped after realizing he may get into unnecessary trouble.

The new president would have to back track on some of his campaign rhetoric. His "corrections to the record" were made easier because he knew the consequences of a lie when he made them and that made him only make little lies. Fibs, as he called them.

Texas it would be. Wells had a lot of planning to do. He started immediately, he worked for Musk now. No room or excuse to waste time. He understood that he, too, would be "sleeping on the factory floor" many times.

Wells got a lot of people working Thanksgiving Day. He needed background checks on the kids, their families, everything. He wanted them by midnight. That meant he would have them by midnight. Miller and Wells would meet in person to go over the information. He was on his way to Lake Charles. There would be no sleeping until after the first meeting of Orion.

Wells asked his mom to make him a plate to eat in his room. He couldn't spare a minute. Johnny wanted to be with his older brother and asked mom to make two plates. She lamented that it was the first time in years the boys were home for Thanksgiving and now she and Kevin were eating alone. "We can eat in front of the TV and watch the game."

"Might as well," she said, shaking her head. "Might as well." She then threw her apron off in a halfhearted display of anger. "Is it too early to put on my pajamas?"

Miller's plane landed to an awaiting black SUV and was chauffeured off to the Rentschler's house. A FEMA trailer was setup and used as the on-site office. It was 11:30 pm when he entered the trailer and saw Wells.

"Hi guy, what'd you find out? Miller talked to Wells three times on his flight, nothing unusual in the reports.

"Take a look at this." Wells was shocked by two items that jumped off the eighth page of the reports that he just read. "The three thirteen-year-olds were born on the same day, same year and time. January 1, 2014, just after midnight." Miller was flabbergasted.

"That's not all." Miller turned and gave him his complete attention. "All three kid's middle names are Gabriel or Gabriella.

Get Gabe over here now. Send my plane to wherever he is. Miller wanted to know the connection. Wells filled him in on how he knew and how he was at both of their homes today. One in Arkansas, one in Nevada. Both in the last 11 hours. I don't know how he can travel that fast. He must travel private."

Wells called Gabe on his cell. He answered from New Mexico. The NSA pinged his phone there. Wells was stunned again. He flew into Arkansas, then traveled to Nevada and now was in New Mexico. It wasn't midnight yet. Oh, he remembered; he ate two Thanksgiving dinners, watched parts of two football games, travelled to and from the homes to the airport before boarding a plane. And called me after sitting down with the two new kids. All in less than half a day.

"Gabe, we need you to be here to meet with us and the kids. We also need you to tell us how you're involved in this. We need you on our team."

"Let me call you back." Gabe was putting him off and he wondered why.

Miller looked at Wells after he hung up. "I'm getting the boys in D.C. out of bed. We need answers on how he traveled so quickly. I need you to call Musk now." Miller got on the phone and Wells called Musk on his cell phone. He thought it crazy that he was going to wake up the richest man on earth by calling his secret cell phone number and telling him he needed to come and meet with them in Lake Charles in hours. A week ago, he was unemployed. He reached Musk right away; he was not sleeping. He was making arrangements to fly out to meet while he was still on the phone with Wells. This man is a quick read, he thought. "This is going to be a wild ride!"

28

Musk was in Lake Charles in 90 minutes. He was dressed in his workout clothes and carrying his "ditch bag." Not with food or ammunition, but with a change of clothes and his toothbrush. "What you got for me?" He was ready for action.

Maggy and Luther would be on the plane in the morning. Will and his dad would be the next stop and on their way to Louisiana to meet Wells, Johnny, Miller, Musk and the president-elect.

Molly couldn't leave her business again; it was too soon. She would allow Maggy two days away from her new home. That was it. She wanted her home and under her watch. She was the definition of intransigent. She was worried how the government might hurt Maggy's progress. These new dreams complicated everything, and Molly was her only advocate. This could go many different ways. Molly had only one way.

Miller put down his phone and walked over to Well's desk and sat next to him. "There is no record of any flights from El Dorado, Las Vegas or New Mexico that comport with the timeframe of Gabe travelling yesterday. No commercial or private. No radar breadcrumbs. Nothing. It's like he just transports himself at will. I also had the rental car companies, taxis, Uber and Lyft checked out to see if any rental services were used by our friend Mr. Arch. Nothing there either. He has no credit history, banking history or criminal history. No birth records or citizenship records. Not even a driver's license. He hasn't any history, for that matter. He's gone darker than any of our top-secret "deep agents." Gabe does not exist!"

The phone rang and Wells picked it up. "Okay, when and where do you want me to come? Gabe would cooperate up to a certain point.

"Where are you? We'll send a plane."

"You know where I am." Gabe was starting off this "new relationship" with deceit. He knew where he was and lied to him to see if he would attempt to conceal his location.

"You're right, Gabe, I'm sorry. Forgive me." He was sincere and Gabe knew it. If he had continued to lie, Gabe would have been a fugitive that no agency could find, let alone capture.

"I'll see you in Lake Charles in a few hours. Is that soon enough for you?"

"Of course it is. We're at the Rentschler's house. We're in the mobile offices on the way in, before the main house. I'll get the plane to you and call you back with a pickup time."

"No need. I'll see you before daylight."

"Can I send a car to pick you up from the airport?" Gabe wanted to know where he would land.

"Come on, Wells, stop being an intelligence agent; you're not very good at it," Miller smirked. Gabe was right—Wells wasn't very subtle.

"Enough said." Wells quit trying to impress Miller. "See you whenever and however you get here."

They hung up and Miller called the boys in DC. He woke up earlier to check every possible way Gabe could get to Lake Charles. "We're on it, sir." Miller knew they wouldn't find anything to connect Gabe. He was certain that Gabe was the key to this whole crazy mystery. He had no idea how he did it, though. "He can't be human." He said silently and that last sentence concerned him.

Johnny was anxious about meeting his two young peers. The three of them certainly had a unique brother and sisterhood among themselves, rarer than the UK nobility peerage found in the Burke registry. So far, only three people in world were in their elite group. Their membership was granted by an unknown entity and the selection process was unknown, too. They would soon meet in Lake Charles and size each other up. Mr. Musk was very interested in meeting the two other kids. He liked Johnny's self-taught geography expertise. Johnny taught him a few things he didn't know.

Gabe knocked on the mobile office door. Wells opened it and looked around outside before letting him in. The only thing out there was Gabe. No car or taxi driving away. Just Gabe, his backpack and his million-dollar smile. "How did you get here?" Wells asked.

"I just flew in." Gabe never lied.

He sat in the chair in front of Miller, and they quickly got down to business. Gabe liked them both. He watched them operate during the last year. He didn't blame them for trying to understand Gabe's illusive capabilities and methods. He knew who E. Reeves Musk was and loved his rockets like a kid would. He sat in the corner of the small office and watched the "interrogation."

Miller asked him directly about the enigma and the three kids. "You know we have invited you here so we can learn about the "correction" and its origins, and we think you know the answers."

Gabe looked at Miller. "I am only a messenger, and I am told what to reveal and not reveal. I work for an honorable man, whose motives are pure. I'm also employed to protect the three children who have been blessed with sight and prophecy. They must never be mistreated, and their wills must be treated with respect. Their participation is very narrow. They will tell you everything they know, and that isn't much. I will always make myself available to you as things unfold. I will not lie to you or shade the truth."

Gabe turned to Wells. "I know you will watch out for Johnny. He worships you. The other two are wonderful. Maggy hasn't had a stable family until now. We need to keep her from feeling left out. Will won't have any problems, except for bedwetting. I think that will go away once he feels safe."

Wells raised his hand a few inches to ask a question. "Why don't you tell us what you know? It would save a lot of time, and we could get the kids back home sooner?"

"I have told you everything I know about this. All the other things you have concerns about have nothing to do with anything. I know you have questions about how I travel. I don't have any records, driver's license, credit information, social security number or any official documents. I will not explain that, it's irrelevant to you."

Wells wanted to ask questions about the source and started at the top of everybody's questionnaire sheet. "Gabe, is this a spiritual battle or test? Is this from above or a man-made phenomenon? I think it's God."

"Yes. I don't know more, except that it's not from the hands of man. Your job should be an extension of mine. You should plan on how to properly warn others about what is coming their way. You won't have any other advance warnings other than what the kids reveal. Things are going to move quickly as the rest of the country is "corrected." You need to have a system set up to deal with shock that will touch everyone."

Miller asked about the rest of the planet. "Would it just be isolated to the US?" He wondered about the antipodes. "Why does this force penetrate the planet and then continue into space?" He kept rattling off his check list. "Is it an energy force? Is it a punishment? Why and how does it stop at the borderline of the states affected?"

Gabe smiled his golden smile and told him everything he knew, which was nothing more than he already told them. He reminded them that he was a messenger and not "running the operation." He was glad the three kids would meet with him later in the morning. He needed to see them again and feel comfortable with the handling of their closely guarded newfound fame.

Miller had special gifts waiting for Maggy and Wills. A Sally Ride training helmet with her autograph on top. And for Will Williston, a signed helmet from Scott E. Parazynski. He was from Arkansas and was on many shuttle missions. Will would like that he was from his home state. Miller had used up all his NASA coupons with these last two historical gifts. He figured if any other thirteen-year-olds showed up, he could get them a pony or a go-kart.

29

12/ 31/2028

December was not productive for the NSA. Johnny, Wills and Maggy became bonded by their gifts of prophesy and their intelligence. Many chess games were played during their off-and-on stays in Lake Charles. The NSA rented all of the cabins at the Loggerhead for the foreseeable future. Jim wasn't complaining about the full occupancy and increased receipts for his bar and restaurant. They also commandeered the upstairs party hall for an operations center. They outgrew the two mobile offices on the Rentschler's property and towed them away. Christmas allowed the kids to return home for weeks before coming back on December 28th. They would be hooked to all the most sophisticated machines they had in the government and military. DC was the predicted target. Three days away.

Mr. Musk was already in town and ready for a hands-on approach to the next midnight announcement. He wanted to monitor his Starlink system personally. The kids sure liked meeting him and the model rockets he gave them. They were all in.

Two days before, DC turned red on Johnny's giant wall map. All three kids had vivid dreams the same night.

New Year's Eve was counting down the clock on the English Bayou in Lake Charles. The operations center was up and running at the Loggerhead and all systems were "go." A giant bank of TV monitors hung over the stage area on the west wall. They would provide live TV shots from DC and the monitoring equipment connected to the children. They had been on-line for two days. The kids went crazy when they saw the seats they would be sitting in. They were exact replicas from the SpaceX labs in Texas. They were a perfect fit for the soon-to-be fourteen-year-olds. They looked as though they were commanding a space exploration mission. Johnny really wanted to wear his helmet. No was the answer again.

Molly and Luther felt like they were on a vacation. Private jet flight to a bungalow on the water. Hanging with E. Reeves Musk. Maggy seemed to be happy with her new friends and her space helmet.

Tammy and Dalton came to be with Will and his parents. He suspected Gabe would show up in his usual dramatic fashion.

The Rentschlers had organized the midnight birthday celebration. They had everyone in the operations center down the street ready to turn off any monitors that might be a bit much for the young minds. Old ones, too. They all were recorded and on the cloud. They could be viewed later when the kids were in bed if the ratings changed to TV-MA.

They were all gathered around the three child-sized SpaceX chairs, watching the monitors. The countdown began at 10 seconds. The kids fantasized about traveling to space. Johnny thought his helmet would help with the daydream to Mars.

All eyes were focused on the monitors. DC would be in shambles if the predictions were correct. The three had no doubts. Either did the Orion Team. Johnny was never wrong and now he was supported by his new friends. In a few minutes, the reporters would be cackling and competing for the loudest and sensational headlines and the chyrons.

The Southeast quadrant was the first to draw blood. Gang activity came to a halt as their dead were piling up on the streets, in cars and homes. Reports came in from Georgetown, Chevy Chase and Bethesda. 12 members of congress were dead. The states they hailed from were, New Jersey, New York, Massachusetts and California. The dead must have done their dirty work while in DC. Senators were also caught up in the punishment along with congress. The toll would be clearer in the morning as the sunlight exposed the guilty.

The ranks of the three letter agencies were the most disturbing. Hundreds were dead in DC and around the world. Many higher up and a few directors ended their careers on a down note. It exposed massive amounts of undercover ops and left behind hundreds of people at risk. Getting them back into the US was a priority. A lot more "dirty tricks" type pros were operating in our capitol as noticed by all the unreturned calls. Quite a few unregistered lobbyists didn't make it home on New Year's Day.

Miller turned off the news before things got too intense for the young ones. They would have the results of their monitoring and see if anything showed up in the brainwaves or electrical impulses of the pretend astronauts.

Maggy had been feeling a little out of place with the Orion Team, it was two boys to one girl. The boys knew it and talked about ways to make her feel more comfortable and included. Johnny thought they could start by letting her blow out the fourteen candles on the cake. They made her the honorary birthday festivities girl. After she blew out the candles, they posed for a photo and just before it was snapped, the two boys kissed her cheeks. That did it for little Maggy; she was the queen of Pickerel and officially part of the team. Her connected monitors started up-ticking. Musk looked at Miller and chuckled. She would keep that photo all her life.

They all sang the birthday song and enjoyed the cake. Nothing like a sugar blast just before bed to keep the kids awake. The Orion Team had a lot of work to do, and they sent the kids home with their parents. So far, the team was batting a 1000%. The most asked question now was, "what state was next."

Morning broke cold and gray. The city was a mix of clouds and light rain paired with the emotional lows and highs of its inhabitants. Your mental condition was dependent on who you were and what you may have done in the past. Like all the other states, the District of Columbia had winners and losers. The most serious offenders were carried off the field without the luxury of having a bad day. It was their last day.

Early totals of the dead included higher percentages of each crime category when compared to the original ten affected states. Murderers and pedophiles were reconciled in shocking numbers. Our government agencies that were known for secrets and cloaked in mysteries were devastated. Enough was known about the tendencies of the "correction" to understand that you couldn't hide. If you committed a crime in DC, it didn't matter where in the world you were. An embassy in Asia or South America had its own "spooks" dead at their desks or dead at their undercover "workplaces."

Many happy marriages were blown to bits on this first day of the year. Hundreds of current and former elected officials discovered their punishment. It seemed that the more powerful you were, the more likely your libido was killed. If you experienced guilt about or wondered how it felt to spay your pet, this would hit home.

It wasn't really provable, but whispers around the district had citizens placing bets on the triple crown winners. Like a hat trick in hockey. Adultery, pedophilia and murder, the big three by one perpetrator. DC took home the trophy as of this day. You really couldn't declare them the unconditional winners until California's time came. Hollywood would more than likely push that state over the top.

So many legislators were caught up in their corrections that the workings of congress were brought to an immediate halt. The United States was at its most vulnerable moment since the Revolutionary War. The only thing holding back Russia, China or the Middle East was the uncertainty about this force. If the US created and used it, then they knew it could be used against them. The leaders that had the power to issue orders to attack would be the first to be corrected on first day of "their" month, whenever that would be. That was not worth the risk in their minds. The old adage, "Win the battle but lose the war," took on a slight and yet significant change to "Win the battle but lose your life." The high-testosterone men running these regimes were more afraid of having no testosterone than dying.

The US was weak and strong at the same time. Its people were sad or happy, and angry or relieved. It all depended on the choices you made in life. The meek were certainly inheriting the world.

The National Cathedral was filled to the arcade vaults holding the roof. The pews were jammed with more parishioners than a 1950s New York mob Christening. There was a revival of belief in God. It was obvious that something biblical was underway. It was now the main culprit/benefactor throughout the world.

Everything else was closed down tighter than the covid lockdown. This new lockdown wasn't government-ordered; it was a voluntary time to reassess everything you ever believed in. The ten other states had fantastic effects on millions of people in their states and the others. The leftover states were affected but in nowhere near the quantities in this DC occurrence. This one touched tens of millions in the US and around the world.

Back in Lake Charles, the kids were in bed sleeping while connected to machines. Musk, Miller and Wells were pouring over the data along with ten technicians. Almost all were borrowed from SpaceX.

After hours of reviewing data and video, there was nothing that stood out except for the flash on Johnny's map and the three flashes that occurred simultaneously in the kid's minds. Their brainwaves changed for a split second after midnight and caused the monitors to flash bright white. Musk didn't think it was a wave or a particle. It was a new force that Einstein never even thought about. It was a new energy force. Reeves immediately turned to the scientists working on the Starlink satellite receivers. It was also detected by the 12,000 satellites that surround the planet. This new energy was from space, but its origins confused the smartest people in the world. The satellites were evenly spread around the lower thermosphere, 350 miles above the earth's surface. The mystifying component was that every one of the satellites received the same "energy" signal at the same time. Starship picked up the same signal at exactly the same time while on the surface of Mars. That one fact changed everything these scientists believed and studied. It was stupefying. What power could do such a thing? How was this possible? The scale of this was wider than the universe and surrounded our solar system.

❖

Gabe was sitting back in the operations center and had to smile. It was just as he thought. It was a "God thing." "What else could it be," he thought quietly. He looked at the monitors in the children's rooms just to make sure they were safe and comfortable. They were sleeping soundly after such a long and exciting day and birthday party.

Gabe walked out onto the large deck overlooking the English Bayou and jumped off. The only thing left on the deck were three feathers from the seagulls that ventured 50 miles inland to find food. It turns out it was not seagull feathers.

It took the Orion Team six hours before anyone asked his whereabouts. It was dawn now and he was gone. They checked his room and saw that his backpack was gone, too. Miller shook his head and jumped back into the Starlink enigma investigation. He would deal with Gabe later.

Miller knew it was time to call the White House. For the first time, they had something to work on. An actual lead that would have the brightest minds focusing on it. Soon, MIT, the Lawrence Livermore National Lab, Cornell and Cal Tech would be setting aside projects to focus on this one thing. Some of these brightest minds didn't like Musk on the project. He was a play scientist in their minds and one who played with rockets. He probably liked dinosaurs too, they thought. He lacked any credentials in their minds.

Those minds were changed when they learned he was the one that came up with the idea to open his Starlink receivers to a broad new spectrum. He theorized that his satellites could intercept anything that was out there. He was right and they were wrong. A few years back, he immediately fell out of favor for joining a presidential nominee that liberals did not appreciate or approve. That would soon be changing.

1/3/29

By the third day of January, the Orion Team was relocated to the hills above Berkeley. It would be the central depository of all things that belonged to the new "Force" investigation. Miller was made the director of this entire operation, and Wells was chosen by him to be the deputy Director of Orion. That made for a good team and Wells was learning the ropes of government pitfalls and opportunities along the way. His people skills were vastly improved by those few encounters with Gabe.

The NSA tracked down Gabe by pinging his cell phone number. It was not connected to any carrier, but it worked just fine. It was like he had his own cell company and was the only customer and it was completely outside the Federal Communications Commission's authority. Like the other times when his credit cards were used, and the businesses were all promptly paid. Those cards were not attached to any bank. They just worked. Everyone seemed to agree that Gabe was part of this. He would have to cooperate if they had a chance to break this crazy code.

The president was picking up the pieces in DC. A huge hole was left in his staff. Evidently, a lot of sketchy people were tugging on the heartstrings of government before the first of the year. A couple of cabinet members were on that deadly dance card. New cabinet member had to be appointed temporarily because there weren't enough members in congress to approve anything permanently. Members still at home for the holidays were caught in the trap. Not returning, meant many questions to be asked, "what did you do?" was the first one. On the other hand, returning might be a surprise to those whose ideas of right versus wrong were defectively self-debated before stepping through the airplane door and whisked off to the capitol.

A streamlined government was the dream of most conservatives. They had their dream now. The ones that survived, that is.

Maggy and Wills were on their way home. They would be brought back a few days before the first of each month. Johnny's map was 11 and 0 now. The dreams for all three were more vivid. Even the silly ones that kids have. They were not at all threatening or frightening. "Interesting" could describe them best. They kept a journal to write everything down before the morning when remembering dreams was stolen by the daylight. Their dreams or visions, as some may call them, were on a broader scale now. They were more encompassing, in both details and locations. Now, their dreams were spread all over the country for the first time. It had been over four months since the last reckoning occurred. They became very close friends and talked almost every day together on Facetime or on Zoom. They wished they lived in the same town and went to the same school. They were so alike in thought and interests. And so different than any other children on earth.

Gabe showed up in Santa Fe the morning of January 1st and after waiting for his favorite place in town to open, he went to the El Farol Bar for breakfast. He ordered oatmeal and began recalling his long life. He was so old, he thought. He wondered how long he would keep working. It felt like a lifetime appointment to him. He was a messenger and a protector. Both descriptions held equal status on his resumé. Gabe knew it was time to disclose why he was involved in this worldly conundrum with no apparent solution. He prayed for direction and for the "why" he was not privy to. His boss kept him in the dark.

30

June 15, 2029
Midnight

Johnny, Maggy and Will woke from their dreams at precisely the same time. They were identical and different from any previous. Their dreams took them across the country, slowing at every state along their "flightpath." They all experienced the same flight. The difference from the other dreams was this one was a view from the sky and two weeks away from midnight on June 30th. They traveled from Maine to Alaska and back onto the mainland US and then back to their homes.

The trio was awakened by an incredible white flash that seemed to be in their bedrooms and inside their heads behind their closed eyelids. Johnny's room exploded in the same bright white light as ten new states on his huge map changed to red. Thirty-one states remained uncolored, including Washington, Oregon, California and Hawaii. The three states on the mainland kept a corridor open between Canada and Mexico. New York left the door open from Canada. The new antipodes extended through the earth and through the Indian Ocean. No other land was included. Guam, Northern Mariana Islands, American Samoa, US Virgin Islands and Puerto Rico were not touched by this latest prophesy. If the entire nation was included in the corrections, it wouldn't be significant in size. The total land area of the US is less than 2% of the earth. Combined with the 2% in the Indian Ocean, less than 4% of the earth would be under the influence of this power. 2% is a relatively small area, but the effect on the planet is huge when the GDP is considered. The US economy accounts for over 26% of the world's economies.

All three children woke their parents to contact Miller and Wells. They had a standing request for immediate notification of new geographic dreams and of course for any map changes. They had a special text number just for that. All three texted within a 60-second timeframe. Miller already knew from an alert that woke him up. The monitoring equipment detected a simultaneous impulse from every Starlink. This force was able to "light up" every satellite at the same moment. It wasn't a directed impulse. It was emanating from deep space and surrounded the earth. This impulse was able to fill our universe. There was no other way to explain an energy that could surround the earth and be detected at the identical time by 12,000 satellites. This was beyond anything ever detected or even pondered by science.

President Hennesy was awoken by his aid. "Director Miller is on the line."

"Put him through."

"Mr. President, we expect 10 additional states to be affected in two weeks:

Montana, North Dakota, Minnesota, Wisconsin, Michigan, Ohio, Pennsylvania, New Hampshire, Vermont and Maine. The three kids all dreamed the exact dream at the exact time. Johnny's map turned them red. The west coast, Hawaii and Puerto Rico are not included.

I'm going to gather everyone in Berkeley to go over this new energy that every Starlink detected."

"First, I want you to meet with me at the pentagon to assess any threats or weaknesses this may cause to our national security. Can you be in DC this morning?" The president didn't want to wait.

"I'm in town already. What time?"

The president would get back to him. A black SUV would deliver him to the right place in the Pentagon and at the right time.

The kids called each other on Zoom and talked about their "visions." They were identical. They were happy to be getting back together early. Maggy missed her two boys, and they missed her. School had ended for the eighth graders, and they were happy to get away from all the questions, notoriety and spotlight they were under. Ninth grade was next and depending on how things went with their new prediction, they would start in the fall. It would be a very crazy summer for the US.

The parents were buying food in bulk before this latest surprise. Now, they had two weeks to make some serious decisions about their future. They would ask Miller and Gabe for advice. Miller would be back in Berkeley later in the day after his meeting in DC. He was sending a plane for the three families to travel the Bay Area.

His meeting was assembled and waiting for the President. It was moved to the "Situation Room" under the West Wing of the Whitehouse. NSA would be in attendance along with the DIA, FBI, DHS, CIA and the Joint Chief of Staff.

The President entered and after a quick acknowledgment, started the meeting.

"Ladies and Gentlemen, thank you for coming on short notice. We are here to talk about the Orion Team and the next prediction. This is the one we've been waiting for. This will test the resilience and character of our nation.

Early this morning, Team Orion's trio of children shared an intense dream at the same time and the famous map on Johnny Rentschler's wall turned ten new states solid red. 31 states were not changed. This premonition, prophecy or prediction, whatever you want to call it, is going to test our resolve and our security. I need threat assessments from every agency in this room by tomorrow morning at 7:00 am.

We are predicting that a total of twenty states will be under this power. Washington, Oregon, California, Hawaii, New York and most of the central US and east coast will not. Puerto Rico and our protectorates are not included. I need to know what to do to protect our citizens from each other and from other nations. We have two weeks to prepare for the expected upheaval. Director Miller will hand out packages to each of you and he will remain to answer questions. Miller."

"Yes, sir." Miller passed around twelve packages sealed in a Top-Secret outer sleeve and waited for them to be opened before starting.

"Here is everything we've got. We expect this to occur at midnight on June 30th. I will leave here today and fly to the National Laboratory in Berkeley to discuss our findings from the Starlink network. I will have a summary report ready for you before 10 pm tonight. It may be important information in your reports to the President. The package you have is comprehensive and thorough. My cell phone number is included for any questions you may have after you have read it. You may call at any time, day or night. Any questions?"

The Joint Chief had one question. "Director, can you tell the military what would happen if a missile were launched into the US from outside our borders?"

"That was the one question I expected you to ask. Here's what we know." Miller looked around the room at the familiar faces and began to speak. "We have two documented instances of attacks from outside our border to a target inside. The first one occurred on January third, 2026. Three days after, the entire state of Texas was affected. It happened on a waterway between Texas and Louisiana. A shooter on a Louisiana boat shot at a rival gang member in a Texas boat. The shooter was in the state of Louisiana and the target was just inside the Texas border. The shooter was instantly killed, and the target was unharmed. He died with the 'Face.' That tells me that an attacker from outside the US trying to kill a person within our border would be killing himself."

"What about a missile attack?"

"We can only make an assumption that the person ordering the attack would be killed. We have no evidence one way or the other. We won't know until someone tries to do that."

"What's your hunch?"

"The shooter would die, and the target would be unharmed." Miller felt certain about this scenario.

"What was the other incident?"

Miller looked at his counterpart at the Department of Homeland Security. "Mark, do you want to tell him?"

"Sure. It was at the border crossing at Eagle Pass in Maverick County, Texas. Two Mexican cartel members placed a backpack on a young girl before sending her across the border. In it was a bomb, a big bomb. They intended to cause a diversion to distract the agents so they could smuggle fentanyl into the US. It was a radio-controlled device. They were over five hundred feet behind the border in Mexico when they detonated the bomb. They were instantly killed and had the "Face." No one else was injured; the bomb was intact but made inoperable at that moment. The girl was used, and she told us everything. We had video cameras on the two dead guys. The instant they pushed the detonation button, they died."

"Thanks." Mark sat down. "These are the only two documented cases. There are others, but we can't determine if they are accurate."

"Any other questions?" No one moved.

"Let's get to work." The President stood up and closed the meeting.

Miller was driven to the airport and took off for the West Coast. He would be meeting with the kids, Musk and Wells, in five hours. They would all be staying in the Berkeley Lab Guest House overlooking the bay.

31

The President was worried about the looming total shutdown of the economy. In two weeks, the country would learn how bad it would be. What terrified him was an attack on our country by a foreign nation, bolstered by the coming chaos. He would order the top leadership into command-and-control bunkers located throughout the country. Never used before, they would now be tested. He wanted them fully manned five days before midnight on the 30th. It caused families that were left alone to panic. There wasn't enough room for them.

Food buying was noticed almost immediately. The President decided that government officials and their families should not have any early advantage over the citizens. He made an announcement that set aside dedicated days for food and supply buying. It was based on a lottery system and the first initial of your last name. It wasn't perfect, but it went a long way to calm down families and present at least a perception of fairness.

That was secondary to the main announcement of the potential "correction" that would be sweeping the rest of the nation. The President was open and honest. It was a real change from a hundred years of deceit from government press offices that were validated under the guise of reducing panic. Any approach less than honesty would have caused unnecessary hysteria. This was different than any other threat before. The Old Testament is not included.

It made no sense that the remaining states were spared. Some thought they were lucky, and some thought they lost again. That view was dependent on your risk of punishment.

Russia, China, North Korea and multiple terror states in the Middle East were struggling to understand the President's message. Like most Americans, they, too, were used to lies coming from the White House. Russia thought it was a trap. The US was secretly begging for them to attack during their "supposed" weakened state. Iran was always plotting to attack through intermediaries and proxy groups. China knew it was true and that if there was a time to retake the Korean Peninsula, this was it. A direct attack on the US was out of the question. They needed the US economy to be healthy if they hoped to avoid a recession that would cause the regime to be overthrown. North Korea never made any moves without its Chinese handler's approval.

Iran was the top threat according to the smart money. Most of the Middle East was right behind.

No breakthroughs with the Starlink data or any secret government listening posts spread around earth and the heavens. That didn't surprise Musk. It was a new force or energy never seen or even fantasized. Information on this new energy would not escape the top secret meetings and strategy sessions. All they had so far was that it was new and all-encompassing and barely detectable, but it came with an intelligence behind it and a power that was indescribable. It was not a shotgun blast to earth; it was a surgical strike as small as an atomic particle. And the most interesting component was that it remained intact with no diminishment of its power over time or distance. What we understand about physics might be obliterated. The only limit to understanding this was the human brain. We would have to rely on machine learning to have a chance.

The meetings in Berkeley made little progress. They were looking at things from a new stance. This was like nothing before. They didn't have a starting place or a stopping place. No goal to achieve except for understanding. No toeholds on hypotheses or theorems. Nothing.

June 30th would be a test for the nation. Ten states simultaneously corrected would strain every institution set up to avoid the wild gyrations of the world's weaknesses and pitfalls. This would not be a dry run or a shakedown cruise. The earlier states started out small and manageable. They slowly increased as time passed. Now, it would be different. Fifty million people would be exposed to the Force and those millions would be judged and sentenced as necessary. It would take less than a minute.

Maggy, Wells and Will, along with their families, would be in a protective bunker and monitored around the clock. Wells brought his old *Rand McNally Road Atlas* along. This was so different from the other midnight callings. Every agency assigned to protect our nation and citizens was well-trained for this day. Communications were modernized to the latest technology and all departments had new equipment. The military was spread out around the nation and the oceans and the gulf that surrounded her were deployed with all naval assets.

The US was prepared to use its Top-Secret Missile Defense System. Its code name was Ronnie. A salute to Ronald Reagan who did not give up when the Dem-controlled senate killed the Space Defense Initiative.

He held one-on-one meetings with every member of the Senate and Congress until he wore them down and received secret approval. He gained enough support as some members capitulated to stop the "harassment" as some referred to it. Now, it was technologically ready and willing to shoot down virtually any ICBM that travelled through the atmosphere. This was the "When you go to bed, put your head on your pillow and know that the government has your back" moment. All the billions of wasted money would be immediately forgotten if the missiles that started flying our way were destroyed before touching a single hair on the nation's population.

Emergency services were on high alert and fully trained for this day. The surrounding states were prepared to help at a moment's notice. Almost three years of dealing with the "Fear" was more than sufficient to learn about it, develop training, practice, and initiate a plan. This was the largest mobilization since D-Day in 1944.

Midnight of June 30th was an hour away. Every citizen knew that a lot of surprises were coming their way. A lot of heartbreak, relief, gratitude, joy, sadness and prayer was coming to ten new states.

The bars were packed around the world for this night. The US would be a safer place in under an hour. The border "wall" would be surrounding most of the country. The only direct access was through New York. California, Oregon and Washington had their own wall. A sanctuary state wall to keep bad people in to torture their tired and weary residents. New York had scrambled to secure its border with Canada. Its legislature quickly passed laws and repealed laws to make it happen overnight. Lawmakers knew their days would be numbered if they stood against a wall and border that regulated who was entering.

The countdown commenced. The bar patrons were shouting in unison as the seconds ticked down. "Midnight!"

It only took a few seconds for the cameras to begin showing images of bodies dropping in the streets and other public places. They knew they would be dinged by the "Force" and treated this New Year's Eve as their "last meal." The ones that would get the "Fear" were mostly in churches or hiding out in forests or offshore boats, waiting and hoping their loved ones wouldn't find the body or find out the horrible crime they committed. The prisoners were separated from the murderers and pedophiles and relocated to different cells. It was surprising to see a relative calmness in the ones that would soon be dead. They realized there was no hiding, no escaping from their bad deeds. They deserved what they got, and they mostly accepted the consequences. For some, this was only the second time they ever dealt with consequences. The first was when they were locked up.

The refrigerated trucks were spaced out around the cities like utility vehicles stationed in various locations awaiting a hurricane to pass over so they can get to work. The CDC was working overtime. People used to working from home didn't like to actually have to work again. Quite a few resigned. The government goldbrickers make it so easy to spot them.

Less than 3,000 died in prisons for murder. Almost 9,000 died in the streets or at home. 12,000 more or less. They would not be missed. Add another 10,000 pedophiles and 7,000 rapists and you're just under 30,000 of America's finest gone for good.

As the night wore on, the less obvious were being exposed. Especially adultery, lying and cheating. That group would cause the most pain. Just like the 30,000,000 in Texas, the stains on society were coming clean.

The banks were shut down nationally as were the stock exchanges. A week would help cool things down. People had enough warning to get what they needed. Credit and debit cards were not impacted. By this time tomorrow, the bodies would be collected along with the DNA collections that were demanded by the CDC. The usual photo of the face was cataloged along with the DNA. TikTok had a field day.

Those left behind and forgotten by loved ones and friends were soon released from prisons as free men and women. If you didn't die at midnight, you were automatically innocent of murder, pedophilia and rape. The false accusers and the law enforcement that fiddled with evidence were paying the price. Politicians knew what was coming and many just resigned or retired, having no chance of winning a reelection. With the honesty ratings and voter fraud stopped, it would be impossible to mount a campaign that could survive the truth for many legislators.

All in all, the ten new states handled things just like they practiced and trained. As its residents worked through the personal shocks, things were returning to a new normal.

No attacks from foreign nations or terrorist organizations. Pretty normal New Year. The President was happy with his country's response and calmness. There would be a lot of problems, but the first few days played out nicely.

Within a week, the bunkers would be cleared out and everyone sent home. The three kids weren't happy to leave each other, but they knew it would only be a short time before the next "dream" would bring them together. The President thought that maybe they should have some Secret Service protection and quickly realized it didn't matter anymore. He didn't even need it while in the new twenty states and DC borders.

They would start ninth grade in late August, and they called or zoomed almost every day. At least Maggy and Johnny did every day.

They missed each other a lot. Johnny's old girlfriend Martha didn't last long. She was way too immature once he got to know her. He was glad to have Maggy and she was happy to have Johnny as her best friend.

He asked his dad about his feelings for Maggy. He remembered when the two of them had the man-to-man talk about girls the year before. "This is what he was talking about; this is exactly what he was talking about." Johnny thought.

His dad agreed and now their earlier talk metamorphosed into actual situations that could happen that they would both regret. "Don't do anything you wouldn't want God to see." He smiled at Johnny. "Or your mom!"

Johnny wanted to grow up and his fourteenth birthday helped with his wish.

Maggy had the same feelings for Johnny. She hoped that Johnny would be her boyfriend one day. She talked with Molly about her mixed-up feelings. Her advice matched Johnny's dad's advice. Maggy loved having a big sister to speak with. Her life was so different now and she was so happy now. She hoped they could be together for their three upcoming birthdays. This year, it was Johnny's turn to blow out the candles. Maggy would kiss his cheek at just the right time to have a photo to take home with her. That's what she wanted more than anything.

10/1/28

Suddenly, all three children dreamt of the remaining states. It was similar to the flyover last June. Their visions were mostly snow-covered and cold. 1/1/2029 was a number planted in all their dreams. January 1st, three years after the first correction. Like all the other premonitions,

Johnny's wall map flashed a brilliant white light just before the states' color changed to red.

It turned Johnny's wall map almost entirely red over the lower 50 states. They all texted Director Miller within 30 seconds. He knew before their parents did. This was the rest of the continental states except for the west coast and New York would be "corrected." This would be a huge population of more than 150,000,000. Mostly, the large East Coast cities and states inflated the numbers. Six states were left untouched by the "Force." Unfortunately for the good people of those states, they would be touched by a massive crime wave that had never been seen before. Most police officers and firemen fled to safe states. It was too dangerous to try and help people in the madness. It didn't take much for the spouses of these brave men and women to gang up on them and talk some reality into their gallantry. As the ranks dwindled down, it became impossible to justify staying and fighting for the helpless.

Most would abandon their homes. With the severe firearm restrictions in those states, Alaska not included, no one could defend themselves from the well-armed criminals that now freely roamed the communities. You could count on your home being ransacked if you left it for a short time. Going to the food store was a dangerous endeavor even in the once safest neighborhoods. It was a total breakdown of law and order that couldn't survive the next "Correction" coming for the rest of the nation.

The country had a three-month warning this time. It would give the government plenty of time to gear up and get the logistics in order. It would also give rogue nations time to plan an attack. The President wasn't looking forward to testing the Missile Defense System or the "Forces" karma system. No one thought the US would be attacked.

The Korean Peninsula and the Nation of Taiwan were of greater concern.

December was different this year. Christmas took on a very serious spiritual direction not seen in hundreds of years. Even atheists were "converting."

The team would be home for Christmas Holiday. They talked their way out of going to a bunker the morning of the 26th as the transfer switch of government was turned on in the below ground facilities. They would be safe in Lake Charles. Gabe promised.

FEMA and the governors of the already affected states helped the rest of the nation plan for the disruptions that would be in their laps five days after Christmas. It was hard to imagine the pain and suffering that would surround those enduring the midnight correction that was most certainly coming. This was on a huge scale and would test our nation's resolve. The progression seemed to make sense now. It gave states a chance to deal with the correction. It gave the nation a way to experience things on a smaller scale and to prepare. The harsh discipline was not sadistic or intended to destroy the survivors. It actually seemed humane because if you had to go through the fire, at least you knew where the exit was. Society's worst would perish without a way out.

Foreign nationals living in the US were leaving by the thousands. Even tens of thousands. Corporate offices were closed early to secure important records, hard drives and let their workers get prepared. Hospitals cancelled all elective surgeries and procedures. Only necessary utilities and services would be available. Military Christmas leaves were cancelled, and all military were called back to their bases. They would soon be dispersed throughout the country to assist.

Looting and theft wouldn't be a problem. Weapons would be left in personnel vehicles and not needed.

The states were as ready as they could be. The NSA was internally predicting over 150,000 deaths spread across the 26 states that were awaiting their correction. The holiday season lacked "spirit" of most in the past. This one would hold more prayers than the regular ones. A new phenomenon was added to this phenomena. Everyone understood how things would work. Thousands of news stories covered the first ten states and DC's own tribulations. Then, the next ten states. Murderers knew their fate was not to be outsmarted. Same with pedophiles. They were as good as dead at the stroke of midnight on New Year's Eve. That understanding caused some to consider paybacks or settling old debts before their own upcoming "Dead Day." These were the ones that had almost three years of wondering when it would be their turn. Now they knew. Why not make a scene on the way out? The punishment was coming anyway, and another murder or molestation wouldn't make it worse. Oh, but it did.

Unlike the earlier corrections, these combined states with a population over 150 million had many offenders ready to release pent-up fears and frustrations that were preying on them since they figured out that their day was most certainly coming. Their planned violence was handled by this mighty Power very swiftly.

A Detroit family man from Asia decided he would go out in style with an "honor killing" before his time ran out. Big mistake. He intended to kill his teenage daughter for dating a young black man. After killing his daughter, he would then kill her boyfriend. He found them sitting in a car outside the young man's home. He approached the passenger side window and smashed it in with a tire iron. Both teens froze in terror when they saw the handgun pointed at his daughter. He was screaming something that neither understood as he pulled the trigger.

The crazed father fell backward onto the sidewalk and started to shriek as a horrid pain raced through every nerve of his body. He wouldn't die until midnight on the 31st. He would live for five more days with a pain so tortuous, that no one could possibly survive it. He wished he hadn't survived. His correction came in two phases. Fully conscience for those five days in agony was his first punishment. When that story hit the online news world, only a few idiots tried a retribution killing ahead of their own correction.

Miller decided to move the kids and their families out of California labs where they were undergoing more tests. It was getting too dangerous. They boarded a helicopter to avoid driving to the airport. Gangs were blocking streets and robbing vehicles. This all changed literally overnight from a "reasonable" crime rate, as the responsible elected officials called the mess they made, to full-on anarchy. A large government jet carried them all safely to Lake Charles, Louisiana.

There had been so many break-ins at the California college and labs that guards were ordered to shoot looters. These labs were filled with dangerous chemicals and radioactive elements that they couldn't risk the catastrophe they would create.

They arrived in Louisiana on Christmas Eve and Miller had to get the kids hooked back up to the monitors. They still had the equipment in the operations room at the Loggerhead. He and Wells ran over and got it.

This Christmas Eve would be on the English Bayou in Calcasieu Parrish. It was a clear night and unusually cold. It made Christmas seem more real. No snow, of course, but the chilly weather made the fireplace the center of the house. A small fake tree stood in the corner. To Tammy and Luther, it was the best Christmas they could remember. Maggy too. Her Christmases were with different families almost every year. Some were okay, but most were a nightmare of foster family anger and alcohol. She vaguely remembered when her mom was still living. This holiday was the best one of her short life. She had her baby niece, Tammy and Luther. And her two boyfriends that were looking toward her whilst smiling. Maggy was growing up and out. Her birthday would be a marker that delineated a child from a maturing teen. She had pretty dresses and new shoes and new happiness. She was pretty, too. It showed up when she put on her dresses and hair bows. She just wasn't the same tomboy anymore. Flannel and jeans and laced hiking boots were giving way to polyester with a blend of Spandex in her yoga pants and ballet-style shoes. A lot of outfits that daddies hated to see on their daughter.

Will and his parents, along with Steph and Jess, sat snuggled in on the long couch. The temperature inside hadn't caught up to the numbers on the Rentschler's thermostat yet. Will was looking forward to the big "fifteen" on New Year's Eve. He was settled into his role as a seer and comfortable with his two best friends. They were so used to each other that speaking wasn't always needed to communicate. It was like they just knew what the other was thinking. Maggy and Johnny were the best at nonverbal comms. Will was close behind, but those two had something different. More intense, more connected. Spiritual.

Johnny walked into his room to look at his map. He was careful to not move the cameras that were focused on it. In a few days, he would turn teen. He had grown tremendously in the last few years. Mentally, socially and physically. He was tall for his age and handsome, even with the gangliness that comes with growth spurts. He had an endearing awkwardness that was tempered by his confidence. Maggy was paying attention to Johnny lately.

The doorbell chimed. Johnny ran out to see who it was. Mr. Gabe Arch walked in through the door with his patented smile and friendly face. Everyone jumped up to hug him and welcome him in. Even Miller. He and Wells looked at each other with as much uncertainty as an expression could express. How could he know they were in Lake Charles? Four hours ago, they were in California. Nobody knew they were on the bayou.

Gabe knew more than he had shown; he always seemed to know everything. He was very close to knowing why and who was doing this. He was in Lake Charles to explain things and to watch over the kids. They possessed a power themselves that worried him. He was happy to see them in such great spirits.

Gabe asked Wells to bring the ice chest he had outside on the entrance deck. He brought Christmas cheer and enough food for a feast. Mrs. Rentschler was relieved. They didn't have much in the house and after cleaning out the fridge before leaving for California, her cupboards were bare.

Miller and Wells wanted him to offer more help than he was giving them. They knew he held the key, and they wanted him to unlock the explanation for all the crazy stuff that was happening. They needed his help.

They weren't ready yet. Their motives were inconsistent with the person or thing behind this. They wanted to "catch" it or trap it or somehow recreate it for their government's personal use. That would never happen.

Gabe had a message to convey. It called for the organization of a meeting with heads of governments and spiritual leaders of all religions on earth. It would be like a United Nations meeting for un-united religions of the world. It would be the first-ever, even going back as far as the written word. A message would be delivered at that meeting. The sooner it was arranged the better; soon everyone would understand who was behind the curtain.

Gabe had brought the exact amount of food and beverages for the Christmas dinner. He even had a Santa hat on as he served everyone. He really enjoyed serving people and this dinner was no exception.

The fire and the furnace kept all cozy and comfy as they sat around the TV to watch Gabe's favorite movie at this time of year. *It's a Wonderful Life* was his top Christmas movie since it was made in 1946. The kids and some adults had never seen it. Some had never seen a black-and-white movie before. Maggy loved it and felt a connection with Mr. George Bailey. She always feared Christmas because of the emotions it would create from her and from her foster parents. It was never a good time for her. She was always on edge and wondering if things would turn bad. They usually did, but not tonight. She was happy and calm and had no worries to dampen things. And she had her two best friends to share it.

It was almost midnight and the skies were clear. Wells wanted to show the kids the location in the heavens that the Star of Bethlehem was in when it led the Three Wise Men from the East. He took them out and pointed to the sky. He told the kids that the star seemed to hover over the men's heads and lead them to baby Jesus. He explained the different theories about what happened in the celestial skies that night. An alignment of Jupiter, Venus and Saturn. That would have provided a much brighter light caused by them coming together. Some think it was a supernova that created a super bright new star. Others attribute a comet. There was no way to know for sure.

"It was a supernova," Gabe said with confidence. "Thousands of light years away. That took some real advance planning." He smiled.

"Nobody knows for sure, but a supernova would create a super bright light in the heavens."

"It was a supernova."

Changing the subject, Gabe looked up in the sky and pointed to the North Star. "They also call it Polaris. It's directly over the North Pole."

Wells chimed in. "It sometimes not directly overhead because of the shifting North Pole." Just as he said that, it flashed five times and stopped for the same number of beats. It flashed again, five times in 5/4 time.

Wells stared in amazement that was coupled with an underlying fear. "How can this be happening?" It was exactly midnight on Christmas Eve. "What is going on?" He ran in to get Miller. He needed to see this and confirm it. He needed to find out if anyone in the scientific community was seeing this.

Miller needed some context. "What am I looking at?"

"The North Star is flashing on and off. It follows a common time beat. Like music. Five-quarter beats in a measure. Then, five silent beats. This is impossible." Wells was stunned. "Find out where else on earth this is happening."

Miller ran to the house and called into the NSA for answers. He would have them in five minutes.

"Wells, I think you're scaring the kids. Please tone it down a notch. This is nothing to be afraid of." Gabe wasn't worried. He knew it was almost time to reveal what he knew. The additional information that was coming to him this night.

"Are we the only ones to see this? Are there any other stars doing this" Why the North Star?"

Gabe looked down from the sky and put his arm on Wells' shoulder and began to unravel the mystery. "The Southern Cross is flashing too. It's on a straight line from the North Star through the center of Earth and then out to the Crux of the Southern Cross. Not exactly over the center of the South Pole, but on to the constellation. No others are flashing. It will stop after seven days on the first day of January, fifteen minutes after each midnight."

"Who are you, Gabe? Just tell me. Are you doing this?" Wells felt like he was being toyed with."

Gabe smiled and spoke. "No, I'm not doing this; I'm a messenger, Wells." He leaned in to start the ball running. "My name is Gabriel--- Gabriel Archangel. I am as old as time. I am in service to God."

Wells looked at him like he should call a mental health professional. He was trying to process this revelation that seemed impossible and possible at the same time. He looked into Gabe's eyes just as Miller ran out yelling to Wells.

"The Southern Cross is flashing too. That's it, no other stars. Astronomers picked it up in Argentina."

Gabe looked at Miller. "It will stop at 12:15 am."

"What time is it now?" Gabe looked at his phone and said, "12:14."

"My dear friends, let's get these kids to bed and we can talk in the morning. I will tell you everything I know. Wells, you can tell him what I told you. Be ready with questions, it's time you understand this."

"It stopped flashing," Wells looked at his watch. It's 12:15."

❖

The President, his family and staff departed the White House early morning to chopper off to a command bunker. He heard about the North Star incident and wanted more information. There wasn't anything new. It lasted 15 minutes and just stopped. In two hours, he would hear from Miller about an extraordinary individual named Gabriel Archangel.

Gabe was up early and so were Miller and Wells. They started asking questions and Gabe asked for a coffee. They went into the kitchen and stood around the coffeemaker, when Wells asked. "How did you know that it would stop in 15 minutes? How did you know about the Southern Cross constellation?"

"Let's go and sit down in the living room." They followed Gabe and sat facing him. "I am a messenger from God. I am the Archangel Gabriel, that you may know from the Bible. I was created by God before the Earth was formed. I announced the birth of Jesus to Joseph. I came to him in a dream. I don't predict things; I announce things."

Gabe's nickname back at the "shop" was Contrapunctus. Translated from Latin as counterpoint in English.  or nagdā in Aramaic. Opposite or contrary is one translation. It should not be confused with the more modern Bach musical modalities and compositions from the 1600s. His messages from God were considered contrary. Contrary to the behavior and attitudes of men. His messages were a counter to the broken people and nations for thousands of years. They were not welcomed by many, but necessary to save lives. These messages were a counterpoint to a world that lost its way.

"Until last night, I didn't know what was next. I do not participate in any planning that God may have. I carry them out when asked. When I'm told, it is more accurate. I have an announcement to make before world leaders and church leaders, to all nations and all religions. I would like your help and the president's help. I need to meet with him. Can you arrange that?"

Miller looked at Gabe. "Can you give something to tell him to make him understand?"

"Tomorrow at midnight, the North Star and the Southern Cross constellation will begin to pulse. This time, it will flash one beat and rest one beat. The North Star will start with one pulse and then the Southern Cross will flash the same way. Alternating flashes will occur tonight at midnight. They will last for 15 minutes. It will occur in the President's own time zone, one hour before we can see it. The President will be in a West Virginia bunker, so he will witness it at midnight in the Eastern Time Zone. If you tell him this, he will agree to a meeting."

"I will do that. I believe you. I'm all in." Miller looked at Gabe again and asked. "How do you travel, and how do you know the President is in West Virginia?"

"I'm an angel; I fly."

"Do you have wings?" Miller and Wells wanted to know.

"The wings thing was left over from 7,000 years ago when humans knew the only way to fly was by flapping wings. Wings were needed to fly. We left it like that to make it easier for people to understand how an angel could travel. It's kind of a cool throwback for angels. We added the feathers left behind for a little drama, an exclamation point. We still do it for fun sometimes. Like I did at the Loggerhead. We actually move around in a Star Trek kind of tele-transporter sort of way. It's mentally controlled, though." Gabe knew to simplify his explanation.

"Oh, and I know he's in West Virginia because I was told he was there. My boss is never wrong."

32

The next day at 12:16 am, the President was on the phone with Miller. He asked if he could come with Gabe to the bunker to strategize bringing together the world leaders. Gabe's prophesy came true, as was expected.

Miller hung up the looked at Wells and Gabe. "Let's hit the hay; we have an early flight to DC."

"I can be there in a few minutes if he wants." He gave the two government men that smile.

"We can leave for the airport at 6:00. Be ready."

Gabe enjoyed the flight on the new Gulfstream G800. 19-passenger capacity travelling at Mach .85 with an eight-thousand-mile range. It was slow for him, but his arms wouldn't be as tired. The 1 ¾ hour flight to Andrews Air Force Base arrived just before 8:00 am. The chopper would have them on site in 1 hour. It was unmarked and somewhat stealth-modified. Greenbriar was decommissioned when the Washington Post disclosed the secret bunker in 1992. It was turned into a tourist attraction. Unbeknownst to the tourists and the Washington Post, a large section was recommissioned after 9/11 and is the President's closest bunker to DC.

The helicopter landed on the property and golf carts took the two men and an angel inside the hotel to meet with the President. The first meeting would be brief. One question summed up the paramount. "Is the United States in danger of an attack?" The President wanted to get that out of the way. His government was hunkering down in bunkers. "How bad is it going to be? Where is all this heading?"

Gabe looked at the President of The United States and answered. Not as a subordinate, because he certainly was not subordinate, but as an equal, even though they were not equals by any stretch of reality. "Not in the way you're concerned. It's an attack on the harmful and horrible people of this planet. It's a judicial equalization. It's a fix on a broken world. America will be attacked spiritually. Think of this as a mid-game realignment. It's not *the* Judgement Day. It is the Creator stepping into the mess that his children caused and calling a timeout. Not a delay as much as a time to reassess and make changes or continue this misguided course. It's a chance to make changes in behavior and attitude. It's a chance to save yourselves."

"Gabe, are you saying you've been sent to us by God?"

"I am a messenger for our Creator. He sees good in America, and he sees bad in America. I don't know why your country was chosen to experience the correction, but I do know it's not such a bad deal. Look at what's happening. Murders no longer occur. Pedophilia is extinct. Adultery has stopped and will give struggling marriages a chance at reconciliation. Lying and cheating self-corrects. I know a lot of people have been destroyed, but a lot of people will be saved from that prison before they make mistakes. Someone will be watching them, and someone will be cheering them on to be a better person. That someone is the most powerful force the universe has ever known or even tried to conceive."

The President sat with his mouth open, listening to Gabriel. He was a believer before meeting his first angel. Now, he was a real believer. Not the once-a-week pew sitter he settled into over the years. This would be a true revelation. He would soon be advocating to religious leaders from around the world to have a meeting that would explain the "Force" that had taken over America.

"Mr. Gabriel, what…." Gabe interrupted the President.

"Call me Gabe."

"Certainly, Gabe, what will happen during this meeting? Who is the keynote speaker? When will this meeting happen?"

"March 25, 2029, in the International Convention Center Jerusalem. It holds over 3,000. It has already been reserved for the weekend starting on the 23rd. Hotel rooms will be provided and are reserved and paid for." Gabe fulfilled his messenger duties and now would oversee keeping everyone safe. He would be protecting religious leaders from all over the world in this mission change.

"A leader will be chosen and soon make known their name. We will invite the head government representative from each nation that sends religious leaders. We want all leaders from all regions to hear this important message. There will be enough room for everyone." Each of the 200 or so nations and sovereigns of the world would be allocated up to 15 in attendance.

Gabe explained to him that he needs to be aware that although not mandatory, this meeting would bring consequences to bear if attending is declined. He told him that a sign would be witnessed around the world. A compelling sign that could not be ignored. "No excuses, no do-overs." That sign will occur on March 20th.

"Can I use that sign to convince these leaders to attend?" The President was trying to formulate a way to get the importance of this into a compelling message.

"You can do whatever you want, if it is honest and truthful. You can "cash in coupons" from leaders that you have been holding for future negotiations. You can coerce and cajole them, just let them know it's important. Try to convince them like their lives and their nation's lives are at peril, because they are. This is that big."

"I understand. Will you be at the meeting? The President didn't want to go it alone.

"I'll be there. You won't see me, but I'll be there."

The President started to create a message to alert the world about the meeting. He wondered why he just didn't force them to go to the meeting. Why did they "need" him to get them there? He surmised that the doctrine of "Free Will" came into play and that forcing attendance would be too much control. People had to decide for themselves. That made total sense to him. He thought about the old saying about leading a horse to water. People had to do this without a spiritual gun put to their head.

He still had many questions and Gabe agreed to be available to consult. His new cell phone would always be on and fully charged. The new number was 1-777-777-7777.

Gabe look directly at the President and told him. "You can give this out to any leader. Consider it a FAQ resource. It will answer as a message to leave questions and concerns that will be answered and returned immediately. Each answer will be in the language of the questioner."

"Thank you, that will help a lot. I like the phone number."

"The number 7 has great significance to us." Gabe stopped and looked at both men. "Great significance."

"You do know that there is no assigned area code for 777? I worked for AT&T while I was in college; that's how I know." The President knew that if Gabe said it, it was true.

"It is now!" Gabe said while trying not to "brag."

Their short meeting ended as Gabe stood up to thank them. "Use the new number anytime. I'm here to help you." He stepped outside the conference room and disappeared without a trace. Wells and Miller looked for Gabe to say goodbye. He was gone. They stepped outside the door and saw the three feathers on the floor. They were lying on top of each other in the shape of a triangle. Wells picked them up after taking a photo and handed one to Miller and then one to the President. The photo would never be found on his phone.

Lake Charles had a cold snap that kept the daytime temperatures in the forties and the three families indoors. For poor Fred, it was a cold night in the bayou waters. He didn't notice it in his state of dormancy. Fred was "out cold."

The temperature didn't stop the kids from their outdoor activities. Anytime children can explore around a stream of lake or bayou, they are happy. Something about looking for fish or watching birds was always a delightful way to spend time. Even at fourteen, they still fantasized about flying whenever a bird flew over. They wondered what flying was like and they wondered about having that ability and always enjoyed those dreams. They looked for Fred, but he was "holed up" somewhere in his mud hole until things warmed into the mid-fifties or so.

Maggie and Johnny were becoming attached to each other a little more than their moms and dads felt comfortable with. It was pure and innocent. All three of the kids knew that they were special. Not a fantasy kind of storybook special. In a very focused one-skill specialty. It was nothing they did or could improve upon; it just happened to them. They didn't place as much importance on their prophecies as everyone else did. It just seemed normal and non-threatening. What was special to them was their ability to communicate without speaking. That's how alike they were; that's how intertwined they were. They all were happy to be fifteen in a few days. That was a big deal to any child. They wouldn't be grown up yet, but they wouldn't be little kids anymore after this life milestone.

The O'Rourke's and Williston's were steering their way into places that Tammy and Dalton never would have imagined. They all felt like they were becoming new family members. Like a long-lost branch of their pedigree, their heritage. In a very cynical and sterilized view, the O'Rourke's were ahead on points. They didn't feel that way; in their hearts, they were still battling their past lives, their failures and the consequences of them. The Willistons sensed that and tried to erase those dark chapters from their day-to-day memories. They tried to push them behind by loving them and forgiving them. It was working and they all were healing, especially when they looked at Steph holding and kissing on baby Jess. For Tammy, those motherly scenes gave her great comfort and increased the excitement of her pregnancy and the birth of her first child. Not including Maggie.

The Rentschler's, like the Williston's, were further along in their lives and family development. They received pleasure in watching the O'Rourke's strange combination of immaturity and wisdom. They were still "in training," but each new day's lessons brought them closer to graduation day. No one reaches graduation day in life until their last day on Earth, but just as a handyman learns something new every day while on the job, so do a husband and wife. So does a single mom, a widow or a man left to live alone in life. The O'Rourke's somehow found a spot in the hearts of their new and unlikely friends. Their new friends felt they had a responsibility to their new "children." There is nothing better than to realize that someone has your back. That someone was looking out for you and loves you. It was all brought about by a kind and eccentric man named Gabe Arch. They hadn't read his complete resumé yet and only knew a little about the man.

Gabe was in New Mexico for some relaxation before the upcoming chaos that was forthcoming. He loved New Mexico in the wintertime.

December 30th brought warmer weather to Lake Charles. The Hood was planning a New Year's and birthday celebration. Any bar, restaurant, bowling alley and club that had big-screen TVs was booked weeks in advance. When attendance dropped to negative profit levels, the latecomers to the party bought TVs to help bolster their business and stay alive.

The President was working on his sales pitch. That's what it was: a plain and simple sales pitch to an audience more diverse than any pitch to a hotel conference room filled with dreamers' hopes of getting rich in a hurry through real estate, time shares or house flipping. It wasn't going well. He was reminded of Abraham Lincoln who said, "You can please some people all of the time, you can sometimes please all of the people, but you can't please all of the people all of the time."

He would have to please all of the people this one time. He picked up his phone and dialed. "Gabe, I need some help with this. How do I translate my message to the thousands of languages and dialects spoken around the world?"

Gabe was waiting for this call and question: "Just write it in English; the recipients will receive it in the language they speak. Sort of a Babylon in reverse. Don't have anyone in your administration try and translate. It will be handled by me. I will send the emails out in your name. I am a messenger, remember? I deliver messages for a living. That's my job."

"Thanks, I feel like a high school kid trying to figure out my assignment. Thanks, Gabe. I'll get back to work."

The President was relieved at first, but the gravity of the message was heavy. He couldn't bring on staff to help; that would cause trouble, and he had to do this himself. He asked the bunker staff to replay the video recording of the earlier meeting with the four of them. It was classified from all eyes and ears except his. A thumb drive was brought in and given to him. He plugged it into the USB drive on the TV panel and watched as it automatically started to play. "Where's Gabe?" He thought as he rubbed his eyes. He had not slept well over the last few days and thought it was his eyesight. Gabe was not on the video. Miller, Wells and the President were visible and heard, just no Gabe. No image, nothing. When they spoke to him, he could hear, and as Gabe answered, silence. Wells wanted to look at the picture of the three feathers on his phone and discovered the same missing image problem.

President Hennessey got back to work on the most important letter he would ever write. He first laid out an outline of the subjects he thought needed as part of his "sales pitch" to the most important people in the world.

1. Update on the US.

2. Talk about the prophesies from the three children.

3. Introduce the messenger, Gabe.

4. Inform them of the "Forces" reach through Earth and out to space.

5. Talk about the pulsing North Star and Southern Cross.

6. The March 20th sign.

7. 1-777-777-7777 FAQ line.

8. Meeting place is in Israel for three days (Friday – Sunday)

9. The US would be pleased to provide transportation on US Jets and avoid the hot zones.

10. Secure Hotel to stay for up to 15 political and religious leaders from each nation.

11. Translators will not be needed.

12. End with a military stand down for all nations during these meetings. If you don't, nothing will happen unless military aggression is instigated. According to Gabe, you will be annihilated.

13. Everyone will be safe and protected while in Israel. As a gesture of my sincerity and belief, I will arrive without Secret Service or any bodyguards.

14. Leave your attendance response with the FAQ line number.

15. Valediction and a direct line of communication to the President.

That was a lot of information for one email. He had to make sure #14 was okay with Gabe. He didn't expect it to be an issue. He dove into it with a passion. He believed every word of his outline. He would not put his pen down until he completed the first draft.

It was now December 31ˢᵗ. Soon, the kids would be fifteen, and the world wondered if they would see another installation of the ongoing saga. They would.

The nation was on full alert again. Prepared for a missile attack, terrorist attack or any attack. If it were to happen, this would be the time.

Midnight was minutes away and the birthday cake was ready for the kids. As routine, the world watched with fear and jealousy. If this worked out for the good, the US could become the number one tourist destination on the planet— minus the five hot spots. Only adultery was holding it from attaining that crown.

5.4.3.2.1. "Midnight" in the East Coast of America and the flyover states. The President was connected to the military command post and prepared for whatever might happen. He wouldn't authorize a retaliatory missile strike until a missile reached the US mainland. He had already authorized the atmospheric destruction of incoming missiles from a rogue nation. He was nervous that if he authorized an attack, it could be interpreted as a murder in the new world he lived in.

This was going to be big. The hardest hit was Boston, Atlanta, St. Louis, Baltimore, Denver, Cleveland, Philadelphia and virtually any large city. Small cities with big problems were not forgotten. Gary, Indiana and Aurora, Colorado, had their troubles purged. The gangs were obliterated. Drug dealers were dead everywhere. Pedophiles were exposed on virtually every street. That was especially sickening and repulsive. Organized crime was so rife with serious criminals that they had their membership rolls purged to unsustainable levels. This continued for hours after the first "Fear" surfaced on the east coast. It was now over the Rocky Mountain states and not letting up.

❖

While the US was in the throes of its largest correction, it happened. Over 100 ICBMs were headed to America from the Middle East, Russia, China and North Korea. The President watched and waited as the missile defense system was put to its first real-life test. Simultaneous launches were initiated and met the enemy missiles over the Atlantic and Pacific oceans. Every missile but one was annihilated. It wasn't stopped in the atmosphere and was headed to Miami, Florida. It could not be stopped in time to save the city from a nuclear attack. South Florida would soon become a very bad real estate investment. The easterly winds would deal a horrible blow to the Bahama Islands as nuclear fallout rained down on its 700 islands.

The President watched as the incoming missile continued on to Florida from Iran. It was called the Fattah and travelled at Mach 15, according to Tehran. Turns out that was theoretical or downright misleading. It was tracked at Mach 5 and would be visiting Miami in a little under 45 minutes from launch.

As it passed over the imaginary border in the sky, the missile was suddenly diverted and turned back to Tehran. The "Force" was protecting the US and Miami. The missile didn't have enough fuel to reach Iran and would likely drop into the Atlantic 400 miles from the coast of France. They would have a lot to explain to America and the world. The UN would accept their "it wasn't from us" alibi.

The missile somehow made it over France and their air force was sent after it. Germany's airspace was violated by the missile. But it was gone before they could intercept it with rockets. It headed south straight to Tehran's missile launch command center. At the last minute, it veered straight into the Presidential Palace and detonated a 1-megaton nuclear warhead. A two-mile radius of destruction was unleashed on its own citizens. Iran would not be a "player" anymore. Not that they ever were more than the bully on the playground. A forensic review surmised that the individual who sent the missile was killed while suffering through a 2,000-degree fire.

The President of the US high-fived his inner circle. The Mayor of Miami had no idea what was happening. He was in the Keys boating outside Marathon at the Sombrero Key Light. Later, when he was eating stone crab at the King Seafood Restaurant while listening to Emily playing her guitar and singing with her lovely voice, an aide whispered in his ear. He literally spit out his stone crab and ran out to make a call. Emily took it personally.

The US restrained itself. Why rip off a few hundred missiles when it had protection from its defense department and the power that was not of this world? The worldwide news was a testament to the futility of attacking the US. They had never been safer since the Revolutionary War. Suddenly, speaking softly and carrying a big stick was a real thing again.

The Middle East, Russia, China and North Korea had a public relations problem. A really big PR problem. America shut down trade with China and Russia. It was now illegal to buy anything made in those countries. Amazon, Apple and hundred more corporations had a major reorganization problem that they would easily survive. Russia was doomed. The US vowed to decimate any country if they made an offensive move on its allies. Suddenly, every nation wanted to be an ally that would follow the lead from Washington. International relations became more of an order-giving endeavor.

The President got back to writing his letter to the nations of earth. He was motivated now.

❖

The candles were lit on the teenager's birthday cake. Johnny assumed his seat at the table. It was his year to blow out the fifteen flames. As everyone sang, Maggy and Will stood on each side. They planned the photo shoot just like the other two. This time, Johnny would be the recipient of the cheek smooches as the photo was taken.

The photographer blew it. Wells snapped it too soon for the picture Maggie wanted. She made Johnny and Will recreate the scene for another try. This one was good but lacked the surprise Maggy hoped for.

The party ran outside to see the pulsing stars for the last time. This had a much different feel. It appeared to be a coded message or maybe just a jumbled nonsensical stellar light show. More work for the men and women in New Mexico. Johnny would ask for a video of both stars side by side. He wanted the challenge of this new enigma.

The birthday party moved indoors to avoid the cold night air. Maggy kept Johnny back and held his hand. "Happy birthday, John." She whispered just before she kissed him straight on the lips.

Johnny stumbled a second and grabbed her other hand to stabilize his stance and once settled, kissed her back. Maggy would keep this "picture" in her mind forever. So would John. He would not be called Johnny anymore. He and his new girlfriend were older now.

Boudreaux, an old Cajun who lived in a fish camp deep in the bayou, compiled the two new teenager's own assessments perfectly into one crude sentence. "They were all growed up."

33

January 1, 2029

President Hennessey finished the third draft. He called Gabe to find a way to send him a copy for his review. Gabe already had a copy in front of him. He made a few grammatical changes and spoke to the President.

"Good job. I couldn't have done better. I fixed a few mistakes for you; they should be on your copy now."

The President looked down at his draft. The corrections were on it. He didn't know if he should be worried or happy. This was the most direct spiritual, supernatural or alien encounter he ever had. He prayed it was from God. He flashed back to the old 1960s TV show called *The Twilight Zone.* It was a show he never missed. He thought about his favorite episode entitled *To Serve Man.* That was the name of a book the aliens carried. It was about landing on Earth to help Earthlings, everyone thought. The comforting first translation of the title was *To Serve Man.* When the book was fully translated it revealed the true meaning. The last line of the show summed it up, "It's a cookbook!"

Gabe sent the message to the world's leaders that evening. He also sent a copy to every news organization still in business. He wanted to include them because he felt sorry that they destroyed their own business with tilted editorials and activism masquerading as "news" reporting. The legacy media was on life support. They were driven into the waiting arms of a handful of apps that thought it better to let individuals decide what was good or bad without the prodding. Hundreds of the huge Heidelberg Printers were available for sale at bargain prices. Nobody read newspapers anymore; nobody needed those commercial printers either.

The responses started quite a worldwide tornado of trouble for some and for others, a feather bed to land on. The bad were panicking and the good were celebrating. The planet knew what happened in the US and the good liked it. Preparing for the meeting in Israel was different than any other meeting before. The RSVPs would be interesting to monitor.

President Hennessey started making calls to the allies first. That would be a good rehearsal for the troublemakers that would shy away from this "confrontation" with whomever they imagined was doing this "Force" thing. He wanted to follow Gabe's desire to try to convince all nations and religions to be represented. Israel was a real stumbling block for some nations and religions. He had his work cut out.

Tehran was devastated by its own arrogance. The world leaders were surprised that they dared to launch a missile at the US. They were more surprised that they had the technology to do it. That would be the final chapter in their military aggression. Even if they could rebuild their programs, it wouldn't be allowed by the responsible adults around the world. They were thrown back into the Middle Ages. Medical teams were gathered from virtually every nation to help with the injured. The remaining leadership, mostly managers, rejected those offers. That was a huge mistake that caused the people to rise up and reject the edicts from this new tattered regime. Free elections were held, and the voice of the people was heard for the first time. This "new" nation would be present in Israel for the most important meeting in history.

Russia was waiting for a military response to their attack on the US. They were on the highest alert for no reason. No retaliation was planned. "Let them worry about the when and where." The psychological torment was better than an attack that would come with its own PR problems. "Let them stew in it."

The Russians were astounded that the US had a perfect missile defense system that defeated every one of their 47 ICBMs that targeted every major city. After the embarrassment of Ukraine, it wouldn't be long before the citizens followed Iran's lead. Russia would be in for major changes.

China was secure from political upheaval. Its citizens weren't aware of a missile attack on its largest trading partner. Economic upheaval would be faster and deadlier to the established leadership and any political demonstration. They were starting to believe that not attending the meeting might just bring the annihilation that the President of the US spoke about in his email. They would wait for the promised sign. Evidently, they thought the flashing stars were a gimmick of some sort. China was walking very gingerly as they wondered what type of offensive weapons they had to complement their new defensive military acumen. Within a month, the problems would begin for the largest nation on earth. Tiananmen Square was not even known in China. Internet censorship and suppression hid that protest from sight. What was coming would be startling to the leadership and their hold on stopping change.

North Korea was, after all, North Korea. Not as much a thorn as it was a pimple. The President would call him, and he would return his call. He sent a dozen missiles over the North Pole aimed at the northern tier states; he had some "esplainin" to do. He wouldn't attend and accused the US of making up stories about the missiles from North Korea. After years of creating fantastic fables about his nation's military capabilities, Kim Jong-un was now feigning the veracity of his tall tales. Nobody cared about him anyway. More than likely, he would be dead soon.

Just as Miller promised, he delivered a side-by-side video of the last week of the pulsating stars to John. Maggy, Will and he would try and crack the mystery flashes. They were only interested in the last episode. That was the most interesting. John was sure to include Will in the mission. Not so much for help but for the cover he provided for him and Maggy's newfound attraction to each other. Will could tell but was happy to be included.

Within an hour, they came upon a somewhat simple solution. The North Star and the Southern Cross were sending out flashes that had different "values," so to speak. Sometimes, the NorthStar only flashed once, sometimes twice, etc. Same with the Southern Cross. They drew the flashes on the whiteboard on the office wall in the house. The video showed them in sync with the flashing for the first time. Before they would flash and then pause while the other flashed. Not on the last night. When viewed side by side and counted to give a number it repeated the sequence hundreds of times. The number 402510 was revealed. Now, the hard part began. "What's the significance of this number?" The three detectives wondered. "What is the meaning?"

The United Nations had no idea what was going on. They weren't even sent the President's email as a courtesy. They were left out of the discussion. The leaders knew their days were numbered. Their credibility was destroyed years ago. It was time to close up shop. Their largest benefactor was the US supporting over 25% of total dues. That would end, and other nations, now wired into the wishes of the US, would soon follow.

Most Christian and Muslim nations responded with credulity. No one knew who or what was doing this. The President's email seemed honest and truthful. No other explanation seemed plausible. This one did. Gabriel was believable to believers. Even the Quran mentions Gabriel as a messenger from God. His announcement of the birth of John the Baptist and Jesus was written in the Bible. Over 4 billion people stretched over both religions knew the name Gabriel. More than half the population of the world. The other half would be the hard part. Intransigency is both a byproduct and a cornerstone of almost every religion. How can you keep an open mind as a Hindu or Buddhist? They had a billion and a half people in their rolls. Same for Christians and Muslims; if this came from Buddha, would Christians give it the time of day? Unlikely. That's why the upcoming sign on March 20th would have to be a compelling argument and unifying.

The news spread around the world. It was given enough credibility because of the pulsing stars that captivated all the nations. The biggest holdback was that this message came from the President of The United States of America. Whether the skepticism came from the truth, jealousy or hatred, the email came from a nation that often lied. Just because it lied less than Russia, China or North Korea wasn't an endorsement. Crying wolf for so long, nations buried the needle on their own credibility.

One by one, nations that seemed the most difficult to convince were coming over to the "open-minded" group. The one caveat was the sign that was coming. It couldn't be weak or open to interpretation; it had to be a slam dunk.

The President thought about all the previous signs over the last three years. "Weren't the tens of thousands of dead, the Indian Ocean, the dead astronaut in the space station, the missile that was tracked by most nations that seemed to break the law of physics and the pulsating constellations enough?"

He knew the reason. Every nation lied, and always for a "good" reason. That's what all liars think to themselves while lying. Some premeditated and scripted, others impromptu. Practice is the best disguise and rewards the most skillful. "The economy is doing just fine," was one of the more recent lies that got him elected.

The place settings at this "marriage of religions" would be more critical than planning the seating chart for a wedding between the Hatfields and McCoys.

34

California was now a failed state. It had been rehearsing for this title for years. Homelessness, drugs, crime, murderers, gangs and pedophiles were too numerous to calculate. Schools were closed across the state. Teachers stopped teaching as the school violence escalated. Most of the police forces were on skeleton crews. Their ranks were leaving their jobs and the state to find work that wouldn't kill them. It was anarchy. The liberals and college students have stopped supporting them now. It was ironic that no one could figure out was anarchy really was. Now, they could see it every time they stepped onto the sidewalk. Weird AL had a new parody hit on the music charts, "California Screaming."

What was left of the media started reporting facts again. When life gets so out of hand, you can't hide it anymore. The "mostly peaceful protests" finally were called what they really were. It turns out that a lack of government wasn't the end-all remedy. Community outreach, cooperative networks or whatever arrogant euphemism you chose could not replace law and order. *Truth or Consequences* had been a popular daytime game show for years. The title of that show was needed in California as a reminder of what broke down. The next election would be a consequence of that lack of leadership as the truth was illuminated.

Now, the people who paid the taxes that supported this twisted state had enough. Enough to force the governor to ask the federal government for troops. They were needed, he said, because the police forces were slashed by 80% and most all from early retirement. No mention of the crazy fiscal and social policies that collapsed their society. Politicians were innocent; it was the police that caused their problems. That was their "truth." Most wanted their "consequences" delivered through a correction that so far didn't count California as deserving justice. Troops would be activated and in the state in three days. It was still a sanctuary state.

New York was a close second in the race to ruin. They seemed to have more sense than their West Coast comrades. The New York City prosecutor was easily replaced in a landslide election. The new governor was Republican, and she closed the border that was an open door into an unguarded house. Female voters got the state into trouble and now they were getting it out of trouble. The governor had overwhelming support from the women of New York. They had a chance now. Too bad the pain and suffering weren't addressed before it got to this uncontrolled mess.

Oregon and Washington State would take a little longer to figure out that there was a correlation between crime and incarceration. It seemed like they all were just hoping that their nutty takes on human nature would somehow become true. They could step over the feces on their sidewalks, but they couldn't step over the damage they caused their citizens. They could walk around the homeless tents and turn away from the rampant public drug use without catching a glimpse of the emaciated users. They could ignore the gangs taking over apartment buildings and deny what was clearly the truth to save facing the reality of their choices. They doubled down on everything that their "loving hearts" told them was wrong because they were in too deep and couldn't admit they failed. They were like friends or spouses that couldn't just admit they were mistaken when it was so obvious. It was their whole life now and to admit that they screwed up would be the same as killing them. The November elections would make or break these two states. Unless the Force swept in to save them before.

Alaska didn't skip a beat. The newcomers were kept on "parole" until they proved they were not there to commit crimes against their new neighbors. It seems everyone owns a firearm in the largest state. It was a preemptive warning that all respected. After one winter, most left to work their way to Southern Canada for warmth. Going to Southern Canada for warmth was a funny string of words that now made sense to these make-believe pioneers and settlers. Canada deported them as soon as they were caught roaming the lower provinces. Before leaving, the Canadian Border Services Agency collected DNA, fingerprints and photographs of each illegal. A new law was passed threatening ten years in prison for any that returned. Now, Canada was off limits to those fleeing their punishment. The world was closing in fast around them and they had no other options they could try.

Hawaii's tourism was decimated. 40% came from California alone. They didn't want them anymore. The legacy media tried to hide it and the implications it carried, but they couldn't outpace the reach of social media. It was the king now, and like all kings, it would last as long as it served a purpose. The value of X tripled for its stockholders, while wages in the Aloha State plummeted. The consensus among the "leftovers" was to get this over with. Bring the correction so they could move on.

"Puerto Rico was different. 80% of its residents were Christians and mostly Catholic. They took this correction seriously. They truly believed this was all from God. They didn't want to wait to clean up the messes. They started at home with their oldest children. Enforced curfews from parents and grandparents were implemented along with dinners together. That was something that went by the wayside over the years. Those two seemingly minor changes made major differences in attitudes and actions. It became the number one topic of videos, blogs and information sites and it was starting to work. That trending topic gave parents a big helpful hand in reeling in their children. One thing Christians understand, is the strength of family to combat evil. Latin families especially hold family ties in great importance and that ancient wisdom found a place to land in these new times.

The consensus was clear. "Let's get this over with now." It was like an old schoolhouse punishment, with the entire class waiting to get paddled by the principal. The first in line were the lucky ones. They got their paddling over while the back of the line was tormented by each new punishment, slowly getting closer and closer to those unlucky enough to have the last letters of the alphabet start their surname.

The teenagers were all back home. The talked every day. Like The Three Musketeers, they had a mission to protect the good citizens. A least a mission to give them a heads up. Maggy and John had a code word during their daily call. It was "Fred." When that was heard, it meant to call each other when Will hung up. They didn't want Will to know about their boyfriend-girlfriend relationship. They didn't want him to feel an outcast, so they hid it. They also didn't want their parents to know. They already had their radar up and spinning, watching for these potential thunderstorms out there.

It was pretty obvious that they needed to be watched. They knew what was right and what was wrong, but self-control is a weak combatant when fighting against emotion and hormones. They were too young to cross over into things that society and advertising execs paraded in front of them every single day of their short lives. Thankfully ads now had a truth rating at the bottom right-hand corner for all to see. That helped them to decipher the truth that was sublimely and unfairly attacking their juvenile minds.

They were good kids and remained good kids. They were smart enough to know what to do.

"John, do you think we will always be friends?" Maggy called him after the three hung up a minute ago. "Do you think that's possible?" It didn't take Maggy long to ask the tough and unanswerable questions. John didn't realize it, but he was in class right now and his answer would be the first "pop quiz" of his relationship with Maggy. How he answered this simple question was the first relationship test he would take in his life. There would be millions more of these dangerous questions throughout his life. He had just turned fifteen with no life ring to grab onto. He carefully formulated a response.

"Maggy, of course we will. The only way it could end is from betrayal, and I would never betray you. That means it's up to you, not me." John took a deep breath, not knowing if he answered correctly. "Who knows where this will go? I'm just a kid with his first real girlfriend." Uh oh, he thought.

"What other girlfriend?" she asked sadly with a frosting of jealousy. "Did you kiss her too?"

"Welcome to the world of relationships," John thought to himself.

"No, you were the first girl I ever kissed."

This back and forth went on for a long time. Each new question confirmed that sometimes it's just best to say less.

He broke the wasted conversation skillfully. "Maggy, I would feel the same if you told me you had a past boyfriend. That's normal because we are so inexperienced and immature. Let's face it: we may be teenagers, but we're both young. Jealousy is an emotion of a child and it's a relationship killer." Up until that jealous finger he pointed at her, all was going splendidly in the classroom.

"I'm not jealous. I'm just curious."

"No, No, No, I didn't mean it like that. I was jealous when Martha acted interested in another boy. My jealousy ended our relationship."

"Her name was Martha?"

He bestowed significance on her when he gave her a name. John felt the quicksand was now up to his knees. He knew he had to stop moving and talking. He needed Wells or even his dad at this moment. He was looking around for a rope or vine to grab onto and pull himself out of this danger.

"Yes, and she dumped me because I was so immature and jealous of something so silly." A brilliant response from such a young and inexperienced child.

"I guess you're right, John." He loved his new grown-up name that Maggy was using. "Sorry, I've never had a boyfriend before."

This time, he thought of his next sentence before talking and decided to end it all on a high note. The high note was silence.

35

March 1, 2029

No premonitions for this midnight. Things were quiet around the world. No one had the stomach to keep battles going when all things could be turned inside out in March. Ceasefires were called and obeyed until all this world meeting passed over. Nobody wanted to be very last soldier killed in a war. It may have been the first time in thousands of years that humans weren't trying to kill each other's tribes or nations.

The National Guard help to keep the roads somewhat safe. Doors to all public buildings were locked until the identity and purpose of those gaining entrance were satisfied. California stepped back a few feet from the edge. For the first time in years local and state law enforcement cooperated with ICE. Slowly, dangerous criminals were being deported back to Mexico. They didn't mess around. Off to the southern border with Central America for these scoundrels didn't take any longer than the bus ride to get them there.

New York legislatures had a little more sense than the West Coast crazies. They welcomed the help. They needed something to help stem the flow of illegals in and the taxpayers out. The correlation was almost one-for-one. They needed taxpayers more than ever. They were running out of people to take money from. The bane of socialism. They hit the wall and finally figured out why.

The Corrected states were recovering nicely. The economies were still in a bit of shambles, but nothing that couldn't be fixed. Throwing off fear and crime was a soothing balm for the weary. Every day brought new possibilities and hope for the future. The upcoming sign and world meetings were welcomed as a meaningful attempt to do what most religions preached about. Peace and love. Not the type Gabe enjoyed watching for a weekend while in Goldengate Park, across from the famous Haight and Asbury intersection. This was world peace and world love, and you wouldn't need an LSD sugar cube to get you there.

Simple things, like leaving your bike outside without a lock. Keeping the doors of your home open without worry. Taking money from an ATM without looking over your shoulder. Meeting a stranger on a hiking trail while alone. Wearing jewelry and watches. Driving with the top down. Walking alone at night. Not worrying about someone adding a drug to your drink in a bar. The list never ends. This new freedom was what the country was founded upon. People from the unaffected states felt an incredible relief when crossing the boundary into the affected states.

The US was enjoying a revival of mental health. Turns out fear was the driving force in most of the suffering. Once gone, it released all the phobias that plagued a human mind. It quieted the phobic slurs that were casually thrown out by activists and the elected to snare and silence political opponents. Now, they would need to debate with an argument instead of an accusatory lie that they confused with a victory when it was only good for shutting down conversations. High school and college debate classes were jammed.

Men began talking to women they didn't know. The fear of danger was gone from those encounters. Women enjoyed a "new" dating scene that was not on one of the swipe apps.

This honesty played out in news interviews, campaign claims, contracts and relationships. A famous anthropologist once said of a tribe discovered in the Amazon, and having no contact with the modern world, that they were so backward that they didn't know how to lie. That was a sad take that should have been the opposite. That they were so pure and honest that deceit and lying were foreign and uncomfortable to them.

The modern citizens of the world would need time to understand the damage that lying and deceit cause at all levels of human life. It was difficult for many to practice honesty, but it didn't take long to stop dishonesty because of the correction that would immediately expose it.

The President's conversation with world leaders was convincing enough that over 150 nations would be attending so far. The holdouts would wait until the sign that was promised was revealed. North and South America were all attending. Most of Europe and Asia. China, Russia and the Middle East were not committing yet. They needed a little more hand-holding. India confirmed after a lukewarm reception. Many non-Christian nations that confirmed knew they could back out if they didn't like the sign or the direction that things were headed.

The Pope and Cardinals said yes, as did many overwhelmingly atheist or agnostic nations. The stories coming from the US over the last three years were hard to ignore or disbelieve. The conversion to belief was easy. Just invite people to walk through a formerly dangerous area at night. They all heard stories of encounters that were now safe. Much safer than their own countries. The single fact that US prisons and penitentiaries were so empty that almost half were shut down and prisons were consolidated because of the vacant cells, was a convincing argument.

Imams, rabbis, preachers and priests were coming together for a meeting. Even cult leaders wanted in on the party. They felt it would give them some greatly lacking credibility. Those were the ones that had to be careful answering questions while in the US and in the corrected states. Pesky and insincere musings from the press on subjects like planets for followers upon death or other wacky assertions of rewards for followers would be ignored.

The only concern most had was the safety factor. Israel and the various nations' political and religious players would be an easy target for a mass killing, or so they complained. Russia, China, North Korea and the Middle East wouldn't mind a massacre. The usual suspects were obviously calculating and strategizing a way to unleash a mass casualty. The only thing lacking was the courage to try it. The CIA had the same conclusion, including one more. Cuba. That wasn't a worry; the Caribbean nation 90 miles off the coast of America didn't have two pesos to rub together. Gabe promised the safety of all, and the President believed him.

March 19, 2029

Tonight was the time for the promised sign that Gabriel was sure would convince the world. The kids were brought together and hooked up to the best technology in the world. So far, it isn't telling anything they didn't know.

The night before, all three dreamt about Israel and John's wall map confirmed it in red after the white flash. Israel was next. The three texted Miller. He informed the President, who called Gabe on his "angel hotline." Israel's antipode was in the Pacific Ocean and not on land.

"Gabe, is it true about Israel? Can you tell me anything about this?" The President liked the idea that Israel would be corrected. If it played like it did in the US, all would be safe in attending the meeting.

"I just found out from the boss. I know that another sign will happen alongside this new revelation. I was told about it." Gabe's rank in the spiritual world was up there, but not at the level of the Trinity. He was a foot soldier and cherished his job. He'd seen a lot of things in his thousands of years working. The upcoming meeting would be on his highlight reel.

The president telephoned the President of Israel to let him know what was coming. He thanked him for the advance notice.

The President called China and told them to watch the news. He told them another sign would accompany this first correction outside the US. He hoped it would change the stubborn leader's mind. There were too many people in China to ignore this meeting. He was on the phone with the Russian President when midnight struck. Suddenly he could hear the sound of a trumpet outside the White House. It was multiple notes from a trumpet. The Russian President heard it inside the Kremlin.

"That must be the second sign. Can I put you down as a yes?"

He couldn't answer, yet he had to consult with his military about the sound.

It was 7:00 am in Vienna, Austria. An opera singer walking her dog was the first to understand the sounds from the celestial trumpet. It was two notes. C and G. It was the Harmony of the Perfect Fifth. C with seven steps up to the G. It was loud but not uncomfortable. It was soothing to all ears, including animals. It was meant as a double entendre and an example of how the world could be in perfect harmony.

Every person on the planet heard the beautiful sound of the harmony. This sign convinced almost all nations except for Iran and Cuba. The meeting would be a success as far as attendance. The two outliers would suffer from their intransigence. They all knew the US couldn't pull off a fake trumpet that all could hear. It was also a trumpet call to the meeting in five days in Jerusalem.

Israel was now corrected and many more died from the fear than any could imagine. Palestinians and Jews were strewn throughout the country. Adultery and pedophilia were much lower than the US. Murder was much, much higher. Attributed to the holy wars and violence passed down from generation to generation. The country was now as safe as the US, and it freed it citizens from the horrible handcuff of not knowing when the next attack would come. Iran took notice and some within the government took a blind approach to the looming meeting. Arrogance and stupidity would be tested by God in five days. Mostly the arrogance.

The Prime Minister and the American President spoke at length about the meeting. He was chastising the US for not including Israel in the planning of this upcoming meeting. He couldn't understand how two allies wouldn't discuss the arrangements in advance and not make it a surprise "party" for Israel.

"Let me stop you there; the US did not make the plans for this meeting. The US did not pay for this meeting or the three thousand hotel rooms. It was arranged by this power that has freed the US from crime and is now blessing Israel." The President was curt in his answer to a good friend of the nation. "You heard the trumpet a few minutes ago this morning. Who could do such a thing? Certainly not the US or any other country. That was meant as a sign and a call for all nations and religions to come together for a chance to heal. Maybe even a final chance."

They both apologized. One for his accusations and the other for his brusque answer.

"We must start trusting. Not blind trust, but genuine understanding and openness. I'm going to need your help at this meeting. You'll see in the next few days how different your country will be. Free from the worry of attack, violence and lies."

"You're right, what happens in the next few days in Israel will make it possible to trust. Until a betrayal destroys it and is exposed."

The President continued. "I appreciate your sentiment, but in this new order, a betrayal will be made known immediately. I've witnessed that myself. I don't know how this will play out, but a man named Gabriel is the messenger for all that has happened. Everything. He doesn't control it; his job is a messenger from God. I don't know if we'll see Jesus or Abraham or a blended deity in five days. I do know that Gabriel is an Angel. He is the Angel described in the bible. He is the same angel of Daniel in the Old Testament and the Hebrew Bible."

"I know that if what you say is true, you cannot lie about it without me knowing." The Prime Minister was interrupted by his aides and said his goodbyes to the President. He was needed to address his nation about the correction they were all witnessing. He knew that he must be honest. He had no other course.

The probes attached to the three didn't reveal anything new. Earthly scientists couldn't understand this power. It would be like explaining quantum physics to a baby.

The kids walked back to the Rentschlers from the Loggerhead along the path next to the bayou. They were glad to be back together again. Maggy and John a little more than Will.

John was very good at communicating difficult subjects. He possessed a wisdom not found in children or teenagers. He was comfortable speaking in front of large gatherings in school and to small groups. Maggy exhibited the same gift and wisdom. The three were invited to speak on social media and they did. Gabe gave them his approval much faster than their parents. Will wasn't as good at it, and he slowly started backing away from the two others. It wasn't Will's calling. He wondered what his calling would be.

The correction in Israel just before the world meeting, raised the temperature of their next broadcast on X. It would surpass all previous ones by millions. This would be a question-and-answer event. When they discovered the estimated attendance, they called Gabe. They weren't prepared for this.

Gabe asked them dozens of likely questions that they would receive from the audience. They handled them with ease. He told them that he would be nearby and bail them out of any trick questions or other evil attempts aimed at harming them. He promised protection. "That's my job!"

They both knew what was happening in the US and now in Israel. They knew it was from God. Everybody did. Most everybody.

Miller wasn't happy with the X event, and he said so. He spoke to their parents in the home office. "This X thing has me worried for the kids. I think you must consider the magnitude of this and the popularity explosion that certainly will follow. I don't think anyone can prepare for that. I know Gabe said they'll be safe and sound. I can't argue against him, but my internal radar is squawking."

Kevin spoke first. "John is turning out to be a great orator. I've seen him in front of a few thousand at his school. He's as smart and intelligent as any his age and beyond. Way beyond."

Molly added, "I spoke with Maggy about my concerns, and she told me that she and John could together withstand any trick questions. They could only answer truthfully and that was enough to defeat a malicious question."

Miller needed help. "Can we call Gabe and talk with him?" Both parents welcomed that call. Miller dialed and put his phone on speaker.

"Hi guys, I can't talk now except to say that Jesus began his ministry when he was twelve!" He hung up as the three looked at each other. Each had a hundred questions about the call they just heard. They all knew, though, that it was an endorsement from Gabe.

Israel was loading up bodies into freezer trucks. The CDC asked that they take DNA samples and photographs of each of the dead. A few attack attempts occurred, and the results were predictable. The borders were quiet as not many wanted to challenge the Force. Everybody stayed put, knowing they were safe inside the country's border. Synagogues and churches were packed and comforting. This wasn't a new thing. It started in the US three years ago. No one was surprised by this. Maybe caught off guard a bit, but certainly not surprised. Some of the dead surprised their families, but all in all, they weren't shocked.

A few more attacks were followed by the instant justice. The social apps covered them with multiple videos and commentary. The Jewish residents of kubutzes near Palestine started returning to their homes. They cautiously welcomed their once-hated neighbors into their homes and villages. The divide between them was still gaping, but with the fear of violence off the table, people could talk, people could explain their sentiments and feelings.

The Knesset called a special meeting. This was the lawmaking arm of the government. It elected the President and Prime Minister. These were the 120 members in control of the country. The modern members were the "descendants" of the Great Assembly of ancient times, whose members were sages and prophets. Today's topic was the correction. The new sages and prophets were in Lake Charles, Louisiana.

Tomorrow was the interview on X. The next day was March 20th. The first day of the three-day meeting in Jerusalem.

Jayson Glass was the slotted interviewer. When Joe Rogan discovered that, he tracked down the Rentschler's.

"You can't let him interview you. He's a known liar that makes up and plagiarizes stories. He shouldn't be rewarded for his deceit." Rogan was pissed.

Check him out before you go live; he's a bad man. He doesn't have a truth review because he's in Washington State.

It only took a few minutes to confirm Rogan. Rentschler called back and thanked him. They agreed he would have been a mistake. They checked out Rogan and asked him if he would host the interview.

"Of course, I would, but that's not why I alerted you."

"We believe you after learning your truth review. Will you do it?"

"In fact, I'll come to your home with a small crew. You can all be in the room and stop the interview if you don't like the line of questioning."

Kevin thought of the first lie-detector mishap. He liked him giving veto power to the parents. "Come on over, Mr. Rogan, we'll be waiting."

"Please, my name's Joe."

That night, the kids watched a movie together. It was a film by a new indie director and friend of Wells. It was called *Unconformity* and Wells never found much time to watch his friend Jonathon's premier directing debut. The title was a perfect metaphor the lives the kids were living.

They were used to being monitored. The Musk equipment was far superior and made comfortable by the wireless capabilities and the 12 smaller patches on the heads and bodies. Reeves was scheduled to visit tomorrow and be with the Orion Team during the interview and the weekend events that would grab the world. He was busy getting ready for a manned flight to Mars. He wouldn't be on the spacecraft; he was needed in the command center. Not for any hands-on control, but as a backup if things went south. His value was in his ingenuity, his quick takes and fearless decisions.

The movie ended and John and Maggy asked their parents if they could stay up a little longer to talk about the interview. They weren't fooled. They were young once, too. Even an outsider could see that they would be girlfriend/boyfriend throughout high school and college. The teenagers would agree with that assessment. Maggy stretched it into marriage, as was her way of planning things. Every detail was carried out to the nth degree with Maggie. She was a very smart young adult and kept her little girl optimism and sweetness. That saved her from the foster care she received from a few bad "parents."

"Okay, but you have a big day tomorrow. Behave!" The chaperones left them alone on the couch and headed to their bedrooms.

"John," Maggy said and paused.

John held his breath and remembered to think carefully before any answer to any questions that started out with his name.

"I hate being away from you. I wish we went to the same school. I think about you all the time."

"So do I, Maggy." Okay, he thought, so far so good.

"I think that's what love is, don't you?" She put his left hand in her right hand and turned to look directly at him.

It was his turn to say something. He took a deep breath. More for an excuse to pause than the need to breathe. He had nothing. He was speechless and worried. Then he remembered Matthew, Chapter Six.

"I think you're worried, Maggy. I used to worry that you would stop liking me until I remembered my dad telling me to read a verse that he gave me. It gave me comfort to not worry about things I couldn't control. Like our interview tomorrow. I am not worried because I am prepared, and you are too."

"What does that have to do with love, John?"

"Everything, Maggy, everything." He paused again. "I have no idea what real love is, and I don't think you do either. How can we? We're fifteen and we are each other's first boyfriend and girlfriend."

"Except for Martha." Maggy smiled and regretted saying that. She apologized.

"See, that's jealousy and we both have to grow up and out of that insecurity." John paused again before he said the next thought that had a good chance at causing trouble for the rest of the short evening they had left. "I'll tell you this much, Maggy. It may be love; I just don't know. I feel that I love you but how can I know? How can you know?"

John Kissed her on the lips and the two snuggled in on the couch. They both fell asleep until Molly rudely woke them around 3:00 am.

"Alright, you two. Get to bed. Sheesh." Molly remembered her own youth and was happy for the couple of confused kids sleeping in each other arms on the couch.

Morning broke early for the kids. Joe Rogan was coming into town before ten and they had to get up and get ready. It was interview day!

They all met up at the breakfast table. John came in before Maggy and sat down. Maggy walked in and sat next to John. She slid him a note under the table. Maggy was happy that Molly didn't tease her about the "couch." John was happy she hadn't told his parents and Wells. He would have teased his baby brother. He put the note in his pocket and dug into breakfast. Will was nervous about the interview that he knew he couldn't handle.

Joe landed in Lake Charles with his pilot and crew. They had everything on the plane they needed to record the interview. It would be on the internet and live. They brought desks and chairs, the famous neon "Joe Rogan Experience" sign, video equipment and lighting. He never did this before. This would be bigger than his Musk/Trump interview in 2024. That garnered over a million live viewers. Conservative estimates were placing this interview into the hundreds of millions. The legacy media could only sit on their hands and watch the final nail driven into their coffin. He would use multiple redundant

Starlink systems to blast it to Austin, Texas, where his studio would handle the process and transfer it out to the waiting world.

Musk arrived a short time later and the two quickly reacquainted. Miller would be watching the interview that was moved to the Loggerhead upstairs meeting room. The President timed his trip to Jerusalem so he could watch it on board Air Force One with fewer interruptions.

Everyone was good to go and after a few sound and video checks, the crew gave a thumbs up. John and Maggy walked over earlier holding hands. The message she gave him at breakfast was short and sweet. "I love you."

Joe and the kids talked for ten minutes or so and they flabbergasted Joe. He would recall later how those two kids had more adults in them than most of the people he interviewed in thousands of sit-downs. He felt lucky to talk with them.

Everything was in place and checked out. The show began with an introduction from Joe. Their combination of humility and intelligence was an unfair comparison to anyone under thirty. John's blond hair, height and handsomeness caught Joe off guard. They had never had their photos in the public domain. Just some old school pictures TMZ paid for.

Maggy wore a beautiful green velvet dress that was age-appropriate, but still revealed her maturing shape. Her brown hair and green eyes were striking. She spoke with such confidence. Not a single "um" was heard from either one of them during the two-hour interview. John looked at her; it was more like stared at her for a little too long. He was in love with her, he said to himself.

Joe could tell they would be a worldwide hit. He was happy for them and worried for them. His business can be so cruel and unforgiving.

The interview started and the very first question caught them both off guard. "Are you girlfriend and boyfriend, because I was watching you two looking at each other during our setup."

It was painfully quiet in the room on the bayou. Quieter than Fred, and he was out cold in a mud hole waiting for warmer weather.

John spoke first. "Wow," he laughed, "I didn't see that coming." He looked toward his girlfriend and held her hand. "That's for us to know and for you to find out." The whole room laughed with John. Joe nodded in respect to the perfect answer to his question. It was a great start.

The questions and answers continued past the two-hour time they had prearranged. The questions were fairly rapid-fire.

"When did you first know you were part of this correction?"

"Were you scared?"

"Did you doubt ourselves?"

"Tell us about the antipodes you plotted to crack the Indian Ocean conundrum as it was called."

"How was it to meet the President?"

"And Mr. Musk?"

Maggy and John handled each question like they were tipped off beforehand. Joe didn't do that sort of thing like the legacy crowd was prone to do with their favored guests.

It ended on a high note as John and Maggy prayed that the meeting in Jerusalem would change the world into a better place. They were ready to turn in their prophecy crowns and return to school.

Before it ended, John brought Will up with him and Maggy and showered him with praise and love. Maggy gave him a kiss on the cheek that would be seen around the world. They all hugged and thanked Mr. Rogan.

"I told you to call me Joe, he laughed."

"Sorry, it seems weird to call an adult by their first name." John and Maggy and Will were headed to stardom.

Their lives certainly changed after that interview. They were known on every continent and country as the American Prophets.

Joe had a photographer with him and with their permission, he asked to release photos of the interview. They agreed before Miller tried to step in and stop it. He quickly remembered they would be safe in the US.

36

The President hoped his interviews with the press would be as successful as the kids' performance with Rogan. He was impressed.

Gabe was already in Jerusalem working on the hundreds of arrangements needed to pull this meeting off smoothly. The opening night was planned as a time to meet friends and adversaries. All attendees knew they would be safe. The earlier reports of attacks on returning members of various kibbutzim and the bad outcomes for the attackers were heard around the planet, not just in Israel.

The airport was choked with aircraft and once they dropped, passengers were routed to other airports in the nation. The President arrived on Air Force One. He took a smaller plane and as was the custom, it was renamed Airforce One while the President was aboard. He was thrilled to see the President of Russia land just behind. He would wait to meet him on the Tarmac. It was no accident; Gabe was at work.

Both leaders paused as they watched a plane from Ukraine land and taxi over. The Presidents of the US and Russia had to wait on the tarmac because of a jammed terminal. They both watched as the young President of Ukraine walked over to them. He noticed his plane was much larger than the President's compact was. The US president quickly took charge and introduced the one-time adversaries. The war between them had ended in 2025 and although the sting still hurt, they shook hands and smiled at each other for the first time. Gabe looked over and smiled his angelic smile. "Another day on the job."

The leaders poured into Jerusalem with hope. This time felt different. Maybe it was the huge scale; maybe it was safety of the newly corrected nation; maybe it was weariness of never-ending violence on Earth. Maybe this time, it would be different. It sure felt different.

Somehow, Gabe got everyone into their hotel rooms to relax before the opening ceremony. Not really a ceremony but a time to look each other over and maybe dispel some objections and mischaracterizations. A time to casually walk over and talk with another leader that was in a dispute or an adversary to their nation. This opportunity had simply never happened before.

This reminded the President of his early years as a litigating attorney. This meeting was like attorneys fighting in court all day and when the crack of the gavel closed the day's hearing, the litigators would head out to a bar for a cocktail and dinner. The litigators from both sides sat together, laughing and telling their own whopper stories from past battles. The next day, they would be back at each other, but it was made malleable by getting to know and understand someone better. Not that they would reduce their passion for their client, but they would reduce their anger at their adversary.

This was happening even while still in the airport. Maybe it had a real chance in the meeting hall this weekend.

The religious leaders were different. The distrust and for some, the hatred of another's religion was palpable and painful to witness. These were the leaders that were billed as the peacemakers. They were more like the Colt Peacemakers sold in the 1870s West. A single-action pistol chambered in a .45 caliber cartridge. Just like these religious peacemakers, the Colt guns killed more people than they saved. This would be an interesting showdown and could make or break the hopes of real peace.

It was 7:00 pm and the meeting hall was halfway filled, mostly by the more insignificant countries and their religious leaders and The President. He thought it would be a perfect time to mingle and meet leaders that he would never have the chance to do again. They just weren't as important as the larger and more dangerous countries. He enjoyed it as much as they did.

As the clock approached 7:30, the larger and more significant leaders entered fashionably late with their religious leader's part of the entourage. It seemed humorous in the context of the weekend. The President was gracious to all. Tonight, he would deliver the welcome speech. After that he had no idea what Gabe had planned. Gabe said he didn't know yet. Saturday and Sunday would be different than tonight.

Practicing Jews would not be in the room this evening because of the day and time that interfered with their piety and traditions. After sunset on Saturday was the start of the meeting. Sunday's meeting would be scheduled to accommodate Muslims' prayer schedules.

The main meeting was on Sunday. It was time to begin tonight's meeting.

The President walked to the podium to great applause. It took him a minute to gather himself. He had never had a reception like this before. He was humbled.

He told the attendees the entire story of the corrections in the US and how they had no idea what or who was doing this. He told them how he settled on God after no other credible reason could be found. He told them about results of the correction and that he prayed the entire world could enjoy this safety and peace that, up until a few days ago, was only in the US.

He talked about the three kids' prophecies and predictions. Everyone knew who they were after the Joe Rogan interview on X. They were famous now.

He talked about his government's failure to understand this phenomenon. He laid out everything he knew and didn't know. He stopped to thank everyone in the room for coming to this meeting. He explained that he didn't know Sunday's speaker. And then he talked about the Angel Gabriel. Jews, Christians and Muslims all knew about Gabriel. His messages were sprinkled throughout the Torah, the Quran and the Holy Bible. He went on to explain his significance in history and this meeting. He told about meeting him as Gabe. An older man with a kind disposition that somehow knew where it was important to be. He told them how his own heart was changed by Gabe. When he learned his real identity, he wasn't afraid. He was relieved to have an answer. No answers were the frightening part.

He told them about his travel methods and credit cards that didn't exist but went through. He told them about the feathers he would leave behind as a fun throwback to thousands of years ago. And he told me how we would not need translators when we spoke to each other. He made it so all of you would understand me in your native language. He told them about the ten-digit phone number of seven sevens that he left if I needed to call him. You can use it right now if you have a question for him. Let's take a minute to have each one of you call him. It's 777-777-7777.

The audience took out their cell phones and dialed the number. No need to repeat it; it was memorable, to say the least. The President stood at the podium and called Gabe himself.

"Mr. President. Very clever; I can't talk now because I'm on the line with more than 2,700 people." He stopped and thanked him for a job well done. "Gotta go!" One by one, the callers in the audience were hanging up, astounded that this guy had talked to each of them in their native language. Gabe and the President made their point that this was real and spiritual. The most important outcome was how he handled religions that didn't have Gabriel watching out for them. He was politely telling them that he could help them with some of the incorrect dogmas that all religions had. He didn't challenge them; instead, he offered to help them have a better understanding of the truth.

So far, a lot of signs were out there for people to see and believe. The correction in the US, the premonitions of the kids, the correction in Israel, the trumpet call and now the talk with Gabriel.

The meeting broke with attendees talking to each other without translators. The start of new friendships wasn't hampered by misunderstandings. Some spent hours together in local cafes and restaurants that stayed open for them. As checks were requested, the servers all said it was taken care of, tip included. A very large tip included. When asked who paid, they all said it was "Their old friend Gabriel."

Morning broke in Jerusalem and tours of the city were awaiting those that had never been or never wanted to be there or weren't allowed to be there. Tour buses took them all over the city to see hear about its history and future. And it was all told in their own language.

Nothing changed with Iran and Cuba. North Korea came along with China, because they were told to. China was worried about Iran. The President of China was convinced they were safe, but something told him he wasn't.

As the day wore on, the attendees were worn out from the night before and the tours. Tonight's dinner would be after dark to accommodate religions that would have been precluded. The host country would be able to attend after sunset. Tonight's agenda was barebones. The meeting tomorrow would be one not to miss.

The dinner was scheduled for 7:30 pm with refreshments in a more casual setting. This would bring everyone together for the first time. A bell was rung throughout to signify the beginning of the feast. The menu was selected for each guest. The favorite food for everyone. Down to the hors d oeuvres, cheeses, deserts and fruits. The food seemed to come out all at once from the kitchen. It was impossible, but it happened. Everything that was supposed to be hot was hot and everything that supposed to be cold was cold. The perfect wines were served along with each course. The desert course as incredible. People were so pleased with the deserts from their own country that they shared them with, friends, new friends and mortal enemies.

Suddenly the air raid sirens were screaming across the city. The President jumped up and ran to the podium.

"Remain calm; we will not be hurt. This will be over in minutes as any person or nation involved will be annihilated. Let's pray to ourselves for peace and unity." The President closed his eyes and prayed to God. Not for himself, but to preserve the atmosphere of hope that was in the room. He wasn't worried about the attacks.

They suddenly stopped, as did the air raid sirens that were part of daily life in Israel.

"When we have information, I'll let you all know." The President of China was impressed with the American leader's Mandarin until he realized the spiritual language workaround. He laughed and that started the room to laugh. It warmed the room for the wrong reason. The other leaders thought he was exhibiting courage while under attack. He wasn't.

A report was handed to the Israeli President. He quickly read it and walked up to the podium.

"Missiles were intercepted coming from Iran and a Hezbollah stronghold in Lebanon. They were not intercepted by Israel or any other nation. They all were destroyed just before entering the airspace into Israel. They were headed directly to our dinner." He paused as an aide ran up to him with a paper. He read it and adjusted the microphone.

"The nation of Iran has been destroyed. Hezbollah was destroyed in Lebanon. The country of Lebanon was spared, but Hezbollah strongholds were obliterated."

North Korean Troops were reported dead at the DMZ. US and South Korean military crossed the border and found dead soldiers with the Face. Kim Jong Un's whereabouts are unknown.

Cuban soldiers were reported killed in all provinces of Cuba. The President of Cuba was reported dead.

The attendees quietly sat and talked about the two announcements. The leaders were glad they came to this meeting. They understood the power of the Force.

Sunday was sunny and warm in Jerusalem. 70 degrees with low humidity. The world's media were focused on the destruction of Iran.

Totally destroyed right up to its borders and not an inch over. Every person was dead within the country. The President of Iran had made the biggest miscalculation of his now-dead life.

The South Koreans and Chinese did not make any moves on North Korea. They both thought it would be best to wait and see what happens with the meeting scheduled for 2:00 pm today. They respected this force. Feared the force might be a more accurate description. They understood enough about the risk of a military move from the stories coming out of America. They knew that whoever gave the go-ahead to invade might just find themselves wearing the Face if anyone was killed. Too many unknowns to step around. Too many calculations ended with "not the worth the risk."

Today's meeting would be broadcast around the world. A satellite feed was available to any television network or internet site. Almost six billion people would be listening live in one form. The other two billion would be asleep. They would view a replay. The language spoken in each broadcast would be in the viewer's native tongue.

Back in Lake Charles, the three families, friends, technicians, Musk and Miller were watching the news broadcasts. They bounced around stations to miss the superfluous commercials. One thing that was noticed when they switched to CNN was their truth rating had improved up three points to 14 out of 100. "At least they were trying," Wells thought the three-point uptick was better than nothing. Not enough to make him watch it, but better than nothing.

John and Maggy were outside with Will. They enjoyed each other's company. Will looked over at the two holding hands and wished he had someone like Maggy to hold his hand. He did have a girl that interested him back in El Dorado, Middle School, but he quickly learned her attraction was based upon Will's fame. He wanted something real. He didn't know what real was. Will was very smart, but too young to understand the complicated equations of love.

Musk was examining the data from the satellites. He wasn't expecting anything. He noticed a weird pulse occurred, matching the exact time Iran was leveled. He went up to John's room to look at the map. Iran, Cuba and North Korea were black.

He sat on the corner of John's bed and called Austin, Texas, to have the engineers measure the intensity of the pulses over the black-colored countries at the time they changed. He had a hunch. They found an anomaly. "Maybe this could be the "fifth force" that scientists in Hungary and at the Cern Collider in Switzerland have been quietly discussing since 2021."

Musk asked to be transferred to Pat Donovan's cell. He woke him up. That was never an impediment to Reeves. "Pat, tell me what you know about the "fifth force" experiments going on in Europe."

Pat was a Particle Physicist and friend of Musk's. He enjoyed batting ideas back and forth with him. Sort of a game of brain badminton. He didn't have to dumb things down for Musk to get the gist. He was a quick thinker.

"It hasn't passed the 5 Sigma level of certainty. Most physicists are wary of proclaiming those experiments as a new force."

"Could this be something that could show up on our satellites?" Musk was hoping it was possible.

"Absolutely not, Reeves. Not a chance!" Pat broke the bad news, but he would spend some free time poking around on his own. "Are you thinking this is connected to the force that just took out Iran?"

"Maybe." Musk didn't want to come off as a total rookie in the field of particle physics. "Just maybe a little bit." He laughed and thanked Pat and he went back to the drawing board, or in this case, the wall map. He made a mental note to research particle physics to learn something new. He was always learning something new.

Today was March 25th, soon the keynote speaker would be addressing the world. Nobody knew who that may be except maybe Gabe. The Orion Team would remain in Lake Charles until midnight on the 31st. No new premonitions yet. Gabe looked in on Slim and Mabel back in LA. They were off the streets, living in a small trailer inside a boatyard. He was the night security. His only weapon was a scary dog and a cell phone. Gabe took them to Nevada and found them both work in Las Vegas. It wasn't safe anymore in California.

His next stop was up to see Earl in Santa Barbara he had workmen loading up his valuables into a huge U-Haul rig. He was heading to Montana. He always wanted to live there. Gabe asked if he could ride along. He didn't want to frighten Earl, but things were getting worse by the day and criminals thought nothing of stopping a truck at gunpoint to ransack it. Gabe protected him to the border with Nevada. They were in Reno. Gabe said goodbye and watched Earl drive away.

Gabe had his plate full today. He was in two places at the same time. He somehow shaped time to his will. Now, he was back in Jerusalem in a sort of advisory role. Waiting for the 2:00 pm final meeting, like everyone else. He didn't know who would be speaking.

It was 1:30 and the hall was beginning to fill. It was stunning to watch old enemies walking together and talking. Language barrios are underrated. The speakers are filtered through language translators and their responses are translated back to the original speaker. At the cost of losing some meaning and breaking the rhythm or normal pace of conversations. The use of translators is not a friend of private and personal discussions either. This weekend was exposing the needless problems that differing languages create. Problems that were easily solved by totally understanding your friend or even old nemesis.

It was 1:45. The US President arrived and took his place. He was seated near the back of the hall. He asked for the tables to not be in the front. "Let the smaller nations have those tables; it will lift them up." He could see the entire room from his hideaway. This meeting wasn't about the US. It was about the survival of the world.

No one knew who would be speaking yet. The room was full as the clock moved toward 2:00.

A huge screen became visible as the stage curtains were raised. It was bright white and as large as any movie theatre.

Suddenly, quiet music began to play through the house speakers as the lights were drawn down. EXIT signs on the side and back were the only illumination in the hall. Gabe was running the show from behind the screen. The video started as the voices of children were heard singing in the distance as the camera drew close to a cemetery. Behind each tombstone was an image of a child. Holographic images of the living bodies of the dead. Row after row of tombstones revealed the children of war. The camera panned out to reveal tens of thousands of stone markers with the corresponding child's name chiseled permanently into the stone. It was a somber beginning to an intense day. The camera kept panning away, revealing even more graves, each with a child standing behind their final resting place on earth.

The camera kept pulling back. Thousands and thousands more of these children's graves extended as far as the distant horizon. As the camera kept pulling back, the sheer immensity of the death of children pulled back to expose the European Continent. As the camera kept pulling back, the graves turned into tiny white circles that turned the land from green to white. Entire countries were white. A legend at the bottom described the scale of death. Each dot was the location of a child that was killed in war or murdered. The panning camera stopped as the video depicted an old movie film catching fire inside the projector.

A new video started playing. This was a football stadium in Spain. Camp Nou in Barcelona. The largest in Europe with a capacity of 100,000. It was filled to its capacity with children. Seating sections were highlighted with a bright white sheet listing the number of children killed. Below that was a name of a responsible country. It started slow, with low numbers as the white veil expanded over more children. It kept increasing and started to gather momentum as more children were covered in white. Now, it was covering the entire stadium. Another stadium slid into the video, then another. All draped in white as the number of the dead increased as the more war-prone countries were highlighted. This kept going until the entire screen was filled with hundreds of stadiums. All in white.

It shamed most as they could see the damage wars and fighting could unleash. These were all children. The video turned white as a voice directed those sitting in the audience to reach out to their number one adversary and talk with them about "collateral damage" that their wars and skirmishes created. Most nations before today thought or convinced themselves that their confrontations were justified. And certainly, many were. Most were not. Border disputes, religious disputes, race disputes and the taking of land to expand nations, were not justified.

Ukraine and Russia went to talk about the ceasefire that was constantly violated by both.

Israel and Palestine did the same.

India and Pakistan spun off to a side room to talk.

Armenia and Azerbaijan left the room to talk about the many ceasefire violations that each blamed on the other.

Sudan and South Sudan had been fighting for decades since the separation of the two areas of Africa. They had a lot to talk about.

Even The United Kingdom sought out Argentina to patch things up in the Falkland Islands/Islas Malvinas.

Impromptu meetings opened up in the main hall. This was the time to take advantage of the current language obstacle that was removed and made communication simple and direct.

The screen remained bright white. No speaker had been seen yet. As the leaders that were outside the hall returned to their seats, the video came to life. The next session is for the world religions and their leaders.

The opening sequence was of the stars and the universe. A trip through billions of light years, finishing with a look at a collapsing Black Hole. As the camera panned back to earth, the music stopped. The video ripped through decade after decade of wars. Wars that directly resulted from religions decrees and teaching. Like the video of the children who perished from war, this was the children and adults that died from "Holy Wars," as they were so perfectly called. The faces of each who died were depicted and started with one young boy in Mesopotamia. At the convergence of the Euphrates and Tigris rivers. "The cradle of civilization," as it is known. A small white dot remembers where the young boy fell. Still in his crude coffin. The first coffin for a war casualty.

The view of Earth changed from a topographical to a geographical image and now the white dot was seen in modern-day Iraq. The images of the dead filled the screen and as the squares filled with the faces of casualties of religious wars. They became so small that the video revealed a single image made from the dead. The final image was of a meteor slamming into the Mediterranean Sea as the screen and the room turned dark. Less than five thousand years of history in thirty seconds.

The screen showed a single star on the left side and four stars of equal intensity on the right-hand panel. The Northern Star and the Southern Cross. They began to pulse exactly like the last time on MarchXXXX,2029. Three flashes from the Northern Star and simultaneously Three flashes from the Cross. It paused for the exact amount of time. Three flashes from each again, followed by another pause. Now, four flashes from each, followed by a pause. Three flashes again for each constellation, followed by another pause that was double the time of the first pause. It repeated. And again, for a total of seven times.

Back in Lake Charles, the three kids broke the flash code. It was a simple message. The Orion Team had the same conclusion. It was a number, and it was 3343. The video of the two stars was confirmed to be a live shot. It was witnessed by two telescopes in the Americas. The Very Large Telescope (VLT) in Chile and the W. M. Keck Observatory, of Mauna Kea in Hawaii.

Musk, Miller, Wells called Berkeley to decode. It didn't make any sense to them. It wasn't coded to the English alphabet or any other that made sense. 3343 was written in large numbers on the whiteboard.

John and Maggy walked in and saw the numbers and laughed.

"What's so funny?" Wells noticed the hand holding as they tried to conceal it with a quick unlinking.

They looked at Wells and said almost in unison."

"Micah 4:3."

"From the Old Testament?" Wells gave a funny look.

"Of course," John answered. "What else is Micah from?"

Maggy spoke with a little less condescension. "It's the thirty-third book, the fourth chapter and the third verse of the Old Testament. 3343."

"We both dreamed of that number last night."

"I saw you guys sitting on the couch dreaming last night."

John blushed and Maggy chuckled. "It's a very old and basic code used for centuries. We started looking for the meaning of 3343 and entered it in Grok AI and there it was, Micah, Chapter 4, Verse three." Maggy and John bowed in front of their admirers.

"You wanna hear it?" John asked and they nodded. He opened the Bible he had brought. Turning to the Book, Chapter and Verse, he began to read.

"He shall judge between many peoples and shall settle disputes between strong nations far away; They shall beat their swords into plow shares, and their spears into pruning hooks; Nation shall not lift up sword against nation, neither shall they train for war anymore."

Gabe stepped into the room unannounced and smiled. They all greeted him with even bigger smiles and confusion.

"Aren't you supposed to be in Jerusalem?" John asked the obvious. "Don't tell me; you just flew in and your arms are killing you!"

"You got me." Gabe turned to the three teenagers and congratulated them on figuring out the number. "It wasn't meant to be difficult to decipher, it was intended to be a message for all the world. Can I tell you about Micah?"

He didn't wait for an answer.

"He was a prophet from the Old Testament or Tanakh to Hebrews. His teachings were about the judgment and eventual restoration of Israel and Judah. His writings include prophecies about the Messiah and themes of justice, peace, and the end of warfare. It is a metaphor for the world we live in now. Micah lived to be almost 140 years. He was a good friend. His wisdom is almost 3,000 years old." He turned toward the door, "gotta go," and vanished. He left three feathers behind.

Will felt left out. He didn't dream about the number like the other two. He was slipping away from the trio.

On his "flight" back to Jerusalem, Gabe was instructed to speak on stage when the video presentation stopped. He was to be the "clean-up batter." He didn't expect to be talking, and he wasn't prepared. His boss told him not to worry; he had his back.

Gabe watched the video end, and the lights turn back on. He slowly walked to a podium that mysteriously arose from the floor. He grabbed each side of the lectern and noticed a few new faces. The Vice President of Cuba was entering the hall. Accompanying him were a few lesser-known, but lethal "terrorists." He would learn later that four of the twelve displayed the "Face" on the plane as it entered Israeli airspace. The Cuban Vice President knew that had Fidel been alive, and on that plane, this would be his new D-Day. D for dead.

They quietly found a spot and sat down. He turned to look at the others at the table and noticed he plunked down at the table next to the President of the United States. He said something under his breath in Spanish. The president laughed. The new table guest didn't know Hennessey spoke Spanish. He didn't, until today. He welcomed the newly minted communist leader to the table and asked if they could talk alone later. "Su español es perfecto, Señor Presidente." He smiled and responded with "de nada."

Gabe looked around the room and without preparation or notes, began to speak.

"The last time I spoke with three kings was Christmas Eve over 2,000 years ago. Here today, we have forty-three monarchs." He stopped to allow the little laughter. He'd been to plenty of comedy clubs and now realized that was not such an easy occupation. He thought of his "tired arms from flying joke" and decided it was best to forgo it. He had no idea what to say next. He just started speaking from his heart.

"My name is Gabriel, and I am an Angel of God." He let that sink in before resuming. "I am the same Angle in the Hebrew Tanakh, the Islamic Quran, The Christian Bible and many, many religions. I was sent here to give a message of unity. That's the job I've had for thousands of years. I am a messenger for God and of God, and a protector of those in need. I'm not here to condemn or praise your beliefs. I'm here to increase your beliefs. I am here to announce an astounding message from God."

Most believed every word Gabriel spoke. They had seen more evidence of the Power of God over the last three years and the last three days, than any ancient king or shepherd or even disciple of Jesus had.

"All of our beliefs cross paths and ideologies. You all know that in your hearts." The hall was in agreement. "We intersect more than we diverge."

Gabe paused for a moment for emphasis. What he would say next would disrupt.

"All of you here are good at heart. That's how all humans begin their lives. Good at heart. Somewhere during our travels, we are enticed away from that by dark forces. Evil forces, Demonic and Satanic forces as some call it."

He stopped again and looked up through the ceiling, toward the heavens and closed his eyes in solemn respect.

"There comes a time when a craftsman needs to be retaught parts of his trade, when a husband or wife needs to be retaught the things that used to bond them but have slipped away over time. When a doctor needs a refresher class and when a sinner needs a new light for their path. That time is here.

Many things have been added to our human thirst for understanding God. Many things have been deleted to make things easier for us to worship our God. You can't have ten editors working on a book. It will destroy the message the author wants to convey. That's what has happened over thousands of years, and it is the main cause of war today. Not wars between nations, but wars between religious ideologies and the evil that loves to confuse and stiffen searching hearts.

We've all seen the obvious fakers. The Mega Church leaders that return to their mansions after a fiery oration in their sanctuaries and defile the Lord with the hidden sins that so easily ensnare the best of men and women. You've heard about the church leaders that were killed in the US by the power they prayed to while, lying, cheating and subverting their robes and $5,000 suits to their followers. The sheer number of pedophiles within our cathedrals, Vatican, billion-dollar evangelical campuses and rented out seedy strip malls in the "bad" parts of town is sickening and a testament to the power of evil."

Gabe looked up again with great thanks that the words he was speaking were flowing from his lips. Great thanks that the Lord, who once again, pushed him into the baptismal lake that Gabe had announced thousands of years ago to John the Baptist and the arrival of Jesus. He pressed on, not knowing where this would end, but knowing it couldn't end badly with the help from above he enjoyed.

"The children we have hurt in war, in our churches, through trafficking and prostitution is enough to confound me that our God has allowed the world to remain in one piece. We deserve death for that alone. In forty-five states in America, and in Israel, those evil abusers of children are dead.

I know a lot of nations wanted the justice that has taken over most of the US and now Israel. I know a lot of you live in fear and torment from war and religious competition. Can't sportsmanship work in every aspect of our lives? I don't know what's next. I'm a messenger, not a leader. I'm a protector, not a warrior. I am an observer and what I observe is wrong and needs to be repaired. Repaired with the manufacturer's original parts. God's parts.

We all saw the pulsating stars during the last few days. What power could make them flash at just the right time? The North Star is 433 light-years away from us. God made it flash at just the right moment. He knew about this time and place on Earth that needed a sign, and he programmed the North Star to flash for us as that sign. Same with the Southern Cross. A heavenly light show to help us believe again.

You saw on the screen, the pulsating stars that occurred during our meeting. Do you know what that meant? I do. It was a simple code that flashed the number 3343, seven times. You know about those three teens in America that have premonitions and prophesies. Two of them dreamed those numbers last night. They used AI from Grok to give them the answer. It was old scripture. It was from Micah and written over two thousand years ago. You wanna know what the message was?"

Gabe paused again to let the "parishioners" answer with nods.

"I'll tell you, it's from an ancient text and the message Micah gave us thousands of years ago, and it is dead on for this place in time. Let me read it to you."

He stopped.

"Wait, Wait, Wait. I need to tell you that this verse is part of Hebrew teachings. And, by the way, we are meeting in Israel for a couple of reasons. Israel was chosen because it has a small population of 10,000,000. Just 15 million worldwide. They are not pressing for a certain religion over another. There is no proselytizing this weekend. The only one recruiting is me. Okay, I'll read you, Micah 4:3 now."

Gabe read it aloud.

"Every one of you here, no matter what religion, sect or group you are a part of, agree with this doctrine, either exactly as written or a close variation. The very words I just spoke are found in every religious text, including your own. Even those nations that don't believe in a superior being believe what I read to you is good. The end to war is obtainable; it's real. The alternative is death. I know this to be true. I was sent here to tell you this message of truth and hope."

Gabe looked around the room as each person was sure he was looking directly at them and no one else. He smiled and asked, "Are there any questions?"

"How would you describe what's going on in the US and Israel? As I look around the room, I see people that probably should have died. I don't mean that as an insult to any person or nation. I'm sure a lot of us have noticed that." The President of Spain was the first to jump up and ask a question. "Also, can we expect more corrections, as it seems to be called?"

"Thank you. I don't know why the US was chosen for this correction, as it's called. I think of it more as a compass recalibration used to plot a course correction. All nations have their problems, corruptions and evil players, as well as good, honest and pure leaders. The US has its share of bad, but on the whole they have a large share of good. They have proven over time that they do not react carelessly very often, and they also have supplied the greatest amount of aid and security to the world in the last hundred years. So, yes, they have the best track record, not perfect by any means, but they would be considered to be the fairest."

Gabe looked at the President of the US and smiled. "I hope our faith in them will benefit the world. As far as Israel, safety and security was promised and has been fulfilled. No one in this room or meeting has had a single hair touched. As far as Cuba and Iran, they were treated differently. Iran was annihilated because of its attack on every one of us sitting here. They were slow learners. Cuba came to this meeting, only after its military was neutralized. They were slow learners, but without the violence this time. The ones who perished crossing the border were obviously punished. I don't know why."

The ruler of Dubai stood up and caught Gabe's eye. "Mr. Gabriel."

"Yes, Your Highness. Oh, and please call me Gabriel."

"I feel silly calling you Gabriel and you calling me Your Royal Highness." He paused and asked Gabe an important question that most Muslims wondered. "I know who you are from my lessons while reading the Quran." He cleared his throat. "I believe you are trying to accomplish what would be considered impossible two days ago."

"What is that?"

"You, by your mere presence here, are trying to unite Muslims, Christians and Jews by using our own sacred teachings. Not against us, but for us. I would never even dream that this could happen in a thousand years. What about the other religions of the world? What about Buddhists, Hindus and other Eastern Religions? Are they included? I ask because I don't believe they are based upon a God. I can absolutely understand that the God of Muslims, Christians and Jews could be from the same God. That leaves billions behind that are atheists or the Dharmic Eastern religions."

'We all believe in right and wrong. Ethics is not a man-made concept but given to man by God. Even Shinto believes in spirits or deities. More than one, you might argue."

Gabe looked at the Prime minister of Japan and watched him nod in agreement. "What about the Holy Trinity, isn't that three as one?

We all have religious similarities and differences. We all look similar, right? But have many differences and races. We're all humans. Although with many variations, most religions are based upon a supreme being or a God. I am here to give you a message from "our" God."

He stood back and said these final words. "Jesus Christ is real, He is the way, and he is salvation. Read his words; they will 'fit' perfectly into your beliefs and in your hearts because he is the truth. Embrace him. He completes everything in our lives and teachings. He is life. He is not here to condemn you; he is here to bring life to you."

He paused again and said, "You can choose life, or you can choose death. It's your choice. You don't have time to capitulate; you must make your choice, your nation's choice and your spiritual choice. Return home with those you brought with you and talk about what I just said."

The questions continued for three hours before Gabe ended the meeting after the last person stood up to ask. "Is the rest of the world going to be corrected?"

Gabe lowered his head in thought then quickly raised it and spoke. "I think you're asking three questions. One: will the rest of the world be corrected? Two: when will it happen? And three: can we do anything to mitigate the things we have done in our lives that surely will condemn us."

Gabe looked directly at the Pope to answer his question and spoke to him and to every person in the room and every person on Earth at the same time. "I don't know the answer to the first two questions. I am a messenger and as such, a message from God regarding those questions has not been given to me. As to the last question. Here's what I can tell you."

Gabe took a breath through his old lungs and slowly let it out. "Yes, some of your sins against your brothers and God can be absolved. First, stop doing the bad things you're doing. You know what they are.

Stop harming your neighbors. Love them.

And trust in Jesus. I know that's a hard one for some. You will be mocked. Believe in him. He is the way and the light. There was a time in the world when we were of one faith. We destroyed that by the decisions we made that were influenced by evil. We diverged thousands of years ago by ignorance, ineptitude or insubordination."

Gabe stepped away from the podium and smiled at the rousing reception and standing ovation. He thanked God for pushing him through this. He also knew a lot about humans. He knew there would be a lot of pain and corrections coming to this "elite" crowd. The believers felt relieved that they had choices and relieved that they made the right choice.

And just like that, Gabe was gone. No one saw him leave. He simply disappeared from the stage and was on his way to New Mexico. He was taking a few days off, unless he was needed. Gabe was always on call.

The great hall was quiet as the attendees looked around the room and around their own tables and in their own hearts. This was a room filled with type-A personalities. Many narcissists, sociopaths and psychopaths. Religious leaders included. Unfortunately, that's what it takes to grab power. These deviant personalities also helped to make battle preparations and strategies to defeat and deflect another hostile nation. Thousands of years of wars with its tears, fears, jubilation and sadness were forced on people that had no choice. Forced by a few that did have a choice. Some right choices and some very wrong choices. The next months would reveal those that chose wisely and those that did not.

March 26, 2029

Most of the leaders and staff left the night before. Many discussions were held with old enemies and many heated discussions were within their own ranks. What they heard on Sunday was a tough tonic for some new-line keepers of their ancient doctrines. The elders were the wisest and open to talk. The youngest came off as the least flexible. No one could deny the "proof" they witnessed the last three years and the last three days. How could you?

As the last visitors boarded their jets and headed home, the world seemed a safer place. It was incredible to witness old enemies step back, take a breath and give peace a "fighting" chance. Not the negotiated, back and forth gamesmanship that was a show of bravado filled with so many holes in the deal to satisfy their constituents. Those pacts had no genuine intention of any long-term deal surviving. This felt real to most involved. The next few days and weeks would determine the future and safety of hundreds of nations. The three-day meeting in Jerusalem advanced the thought process of peace farther than anything the United Nations had accomplished since its inception. This meeting showcased the watered-down and activist-tainted organization for what it really was. A liberal think tank with little dimension or substance. The exposure was glaring and would help to dismantle the failed experiment that was bloated beyond repair. It had outlived its usefulness.

The European Union had a reckoning. The migrants that were so easily allowed to enter their countries were becoming a serious problem. Not for the leaders, but for the voters. They were turning on the governments that violated their trust. It became clear that a peaceful assimilation into these host nations was not these "newcomers" intention. The citizens on the front lines had a different take and it wasn't compatible with that of their leaders. No one seemed to have answers to the obvious questions. Why are you allowing this? Why do you want to dilute our heritage and our culture? Why are you doing this? Why do you hate us? The media didn't dare ask. Those questions were never posed because they knew their answers would expose.

The daily life on Earth was about to get interesting…

37

March 27, 2029

Cuba's antipodes were mostly in the Indian Ocean. It grazed Western Australia and the Keeling Islands and affected a few thousand people. Cuba was a different story. It turned red on John's wall map Sunday night. So did Jamaica and Haiti. Maggy and John shared a similar dream about beaches and palm trees and pirate ships and Reggae steel drums. Their dreams were not shared by Will. They also didn't reveal the crime and violence that was overtaking the good people that lived on these islands. That was about to change in four days at the stroke of midnight.

Will was losing his ability to "see" the things the other two did. He lamented that and felt more outside than ever as he watched Maggy and John's relationship blossom. They were still good friends, but their brotherhood was slowly dissolving, and Will knew he would not have the same notoriety that his teenage mind enjoyed. He was sadder about losing his tight friendship than his now fleeting "fame."

Maggy and John sensed that and made it a point to include Will in all their activities. Will appreciated that. So did the parents of the two "soulmates" that needed looking after. Will would be a stand-in chaperone for them. It was a good deal that allowed more freedom when away from the adults.

The twelfth mission to Mars was successful. A manned habitat was operating smoothly and even a launch control facility was operational to assist in return flights back home to Earth. John and Maggy were captured by the Mars mission. They spent hours talking with Musk about every aspect and even had their suggestions incorporated into the working "village" that was generating its own power and water. An agriculture facility was supplying food and nutrients to the early inhabitants. Space travel was not extraordinary anymore. The most difficult part was the travel time to get there from Earth. Originally, six to eight months was reduced to three months. Not even worth to be in a state of suspension. Passengers with no experience in space flight were able to travel with ease and comfort. Musk had done the unimaginable. He made it almost commonplace to travel in commercial spacecraft. Safe too.

Musk was planning a trip himself in the next year. Daily launches were supplying the pioneers with everything they needed and a lot of extras they didn't. Humankind in space was up and running and it seemed that nothing could stop it and its march forward. The richest man in the solar system was now the most famous. Maggy and John were making their own plans to visit the 187 residents of the red planet one day. It was a perfectly normal expectation in 2029. Musk predicted over 5,000 residents within the next three years. They would be ready for them.

March 31st, 2029

Cuba handled their correction better than Haiti and Jamaica. Especially Haiti. Within three months, all three island nations would be experiencing a massive influx of capital and explosive real estate and tourist expansion. All three would soon be the hottest tourist locations in the Caribbean. Cancun was out of fashion now. Cartels and crime killed that golden egg.

Cuba repatriated thousands of its citizens that escaped the harsh government control and violence of the communist regime. Fair elections shocked everyone as the results of their island's correction put things in good stead. It's hard for communists to keep control with fair elections getting in the way. Haiti was relieved of tens of thousands of killers and kidnappers that destroyed any sense of safety and confidence. With the bad elements underground displaying their "face" to the earthworms that stopped by their graves. Massive projects were able to be financed. Projects that built roads, schools and reforested the barren and ravaged landscape. Soon cruise ships would return after a years-long hiatus from the mainland.

Properties in Jamaica that hadn't sold in years were suddenly hot properties. Even Montego Bay was closing deals not seen in decades. People bought properties and closed without attorneys. No cheating or fraud was allowed these days. Airlines were increasing flights and hotels were expanding. Going to the beach and sticking your wallet in your shoe while you swim still keeps the sand out, but now your valuables remain untouched and safe in your beach wear.

Peace was breaking out in four "corners" of our round planet. More people were now gone from the Correction than actual wars that plagued the populations. Land grabs that were attempted and made successful by a strong military were pointless now. When a Correction appeared, it all went back to previous boundaries. Since the meeting in Jerusalem, countries and religions were on notice and risked more trouble than it was worth.

The next two years were a quiet time. Pockets of crime and war were still erupting. South Africa, Somalia and the Congo started up again and as time went by, more nations were starting to fall back into aggressive moves and shows of force. It did not go unnoticed in Heaven and on Earth.

California, Oregon, Washington and New York were suffering from outrageous levels of gang activities, murder, rape and drug sales. Most of the good citizens were already gone and each day the ranks of criminals increased. The borders were sealed into Mexico and Canada. The west coast was a prison without bars or guards. The Pacific Ocean was the only escape route without risk of correction. New York had no path to safety for their "at risk" residents except for the St. Lawrence River to the North. A boat was needed for that crossing and Canada didn't want them.

A few nations started jabbing each other like a brother and sister in the back seat of a station wagon while on vacation with their parents. Nothing caused damage except to egos and maybe dignity. The Middle East was full of squabbles and name-calling. If the Iran destruction was a warning to knock it off, that was loosened up by the peace across the region. Nations were behaving better than religious leaders. It felt like the "good ol' days" where a little roughhousing was tolerated but careful not to cross the line.

India and China were throwing insults at each other again. China had border disputes for years with them. Pakistan had disputes with

India in the Kashmir region. No one made a move since the Jerusalem Summit. Too risky to take a chance. Maybe things would hold.

SpaceX created a school program for kids interested in space travel technology. It was a new science created to solve the problem of space flight and planetary living away from Earth. Headquartered in Austin, Texas, it included dormitories and boarding for the students. Maggy and John were invited to be in the first class of 2033. They both hoped to be a part of this new curriculum. Musk enjoyed the joy they experienced whenever they dreamed of traveling through space. They didn't know it, but he was already planning with their parents to take them with him in the next year to Mars. He thought of the two as young ambassadors and future teachers in the new world that was being created. He promised the parents that he wouldn't take any chances with their safety. He would bring one of his own children along for the nine-month trip to and from the red planet. Language classes were a central component of the program.

Maggy and John had no new prophecies since March. Almost seven months since the summit. John kept his road atlas nearby and now he had a small world globe that he kept. It was the size of a softball and yet it did not have any red areas of "correctness." John thought it would turn red if another correction was called by God.

Gabe was slowing down and hanging out in the mountains of New Mexico. He was spending the winter there after a relaxing visit to Montana. He enjoyed Northwest Montana in the summer months and New Mexico in the winter. After thousands of years of dedicated service, he was winding things down a bit. He wasn't retired or resigning; he would always be in the Reserve Corp and ready to be called up for service.

Team Orion was still operational and monitoring the kids and the heavens, but it became apparent at the summit that God was behind everything. It was like any other government institution. Once started, they never end. Wells was winding things down and gearing up to return to Berkeley to finish his PhD program and research. The California operation was in the process of moving to a safe location in Nevada. It was too dangerous to stay and chance the crime and violence. Sacramento was turning into a gated city surrounded by the National Guard. An actual wall was proposed to be built to keep the legislators protected. The irony did not go unnoticed by the public.

The Sunnis and the Shias were posturing again but their contempt was kept under wraps by the force they feared. Small incidents between them went uncorrected and that surprised many. It caused some "testing the fences" in small ways and in small numbers. "Was the force unplugged?" They thought silently.

A murder in Arizona startled the US. That wasn't supposed to happen anymore. They were corrected and protected. It was a domestic dispute that went south when the wife of a wounded war vet lost control and lashed out at his verbal abuse. She picked up an iron skillet and swung but didn't miss. He was knocked to the floor dead. She was still standing. Something had changed. The doctrine of free will is a fundamental part of most religions. Forcing an individual to believe is counter to almost all beliefs and Christianity is no different.

The first term at the Space Technology Academy was remarkable. The quality of instructors that the program attracted made it instantly a prominent and preeminent academy in the physical sciences. It was able to present world-renowned scientific minds because the headquarters for Musk's companies was in Austin. It didn't take a lot of arm-twisting to deliver the finest minds to a nearby school loaded with the finest student minds. That's what Maggy and John were. They tested in the top 1% of all students. John's combination of curiosity and solution skills was fun for his instructors to watch. Maggy was different. She was brilliant, but not in the obvious way that John was. Her brilliance was her ability to hone in on a problem without being distracted by all the shiny distractions swirling around and diverting focus away from solutions. She was like a hunting dog pointing to the prize. Slowly and steadily, moving towards the game without ever looking to the side. Moving so deliberate and gradual that it appeared to be stationary until the "strike." Other than that, they were simply two young adults in love and with no experience in things related to relationships and emotions. Other than their combined brilliance, they were just two ordinary kids. You could say, just average.

Days were spent in class and in the engineering labs at SpaceX. Evenings were spent reading and studying and nights dreaming about each other and wishing they were older and allowed to be more intimate. They were attached at the hips and their cerebrums. They held conversations without speaking. Mornings made their compatibility even more obvious as entire silent conversations were recreated from the night before while in different buildings, lying in bed awake in silence and darkness. They both thought that all boyfriends and girlfriends spoke to each other in silence. They both thought their bond was special, but ordinary. It was one of the few things that they didn't understand.

Will was back at his own school in Arkansas. His talent for prophecy was fading little by little. He didn't have the same feelings or ability to communicate without speech anymore. He was settling back down to pre-corrections days. His parents and especially Steph were happy he wasn't living in Texas.

Dalton and Tammy had their baby boy and named him Gabriel. They both came up with the name from the day Tammy learned about her pregnancy. They both knew they would be in a different situation without Gabe. The barnacles of drug dealing, horrible decisions and the death of Jesse Williston would have dragged them both down to the bottom to die, without their Angel resuscitating them.

Molly and Luther were in the "Lost and Found" department of life. They, too, owed a debt that could never be repaid. The old man who knew things untold, dragged them from a church to restaurant to his apartment that he gladly relinquished to them. They were glad he was an Angel. They were confounded by everything about him. So confounded that only a crazy explanation could make sense. An Angel was that explanation.

John's parents were glad to claw back some of the normalcy that was a trademark of their life in Lake Charles. Wells was back finishing his work and moving to Nevada. It was a lot quieter with John gone. They missed him but understood how special he was. Sometimes, it's hard to spot genius when you're too close to the center. They knew John was in the best hands he could be. For the first time, they looked at Maggy as his life partner. They could see the forces that bonded them, and it reminded them of their first years united and how they knew they were in it together—together forever. It didn't make them less worried about the spark they shared and the flammable love they felt.

Bad things were trying to return to "normal." Nations were sliding back to the old way. It was alarming to Gabe and the President. The

initial reports of violence not corrected were disturbing. The US was used to the new justice system. They didn't want to go back.

After a murder inside the Arizona border with Mexico, alarms went off in state governments. Was the Force losing its power?

A Mexican wanted for murder in California drove into Arizona to see for himself. He survived. He wanted to return home to Texas and restart his drug business. He didn't make it past the New Mexico border. What was going on in Arizona? Why was New Mexico corrected but not Arizona? This caused great uncertainty across the nation. Governors and law enforcement liked things the way they were in the new age of no crime. They wondered if it would all start to slowly unravel state by state. They were unprotected and vulnerable. Except for the five uncorrected states, the rest were self-regulated and safe.

The President phoned Miller. "Put the team back together until we figure this out." Miller knew who to call.

The President spoke with the governor of Arizona and was preparing to send in the National Guard to beef up the totally depleted law enforcement ranks. He wanted them in position before word spread and would attract predators to the prey. The wolves would overpower the lambs in short order. He wanted things in place to be ready, just in case. Only one accidental murder so far. Maybe it was a fluke and the dead man's behavior was considered justified in the eyes of the Judge. Hopefully, this was just a scare and nothing more. Hopefully.

John's small globe changed the color of Arizona to black. He noticed it just before dawn. The night before he and Maggy dreamt about the state through a gray fog that gave it a somewhat ominous rendering. Maggy texted John when she was woken and startled by her premonition. John was awake and trying to make sense of the same dream he experienced. He called Maggy to meet up at the cafeteria steps. He first called Wells to describe things. The next call was from Wells to Miller and then from Miller to the President. The globe had turned the state of Arizona black. This was a new warning.

The wall map in John's room remained unchanged. Nothing was picked up from cameras or radio waves. Only the globe changed and only the state of Arizona.

That morning, the internet was abuzz with the death of the vet. Much speculation and fear-mongering about this aberration. A police officer decided to see for himself and drove a prisoner to Blythe, California before crossing the Colorado River and over the border into Arizona. The prisoner did not die. The State of Arizona had fallen back into pre-correction status. This would have an enormous impact on the nation.

John and Maggy were moved to the Lake Charles control center to be monitored by the Orion Team. They would have no privacy in Louisiana, with all the monitoring and video cameras. It was like they were in a different location from each other, and they hated being so close and so far away at the same time. Miller and Wells would join them that evening. Even Musk would stop by on his way to Austin.

As Maggy and John sat in the reclining chairs, he put his left hand into her right hand and gave it a squeeze. She leaned over and kissed his cheek as they both watched the monitors awaken with beeps and lights. The technician tasked with the monitors was chastising the kids as Musk walked into the room.

"Leave us alone for the next hour." Musk didn't like the techies' attitude and the man picked up his negative vibe while leaving the room.

"How are my favorite students doing?" Musk knew the answer. They were annoyed to be shuffled around the country every time something "happened" in the world.

"It is what it is, Reeves." They were getting used to calling him by his first name. They felt as if he was a parent and that made it weird to them. If he wanted to be called Reeves, they were happy to comply.

"I just spoke to both of your parents in the house a few minutes ago about taking a little trip to Mars." The zoom call to Maggy's "mom and dad" was a checkup to see about the space mission for the kids. It went smoother than anticipated and Reeves was happy to announce they were "good to go." The Rentschlers were a little more work, but they agreed to let the kids travel to Mars with Reeves. It would be eight months total with six weeks of travel time each way, there and back. They would be on Mars for five months. Not as tourists, he stressed, but as scientists conducting experiments on themselves and others.

Maggy was excited to try out her idea of energy creation from exercise equipment and John had a program to monitor things. It would challenge the participants to increase the exercise and give them more credits that could be traded for just about anything available to them on Mars. The gravity on Mars is 38% of that on Earth and muscle maintenance and bone health were issues that could be examined using the special exercise equipment they designed at the Academy. The SpaceX program built the designs, and they were ready to test on Earth.

These experiments would be crucial to understanding the effects of lower gravity over time. Although the gravity is significantly higher on the International Space Station compared to the surface of Mars. 89% of Earth's gravity on the ISS was enough to exhibit some short and some long-term effects on humans. Mars would present a challenge for long-term life. Reeves chose five months on Mars as a safe time period for young adults and long enough to process the results of the experiments. Reeves would bring one of his own teenagers along. That was comforting to the Rentschlers and pushed them over the finish line for John to travel.

"When?" John and Maggy exclaimed. "When?"

"In a few months. We will need to increase your exercise regimes before we leave. All of us need to strengthen our muscles and increase our stamina. It's not gonna be easy. Get ready to work hard. Your designs are on their way here; we will train on them and make any changes, if needed. I'll have my own equipment in Austin." Reeves was as excited as they were. This would be his first time launched from Earth by a rocket.

Cardiovascular deconditioning and mental preparations for cramped living and travel would be essential, along with centrifugal workouts to lessen the impact of space travel and the return to a higher gravitational environment.

These were very important experiments and John and Maggy were integral to the success of future missions. John's software analysis program was ready for stress testing on the new equipment.

January 1, 2030, was the scheduled liftoff from Florida. The largest rocket ever built would carry seventeen people on a six-week voyage to the red planet.

John and Maggy wished they could just be alone for a few hours. Nobody monitoring, nobody watching video cameras and no eavesdropping on their private conversations. Having a prophecy talent with national interests at stake, was the best chaperone a parent could ever want. Life on Mars would be even more restrictive than it is now on Earth. The parents' only worry was for their health and for their safe return home.

38

The workouts began and both noticed how weak and pampered they were. Pull-ups were especially disappointing to John. Maggy needed to chair to help. Two weeks later saw drastic improvements. Four weeks of workouts increased pull-ups, and push-ups to well above average for kids their age. That made the workouts more fun and encouraging. Reeves and his son, Ocean, were experiencing the same improvements and increased stamina. The new machine designs allowed for ultra custom resistance settings and John's tracking software made analysis simple and concise. The settings were computer-driven and seamless. Their designs for space conditioning while in space were now the standard for preconditioning on earth. Every machine change was handled automatically and unnoticed by the user. No more stopping to change weight or speed. John's software handled it so seamlessly and transparently that the increases in strength and stamina "earned" by these space gym rats didn't seem real until they reviewed John's stats and spreadsheets on their newly created phone app.

Maggy was looking at John's progress and smiled. She touched his stomach under his shirt and burst out laughing.

"What's so funny, space girl?" John was joking but wasn't sure what was so humorous to his girlfriend.

"You are ripped, space boy!" She said as she felt under his shirt again and pulled it up to reveal a six-pack like in the movies. "You're what you call a hunk, big John!"

Maggy lifted her shirt, revealing her own six-pack. The two of them laughed so hard they had to stop and use the bathroom. But not before John reached over and felt her stomach muscles under her soft skin.

This was the most touching the two had ever done and they both enjoyed it way too much.

If they needed motivation to work harder, this was it. Checking each other's abs was a daily indulgence for both overly charged teens. They would be ready for space travel on the first day of the new year. Sixteen years old and boarding a rocket to Mars. You can't make this up. It would be their first real date, along with fifteen other passengers. Space travel was becoming so common that the name for these pioneers was downgraded to "passengers." Soon, "accommodators" would be the euphemism to describe the ever-changing job description that started as "stewardess" almost a hundred years before. No one needed tickets yet, but each new mission was inching to that final step in killing the spirit and risk of space travel.

Musk and Ocean were looking good, too. Zuckerburg wouldn't stand a chance in a match now.

Old wounds were opening again in the Middle East. Israel was protected for the time being. Old habits were still habits. Little skirmishes were converted into big skirmishes. The world was changing back. Eight months ago, the world was challenged to be different than the scores of generations before them. The challenge seemed to be more than they could accept. It was like quieting a raucous child for a few minutes, only to watch them explode back without skipping a beat.

The continent of Africa was testing the boundaries as if they had a justified pass. The Congo didn't have enough trouble. Sudan and South Sudan had too much peace. They played tough guys and were strutting like they meant it. It was all just a game as if constructed by mankind to justify violence, to fill in the boring parts of life with death. It was the model for video games and dominant males.

The US didn't have any changes since Arizona. That was a pretty tenuous situation, but the state was assisted by the Guard. John and Maggy had no new premonitions. That made them happy. They were worried the trip to Mars might be interrupted. They wanted to leave Earth behind.

As each day came without premonitions, they became more committed to their preparations and studies. Each day that brought them closer to launch inspired them to work as diligently as possible as two teenagers distracted by each other could. They were growing up as fast as their strength and stamina were.

Christmas Day gave them a break from their work and time to spend with their families who waited in Lake Charles for them to arrive. They would be gone for eight months, and the only unknown was how they would handle homesickness. That wasn't so difficult for Maggy. Most of her young life was spent alone in foster homes. John had no such childhood sadness to punch at. He would be homesick within a week of the launch, but having Maggy next to him would satisfy his fears, except for those hidden behind the veil of a young love. That was more mystifying than space travel, premonitions and pulsating stars in the heavens. Maggy, too, but she was energized by that same mystery.

"John," Maggy whispered to him on the plane heading for Christmas on the bayou. "I am so happy that you will be with me on this crazy trip to another planet. I hope nothing will change between us except for our closeness."

"Why would you think our closeness would change? Why would you want it to change?" John was experiencing another mystery of the female mind. It seemed so dark to him. Why would she want that to change?

He reached for her hand to make himself feel better than to express his feelings to her. "Let's talk later; I'm exhausted from today's preparations." What he silently thought was his exhaustion from the ups and downs of being a boyfriend to such a beautiful and smart and kind young woman and the rigorous challenges she made to his rapidly maturing body and mind. Maggy wasn't as strong as John, but she was at least two years more mature than him. He didn't understand the advantage that it gave Maggy in their relationship. All he understood was that she was his life now. After this trip, he would transfer his instinctual family love from his mom, dad, and siblings to this new and instinctual attraction named Maggy Gabriella O'Rourke. The girl with the exact birthday and mental "wavelengths" that he possessed. Not many lifetime relationships begin this young. Most who fall in love, only see the attractor of their heart as a young girl or boy through photographs. Pictures that are only guesses into what they were before growing up. Speculations as to who they were. Conjectures about who they were through the funny smile or glint in their eye as they posed for school photographs in their "best" clothes.

Not these two. They went back a long time. Two years was a long time when you were sixteen. Throw away the first two or three years of early life and that made their relationship over 25% of their existence. Each year would shift that equation and the chips from the dealer side of the table to the gambling side. The gambler finally had a slightly better chance of a long life together, even if only by one or two points. Every advantage, no matter how small, would be needed in this new world, seemingly stacked against anything that was good and pure.

The plane was getting ready to land. Maggy was asleep when John whispered in her ear. "I love you so much, Maggy. I always want to be with you." Maggy was not sleeping. She kept her eyes closed as John professed his feelings toward her. She wanted him to keep going without the distraction of speaking directly, that sometimes ripped away confidence into pieces. The young are good at that.

It's curious to think that the young view their chances of securing the love and devotion of the other sex can so easily be quashed by chance or conditions beyond their control. Somehow, they believe that the circumstances that allow them to engage with each other can be more significant than the attraction that undergirds the passion. Almost like a game of chance that is as unpredictable as the weather and the predetermined odds. It would be frightening to think that a difference in minutes could steal or propel a lifelong love.

They were brought together by an Angel name Gabriel. Time didn't matter. "Odds" wouldn't be a word that would interfere in their devotion to each other. It might have seemed unlikely to others around them. Even their parents, but their devotion was spread across all the emotions they possessed and soon the solar system they would be travelling through.

The Christmas this year was different than any other. Tammy and Luther were flown in, courtesy of the government's generosity. They were all home and together again. Will was not there with them. He wasn't a distant memory, but he was pushed aside by waning skills of prediction and time spent away from Maggy and John. He was a little sad, but smart enough to know his place and mature enough to deal with it in a healthy and proper way.

As both families gathered around the fireplace and big screen TV, Gabe's favorite Christmas Movie started to play on The Movie Channel. The doorbell rang. They all knew who it was. Gabriel, of course. He walked in and was smiling as big as ever.

"May I join you all? I heard you might be watching my favorite Christmas movie of all time. Am I late?" Gabe acted like he was a part of the family. Like a great uncle that could never stay away for long. He was in town for Maggy's sake. Tammy was getting cold feet about the mission to Mars. She knew she couldn't cancel plans, but that didn't help her feelings of abandoning her Maggy. She wondered what mothers thought when they would send their children off to boarding school for the year. This was almost as long and definitely much farther away. Gabe would help steer her through her emotions with comforting words and a promise. A promise from an angel was unassailable, more so than any human vow that appears sincere until it becomes time to break it and betray. That's the kind of thing heaps are made from. Garbage, trash and broken vows.

"I brought popcorn." This was a family member that didn't come with any baggage, let alone even a suitcase. He came and went with such ease and left no footprints. "What bowls should I use?" He said that to get Tammy to come into the kitchen to help.

"I'll help, Gabe." She knew where everything was in this kitchen. She been over so many days and weeks. "Use these."

Gabe looked at her, and with only his eyes, drew her in closer to him. "I want you to know that I will be with Maggy on the voyage to Mars. I may have to return to Earth for "work," but I can be there in less than a second. I promise you she will be safe and protected by an angel. Safe from all danger, even John." He winked at her and smiled. "You better start getting used to Maggy having a man in her life. This won't go away until the "Death do us part" part of their lives. I have been instructed to keep those two safe and to be their mentor while away from you and Luther."

"Oh, Gabe, I really needed to hear that. How did you know what I was going through? How do you do that?"

"I don't do that. My boss does that." Gabe put the first bag in the microwave and hit start. "I'm a messenger and also in charge of security."

He knew when to stop talking. He closed the deal already. Tammy was on board and relieved that Gabe was overseeing her little sister. He would have a similar talk with John's mom. Both fathers were oblivious to worry and concern about the upcoming trip. Most strong dads and their boys are risk-takers and thrill-seekers, not injury-seekers. They were too smart for unnecessary risk. John had the right mix of both and that made for a dependable man who avoids stupid risks and challenges. Both teenagers would require little safety advice from Gabe. Relationship questions were a whole different subject. Neither of the two hand-holders knew much about that. They would follow their hearts and urges into danger if left alone. Gabe was there to lead them not to block them.

The movie ended and Maggy and John separated a little bit from their movie closeness. Gabe stood up and asked to speak with them. It wasn't what the "moms" thought. It was about the next correction that was "scheduled" for the New Year. They would not have forewarning. Gabe didn't know why; all he knew was they wouldn't have dreams and no maps would change. He didn't want to lie to them about the reasons. He only wanted them to be focused on the mission. He suspected something was going to happen, but he wasn't told anything. He let them know he would be with them during the next eight months and that it was a promise to John's mom and Maggy's sister.

Christmas day was different this year. It had a more serious tone that relegated gifts to take a back seat to the spiritual. The world had been through a tough year. Things were starting to reverse from the promises of peace and the end of war. Even with the understanding that God was running this show, the two families on the English Bayou outside of Lake Charles, Louisiana, were on edge. The unknown seemed to be the way of life that started four years ago. It seemed like they didn't believe that the miracles in the bible were true and the miracles they witnessed didn't count. Not the first time this has happened in history.

39

Christmas Day 2029

A fifty-passenger Boeing Business Jet picked up the Louisiana group from the Hood. Each of the neighbors boarded the plane for a week in Florida. Not to work on their tans or drink too much on the beach, but to watch the largest rocket ever built launch from a pad in Cocoa Beach. That was Miller's idea, and it was well received on Pickrell Lane. Reeves Musk would greet them at the airport and bring them along as VIPs for the launch. Their Louisiana charm and humor made them an instant hit with all the celebrities invited to witness this historic launch. Mike was elected the leader of the group by the famous actors and elected officials invited to the event. The Hood had the front row seats and that did not go unnoticed by the forty other people that were much more important than them. More important, in their own minds. Ben and Trish had already become friends and set up a Caribbean cruise on private yachts for the next winter. They would soon be hanging out with the "other half" while mixing Margueritas on board the Contraband. The Hood was expanding their Cajun influence and now going international. Even Kenny Chesney wanted in with his black-hulled eighty-foot Italian yacht. The Hood agreed and accepted his terms of providing live music for a couple of evenings while afloat.

Those impromptu concerts would be transmitted to Mars and through Musk's Starlink system to any who wanted to watch.

The next few days were intense for the two teens. Musk had them and his son working the simulated helm. They would know how to run certain aspects of the mission while watching the myriad of details that were part of something this big. Watching was mainly paying attention for warning lights and sounds. Initiating landing and returning to Earth sequences were canned programs that needed very little human interaction. Once out of Earth's gravity, John would commence the exercise regimens that were needed to abate muscle atrophy. He would be the anti-gravity fitness center director. Maggy would be the energetic coach that guided and cajoled her exercise classes, headed to Mars and traveling at 38,000 miles per hour. They would learn to avoid her eye contact later in the voyage. She was very demanding.

December 31, 2029

The crew woke at noon for the midnight launch. So far, all indications were a go for the launch. Weather and wind were behaving and the thousands of pre-launch tests were normal. A few peculiarities were detected and software tweaks brought them to heel. Musk showed up in great shape and it was obvious he took his exercise seriously. Everyone was assembled in a large white room for the final pre-launch meeting. When the President walked in with Will, and shook John and Maggy's hands, the photographers went crazy. This would be a lifetime picture for the three of them, although Maggy held the birthday kiss photo in higher esteem. The press was buzzing over rumors of a young love relationship on the rocket and when a birthday cake was wheeled in and the candles lit, and songs sang, they were ready for an iconic photo.

It was Will's turn to blow the candles out and he was ready. He was also shocked by the physiques of his two friends with the same birthday. He knew he would never have a chance with Maggy now.

He leaned over after making a wish for their safety in space and blew them out with a forceful blast. Maggy gave him a kiss on the cheek and not to be outdone, so did John. Cameras were still flashing when Maggy grabbed John's face and pulled him in for the most serious kiss of his life. It lingered a bit too long for the parents and it wasn't just a cheek kiss it was a direct hit on the lips. The five seconds seemed to last an hour for the parents and about a half second for the two lovebirds. The Theory of Relativity explained in one sentence. That pic was on the front page of every newspaper that was still in business and on the internet that was slowly killing them. Speculation would extend to betting lounges in casinos as the odds makers found another reason for people to lose their money. Vegas didn't build all those glitzy hotels by making mistakes. The smart money was on marriage. The "Sharps" weren't usually wrong.

Everyone was ushered out except for the travelers. It was time to start the long process of dressing for success. Spacesuits surrounded their bodies to protect them from temperature changes and to prevent any catastrophes from lack of oxygen, pressure variations that could cause injury and to handle body waste. Maggy wanted to wear her helmet from Miller. Not happening; it was forty years old and didn't mate with the new suits. She knew the answer but had to ask.

"Maggy." John wanted to talk to her one more time before they would be on a helmet microphone broadcast to the control room. He leaned over her from the front and grabbed her uncovered hands and quietly whispered three words that any young woman wants to hear from someone she cares for more than anything or anyone. "I love you."

Maggy started to cry as she spoke to John. "I love you too. I was afraid to tell you. Thank you for telling me that. It's just what I needed to hear before launch." She was relieved of the worry of being rocketed into space by those three little words. John felt the same relief. His girlfriend loved him. Neither really understood what love was, but they knew that they were on the right trajectory.

The sportsbooks were, too.

Three hours before the final launch sequence would commence. All were fully suited and located in their custom contoured crew seats. Maggy, John, Reeves and Ocean were in the second row and would not be taking part in any of the launch procedures. They were passengers, special passengers.

The first day would be full of tension and excitement. The G forces would be significant, and the training would help them understand what to expect. That would prepare them to handle the forces. The initial rocket launch and two subsequent stage ignitions needed to get into earth's orbit would fill the cabin with intense noise and shaking from the terrific power of the engines. Once they started the Trans Mars Insertion (TMI) a few hours after orbiting earth, the TMI burn would propel the spacecraft towards their new home.

Hundreds of systems checks on land and space were conducted in the first 24 hours. Everything was checked out. A voltage drop in the multi-function screen displays was easily patched with a restart of the power supply.

Soon, health checks and light exercise would begin along with hydration plans. The first meals in space would be a learning experience for the travelers.

Maggy, John, Ocean and Reeves made it through the G-forces that had them concerned. It wasn't pleasant, but it wasn't as bad as a tooth extraction. That was the major milestone of the trip. Soon, they would fall into a sleep and activity pattern that was prescribed for each traveler.

The all clear was given to shed the spacesuits required for the launch. One by one, the suits were removed and stored. Maggy was first, followed by John, Ocean and Reeves. Reeves joked that he should first. It was his rocket.

They were taken to their small sleeping quarters to preview their next six weeks in space. Maggy's was next to John's and that surprised her. She was happy with that. So was John. They had each spent a night in the mockup version weeks before.

John saw his globe that was secured on the small shelf. He looked at it and froze. All of Europe was black. He called Maggy in to see.

"It's black, Europe is black. It must have happened during our launch. Something big is happening. Gabe said he knew something when he talked to us."

"Gabe doesn't lie." They were worried for Earth and for their families.

The president had been alerted by Gabe. He was prepared as he sat in the Situation Room, watching the monitors and fielding calls from leaders of nations and religions. He was more worried about the economies that would certainly collapse. The ones that died deserved it and weren't even a second thought. The US survived their corrections. He wondered about Europe. They weren't planning for it. They would be tested. Parts of New Zealand and the South Argentina and Chile were in the antipodes. That was it. The antipodes of Europe were mostly in the South Pacific Ocean.

Russia sent a nuclear missile toward the Ukraine. It exploded with a nuclear mushroom not seen in battle since 1945. Eighty-five years later, the memory seemed to be faded. The horror it unleashed devastated a large part of Europe and left Ukraine destroyed.

China hit the Korean Peninsula with its own version of hell. Their missile was permitted to devastate Singapore and most everything in a one-hundred-mile radius. The world was at war.

All air traffic was closed. Anything picked up on radar was fair game and immediately pounced upon. Most got through. The US Missile Defense System was on high alert and ready to prove Reagan's brilliance again.

Canada and Mexico were snuggling up to their troubled relationship with America. It was like a newly divorced mother realizing that she needed the help and support from the husband she betrayed. It was sincere, but very eye-opening. And like any good father, the US would shield them from the realities of the evil that lived from good and seemed to thrive everywhere. The father just didn't respect his neighbors.

The world waited for the next attack. It didn't take long for Pakistan to hit India.

Russia pushed the button on warheads aimed at the US. All but one was stopped. It destroyed the Silicon Valley. The US retaliated and that caused China to release their own nuclear hell. The world was spiraling down a death hole. The planet would be surrounded by a nuclear cloud that would travel to every continent in less than three weeks.

China's missiles didn't penetrate America's defenses, but it wouldn't matter. Seventy nuclear missiles were detonated and would end most of life on the planet.

The Mars mission started its trajectory corrections with the ground team at Kennedy Space Center in Florida's Complex 39A.

They received no reply signals. No communications. The Mission Commander was brought into the flight deck to oversee. Musk moved closer to see what the commotion was about. This problem had never occurred on any of the hundreds of prior missions.

They attempted to contact SpaceX's Mission Control Center in Hawthorne, California. It was used as a backup for the last few years.

"Hawthorne, this is Mars Mission 12, over." Nothing. "Hawthorne, this is Mars Mission 12, over."

"Keep trying both of them." The Commander was as baffled as Musk. He wasn't worried about any trajectory corrections; they could handle that manually from the flight deck.

"Bring in Joplin. He knows more about the circuits and the electronics beneath these screens we're looking at than just about anyone. He's crimped more wires than an old man trying to maintain an old yacht." The commander chuckled. He and Joplin went way back to their NASA days in Houston.

The seeming lack of concern from the Commander eased Musk's concern. The teens picked up on it and breathed easier. "Keep trying Florida and California."

Mike Joplin was on the deck now and knew too much about these things to not be worried. "Anything?"

"Not yet."

"Hawthorne?"

"Same." The commander said and looked at Joplin. "Can you fix it?"

Joplin knew there was nothing to fix on his end. "It's not us. Something is seriously wrong on Earth. Both command centers couldn't be down at the same time. They have backup power, obviously. I don't think they are manned right now. It's not a dead signal; it's no signal. The only reason I can come up with is they were shut down in anticipation of a directed Electromagnetic Pulse. I don't want to think about it, because that would mean a nuclear attack was imminent or already perfected. The first scenario means no radio comms for months and the second means no radio comms until the danger has passed. We better hope it's the second.

See what you can get from the Internet. We have high-gain antennas; we're still in range. The latency will slow things down, but we should be able to make contact. Go to the US Emergency site. They'll have it on the homepage if there is a serious problem with the electrical grid." Joplin stood back and looked at Musk. "What do you think, Reeves?"

"It's no big deal." He said while winking his left eye and then, without moving his head, pointing both eyes toward the teens who were nervously waiting to speak. "You'll figure it out. Keep trying to reach both bases; they'll get back online soon enough." Musk was worried, this wasn't a glitch, this was a crisis.

"Mr. Musk," John asked if he could speak alone.

"It's fine, John; they're just having some radio problems."

"It's not that," he paused while looking at Maggy. "My globe has all of Europe colored black as well as other countries. I just noticed it. Can we let Miller know?" John was worried about his parents and siblings back home. He didn't believe in coincidences. He knew the globe and the radio were connected somehow.

Musk looked at him and spoke. "We'll figure out a way. We are prepared for these types of things." He wasn't very convincing.

Ocean had a printout from the US Emergency website. It took 12 minutes to receive the weak signal. The news was disturbing.

"The United States Department of Homeland Security advises all citizens to shelter in place. A series of nuclear explosions have occurred across the world. One Missile survived the Defensive Shield and detonated above the Silicon Valley of California. Initial reports have been limited, but some suggest the total destruction of Menlo Park and Palo Alto. We have not confirmed these reports. All communications are down and we are unable to obtain reputable reports. We have established a hot-line for other reports."

Musk looked at his son and thought about his other children and their mothers. His expression said it all. This was serious. "This is big, Ocean. The corrections and the protection they provided are down. They must have been stopped. If a missile made it through the defense shield, the US is under attack."

He looked at John. "I'm sorry to frighten you and Maggy; something terrible is happening on Earth." He paused again. "John, will you bring me your globe? I want to see it."

"Yes, sir." John started to leave and noticed Maggy hanging onto his arm. He took her hand and led her with him to find the globe and bring it back. She was shaking. "Gabe is on our side; he will protect our families."

They were still getting used to the weightlessness and had to slow down. John looked back at Maggy and saw droplets of water floating around her face. She was still crying. "Maggy, I'm here with you; we're gonna be okay."

"I know Johnny. I know." She hadn't called him Johnny in months.

"It's too early to do this. We need to keep it together. We're astronauts, Maggy." He looked at her intently and told her he needed to tell her something. He couldn't come up with the words. He was frozen like in a dream when someone was chasing you, but you couldn't run away. He touched her shoulder and began to hug her. That helped his composure. He still couldn't speak.

"What do you have to tell me, John?"

John pulled back a little and looked her squarely in the eyes. He still couldn't speak, but he was able to communicate. He swept her hair away and lined up her mouth with his and kissed so passionately it even surprised him. He gave her a big boy kiss. She started to tremble. Not from the fear or sensual tension, but from the emotions that pierced her weaknesses and threw them on the metal floor to be trampled over. They were floating and pressed together so tight, that it gave them an almost prenatal feeling of safety and love. It was a mother's kind of love. The kind of love that can defeat even the most deadly attack on two souls.

xxxxxx

John grabbed the small globe and the two of them headed back to the flight deck to see Reeves to show him. Maggy had reset her brain with the help of John and was ready to work on the glaring problem staring them down.

Musk needed to give a talk to the crew and three young adults. He had already assessed the situation and had the big picture flyover. They would be okay. They would make it to Mars and be safe. He didn't know about their home called Earth.

"Mike, I want to speak with everyone aboard. Can you make that happen?"

"I sure can. I need to alert the crew to put on their headsets. I'll tell you when it's time." Joplin was always a team player and helpful. He looked at the panel and said, "Everyone's on; you can talk now."

Musk looked at the people on the flight deck and began his talk. "Some of you are not aware yet of a situation that is developing. We have no communication links working with the command center in Florida or California. It appears that a nuclear explosion has occurred at many places on Earth. One missile from Russia penetrated the defenses of the US and detonated over the Silicon Valley in California. Also, multiple nuclear missiles have been launched and detonated over the world. We don't know from who or where they have hit.

This spacecraft is fully self-contained and will land safely on Mars. We can return to Earth on our own. We are monitoring the internet as best we can from our location in space. It will be slow, but we will get more information and hopefully soon.

I'm sure you are all worried for your friends and families as I am. I don't have anything new to give you, but I will as soon as we receive updates. The US was hit, but so far, only one missile has made it through our defenses. That will help to diminish our casualties, but I worry for the rest of our planet. Please pray for humanity."

The President got the message out before the anticipated Electro Magnetic Pulses or EMP could cause a radio blackout. That's why the command centers were shut down. Those pulses could permanently destroy the command equipment and take months to replace.

He signed off, sounding sad and frightened. They all were. Here was a group of elites encapsulated on a planetary ship, safe and sound while their families faced and unknown terror and most certainly the risk of death.

The next internet information would hopefully clarify things. It wouldn't be able to update the ship after the next twelve hours. Mars Mission 12 would be out of range and left hanging.

The Mars homestead would know less than the Mission 12. Their communication was even sketchier. It took days to receive communications from Earth. The Mars Mission would be able to contact them in one week.

The President was hunkered down in the Greenbriar Hotel vaults. The reports from around the world were getting more dire. Russia and China were on the offensive. Every retribution that was caused by some silly squabble decades ago was being settled now. It was like a floodgate opened when the reality of an uncorrected world was in play again to exact whatever violence was thought to be a good and painful measure. India and Pakistan were killing each other in unbelievable numbers. The nuclear cloud would finish the job.

The Rentschlers, Molly and Luther, the Willistons family and Dalton and Tammy were hustled out of the launch site to a protected underground survival shelter. It was Reeves' idea a few years back. He built it to help a friend who started a survival-home construction business and thought it was pretty stupid. Today, the teenagers and their families would be staying with all of the Musks. Reeves knew the plan; it was his idea. Gabe was called up by his "boss" to check on the new residents. He would be a messenger again, relaying messages back and forth from Mars to the shelter. Now that they were all safe, he was free to travel.

The second day of the launch was somber. The excitement stripped away by humans that seem to never learn from their centuries-old mistakes, brutalities and savageries. It felt like God was engaged in a grand experiment to see how far humanity could slide toward darkness when left alone to make their own plans. God doesn't work like a spreadsheet seeking answers to all the thousands of "what-if" scenarios. God is all-knowing and perfect.

After the last few years of Corrections, humans were given a model to follow to live peacefully and happily. Nope, not enough to feed egos of the commanders and their followers. Most religious leaders were distraught and had given up. "End this game that pretended humans could live together." Even the Pope had thrown in the Papal towel along with the other so-called enlightened "insiders." "Burn it down," was the desperate consensus of most pastors, priests and pretenders. "Enough," was the concise conclusion reached by the mostly good. The old dependable mantra found on signs and graffiti; "the end is near," would hopefully, to them, be replaced by a new dream, "the end is here!"

God had an entirely different wisdom-driven plan, as was his custom. A more accurate assessment was that man had a different sin-driven plan as was his custom. They would have to wait and see.

Maggy and John's sadness and worry brought them even closer together. They spent most of the time looking at each other and understanding each other in a way that was so different than young teenagers with a crush. They understood that their youth precluded them from taking relationship steps that were too soon for their forming bodies and emotions. They were prepared to wait for things that would be disclosed and understood later in life. They had fully formed minds, it seemed. Knowing that you don't know is a major component of the wise.

"John?" Maggy broke the long silence and held his hand tightly. "What will happen to us? I feel like we were brought together so we could survive." She leaned over and kissed him on his lips. "Are we special?" Maggy was thinking out loud again. "Do we have a purpose?"

"You are special, and if you like me as much as I love you, then that makes me special too."

"No, I'm serious."

"So am I. You own my heart. You're all I think about. And I mean all I think about." John squeezed both her hands and slowly breathed out a slow sigh. "I can't imagine worrying about my family and friends back home. Worrying all alone. Thank God and Gabe for bringing us together to survive this." He thought about Gabe and wished he would just stroll into the crew's quarters and give his surprises and display his calming smile right now. "We need Gabe, honey." Maggy nodded and smiled at John. She liked it when he called her Honey. That word made their relationship seem like older people's affectionate responses. She wanted to be older. They both needed someone, or an Angel named Gabriel, to give them answers to the things that they didn't know. The things they knew they didn't know. "Let's go see Reeves and Ocean." John wanted to be on the flight deck in case something came in from home. That's what they called Earth now. Home.

"Can you pick up any communication yet?" Reeves knew the answer but felt compelled to ask again. He had a large family to worry about. He hoped they made it to the shelter. He watched John and Maggy duck down to enter the flight deck. "It's like you two are connected at the waist and your brains." He laughed a bit to make them feel better. Reeves always struggled to tease. He liked the way it made people drop their defenses and smile. "Should we cut a hole in the wall between your sleeping quarters so you two can hold hands all night?" That flopped. Reeves approached human relations like a rocket designer. He always pushed the limits and always won when experimenting with the things that couldn't be done. Reusable rockets that safely land back on earth or on the pad of a moving ship in the ocean were a perfect example. Building a homestead on Mars was another. Purchasing Twitter was touted as his supreme failure. No, no, it wasn't. It helped to stop the backward wandering that was stepping on the First Amendment. He may have even saved it. Electric cars, Neural implants and tunneling technology were all on his incomplete resumé of accomplishments.

John and Maggy felt better. If the rocket guy can joke around, so could they.

"Everybody needs to get to their exercise equipment. You all have your schedules. We can't stop because the radio is silent. Joplin, you're up first, along with Reeves and Ocean. Get going!" Maggy wasn't the type to get overloaded and freeze during a crisis. That was most of her life. Surviving in good and bad foster homes. She wasn't worried about her own life. Now, it would be saved for the ones she loved.

"Yes, Ma'am." Reeves saluted the fitness commander and walked toward his quarters to change. He actually "handled" his quarters by moving from one handhold to another while playing in the weightlessness that was a childhood dream.

"Hook 'em up, John," she ordered in the demeanor of a drill sergeant while winking at her cute boyfriend.

"Roger, Wilco." John loved the military jargon that carried over to space exploration. Learning to obey orders from Maggy would come in handy as they grew older together.

As the flight deck cleared out, the lights flashed off for a second. Not long enough to panic, just long enough for Gabe to settle into one of the launch chairs.

"That was me," Gabe smiled. "I always love a little drama."

John ran over and hugged him. He didn't doubt that he had information from Earth. Message was the term Gabe, the messenger, liked.

"Can you put me on the interior comm headsets so I can speak with everyone?"

The wait was noticeably nerve-wracking. He didn't say everything was bad, but he didn't say it was good either. He waited until all could hear him.

"All set?" Gabe didn't need a headset. His message would somehow travel to each of the seventeen space travelers clearly.

"My name is Gabe. I know a few of you and I look forward to meeting with the rest." He slowly began to speak to the waiting and worried. Gabe normally started off with an icebreaker. Not this time; the "I just flew in" joke would crash and burn in the elevated oxygen environment.

"I am an Angel of God, and I came here from Earth to bring you the information you all want and to bring a message of hope that you all will need." He looked at the seven people in the room and began. "Yesterday, several nations launched nuclear weapons toward the US and other nations. Dozens of missiles were stopped by the America's defense shield. One got through and landed on its target: the Silicon Valley in California. Tens of thousands are dead and a nuclear cloud is slowly moving toward the east." He stopped when he heard the gasps and crying from those with friends or families in that part of the state.

"I want you to know that your families are safe. Only God knows what will happen next." Gabe didn't know more. He changed course to talk about the ground command.

"Communications are down and out for the time being. Florida and Hawthorne, California, are down. Hawthorne is unmanned. Florida is assessing the EMP risk. If it is positive, they should be back up within the next day. Power plants were shut down to protect them and to assess the possibility of future potential attacks. The St. Lucie reactor was one of two nuclear reactors. It was close to the command center and its primary source of electricity. The Turkey Point facility was south of Miami and went to standby mode until the regulatory commission greenlighted restarting."

He answered as best he could, all their questions. He was able to dissipate most concerns and calm things. He would talk with John and Maggy alone about the location of their families. He learned that something big was in the playbook for the two teens cruising through space at 35,000 MPH. Heading to a distant planet without direct communications with Earth. His job was to protect them and by association, the crew of Mars Mission 12.

This news brought a halt to the prescribed conditioning workouts. The crew gathered around the flight deck and wondered what would happen to them. Sure, they were told their families were safe, but without talking with them, it seemed hollow. Even though an Angel brought them the news, they couldn't believe it without "proof of life" evidence. The ancient flaw of the unbelievers was now expanded to space.

Maggy and John didn't worry. They trusted Gabe completely. From the first day they met him, they could tell he was a special man. They weren't surprised to learn he was an Angel; that made it all make sense. The teens did their best to convince their crewmates that Gabe's word was golden. He appreciated his two "protectorates" standing up to doubt and giving testimony to quell the ranks.

The two soulmates were holding hands as if they were glued together. That bond was stronger than the best adhesives on the market. Maggie would plot out their future together to hold back her desires. Those daydreams culminated with her wedding day and honeymoon. John was a typical male and his mentality was not as intricate in matters of love. It didn't mean he didn't love her as much as she him; it was just a different perspective. He often thought about marrying Maggy. Not so much as a fantasy than as a soothing balm to cover his lack of confidence in these things. His participation in his wedding dreams was similar to his would-be participation in his future wedding plans. Marginal. All he needed to dream about now was his life with Maggy and one day sharing her bed. His dreams were not cluttered with babies, in-laws, jobs and the day-to-day struggles to overcome doubt and second-guessing that can plague a union in the months after the vows are declared and carved in marble. They both thought they had love under control. Youthful planning is so precious and innocent. And humorous.

Gabe floated over to the kids. No handholds for him. He just moved flawlessly to where he wanted to go. "Maggy, are you okay?"

"I'm so glad you are here with us, Mr. Gabe. I'm so glad." Maggy truly felt the comfort of an Angel's protection. The protection wasn't always the sword and shield kind. This was the heartfelt, soul-comforting protection that she needed.

The same question was put to John. "Yes, sir, now that you're here with us, I feel so much better about all this craziness going on back on Earth. You make it all more manageable and less frightening."

Gabe looked at the two standing together and noticed the changes in their bodies and minds that had evolved in such a short time. Maggy was maturing into a stunningly beautiful young woman. John matched her with his handsomeness and size. He was strong and tall. What Gabe also knew was that they were even more beautiful in the contents of their hearts. He would do everything to protect them and guide them. He didn't know what God had for them, but he understood why he chose them. They were what you called "really good kids." That's because they were "really God kids."

Gabe explained he would be leaving soon but promised he would be looking in on them and their safety. He asked them to convey that to Reeves, Ocean and the rest of the crew. He would be the messenger and security for the Mars 12 mission. It was his mission.

Gabe was back in the Musk shelter to deliver some comforting words to the families and friends hunkered down. Until this week, they all trusted Musk more than anyone on the planet. They were witnessing the fragility of life and that stark realism changed that notion to all things God. Gabe made that a lot easier. Most "Smart"

people needed proof and the "rest of us" were content with faith, even if sometimes it proved to be a difficult task.

Reports from around the globe were sketchy. Ham radio operators were back in vogue after years of being relegated to obscurity. Their transmissions were more reliable now. Suddenly, a crystal radio and a Ham radio tower within a few hundred miles and if the Ionosphere conditions were reflective, could be your only information source. If no helpful boost from the atmosphere materialized, it would be greatly reduce reception. The nuclear fallout in the atmosphere was plotted and forecasted its direction and speed. The fickleness of the upper winds would determine the number of casualties and the quality of radio communications. The planet was at the mercy of a handful of world "leaders." World killers was a more accurate assessment. Lack of information was always a welcome companion to leaders. It helped to quash dissent and truth. A nuclear attack was conveniently disguised by the silence.

As the second night in space approached, appetites and enthusiasm diminished. Days and nights in space are just relic terms from home. Crews worked in shifts and resting was not determined by sunrise or sunset. The sun was always in view and couldn't be used as a clock anymore. John and Maggy were on the same schedule and although they ate only a little of the strange foods, it was enough. They sat on Maggy's bed and went over the exercise and fitness protocols that were needed to be in place. They had an important job that couldn't be delayed by an emotional/sick day. They handed their responsibilities like adults. It was a great distraction from all sorts of negative thoughts.

They both went to each of their beds and hugged and kissed before closing the curtains on a crazy day. The launch from Florida, the emotion of feeling the power of the rocket that propelled them, the weightlessness, the nuclear war raging on earth and a personalized visit from an Angel. That's a lot to take in for a battle-tested commander, no less for a teenager. It wouldn't be easy to fall asleep with so much spinning through their brains and hearts.

John fell asleep first. Maggy couldn't release all the tension of the last 24 hours as easily. She wished Gabe had cut a hole between the flimsy wall that separated their beds so she could touch her Johnny. They were so close yet so far away. They prayed together before bed and stopped using words. Their minds were synced and as if they were one person praying.

In less than an hour, Maggy took off her sound muffs, got up and looked in on John sleeping peacefully a few inches from her. She wanted some of that. Actually, both of that: sound sleep and her Johnny.

She crept into his cramped quarters and closed the curtain behind her and quietly crawled into bed. He was facing the side wall. She wanted to see his face but decided to put her arm over his back and kiss him a "good night" on his cheek.

John was awake and too scared to open his eyes. Today was the best, the worst and now the best day of his young life. Maggy's brain picked up on his thoughts and agreed together with her "man." He rolled over to kiss her and hold her. They fit together perfectly in each other's arms. They both wished they were older.

Suddenly, Gabe peeked in between the curtain and whispered. "You know I'm watching you two." He vanished as quickly as he came.

They both laughed and kissed each other for over a minute. That was how they teased their Angel friend. Maggy was happy he was watching them; John was relieved.

40

A week had passed since the wars on Earth. Gabe visited multiple times and soon became friends with the entire crew. He was their only connection. No communication was working except for the Archangel named Gabriel.

The crew was beginning to settle in the best they could. John and Maggy slept together every night now. Gabe approved after he "offered" some mother and fatherly advice to the young ones. They got it. Boundaries were to protect, not restrict. Gabe recalled a social experiment in England from the early seventies. A grammar school outside London decided to take down the fence surrounding the playground. They felt it was too restrictive and stifling to be compatible with the ultra-liberal curriculum promoted by the sixty's era educators. The staff at the Summerwind School had the answer.

They dismantled the fence and took it away. They were shocked that the "stifled" children, who as recently as the day before hung around the fences. It was their preferred location in the yard. Now, a day later, they were huddled in the center and were afraid to be "unprotected" by a fenced safety net. A boundary that gave them comfort.

Two weeks in space returned everything to as normal as could be while lacking any outside information that wasn't provided by Gabe every few days. No more missile launches. Now, it was more of a hand-to-hand combat situation as humans protected their lives and property with whatever they had. The US was at the forefront, as usual. Close to half a billion guns were in the hands of three hundred million plus good citizens. That number included also a lot of bad citizens.

The nuclear clouds that were surrounding Earth would be detrimental to over half the planet. When and if the Mars 12 Mission returned to earth, it would not be recognizable. It would be a whole new world. The Jet Stream dipped south and carried its airborne death to the Gulf of Mexico. It stayed for weeks before returning north to harass Canada. The Southern Hemisphere was affected, but much less than the Northern.

Bartering was driving commerce as much as gold and silver. Government paper was considered useless and would remain so until a government could be restored.

Maggy kept the exercise program on track. They all understood the consequences of slacking. They were eager members of the "Mars Fitness Club," as they affectionately called it.

The third week brought the crew closer to their new home. Even though the three-week trip was longer than voyages across Earth's oceans, the anticipation and the unknown bonded to make a strange emotional brew.

As Mars drew closer to the naked eye, the beautiful color was a welcome change to the sameness outside the portholes and video screens they had viewed for. In three days, the landing countdown would begin and if all went as the engineers had planned, they would be the first visitors inside the "Homestead."

Maggy and John couldn't wait to get to their sleeping schedules. They were behaving and Gabe was watching. He only had to warn them one time when their hands started exploring the bumps and valleys of their own private planetary surfaces. They knew better and now the price they paid for that short dalliance into the grown-up world was something they couldn't put behind them. Once teens get a taste of things to come, there is no going back. You can't undo it or unsee it. In ancient times it pushed forward many a marriage and many a baby or three at early ages. Mary gave birth to Jesus at fourteen and by some accounts, even younger. This old birth control was replaced with a new and dependable version. Young marriages were not as important to participants that didn't see the need to "buy the cow" when the butter was free.

They were happy to see Reeves assigned them bedrooms next to each other. They were worried they might be in different structures and that scared Maggy. They promised to behave to seal the deal.

It was now 24 hours before touchdown on Mars. They all knew the procedures and what to expect. The "seven minutes of terror," as it was affectionally called. This was the event that was not computer-driven. Hands-on control was required by the commander as the craft entered the atmosphere. This occurs as a plasma cocoon surrounds the craft and blocks signals. It returns after about seven minutes as the plasma dissipates as slower entry speeds occur. Normally, the command center contact would verify and make slight changes to the trajectory. Not on this voyage. The crew was thoroughly trained to handle things during an unexpected emergency communications blackout like this. Computers made most of the calculations required to build the rockets and control them. Humans were not obsolete quite yet. The Mars 12 Mission couldn't safely land without them on this flight.

The crew returned to their space suits and helmets and crawled into their seats for the landing. John was happy to be next to Maggy again. It soothed them both. Musk was his usual calm and Ocean was too. When your dad lives and breathes space travel, the experience is almost rote. Almost!

The commander went through the usual checklist, even the communications with the non-existent earth command. He knew no one would answer, but his training demanded the attempt be made. The crew understood the procedures thoroughly and were mentally prepared to touch down on Mars.

The Mars Station communications worked flawlessly out of the cocoon that was left behind them. The parachute was deployed about six miles above the surface. This would take three minutes to slow the vessel for the last procedure. They would deviate from the normal protocol and not jettison the heat shields.

The final phase would ignite the retrorockets, deploy the landing gear and allow the capsule to gently land on the surface within two minutes. If all went well. It did.

Before you could say the word Angel, Gabe was onboard and floating around with the skill of a Las Vegas circus act. John and Maggy breathed easier, knowing he was with them.

The craft landed smoothly and flawlessly. Gabe decided this would be a good time for his tired arms flying joke. This time, it worked. The pent-up emotion during the landing procedure was released and that relief soon turned into laughing at Gabe's stupid joke. Gabe would hang around to deliver messages to the crew and to make sure all went smoothly during the transfer from the capsule to the Mars structures. Their new home for at least five months.

❖

Life on Earth descended into chaos quickly. No more nukes were thrown; now the battles changed to a more personal street fight. It was shocking to see the depravity that humans can perpetrate on humans. Shrinking resources reduced the calendar of civilization back five thousand years. No fuel and contaminated food supplies would be the future of the planet for years. No one really knew. This was the first global nuclear war. The US was one of the only nuclear-capable nations that kept decades of promises to never use nukes. France, Germany, Israel and the United Kingdom were a member of the club, too. North Korea was gone and didn't count. Soon, large parts of Russia and China would be ravaged.

The US was suffering from only one missile that penetrated the Missile Defense System that decades earlier was somehow conflated with an offensive weapons system. The remaining living Democrats that voted against it would be humiliated. The dead ones would have an asterisk next to their legacies.

Musk's shelter could sustain the temporary residents for two years if needed. That thought was pushed aside to be handled later.

The space travelers settled into their new homes. There was great concern over the ability to return if life remained untenable on Earth. It was still too early to get caught up in the problems you couldn't control. But it did hang over everyone's heart on a faraway planet called Mars.

The first few days were filled with learning how everything worked and flowed in gravity that was 62% less than on earth. A two-hundred-pound man would weigh under 80 lbs. on Mars. That would take some getting used to. The fitness regimens were a welcome distraction and escape from worrying about the fate of civilization. There was enough to worry about on Mars and that forced the focus of attention to the immediate tasks and duties. It wasn't able to reduce the sadness that seeped in and soaked these routines.

41

Earth was radio silent. Not even static could be detected. It was as if it didn't exist. Was the Mars Homestead the last stand for the human race? No one actually believed that yet, but what if they never heard from their home planet again? They had Gabriel. Where was he? Why wasn't he helping them understand? They needed him now.

John and Maggy were their own distraction to conquer fear. They were two hearts in the "heavens" that synced the thoughts and emotions that revolved around the love they held for each other. Everything they did was pulled into perfect alignment with each other. It was as if they were a mathematic equation that had never been seen. An equation that had never been solved. They both knew that only one thing was missing in order to solve their "problem." That one thing Gabe told them not to do. The one act that Gabe warned them to avoid.

They slept in each other's arms every rest shift. They knew the boundaries were clear and unambiguous. They were exploring each other, but never stepping out of bounds. Like the children of the Summerwind School, they leaned against the fence, but never climbed over. They weren't old enough to understand what was on the other side. They thought they were mature enough, but they really couldn't fool each other. Soon, they would sleep without clothing. Intertwined and interlaced arms and legs pressed together. Frightened by their desires, but happy to be so close. It could best be compared to a young student pilot on a first solo flight. Scared as the plane approached the landing for the first time alone. Nobody to blame if things were misjudged or miscalculated but the person in control. As frightening as that first attempt may be, the same pilot exhibits a giant smile on their face that exposes the pleasure of conquering a fear. Young lovers are the same. They were stepping very close to the other side of the fence. Their hands were grip-testing the best way to climb over to the other side. For now, they only looked over that boundary as if that could quelch their urges. Yearning would bring learning and help them navigate the warm and inviting waters surrounding them.

Gabe showed up with news from home. It was bad news. More wars broke out. People were fighting over food and medicine. In the US, it was the same. California was almost tribal. That word can be interpreted as a kinship or culturally compatible group. It can also be described as primitive and backward. It was a blend of both in California and America. The Second Amendment was being used to defend against your own neighbors trying to steal your supplies. That wasn't our forefather's intention. It was put in place to survive an out-of-control government. The government lost control and now its citizens were testing life without laws. As always, the well-prepared do better. The "preppers" felt justified and now the slings and arrows from neighbors and civilization that targeted them were depleted by reality.

"Gabe!" four or five on the flight deck chimed in. "What's going on? We have no contact from either space command. We are totally in the dark. We need to ……"

Gabe interrupted and simply said. "Earth is almost unrecognizable. Your families are safe, but 99% of the world is in bad shape. Wars broke out everywhere for basic needs and food. The upper and lower atmospheres are transporting nuclear fallout around the globe. Soon nothing will be left to return to. Humanity will soon be ending without an intervention from God. "Society" has managed to commit suicide on a global scale. You cannot return home now. There is nothing to return to except for your families that have limited resources needed for their own survival. They are in the exact same situation you all are in. Just on different planets."

Gabe stopped after seeing the expressions on the flight deck. "We need a general meeting with the entire crew. They all must hear my message."

He was pelted with so many questions, he stepped back and told them to hold the questions until the general meeting. They agreed.

Gabe floated over the John and Maggy's compartment and "knocked" on the curtain before peeking in. "I'm watching you two."

Maggy jumped up to hug him and realized she was naked. She pulled the covers over her body out of shame and looked away from Gabe's eyes. She never looked away from Gabe. It always gave her comfort and a feeling of safety.

John looked at Gabe and spoke. "We haven't done anything wrong, Gabe. We both know we were pretty darn close to it, but we have not crossed over."

 "Guys, it's okay. I know you haven't. I'm not here to scold you. I'm here to help you. Your families are okay; they're safe. We will have a meeting in the community room soon and I will update everyone together. Get dressed and come on over."

They both looked at Gabe as best they could. They felt bad that they had so little self-control. Actually, it was the feeling they let Gabe down that made them feel bad. What they were doing wasn't "technically" wrong in their young minds.

John asked Gabe how old did they have to be to "you know." Gabe silently chuckled and spoke, "If you're not married, never. You need that commitment."

John understood that and re-asked his question. "What I meant was, how old do we have to be to get married?"

"It depends on whether humanity needs you to." Gabe left it hanging, not as parable, but as a mystery. He didn't want them to worry about their future. He didn't want them concerned with the mess on Earth. He wanted them to continue innocently loving each other. He enjoyed their slightly diluted purity. It was still pure, and it was still innocent. He didn't know what would happen to them, but he did know something special was in the master plan. They would be a counter to all things evil if they could overcome their temptations.

The general meeting was set and would be an answer to the unknowns that were racking their minds. They were worried and relieved at the same time. No news is not good news when you're on another planet and three weeks away from home. A communication blackout jolted them and presented the reality of never returning to Earth.

Gabe apologized and excused himself just as he was beginning his talk. He needed to be alone for a minute. Something bad was happening back at home and he "received" reports that were disturbing. Nuclear missiles were flying toward each nation, that was a threat to the attacker. Every nuke was launched and heading toward the final minutes of civilization. The US was drawn in as hundreds of missiles that were penetrating the shield. It was rendered inoperable by the chaos. The world was at the end of its lifespan. The human race was not killed off by global warming. It was not killed by pollution or fossil fuels. Or the ozone layer and the threat of an ice age. It was not destroyed by exaggerated weather events. It was not annihilated by racism, bigotry and cultural appropriations. Society collapsed because of the hatred of its neighbors and cultures. Earth would be barren and lifeless for years. A fitting end that was well deserved.

Gabe knew this day was coming when the correction failed to convince. When turned to their own short-sighted desires and temptations, they had a track record that couldn't be ignored or dismissed. A great flood was coming, and the only ark was on another planet called Mars.

Now Gabe had to tell the last survivors of humanity their new mission. He would stay with them and guide them and protect them. His messages would be from God. Innocent and guilty would soon die together. Weeds would grow over and conceal over 5,000 years that created the "wonders" of mankind. It would all be forgotten within a few years. Leaving behind the few traces that would be found of this dead civilization.

Gabe came back to the meeting and walked in with John and Maggy. He needed to be next to them. Gabe started his talk after a moment of silence that felt very long.

"I bring a message from home and from above." He paused again and without any whitewashing or dilution, he restarted. "The Earth is doomed by people chosen and unchosen to look after its citizens. The people charged with making decisions to benefit those people made the decision that a world war waged with the most powerful weapons ever imagined was a good decision." Gabe stopped to let the space travelers that were more than 140 million miles away from their home, process what they had just heard. It didn't take long for the crying and fist-pounding to erupt as they thought of their friends, families and countries.

Some were standing next to citizens of a country that launched missiles at their homes. They were angry. Not at the person next to them, they were angered by the stupidity of the world.

"The residue of a nuclear missile will finish the work that these evil people have begun. You will not be able to return home for years, maybe never. I will help you on this distant planet to survive and thrive."

Gabe was very emotional now and lacking his usual enormous smile, he almost seemed weak. "Throughout the millennium, I was tasked with making joyous announcements. Some are in the Christian Bibles and some are in the Quran. Those are only a few of the thousands of messages I have delivered for God.

I never imagined I would be called upon to deliver this message. The announcement of the great flood was my most difficult assignment until today."

John and Maggy were staring wide-eyed into each other's faces. They barely blinked as they listened to their friend talk. They were holding each other so tight it began to discomfort them. They didn't let go; they needed to squeeze hard. Not to hurt, but to hang onto each other out of fear of the slightest separation that they couldn't survive. It was as if they were hanging over a cliff.

John and Maggy understood the ambiguous comment Gabe made a few minutes ago when he said, "Not unless humanity needs you to."

"John." Maggy squeezed tighter. "Are we gonna be Adam and Eve?" They both had streams of tears running down their cheeks. They both understood that they might never see their families again.

"I don't care what we are as long as I'm always next to you and you wanna be next to me." They closed their eyes and longed for the time they spent in Lake Charles. They longed for the yesterday that they could never return to. They still had each other. That would keep them able to press on, to help Earth start over again. Hopefully, without repeating history.

Starting Over Again is the upcoming sequel to *The Master of Counterpoint.* Expect it in the fall of 2025.

JK would love to hear from you. You can contact him at jkworthauthor@gmail.com. He can also be reached on X at jk_worth.

jkworth.us and on Facebook at JKayworth.